Praise for *A Haunting in the Arctic*

"Rich, chilling, and gorgeously gothic. *A Haunting in the Arctic* is the kind of enchanting, terrifying mystery I just adore."

—Chris Whitaker, *New York Times* bestselling author of *We Begin at the End*

"Cooke delivers yet another spine-chilling treat in this lushly imagined, terrifying novel. The characters will haunt you long after the final page is turned."

—Emilia Hart, *New York Times* bestselling author of *Weyward*

Praise for *The Lighthouse Witches*

"If you like your thrillers chilling and gothic, *The Lighthouse Witches* is a creepy and atmospheric read." —Book Riot

"This chilling tale weaves a web of superstition and truth that fans of gothic horror won't want to miss." —*Library Journal*

"In her deeply atmospheric new novel, Cooke weaves together multiple genres into an intriguing story about longing, lost love, and family. . . . Cooke does an excellent job of bringing together three time periods and multiple storylines. Readers of Audrey Niffenegger's *The Time Traveler's Wife* and students of Scottish history and myth will love this read." —*Booklist*

"The story is executed like a dream. A frightening, suspenseful, and otherworldly dream. It was very difficult to put this book down and go to bed at a reasonable time." —Culturess

"*The Lighthouse Witches* captures the essence of how fear can bring out the worst in ... generations."

... *San Francisco Book Review*

Praise for *The Nesting*

"A taut, scary thriller that winds the suspense so tightly you can barely breathe. I was rooting for the heroine all the way to the terrifying conclusion. This one will definitely keep you up at night."

—Simone St. James, *New York Times* bestselling author of *Murder Road*

"[A] hypnotic psychological thriller. . . . Readers will keep guessing what's really going on right up to the surprising ending. *Rebecca* fans won't want to miss this one."   —*Publishers Weekly* (starred review)

"Dive into *The Nesting* for some creepy full-body chills."   —Shondaland

"An atmospheric thriller."   —*New York Post*

"[A] nail-biting gothic suspense novel."   —*OK!*

"[A] fast-paced, gripping plot."   —*Chicago Review of Books*

"A thrilling blend of lore and suspense, *The Nesting* is a gripping, deliciously tense page-turner that will give you chills."

—Rachel Harrison, *USA Today* bestselling author of *So Thirsty*

"Norwegian fjords and folktales are beautifully evoked in this vivid and compelling novel."

—Rosamund Lupton, *New York Times* bestselling author of *Three Hours*

"*The Nesting* is at once a taut psychological thriller, an eerie Nordic fable, and a thoughtful meditation on stewardship. . . . Cooke tells her story with a spare, elegant prose that betrays a poet's ear and also a poet's discipline. . . . The characters are heartbreakingly three-dimensional. . . . A quick read with a long echo."

—Christopher Buehlman, author of *The Daughters' War*

ALSO BY C. J. COOKE

I Know My Name
The Nesting
The Lighthouse Witches
A Haunting in the Arctic

THE
BOOK
OF
WITCHING

֎

C. J. COOKE

BERKLEY

NEW YORK

BERKLEY
An imprint of Penguin Random House LLC
penguinrandomhouse.com

Copyright © 2024 by C. J. Cooke

BERKLEY and the BERKLEY & B colophon are registered trademarks of Penguin Random House LLC.

Book design by Nancy Resnick
Ornament by Anne Mathiasz/Shutterstock.com

Library of Congress Cataloging-in-Publication Data

Names: Jess-Cooke, Carolyn, 1978- author.
Title: The book of witching / C. J. Cooke.
Description: First edition. | New York: Berkley, 2024.
Identifiers: LCCN 2024017708 (print) | LCCN 2024017709 (ebook) |
ISBN 9780593816967 (trade paperback) | ISBN 9780593816974 (ebook)
Subjects: LCGFT: Gothic fiction. | Novels.
Classification: LCC PR6110.E78 B66 2024 (print) | LCC PR6110.E78 (ebook) |
DDC 823/.92—dc23/eng/20240422
LC record available at https://lccn.loc.gov/2024017708
LC ebook record available at https://lccn.loc.gov/2024017709

First Edition: October 2024

Printed in the United States of America
1st Printing

For you, dear reader

In 1594, a woman was accused of assisting a man in his plot to kill his brother. The man was acquitted. The woman was executed at Gallow Ha' in Kirkwall, Orkney.

Her name was Alison Balfour. She was the first of over seventy women to be executed in Orkney on charges of witchcraft.

The more women, the more witches.

—Henry Holland, *A Treatise Against Witchcraft*, 1590

THE
BOOK
OF
WITCHING

August 21st, 1594

To His Royal Highness and Majesty, King James VI, Most Glorious and Sacred of all God's Creatures,

I beseech thee, Cousin, to consider this letter when I know you remain displeased with the persistent matter of my debts—verily, these will be resolved swiftly—but a matter has arisen here upon the isles of Orkney that forces my hand, and which I trust may find you in a temper of compassion. This past fortnight I have been gravely ill, struck with an ague such as I have never endured. It is the will of God that I remain upon the Earth. Having been treated by physicians from Edinburgh, and having consulted with my household, I have learned that my brother, John Stewart, our own Master of Orkney, has waxed strong in his urge to usurp the earldom that I have so rightly claimed, to use for his own gain. My enquiries have proven that his urge has taken shape in the form of witchcraft.

I thought of you, Dear Cousin, once I learned that witching was behind my distemper . . . I am and ever will be thankful, even indebted to God, that you did not lose your own life upon the North Sea, and that you wrought justice upon those who sought to take it from you. I write therefore to inform you that a similar method must be pursued to correct this course, with those who would see me murdered sorely punished.

I trust, Cousin, that you understand that the impious
and unholy abomination of witchcraft cannot be tolerated
on the isles of Orkney, even as you have thrust it from the
shores of Scotland. God bless you in all safety.

Your ever devoted and most true servant, always,
Patrick Stewart, Earl of Orkney

PART ONE

FYNHALLOW

CHAPTER ONE

Fynhallow
Isle of Gunn, Orkney
May 2024

It's almost sunrise.

A magenta streak across the horizon, a smooth, glittering sea.

The ranger's dog is barking, a wild, staccato squeal that splits the calm.

She shouts at him now to be quiet, her voice growing louder, her pace quickening as she moves toward him. He's a springer spaniel, two years old, easily roused. But he's never barked like this before. As though he's afraid.

Fynhallow's sand is soft, silken white, a seam that joins the Isle of Gunn to the North Sea.

The silhouette of the dog noses and whines at a dark shape by the caves that run along the outcrop. It must be a dolphin, she thinks, perhaps a pilot whale. Except there's no fin, no shape of a tail.

She sees the shape of two legs, and gasps.

The curious odor that she caught earlier registers: something has been burning. The wind was in the wrong direction before, but now she catches notes of flame and meat. The dog paws the ground near the body; she sees the hands are bound together at the end of bent, blackened arms.

Her pulse racing, the ranger reaches for her phone and flicks on the torch, and when the harsh white light falls on a charred grimace she drops the phone to the ground with a shout.

It lands upward, the white glare of the torch falling on the body. It is clear that the person is dead.

And her torchlight picks out another shape farther along the bay. She breaks into a sprint, talking to the dog as he follows her, soothing him.

Somewhere, embers glisten in a nest of twigs like rubies.

She lurches to a stop, just where the tide meets the sand. At her feet is the body of a teenage girl, a *Nirvana* print visible on her sooty T-shirt, tattoos of mermaids and beer cans on her forearms. Her face is encrusted with blood. The ranger crouches, noticing the dog is licking the girl's foot and whining.

Oh God, she thinks, fear thumping in her throat. Was this an accident, or murder?

She moves her fingers to the girl's neck, gasping with relief as she finds a faint pulse.

The girl is still alive.

Quickly the ranger snatches up her phone and begins to dial.

CHAPTER TWO

Fynhallow
Isle of Gunn, Orkney
January 1594

ALISON

I wake to the smell of fire.

I rise quickly, scanning the earthen floor of the cottage lest the carpet of ferns I have placed to hold the heat has set alight. Silver moonlight pours through the cottage window that overlooks the bay. Above my bed, the posy of herbs I fastened to the beam is silvered with frost. The air is filled with winter's teeth.

I wrap my shawl across my shoulders against the chill and make for the stove, enjoying the warmth. It is not yet dawn, and no one else stirs, not even the chickens in the rafters nor the calf that Beatrice has taken as a pet. Outside, an owl calls, and I stiffen. An owl is an omen. It brings a message.

I hold my breath, listening for the owl's tidings. These should unfurl inside my mind as a thought with edges, an instinct. But only the faces of my children come, and I realize with a start that I cannot hear either of them. Edward and Beatrice are restless sleepers, often calling out in slumber, even responding to each other, as though they inhabit the same dream. But tonight, there is only the call of the owl and the distant wash of the sea.

Edward's bed is empty. I tear back the coverlet and search beneath the straw mattress lest he has fallen beneath the ground, dissolved into vapor. He is not there.

"Beatrice?"

She does not stir. I lunge toward the gaping square of the neuk bed, set into the stone wall of the cottage for warmth. The calfling is curled up on the coverlet, where it usually is, for Beatrice likes it to sleep with her. But my daughter is gone.

A cold terror sluices around my shoulders, enclosing my heart in ice. Have the children been taken? William is yet in Kirkwall, repairing the stonework in the cathedral. When last we spoke, he had redoubled his efforts with the cohorts there who seek to overthrow the earl. And although the plot has yet to take shape, their consultation has not been without danger—the calfling that sleeps now in my daughter's bed was born of the milking cow we found put to death outside our front door five nights afore. Her throat had been cut from ear to ear.

I pull on my kirtle, cloak, then my cap and boots, before dashing into the night air, scanning the field and the byre for any sign of the children. No sign of them. William tore out the hedges that ran along the bank so we could keep watch for approaching visitors, but in the dark no such view is afforded. The black sky is clear, a full moon fixed above, creating pools of light and wells of deep shadow.

"Edward? Beatrice? You must call if you hear me!"

All is silent.

And still, the wind carries the musk of an open flame.

I hasten after it, heading first to the caves that run along the outcrop above the beach. Behind me, the owl lifts silently toward the moon, its white wings set aglow by moonlight. But then it curves around behind me, headed toward the brae behind our cottage.

That is where I am to go.

Voices swirl in the air as I near the top of the brae, though the clamor of my heart is enough to drown out almost all sound. The climb to the towering rocks is fearsomely steep, and for much of the year it is almost impossible to traverse on account of ice or flooding. The children often take their sledges out in the snows and hurl themselves down apace, and I watch, praying for their safety. It is sheer desperation now that helps me climb to the top, tearing my boots on the rocks as I do. Drenched with sweat, I grasp the base of the rock that stands at the top of the hill and pull myself to the summit.

I am careful to conceal myself as I peer down into the fairy glen below. The glen is named for the spiral of rocks found there, which legend says marks the spot where the fae meet. Tonight, it seems a different kind of gathering is occurring. Two score men and one woman congregate around a large fire in the center of the spiral, smoke pluming toward the sky. As my thoughts begin to untangle from the snare of blind fear, I remember—tonight is no ordinary moon. It is the Wolf Moon, the first of the year, marking a season of change, bravery, and loyalty.

I crouch behind the rock, aware that someone is drumming, and someone is speaking. It is difficult to hear their words, but then a figure amidst the crowd takes a familiar shape, and I realize that it is my mother. She is wearing a long cloak made of wolfskins and a helmet of deer horns. She approaches the fire, holding hands with two others. A girl, and a boy, both wearing cloaks of wolfskins.

Edward and Beatrice.

I open my mouth to call out, but then I recognize others in the group. The woman singing and drumming the bodhran is Jonet. She and I played together throughout many a summer on Fynhallow when we were children. The two men standing in front of the fire with crossed halberds are Solveig Anderson and David Moncrief, the blades of their weapons glinting in the flame.

The gathering is the Triskele, the oldest clan of magic-wielders in the world. And they are initiating my children.

I creep down the other side of the hill toward another rock, my mind wheeling for answers. I am outnumbered, and the Triskele will not halt an initiation ceremony at my bidding. They will not hesitate to cut me down if I attempt to stop it.

Even though I was once one of them.

So I watch, my heart in my mouth, as the children answer questions posed to them by the halberd bearers. They must answer the questions correctly, or face being impaled. I scramble to my feet, the impulse to protect them overcoming my fear of their weapons. But as I move from behind the rock, poised to hurl myself down amidst the crowd, I see David and Solveig stepping aside, and the children kneel by the fire, their hands in the air in supplication.

The drumming grows faster, and a wild cry rises up from the group.

I watch on as Duncan, one of the older members of the group, large as a bear, approaches Edward, carrying what looks like a black slab of stone. But I know it is not a stone—it is a book. A book with black pages, its binding made from a tree.

The group begins to sing along to the drumbeat, a long, sustained note held in unison. My son holds the book to his face.

Suddenly, he lets out a long scream, a cry of anguish. My instinct is to race to him to see if he is well, if he is injured. But then Beatrice also shrieks like a wounded creature, and some long-buried memory rises up of my mother telling me to do the same.

My children are not merely being initiated into the Triskele. They are being ordained as Carriers, by signing the book.

One's purest signature is the sound of one's fear.

And *The Book of Witching* holds them all forever.

I lie still in bed, nerves jangling, anxious for my children's return. When dawn inches across the fields like a gold sheet drawn across a bed, I hear them tiptoeing into the cottage, trying not to rouse me. I force myself to lie still instead of jumping up to drill them with questions. Beatrice is merely six years of age and does not know my mind on the matter of the ritual. But Edward, at twelve, knows I will not stand for the Triskele.

I refuse to be wounded by his decision, however. He is yet young enough to be persuaded, and my mother is very persuasive. It is she who is responsible for this infraction, not my children. They are simply caught up in a family dispute.

It takes a great deal of patience to wait until I am free to head to my mother's cottage. She is choleric in the mornings, and besides, I need time to soften my anger. And I ought not to abandon my chores. I go into the field and let the sheep and goats out of the byre, scattering oats for them across the frosted ground and breaking the ice in their water trough. The well is similarly frozen over, and I gather a bucket of stones to break the surface before drawing water and carrying it home in buckets.

Beatrice and Edward are usually up by dawn, the noise of the chickens a blare through which even the dead could not sleep. But today they do not stir, exhausted from last night's initiation. I think of William, and how I dare not tell him. What if he had been here? Would my mother still have taken the children from their beds?

Unlike me, William would not have hesitated at the sight of the weapons wielded by the Triskele. He would have risked his life to stop the children being initiated.

I serve them oatcakes at the stove, picking motes of ash out of Beatrice's hair—remnants from last night's initiation.

"Are you well, Mother?" Edward asks. He can see I am ruminating.

I kneel between them. "I saw you last night. In the glen. You know my mind on the Triskele."

"But you *are* Triskele, Mama," Beatrice says, flicking a look at her brother. "Grandmother said you would be pleased."

"No, she didn't say that," Edward scolds. He glances at me, guilt written large upon his countenance. "She gave us a choice. She said we ask your permission, that you would likely say no. Or we could go with her in secret."

"And you chose to go in secret," I repeat slowly. "Despite knowing I would be displeased."

His cheeks burn, and he lowers his eyes.

"I want to be like you," Beatrice says, reaching out to touch my hair. She hates that her own hair is blonde, like William's, and not dark, like mine and Edward's. "And it was fun, Mama."

Edward scoffs. "You were scared."

"I was *not* scared," Beatrice flings back.

"You said the fire was scary."

"I said it was *hot*," she snaps, eyes blazing.

I tell them to be quiet, for my head is throbbing after a night of little sleep. "You must not tell your father," I say. "Agreed?"

"Why?" Beatrice asks, puzzled. "Will he be cross?"

"Yes, but not with you."

"With who, then?"

"Grandmother," Edward answers.

I head across ice-hardened fields under a glancing white sky, the mountain's round head blanched by a scree of cloud. The weather is wild again this morning, hard rain driving sideways as I make for the brae where my mother's cottage stands. Much of Orkney's land is fen, swamp, mire, sinuous lines of sandstone and basalt rimming the coastlines. But Gunn is heavily forested, copses and boscages undulating through deep valleys to the cliffs. Storms have rendered this woodland treacherously muddy, tree roots roping across the path. The old wych elm that marks a hundred paces to the pool has shed its golden leaves, standing naked save its fresh coat of lichen and beard of rooty branches. I am mindful always when I take this path of the coal seam that runs alongside, the signature of a dead forest from long ago. I appreciate the black line of it, the afterlife of all the trees and leaves that once flourished like the wych elm providing warmth and light in our homes so many years on.

I have been wary and cautious since I was a bairn. The only one of my mother's six weans to survive past adolescence, I sense I was her least favorite, or the one who inherited the fewest of her traits. I am more like my father was—quiet, preferring to wander the halls of my own mind than those of any dwelling wrought of stone or wood. My mother is bold as a wildcat, born for war—our family heralds both from the old clans of Orkney and the Vikings that usurped them, and surely my mother would feel at home on a longship, wielding an ax. Her nickname for me is *peerie moose*, which means "small mouse," on account of how quiet I was as a child. Or at least, that was how she explained it. She said I had a penchant for both hiding away from her and keeping so still and so quiet that I could never be found. I would both infuriate and scare her half to death, slipping inside a bale of rushes or a coffer while she called my name, frantic. When she shares such tales—laughing at the memory of it while using it to illustrate what a torment I was as a child—I wonder why my younger self sought to worry her so. I must have heard the fear in her voice as I hid in the dark, quiet as a rock.

The Triskele is the oldest clan in all of Scotland and, I daresay, the whole wide earth. This is not the main characteristic of the Triskele, however—rather, it is the knowledge and practice of old magic that the Triskele is known for. And while magic is as pervasive as the grass in the fields and the leaves on the trees, the Triskele are the only clan to be entrusted with the most important of magical artifacts—*The Book of Witching*. And it is this I witnessed my children swearing to carry last night, by screaming their own fears and darkness into its pages. Many who are initiated to carry *The Book of Witching* are not called upon to do so, but my mother is the chosen Carrier for this generation, and she foresaw that I would be next, and then my children.

But I left. I told the Triskele that I was no longer a member, tearing the cloak they made for my initiation in two. And my mother has never forgotten it.

She is not alone when I arrive, judging from the donkey tied up in the byre. I consider turning around and heading home until I can speak to her without company, but she pulls back the wolfskin from her front door and waves to me.

"Good morrow, Alison."

She is smiling, and I see her mood is fair. She is bright-eyed, despite the sleepless night, on account of the clay pipe in her mouth. A long black braid of hair sits over her shoulder like a pet snake—she refuses to wear a coif or forehead cloth, though she knows well it sets the gossips' tongues ablaze—and she wears her woolen shawl the color of poppies, a forbidden color for peasants like us. The sumptuary laws state that only the rich may wear such colors, and by wearing her shawl my mother risks a fine of ten pounds a day and three months' imprisonment. But, as ever, she does not give a damn.

"Come inside, Alison," she calls, blowing a thick cloud of pungent tobacco smoke in my direction. "I have fresh oatcakes in the pot."

I follow after, finding a young man sitting by the fire. A client, come to seek my mother's assistance with an ailment or affliction. I wonder if he is local to Orkney, or if he has traveled from afar. Her clay pipe was payment from a Frenchman who sailed from Normandy to procure a spell for plentiful rain for his new vineyard.

"This is Gilbert," she tells me, as though I should know who Gilbert is. She gives him a stern look. "That wax won't stir itself."

He reacts with a start, leaning forward to a pot on the stove that bubbles with liquid wax.

"This is my daughter, Alison," she tells Gilbert. "She is also a witch."

She winks at me, for she knows I do not like the term. These days there is a new meaning put upon it that chills my blood. It is a mere two years since the king put scores of people to death in North Berwick for apparently driving storms across the North Sea while he traversed upon his ship, declaring them witches, and invoking the Bible's command to kill anyone who is one. Many of the witches were women, and the king has made it known that he believes women and girls to be more inclined to Satan's wiles than men. Every week since, the Sunday sermons declare witches to be a scourge permitted by God to separate the wheat from the tares. And yet the parson himself visits my mother seeking magic for his humors, for charms to rid his well of rot, for his dreams.

I cannot remember a time when the divide between magic that is of God and that deemed of Satan was so entangled, so difficult to discern. It is said the king has his own magicians, and his own witches, and that he consults with them and seeks their counsel. And yet, he declares that witches must be put to death. It is maddening to think upon.

I sit upon the old oak coffer in the corner by the pig, who lies on a bed of rushes. He is too old for anything but slumber and prefers to be indoors with Mother. Worse is his name—he is called Magnus, which offends almost everyone who discovers it, aghast that Magnus the Viking earl, Magnus the patron Saint of Orkney, now shares his good name with a pig. But my mother is inclined to such things as offense for its own sake. And, she will tell anyone who listens, St. Magnus's forefathers usurped the islands of Orkney from the Triskele, claiming power that was not his to wield. It is proper, she'll say, that a pig adopts his name.

"Here," Mother says, passing me a cup of malvoisie. "It's sweetened with sugar. Just as you like it."

She sits on a stool next to Gilbert and passes him a handful of herbs, pebbles, and berries. "Crush these up and drop them into the wax," she tells him. I know what comes next. Gilbert is making a wax figurine of someone he wishes to love him, or perhaps someone to whom he wishes harm. I still know the words of the spell. He will need something that belongs to the person. A lock of hair, or a piece of clothing. Perhaps a tooth, or a small bone.

I watch as he removes a cotton sack from his pocket and takes out a small white button. He looks at it tenderly, then glances at me.

"My son's," he says. "He has chincough."

I draw a sharp breath—my own son was poorly with chincough ten years ago this winter. I am not certain this spell will work against such sickness. It did not work for me.

None of the spells worked. He was named William, after his father. Just eleven months older than Edward. They were such great friends, and Edward looked up to him enormously. We buried William on a wild, wet day such as this, in the graveyard in Gunn. Edward was so young that I thought—or hoped—he would forget his older brother. But even now, he will murmur his name in his sleep.

Once Gilbert has fashioned the hot wax into a shape resembling his son and uttered the spell, he pays my mother with a bag of coins and departs. I wait until I hear the clop of the donkey's hooves on the path before challenging my mother.

I waste no time on pleasantries. "I saw you," I tell her. "Last night. In the glen."

She bends to sweep remnants of wax from the floor. "I know you did."

"You took the children without telling me. *My* children. You came into my home and took them in the middle of the night."

She cranes her head up and stares at me. I swore to myself that I would not let ire overtake me. That I would speak with her in a calm manner and not debase myself with fury.

But I feel undone by it.

She shrugs. "Well, if you saw it, why didn't you speak?"

I don't offer an answer.

"I thought that if you'd wanted to join us, you would have said something." She smiles, and I feel a heat rise up the back of my neck. She is using pleasantries to disarm me, to deflect from the wrong she did against me last night.

"Gilbert should have come to see *you* about the matter with his bairn," she says, scraping the remnants of wax into a sack. "You always were the better witch."

I tut. "I am no witch."

"No?"

"I am a spaewife."

"Same thing, no?"

"You know very well they are not the same."

She throws me a knowing smile, and for a moment I see my daughter's face staring back. "A spaewife, eh? When Dougal Netherlee wanted to spare his cattle from the pestilence, who did he ask for help?"

"It was many years ago," I say quietly.

"He said, 'I wish to find the greatest witch in Orkney,' did he not? And that brought him to you."

I look askance, my cheeks flushing. I do not wish to be reminded of this.

"And you put a cross upon each of the cow's foreheads, all sixty-nine of them. And how many did die?"

I sigh. She has told this story a number of times. Interjection only makes her say it louder.

"None," she says, wagging her finger. "Not a single one of Master Netherlee's cows died of the pest. Because of you."

"I also put a cross on my own cow," I tell her bitterly. "And that did not stop her throat being slit a few nights before last. You understand, Mother?"

"Understand?"

"That magic does not and cannot meddle with the actions of men."

"Oh yes it does," she says. "And you know very well that a single hex can change everything. It can change history. It can undo what has been done."

She speaks fiercely, and I lower my head. "Only if the person hexing is seemly."

She falls silent, because I am right—a spell or a hex is much, much more than talent, or a sack of ingredients. It is more than wax or teeth or locks of hair. It is why my own spells to save my children did not work, despite my best intentions. Some magic requires circumstance; it works only if the sorcerer is in love, or with child. Some work only if the sorcerer is a murderer, or a priest. There is still much about magic that we do not know.

"You know the children will tell William," I tell her. "And he will be furious."

"Perhaps he should join the Triskele."

I make a noise of shock. *The very thought of it!*

"You know William would *never*."

"Never is a very long time, lass."

"His concern is with the rebels," I say, bristling. "As the Triskele's should be."

"The Triskele is concerned with the situation," she says.

"Concerned? Will this concern take the form of action?"

"Timing is of the essence," she says with a smile. "You will see."

I shake my head. "You must not draw Edward in." Then, in case she thought I was not serious: "As his mother, I will not allow it."

"And why not?" she says. "Joining the Triskele is a great honor . . ."

"By teaching him this art, you are placing a weapon in his hands. And you are making him a target. You know what the king has done."

She gives a scoff. "We are all targets. The king has decided that magic caused the storm that almost killed him. But this is folly, Alison. We all practice magic. Even the king practices magic! Perhaps he should put himself on trial."

She says it with a sweep of her arm and a wild laugh, but I cannot join her. The image of my children screaming into the book sends chills up my spine. They have a solemn responsibility now. The book may choose them to carry it. There are stories yet of the book driving its Carriers mad, whispering dark impulses. There are tales of Carriers murdering their families. The book, they would say later, drove them to it. The evil emanating from it is hard to resist, even for a Carrier.

"It's a heavy burden to carry, Mother. And Beatrice is only six."

"All of our family have been initiated into the Triskele since . . ." She waves a hand, though does not finish her sentence.

I fold my arms. "You are forgetting that I left the Triskele."

She breaks the pieces of wax into the pot, ready to be melted a second time. Then she holds me in a look of piety. "Oh, Alison. We both know nobody leaves the Triskele." She leans closer, a twinkle in her eye. "The book knows, too. And it will come for you. When you're ready."

CHAPTER THREE

Glasgow, Scotland
May 2024

CLEM

Clem is watching the birds when the landline rings.

The raven that visited the garden yesterday is back, an ominous presence on the fence dividing Clem's little plot from next door. But today, it seems to have fallen foul of a gang of jackdaws. It's mesmerizing, this sudden standoff on her patio between the large, black birds, and even though the baby is sleeping she lets the handset burr, plucking her mobile phone to record the raven backing away from the feeder as the five jackdaws squeal and lurch at it. Suddenly it unfolds its magnificent black wings and flies off to settle on next door's roof.

Clem hits stop and makes for the landline bleeping by the sofa. It'll be one of her bosses calling, either the school office where she works during the day or the café where she works at night, asking her to do overtime. Or maybe it's her daughter, Erin, calling home. Erin is nineteen and is currently hiking in the Orkney Islands with her boyfriend, Arlo, and her best friend, Senna. Erin is a prolific sender of WhatsApps, usually in the form of TikToks that she shares with Clem to make her laugh. But she's not sent anything since Monday, which was four days ago, and the WhatsApp message Clem sent yesterday morning (hey love, you OK?) is still unread.

"Hello?"

"Am I speaking with Clementine Woodbury?"

"Yes?"

It's not Erin, nor is it either of Clem's bosses. The caller is a man. Probably someone trying to sell her broadband. "Who's calling?"

"My name is Dr. Miller and I'm calling from the Burns Unit at Glasgow Royal Infirmary. Can I check that I'm speaking with Clementine?"

The Royal Infirmary? Burns Unit? Why would they be calling? "Yes, yes it is," she says, the heat in her neck rising. "Why are you calling, please?"

"It's about your daughter, Erin. Can I ask if you have someone with you just now?"

Her stomach clenches. "What's happened?" she says. "Is she okay?"

"Erin is in the Intensive Care Unit," he says, his tone shifting, steady, authoritative. "I'm sorry to say she has suffered extensive burns on her arms and legs."

"Oh my God," she says, reaching out to the wall to steady herself.

"The air ambulance delivered her here earlier this morning. We've placed her in a medical coma for now."

This news lands like a pickax to Clem's heart. "But she's alive?"

"Yes, she is."

It feels as though the frame of the house is tipping toward the core of the earth. In the small box room at the end of the hall she can hear the baby stirring, calling out *Mama! Mama!*

"Just a minute, Freya," she calls, before turning back to the handset. "What happened?" she asks. Then, hastily: "Can I come and see her?"

"Of course," he says. "But . . . please be prepared. It can be a huge shock seeing someone after they've experienced burn injuries. I'll meet you at reception and take you to her."

The Glasgow Royal Infirmary is where Erin was born on a wet September morning in 2004. Clem races blindly now through the front entrance, fifteen-month-old Freya bouncing on her hip. Clem is wearing odd shoes, forgot to put on her glasses, didn't lock the front door, or the car door. None of it matters, none of it. The world has fallen away once more, distilled entirely to the length and breadth of her daughter's life.

The man waiting at the reception of the ICU is younger than she'd envisaged. He doesn't offer a handshake, calls her Clementine, looks at the baby, puzzled.

"Where is Erin?" she asks, breathless and numb.

He nods at a small room to their left, and she follows, her confusion mounting when she finds it is a storeroom. He hands her what looks like a yellow bin bag. "Burns victims are at a high risk of infection. This is for her protection."

Now she realizes—the yellow bag is a plastic gown which he ties for her at the back before handing her a pair of blue latex gloves.

A nurse appears, her eyes settling on Freya. "Shall I look after the little one while you go in?" she asks.

Clem nods and passes Freya to her, who fusses. Usually she would console her, but her focus is too fixed, elsewhere. As she snaps on the gloves she feels a fierce tightness in her chest, as though her ribs are being pulled together like a corset. She stops, taking a moment to breathe, breathe.

"Are you okay?" the nurse asks, and she nods, pressing a hand to her chest, feeling the stuttering of her heart.

"I'm on medication," she says, feeling the tightness begin to ease. "For my heart."

"Which medication?"

The names of her prescription pills slip and slide through her mind, muddied with panic.

"Um, Entresto and metoprolol."

"Well, you're in the right place, darling," the nurse says. "You want to make a note of your dosage and I can fetch it for you?"

Clem takes a breath, holds it, willing her heart to be calm. This is exactly the kind of nightmare that her cardiologist said she must avoid. *No smoking, booze, or stress.* There is no avoiding this, however.

She tells the nurse her dosage, and they proceed hastily down the corridor. "Has she woken up yet?" she asks, forgetting what Dr. Miller said on the phone about the medically induced coma. Everything's mashed together, confusing and too real to grasp.

"We've placed her in a medical coma for now," Dr. Miller says, nodding at the stretch of corridor ahead of them.

"Why?"

"Anesthetic sedation is beneficial for pain control."

"When did this happen?" Clem asks, glancing at Freya in the nurse's arms to reassure her. "Where was the fire?"

"Yesterday, in Orkney. A ranger found her in the early hours of the morning."

Clem reels. "Yesterday?"

"About four or five in the morning," Dr. Miller says. "On one of the islands. They took her to the hospital in Kirkwall, then air-ambulanced her here by this morning."

Clem can't get her head around that. "So she was found over twenty-four hours ago? Why did nobody call me?"

"She had the number for a Chinese takeaway listed as her next of kin," he says. "Which unfortunately led to some confusion . . . It delayed us reaching you."

An odd compulsion to laugh blooms beneath her horror. A Chinese takeaway. Typical Erin. Clem wants to explain to the doctor that Erin does things like that, just for laughs. Erin's defunct Facebook profile has her listed as married to Bilbo, their late family dog.

"One last thing," Dr. Miller says, coming to a stop midway along another corridor. "Erin has been assigned a police officer to be present in the room with her at all times."

"What? Why?"

"It's part of the investigation, a formality. Until we know she's safe, Constable Byers is with her."

Clem's mouth falls open. "Until you know she is safe?" she repeats. "That doesn't sound like a formality. Was she attacked? Are you worried someone might come and attack her again, here in the hospital?"

A door opens in front of them and Dr. Miller falls silent, beckoning her into a hospital room with chirruping machines and snaking tubes and a single metal bed in which Erin lies, swaddled thickly in bandages and heart-wrenchingly still.

"I'll be right outside," the nurse says, still clutching Freya.

In a corner, a man—Constable Byers, Clem realizes, the promised protector—stands somber and gowned as she is, his uniform just visible through the transparent sheet. He gives a polite nod which Clem returns, but her attention is pulled to Erin in the bed, horror yanking her up out of her body. "Hello, sweetheart," she attempts to say, but her words are strangled, stolen by a sudden flourish of shock that rushes throughout her body.

Her bravery crumbles, the whirring of the ventilator, the rustle of the plastic gown, the sound of distant traffic a jarring mash of impossible realities.

Clem stands a little away from Erin, though her impulse is to rush to her, cradle her in her arms. But she registers how delicate she is, how the IV and the ventilator are working hard to keep her on the side of the living. There is barely an inch of her that isn't swaddled by bandages and dressings. Her pink curls have been shaved. Erin will be livid—it took three boxes of bleach and then a costly visit to the hairdresser to get her hair that shade of pink. A green toenail flashes at the end of her left leg dressing, but the other foot is an odd shape—truncated, smaller.

It's only when she sees Erin's hands—pawlike, a black hook peeking out from the bandage that turns out to be a badly burned finger—that she realizes the toes of that foot are missing, gone completely. And Erin's eyes—why are they like that, like a doll's, swollen and fringed by long black lashes? Clem stares, realizing with a gasp that they've been sewn shut, a macabre seam of black stitches running along the skin beneath her eyes.

The room seems to dissolve around her, the walls bleeding into the floor.

Dr. Miller appears beside Clem, and when he starts to speak she realizes that she had not heard the door or seen him enter; in fact she seems to have blacked out for a moment, coming to midway through his sentence.

In low, measured tones, he says words that she can barely comprehend. Fourth-degree burns on 20 percent of Erin's body, third-degree burns on another 20, mostly the arms and legs. Some of Erin's digits were necrotic, requiring urgent amputation at the hospital in Kirkwall to reduce the bacterial load on the wound surface. The burns team in Glasgow will monitor the level of injury to her deep tissue, which means that Erin may yet lose more fingers, more toes.

Clem hears herself ask about legs, arms, ears, whether her face will remain as relatively uninjured as it is, and then she feels her knees giving again, and a nurse materializes at her right, steadying her, with Dr. Miller on her left.

Somehow Clem finds herself in a chair, in a different room entirely, her protective robe and gloves removed.

The room feels icy cold, her body numb from head to toe. Where is Freya? Is this all really happening? She lurches in and out of confusion and back to the too-realness of this situation, of the hospital with its signs of neglect and echoing corridors. Dr. Miller and a nurse from the Burns Unit, Nurse Lewis (*but call me Biola, or Bee for short*) sit opposite, telling her things that she registers are important, things she is supposed to be taking in. A cup of water sits on a table alongside a vase with plastic peonies.

She has so many questions, but they lag in her brain, snared by the maelstrom of this vicious new reality.

"Her eyes?" Clem says finally. It's as much of the question that she can bring herself to speak. She looks up at Erin's nurse, Biola, who nods sympathetically.

"Erin's eyes have been sutured for protection," she says. "Infection after a bad burn is an extremely high risk. And the eyes can dry out. We suture them until that risk has passed."

"Will she be blind?"

Bee glances at Dr. Miller. "We don't know yet."

"Will she be able to walk?"

"We just don't know."

"But . . . how did this all happen?" she asks. "The fire, I mean. What *happened*?"

"The police will be here soon," Dr. Miller says. "They're investigating the area as we speak."

"Can we call anyone for you?" another nurse asks from a corner. Clem starts—she hadn't realized the nurse was there, holding Freya, who is fast asleep.

"No," she says, confused for a moment why she should want to call anyone.

"Is Erin's father in touch with her?" Dr. Miller asks. "Perhaps we can call him for you so you don't have to answer questions . . ."

She wants to scoff at the question of Erin's father, but is too numb, too shattered, to do anything but stare at the space on the floor by her odd shoes. Quinn, in touch with Erin? Barely. But he'll have to be made aware of this. And Heather, Erin's stepmother, and their boys, Erin's half brothers. Siblings Erin yearned for and barely knows.

"It was a hiking trip," she says in a thin voice, mentally trying to answer her own question. "Just . . . just a hiking trip. Up north, around the Orkney Islands. Turns out my side of the family is from there and she wanted to explore, maybe see if she could find some ancestors. She . . . she had friends with her, where are they?" Clem straightens up, her hands dropping from her face. "She was . . . was with her boyfriend. His name is Arlo, Arlo McGrath. And a girl, Senna, Erin's friend. Were they injured?"

Dr. Miller frowns. "I've not heard anything about the girl," he says, glancing at his colleague. "But I'll note that name down for the police. Senna, you said her friend's name was?"

Clem is finding this very difficult to comprehend. "She wasn't with Erin when they found her?"

"I don't believe so. Do you have her parents' number?"

She shakes her head. "What about Erin's boyfriend?" She adores Arlo. He is nerdy, sporty, polite, funny. Everything she could have wished for her daughter. "Arlo McGrath. He's twenty, into sports, really strong. Wears glasses. Do you know where he is? Is he okay?"

Bee leans forward, her dark eyes creased with concern. She reaches out to take her hand. "I'm afraid Arlo was already dead when they found him."

Clem slumps back in her seat, all the air pushed sharply out of her lungs, the walls of the room seeming to fall in. She can't believe it. Arlo, dead? It's unbearable. He's too young. He's in his first year at university, has a part-time job in a café just around the corner, where Erin also worked. He always offered to do the dishes when he visited their flat. He's about to take his driving test, had showed her pictures of the car he was saving for. What was it? A Ford something, a decade old. She had sympathized with him about the cost of the insurance, over a thousand pounds. *But it's worth it*, she had told him. *To get your own set of wheels. Your own freedom.*

"Where is he?" she asks, an invisible curtain of ice sweeping across her skin. "The . . . body?"

Dr. Miller lifts his eyes in a dark look. "He's at the mortuary in Kirkwall."

"Oh my God." She begins to tremble from the shock of it. "Did he die in the fire?"

"From what the police have said, yes—it seems he was killed by the same fire that injured Erin."

"Do his parents know?"

"Yes. They are with him."

There is no processing it, no accepting the horror of it.

Erin will be absolutely ripped apart.

Freya starts, as though the stunned silence in the room has

bothered her, and Clem motions to the nurse to pass the baby to her. The nightmare pauses.

"Is she your youngest?" the nurse asks warmly, lowering to settle Freya into her arms.

"She's not mine," Clem says, feeling the tightness in her chest begin to ease as Freya curls into her. "She's Erin's baby."

CHAPTER FOUR

Isle of Gunn, Orkney
August 1594

ALISON

Late summer, and still the gardens outside are bursting with color, the rosebushes drowsy with fragrant blossoms. Orkney in August is a heaven in its own right, a place where you can easily imagine angels sitting on the hilltops, the fae gathering in the valley. This is the time of year when I feel I can breathe, when the warm sun turns the sea into a gold disk, when the brae is cloaked with sweet grass, and heather makes the valley seem to blush. The stones at the fairy glen disappear out of sight, swallowed by the wildflowers that push up, like a remembered song.

Today we are to travel to Kirkwall, where William is unveiling his work at the cathedral. It is an important day, not least because we will fetch him home. After many months of working tirelessly on the new quire, he will unveil it before the townsfolk, the clergy, and John Stewart, the Master of Orkney. I am so proud of him, but secretly I am more pleased to be bringing him back to Gunn. So many months apart has me longing for his company, for the feeling of safety he brings to our home. For his touch.

It is this that has me singing this morning as I hang the

coverlets and garments out on the line to dry, and when I see Edward return from the byre, I notice he is smiling, too. This pleases me greatly, for he has been melancholic of late, caught up in a dark mood. He has been since he turned thirteen. My mother tells me I was thus at his age, but I worry he is overhearing too much talk of strife in the isles. Gairsay, the isle next to ours, is the most fertile of the isles, and often the earl has made mention of it. Last month, a fierce blaze consumed seven cottages and fourteen acres of crops. Two men died, and their families have been left without food or shelter. We offered to take in several of the children, an offer that was not made lightly—our own supplies have been stretched this season. Without a milking cow, we have no milk, butter, or cheese, and Earl Patrick keeps raising the skat. Edward and I have been working in the udal fields to the south of the island, stolen by the earl.

In the end, the people whose cottages were destroyed went to stay with relatives on other islands. I have no doubt that they will yet be liable for their own skat, despite the destruction of their lands. And when they cannot pay it, Earl Patrick will then seize those lands against the skat. It is easy for him to do, given that udal law means that land is passed on verbally, without written deeds. It is an ancient practice upheld by trust, but one that allows the earl to usurp our property.

When William is not in Kirkwall, he is busy in the quarry, or meeting with the men from Gunn and other islands who seek to redress the earl's tactics. When William is home, they meet oft in our cottage, sitting by the stove, discussing ways to petition the king. It has become apparent that the king is not sympathetic to the plight of Orcadians, which makes our situation doubly precarious—a tyrannical earl and an apathetic king make us easy pickings.

But I fear that Edward has overheard too much of his father's conversations. It is a double task, living in such times—protecting my children both from the consequences of an avaricious tyrant and the bitter rage that fills the hearts of simple folk because of it. Edward is softhearted and still tender of age.

But today, the sun has lifted his countenance, and he is holding one of the hens in his arms, still smiling as he approaches.

"What has you in such a fair weather?"

It is Beatrice's voice, and I turn to see her addressing her brother, her fists on her little hips.

"Kirkwall has me in a fair weather," he answers. "And . . ."

He pulls a gleaming red strawberry from his pocket and drops it into his mouth, making both Beatrice and me gasp, but for different reasons.

"Give me!" she shrieks, and I chide him for picking the strawberries too early.

"It's only one," he says, laughing as Beatrice attacks him, and I tut and say no more. He races off, Beatrice chasing after, the hen flapping out of his arms. I mark the way his tunic has started to slip above his knees, his legs growing faster than I can weave.

"Good morrow, Alison," a voice calls. It is Agnes, making her way across the field, accompanied by a shaggy kyloe heifer tethered by a rope. Agnes lives on the other side of Gunn, and I have known her all my life. She is not Triskele, which endears me to her even more since I left. Before, all my friends were Triskele. My mother encouraged me to play with only Triskele children, to speak with only Triskele adults. It made leaving all the more difficult.

"Good morrow," I say, greeting her with a kiss on the cheek. "Is this your new steed?"

"This is your new milking cow," she says, and I stare, agape.

"I can't accept," I say, reaching out to scratch her fluffy nose. "This is too much."

She turns to Edward, who races past as Beatrice chases him with a stick. "I missed a certain young man's birthday," Agnes says, winking. "But what better gift than one that provides milk."

Edward and Beatrice stop running and stare at the heifer.

"She's such a bonny color," Beatrice says, rubbing the ginger flank.

Edward reaches out to touch the kyloe's horns. "Is she ours now?"

"No," I say, but Agnes says "Aye" at the same time. "She is," Agnes tells him, passing me the rope, and I take it, reluctantly.

"You are too kind," I tell her quietly. "I will have to repay you."

"The point of a gift is that it is not repaid," she says with a smile. She watched me cry after our own cow was killed. It was a brutal thing to happen—we loved her, had made the mistake of naming her. Penny, she was called. We couldn't afford to replace her, and so have depended on my mother's donations of milk and butter these last eight months.

"Will you be coming with us to the cathedral in Kirkwall?" Beatrice asks her. Agnes reaches out to touch Beatrice's blonde braids, fastened with a little piece of white ribbon at the ends.

"Sadly, I shall not," she says. "The boat unsettles my stomach. You must bring me back some sweetmeats."

Beatrice nods obediently. "I shall."

"Why are you *not* Triskele, Mama?" Beatrice asks. We are on the boat to Kirkwall, traveling with others who are going to the market. Beatrice is weaving stalks of barley into a doll, her little hands expertly braiding and tying until she is satisfied that the doll is made as she wishes.

"Papa isn't, either," Edward interjects.

"You mean, why did I leave?"

"She was born into the Triskele," Beatrice tells Edward. Then, uncertain: "Weren't you, Mama?"

I make to answer, but Edward gets there first. "You don't have to be born into it," he says. "Anyone can be initiated. Isn't that right, Mama?"

"Yes," I say. "Anyone can, so long as the other members of the Triskele approve."

"How many members are there, Mama?"

"Well, that is difficult to say. The Triskele are all over the world."

"Even in Persia?"

Beatrice has been learning about the countries of the world. I have taught the children since they were five, ensuring I gift them the education that was gifted me. With a pang, I remember that the only reason I received an education at all was because I was Triskele.

"Yes, even in Persia."

"What about Egypt?"

"I believe so."

Her eyes widen, and the questions tumble out of her: Do the Egyptian Triskele hold fast to the same traditions as the Triskele here in Orkney? Do they speak the same language as us?

"It matters not, Beatrice," Edward chides. "The magic is the same, and that is what matters. Isn't that right, Mother?"

I hold back from saying what I really want to say, because I know it will get back to my mother—that the Triskele are no longer regarded as a noble, warrior clan of magic-makers and spell-wielders. Instead, they are seen as feral and barbarous, their wisdom outdated and their methods peculiar.

And while Orkney has suffered under a litany of tyrants, wicked men purchasing their authority from the king and using it to seize land and starve the people, the Triskele has done nothing to stop them. Once, I believed they did not act because they were disinterested, that they considered themselves different from Orcadians, and therefore stood impassive to the earl's evil upon this land. Now I believe that William is right when he says that the real reason the Triskele do not support the rebels is simply because Triskele magic is not as powerful as I once believed. They are not a noble clan, the Protectors of Ancient Magic, but a group of cunning folk. Nothing special at all. Rather, they are shameful.

"Mama?" Beatrice says. "What is *The Book of Witching*?"

My jaw tightens at these words falling from my daughter's mouth.

"Well, it's a book," I say simply. "I think you saw it on the night of your initiation."

"It was very dark," she says, disappointed. "Grandmother says it's the most important book in the world."

"I know what it is," Edward says proudly.

I turn to him. "You do?"

He pulls his cap down over his eyes and wraps his scarf around his mouth, wiggling his fingers beside his head as he affects a deep voice.

"Not long after the earth's violent and fiery birth, a book came into existence. With a binding made from the bark of the first tree, and with pages black as moonless night, this book held the secrets of dark magic practiced by the earth's inhabitants. Whispered tales claimed the book was crafted not by human hands, but by spirits of darkness. It was called *The Book of Witching*."

"Is that true, Mama?" Beatrice asks. "The spirits of darkness made the book?"

I hesitate, neither wishing to add to Edward's dramatic recitation nor to lie. "What I must remind you, my dear, is that your father will be very displeased if he hears that the two of you were initiated into the Triskele."

"But why, Mama?" Beatrice says. "Why must we not tell him?"

"Because he will be angry," Edward says. He throws me a sullen look.

"You are both simply too young to understand his reasons," I say. "And this is a special day. We are here to see the work he has done at the cathedral, and to celebrate it."

The ship begins to slow, and the docks come into sight. A crowd of people wait there, many of them already waving handkerchiefs to signal to their loved ones. I scan the many faces and spy William, anxiously looking for us.

"Daddy!" Beatrice calls, and he sees us, his face lifting. He races to us, scooping up Beatrice and wrapping an arm around Edward. I hug him, and all four of us are joined together once more. It is the sweetest feeling on earth.

We walk along the cobbled streets toward the cathedral as Beatrice and Edward chatter to their father, telling him about our cow and their sighting of eagles from the brae. William and I can't get a word in edgewise, but he throws me smiles and winks as he answers the children's questions. It lifts my spirits to be in Kirkwall, with its crowds and enterprise, the hard stone of the streets calling up hooves and wheels, such a foreign sound. I am used to grass underfoot, and nothing but the rush of the sound and the call of the owls for days on end. And the cathedral, a vision of red and yellow sandstone, its magnificent spire thrusting up to the clouds and the stone gargoyles staring down. I had forgotten how big it was, how resplendent.

"Did you build this whole church, Daddy?" Beatrice asks when we reach the cathedral gardens, which causes the rest of us to laugh.

"I did, aye," William says. "Only took three months. Impressive, isn't it?"

Beatrice's eyes go wide as she stands in the cathedral gardens, staring up at the spire.

"It's only a wee jest," William says, and he tells her about the hands that made it, and why. "Vikings built that spire," he says. "They wanted to build a church that would be a light in the north, and a home for the body of St. Magnus. His bones lie inside a pillar, holding up the spire itself." Beatrice pulls a face, so he bends his knees to lower himself to her eyeline. "The reason they buried him here is so that, even in death, he would be seen to still be holding up a light to Orkney. And because he's a saint, his resting place brings people from far away to visit."

"Why?" she asks.

"Because it brings them hope. They feel that, if they touch the pillar wherein his body sleeps, they will be nearer to God."

Beatrice's eyes widen. "Can I touch it?"

"Of course."

Her hand in his, William takes our daughter inside the cathedral, Edward and me following after, to a pillar marked with a skull and crossbones.

"This is it?" she asks, and he nods. She stands still before it, contemplating what he told her, before reaching her hands out slowly to touch it.

"What did you feel?" Edward asks, visibly tempted to do the same. "Did it bring you hope?"

She nods, her face breaking into a smile. "It did."

Today it is market day, and so the cathedral thrums with people and animals. I love to admire the fabrics, both on the stalls and those worn by the people of Kirkwall. The peasantry may wear only wincey or hemp, dyed in shades of bracken, slate, sable, or thistle. But many elite reside in Kirkwall, and so there are garments of every color: kirtles of red silk, doublets with pink tassels, bodices made of whalebone instead of reeds that scratch the skin. I see Beatrice is similarly breathtaken by the girls her age wearing purple dresses hemmed with rabbit fur, the boys in lace breeches. Such clothing is certainly not washed in lye soap, and thus does not reek of pig fat. The cathedral is full of foul smells, however—the earthen stink of sheep and cows, and the dead, who are buried in shallow graves beneath the flagstones in the nave, the odor of rot faintly detectable beneath the lush garlands of tansies, trefoil, and willowherb hung about the pillars.

William introduces us to his employer, Mr. McNee, the master stonemason in Kirkwall. He is a courteous man, shaking the children's hands and taking time to praise them for having such a talented craftsman as their father.

"I like masonry, too," Edward says, and McNee turns to him.

"Do you, now?"

William places a hand on Edward's shoulder. "Finest dry waller on Gunn," he tells Mr. McNee. "And nimble in the quarry. We have yet to train him in the ways of the ax and point, but I daresay he'll master those as he has dry walling."

Edward's cheeks redden, and he shifts his feet.

"Well then," Mr. McNee says. "Perhaps we might have work for more than one Balfour. But first, let us celebrate your father's achievements."

We follow him to the quire, where fifteen stone arches have been newly sculpted, the pillars carved with designs that match the older patterns around the outside of the cathedral. Mr. McNee holds up a brass bell and rings it three times, drawing quiet across the crowd in this part of the cathedral. He waits a moment, allowing the people to gather. I see a number of masons join us, greeting

William—his colleagues, I realize, though I do not recognize them. Clergy and nobles join us, too, interested to discover the reason for the salutation.

"Orcadians of Kirkwall," Mr. McNee shouts. "I wish you all to join me in a public offering of thanks to our newest stonemason, whose mark you see here at the base of the pillar. We thank thee, William Balfour, for the craft you have bestowed upon the cathedral, and present you with this gift from the earl, a token of thanks from all of Orkney." Mr. McNee reaches for a wooden box at the base of the pillar and presents it to William. He appears to be surprised, opening it to find a gleaming silver ax therein, holding it aloft for all to see. A round of applause erupts from the crowd, and William shakes Mr. McNee's hands in thanks.

"Can I fetch sweetmeats, Mama?" Beatrice asks me.

"Sweetmeats?" Beatrice has never tried these.

"For Agnes," she reminds me.

William takes my hand and squeezes. "Edward, you go with your sister," he says. "Your mother hasn't seen my lodgings in the upper chambers."

I watch Edward dash off, and when I turn I see William has a familiar look in his eye. A look of longing. Silently, he leads me upstairs, introducing me to the workmen and clergy we pass by.

We reach a small room at the very top of the cathedral, where pigeons roost on joists, and where the floors below look terrifyingly far.

"Here we are," he says, opening the door.

"What snug lodgings . . ." I begin to say, but the rest of my words are stolen by his lips on mine, his hands searching for the hem of my dress. I know what he wants.

And I am glad of it.

. . .

"I do wish Mr. McNee hadn't presented the ax on behalf of the earl," William says as he fastens his belt. "I won't be able to use it now."

"You know Earl Patrick has no knowledge that you or the ax exist," I tell him.

"Even so."

"What is the talk of rebellion here in Kirkwall?" I ask him, careful, even in this small space, to keep my voice low.

"Still more talk than action," he says. "But we are gathering in number. The udallers are displeased with the earl."

"Of course they are," I say. "He has stolen their lands, after all."

He frowns in displeasure at the thought of it.

"I think the udallers are beginning to understand that rebellion is the only course of action for Orkney," William says. "Some of them still believe the Triskele will wave their wands and magic the land back into their possession."

He scoffs, and I look away, fearful that he may read my mind and discover what my mother has done.

"The Triskele has done nothing," he says, anger creeping into his voice. "They have stood by while the earl has driven the Orcadians to their knees."

I watch him pack his satchel, reminding myself how good it is that he will join us once more, that we will be a family again. And I make a note to tell my mother that my children's initiation does not hold, that they are not to be considered Triskele. William's ill wishes toward them are shared by many.

I do not wish that for my children.

We head downstairs, and I tell William that I will light candles while he takes his leave of his colleagues.

The north transept is quiet and vacant. Images of saints shine down from the stained-glass windows, and the candles shimmer for lost souls. I light three to remember our lost children. I whisper their names: the boy I named William, and the two little girls, both small as fairies: Eliza and Viola.

As I kneel at the altar, I hear footsteps behind. A priest approaching me, perhaps. But when I turn, I am astonished to see David Moncrief. I last saw him many months ago—January, the Wolf Moon—in the fairy glen on Gunn, when my children were initiated into the Triskele.

We are the same age, born a month apart. He has the same high forehead that bothered him as a boy, and the same kind eyes and deep scars upon his face from the pox that almost killed him many years ago. He received schooling for a time with me when his mother took ill, both receiving tuition on the Triskele language in my mother's cottage. She wanted me to marry him—Triskele members are strongly encouraged to marry within the tribe—but I met William and fell in love.

"Good morrow," I say, but he approaches no further, instead touching his chin—a Triskele greeting for *I wish you well*. I return the gesture.

"Madam Balfour," he says then. "John Stewart wishes to speak to you in the gardens. Will you follow me?"

"John Stewart?" I say, astonished.

"Aye, madam," he says, catching my eye a moment longer before beckoning me to follow.

David leads me to the gardens, where I see two men standing beneath a sycamore tree. One I recognize—he is Thomas Paplay, a man I healed some months ago. He is better now, a broad smile upon his face and his black hair swept back from his face. The other is of short stature, shorter than I, and broad as an urn, with unruly copper hair to his shoulders, a scraggly beard that touches his chest.

"Madam Balfour," David says, "I present you to John Stewart, Master of Orkney and cousin to His Majesty, King James."

"My lord," I say, bowing and averting my eyes. I cannot imagine what reason John Stewart has to call upon me, and I wait for him to tell David that he has brought the wrong person before him.

But he makes no such comment, and I see his hand extended, the gleaming jewels upon his fingers. I take it with a nervous kiss.

Thomas takes my hand next, pressing it to his own lips. "Madam Balfour, you know you have my undying thanks." He glances at John Stewart. "I have told my master of how you saved my life last winter."

I recall the scene that met me at Thomas Paplay's home last December. A man clinging to life by his fingernails, his body riven with smallpox, his pulse no more than a whisper. He had been treated with leeches and drained of blood. I kept a cloth tied across my mouth as I boiled cow's milk and sheep dung on his hearth, then fed the mixture to him, spoon by spoon. An old remedy, utterly foul to both smell and taste, but effective.

Evidently, he recovered.

I had no idea that Thomas Paplay was a servant of John Stewart's, however, nor David.

"I have a request," John says. "Walk with me."

"Of course."

I glance back at the cathedral, wondering if I should tell William. But John is already walking ahead, and I follow, keeping apace. We move deeper into the gardens, leaving the noise and bustle of the cathedral market behind. I am flanked by John and Thomas, with David following after. I find my heart is racing, not with curiosity, but with a sense of foreboding.

"I have heard that you are skilled at potions, and charms," John says at last. "Thomas tells me you restored his health, long after the physicians gave up."

"That is right," I say.

"I am glad for it," he says, glancing at Thomas. "I was hopeful that I may ask for another of your charms."

I stop then, noticing that a raven has perched on the branch of an oak tree ahead. A navy eye turns to me, and I feel a shudder pass through me. It is a warning.

"A charm," I say, and he nods. "May I ask the nature of the charm?"

I turn to face John and Thomas, ensuring that my expression is easy, a slight smile on my lips. I do not wish to seem unreasonable, or impertinent.

"You do not wish to discuss payment?" John says.

"My lord," I say softly. "It would be improper to discuss payment before I ascertain whether your request is within my capabilities."

I see a hardness pass across John's face. He flicks a look at Thomas, who steps forward.

"Your charm saved my life," he says. "I would say you are capable, madam. We know you possess the skills we require."

"You wish me to save a life?" I say lightly. The raven has not moved, though we approach it.

"Not *save* a life," Thomas says, glancing at his master.

I stop and hold him in a deep look, searching his face. "You wish me to prepare a charm that will take a life?" I whisper.

His eyes slide to John's once more, and then he gives a small nod. John's gaze does not move from my face. David steps forward.

"Madam Balfour, it would be prudent to accept this request."

A heat grows on the back of my neck. My hand is being forced, I can feel it. I am indeed capable of such a charm, but the thought of it makes me gravely worried—the Master of Orkney has power to hold any one of the citizens of Orkney in prison, or to remove us from our homes, or even to starve us to our death. That he should then require *more* power leads me to believe that this charm is not for use on someone who holds less status than he.

It is for someone who stands above.

I bow deeply, trying not to reveal the fear such thoughts have caused to sink into my bones.

Who could John Stewart wish to kill?

"My lord, I give you thanks for holding me in such high esteem as to make this request. But you see, this charm can only be made by someone who has not witnessed death. And as I have witnessed much, I am unable."

It is a lie, but I have no choice. *May God forgive me.*

John holds me in a dark look. I sense he is angry, but I return his gaze with an apologetic expression, though my heart is hammering in my chest. I have deliberately answered in a way that prevents him from seeking out my mother, and indeed most of the practitioners of magic. I sense that he is quite prepared to use force if necessary, which is why I chose to lie.

"Thank you, Madam Balfour," Thomas says, disapprovingly. "You may leave us."

"My lord," I say, bowing again. "I wish you well in your endeavors."

I bow again, trembling now, before heading quickly back to the cathedral.

CHAPTER FIVE

Glasgow
May 2024

CLEM

It is a wrench to leave the hospital, but Freya is growing fractious, and Clem knows there are people she needs to call and share the terrible news with.

Clem sits for a moment in her car outside the hospital, listening to Freya wail in her car seat.

"It's all right, darling," she tells her, reaching back to hold her hand. Freya is due to have lunch. She will take her to nursery, that's what she'll do. It will give her headspace to think about whom to call. She'll need to take time off both her jobs, the one at the school and the other at the café. She'll inform Erin's employers, her friends, find out whatever she can from them. And the police, she'll need to speak to the police. The nurse at the hospital wasn't able to get Entresto, so she needs to go home. She's already feeling faint.

She drops Freya off at nursery, apologizing for her lateness. She sees the smiling faces of the nursery staff, the other children playing in ball pits and at the sand table, and decides she must lie. No mention of Erin, not now. She'll fall apart, and these poor people won't know what to do with her.

Clem was with Erin when she delivered Freya, holding her hand and whispering words of comfort. Her focus had been entirely on Erin, but as soon as Freya came into the world, she felt it, the heat of a different element.

As though a new color had been introduced to the world.

She waves goodbye to Freya, blowing kisses through the window, her heart lifting a little when she sees Freya running to join in at the sand table.

Clem knows she should call Quinn. Quinn is Erin's father, living happily with his wife and sons in West Yorkshire. Her marriage to Quinn lasted just eighteen months, falling apart while Erin was just beginning to wean. His efforts to be a father to her have been a study in ineptitude. Watching Erin teaching herself to be content with the crumbs of Quinn's affection has been a protracted explosion of any feeling Clem once had for her ex-husband. She wanted Erin to cut him out of her life, had to hold herself back from urging her to do so. But Erin has craved her father, has moved through her own cycle of hatred and love and bitter disappointment, and all Clem has been able to do is watch and despair.

She sits in her car and stares at Quinn's number on her contact list, trying to summon the strength to call him and let him know what has happened to his only daughter. But just then, the phone rings in her hand. A number she doesn't recognize flashes on the screen.

"Hello?"

"Yes. Hi, this is Senna's mum, Elizabeth. Is that Clementine?"

She gasps. "Hi, yes. Have the police contacted you about Senna?"

On the other end, Elizabeth begins to cry, and Clem waits, a hand to her mouth, for Elizabeth to speak. She's never met Senna's mother, has met Senna only a few times, and always in passing.

She and Erin first met a few years ago. But now she feels connected to this woman, both of them sharing the same nightmare.

"There are police with sniffer dogs in Orkney," Elizabeth says, her voice shaking. "They can't find Senna."

Clem's mouth falls open. "What do you mean, they can't find Senna?"

"Does Erin know where Senna is?" Elizabeth asks.

"N . . . no. She's . . . she hasn't woken up . . ."

"I'm so sorry," Elizabeth says. "This is all such . . . such a shock. I don't know what to do . . ."

"Do you have any idea what happened?" Clem asks.

"I've no idea," Elizabeth says, her voice thick with emotion. "They went to Orkney for their trip. Senna said they were camping." She trails off, her voice breaking. "I'm just so worried."

"You must be. God, Elizabeth. I'm so sorry."

"I gave my phone to the police with all the texts. She texted me on Tuesday."

"What did she say?"

"Senna said she wanted to come home."

The back of Clem's neck prickles. "Oh? Did they have an argument or something?"

"Yes, the girls did. But, you know, three teenagers on a hiking trip . . . I thought nothing of it. That was the last message I got." She takes a breath. "And Arlo is dead. I never even met him. His poor parents . . ."

"Elizabeth, do you know why Senna wanted to come home?" Clem asks, her mind flinging to an imagined scene of the girls, and Arlo, on a beach in Orkney. Why would they have argued? The weather was glorious, a balmy twenty degrees, and the photographs Erin had sent were of postcard-pretty landscapes.

"I can't remember," Elizabeth says, her voice catching. "I'm

THE BOOK OF WITCHING 49

going out of my mind. I've been ringing her phone nonstop, and it just goes to voicemail. I mean, where could she have gone?"

Clem bites back a reply. She imagines Senna caught up in the fire that claimed Arlo, and rushing into the sea. Perhaps she drowned. It's a harrowing thought.

"Please tell me if Erin tells you anything."

"I will," Clem tells her, and hangs up.

The clenching in her chest starts up again, the frightening stall between heartbeats. She needs to take her medication, and quickly.

She drives home, parks up, rushes blindly into her flat. She swallows her pills with a glass of water, holding firmly to the side of the sink in case her knees give. She feels faint, but bats the thought of it away. She can't faint. She has a daughter in the hospital and a granddaughter in the nursery, and they need her.

Once she feels strong enough, she heads into Erin's bedroom, a sob in her throat. Elizabeth's voice echoes in her ears. *The girls had an argument.* She tries to push away the idea that an argument had something to do with this terrible tragedy, but it scratches at her mind, like a cat wanting to come inside from the cold.

And so she stands in Erin's bedroom, looking over the baby ephemera, clothes scattered on the floor, endless Shein bags. A pile of tarot cards, crystals arranged in a cabinet. Runes in a jar. Erin has always been into all things mystical and pagan.

Her eyes are drawn to Erin's mixed media canvas hanging above the cot, the one she made for Freya a few months after she was born. It's a meter long by a half meter wide, spelling out PROTECT ME FROM WHAT I WANT in large, wobbly letters. Such a curious thing to put above a cot.

Clem hadn't thought much of it when Erin hung it on the wall last year; her mind, obviously, was consumed by the prospect of the baby, the insanity of becoming a grandmother in her midforties.

But now, as she steps closer, she sees that the mixed media is in fact bits of nature, dead leaves and feathers stitched into the canvas and sitting outward from the letters. The final letter *t* is a fine animal bone stitched into the canvas.

Clem shudders. Why hadn't she noticed that before?

There is nothing in the room to ease her mind on the matter of Senna, and the argument. She finds Quinn's number on her phone, and when it starts to ring she feels a familiar twist in her gut, preparing her for a fight.

The call doesn't go through; a message pings up on her phone, a virtual slap in the face.

I'm sorry, I can't talk right now.

She rings again, and when the same message flings up she types a message.

Erin's in intensive care. Answer.

Quinn phones her straight back.

"What?" he barks. "Erin's in hospital?"

"I got a phone call this morning," she says, and tells him everything she knows.

"I'll drive up this afternoon," he says, and her heart lifts a little at the relief of this. Even someone as hapless as Erin's father is better than dealing with this alone.

CHAPTER SIX

Fynhallow, Orkney
October 1594

ALISON

Samhain: the Witch's Feast. Edward carries the apples from the orchard in a basket and drops them in front of the fire. They are to be buried beneath the threshold of the house, as we do every year, before going guising and dooking for apples.

"How do I look?" Beatrice asks, twirling in a long white sheet that has been pulled over her head like a ghost. I'm about to chide her for putting holes in a good sheet when I notice the eye holes are coal marks.

"Very ghostly," I say. "But how do you expect to see?"

"I can see a little," she says, hitting the coffer with her shin.

"Come here," I tell her, and I use coal to black the sockets of her eyes and her lips, and ash to whiten her cheeks, before tying the fabric around her neck. I do the same for Edward, and then William appears, wearing a dark bandanna, his eye socket blackened like a pirate.

"Argh!" he roars, and Beatrice gives a shrill scream in response. "I hear tell a banshee haunts these parts," he says, swiping the air with a wooden cutlass.

"Woooo!" Beatrice says, spreading her arms out wide.

"I think a banshee is meant to scream," I tell her, cutting an apple into pieces.

The four of us head to the vegetable patch on the field overlooking Fynhallow beach. A row of children are pulling up kale stalks, and Beatrice does the same.

"You have to close your eyes!" little Gundrea tells Beatrice, who immediately squeezes her eyes shut and pulls up her stalk, which is almost as long as she is.

"You're going to marry a long, thin man," Gundrea says, appraisingly.

"And look at all the soil at the roots," Abigail cries, gleefully clawing at a handful of earth and holding it aloft. "That means he'll be rich!"

Beatrice claps her hands, and the three of them run off toward the bonfire along the bay, white sheets streaming behind them. Edward walks along with me, a little somber. I see his friends Adam and Caleb, dressed in black cloaks and guising at the door of the MacCrimmons' cottage.

"Why don't you join them?" I ask him, but he mumbles something that suggests he doesn't want to. Adam catches sight of Edward but looks away. My heart aches for Edward—they were always so close, so similar in temperament, and now it seems they're no longer friends.

"William?" a voice calls, and we glance at the cottage opposite, where the orange glow of a lantern lights up a familiar face. Duncan. He waves at us, and we head inside.

By the fire of Duncan's small cottage, we find a gathering of six others, all rebels—Dougal White and his wife, Ola, Isaac Henderson, John Rathmire, Robert Kent, and Jack McKinnon. The mood is heavy.

"What has happened?" William asks, seeing the looks on the men's faces.

"Come inside," Isaac says grimly.

We sit down next to the fire, and Ola passes us both a bowl of hot broth.

"Earl Patrick has put a man to death," Jack says. "Thomas Paplay. He was executed this afternoon in Kirkwall."

I start at the name. Thomas Paplay? I think of our meeting in the gardens of the cathedral this past summer. The way he petitioned me for a charm to take a life.

"Thomas Paplay is a servant of John Stewart," I say, astonished.

"Why would the earl put his own brother's servant to death?" William asks, shock in his voice.

"It is rumored that he attempted to kill the earl."

I feel my heart begin to beat faster, a feeling like ice spreading across the skin of my arms and shoulders. I think of the raven I saw in the gardens, the warning I knew it carried as I conversed with the men. Their strange request, and the way John looked at me.

I knew that John would seek out such a charm only for someone who held more power than he, but to attempt to kill his own brother? Surely not.

"Do you think John Stewart knew of this plan?" Robert asks, folding his arms. He speaks with a wry tone, for there have long been whispers that John sought to be earl instead of his younger, legitimate brother. He has grown up being called "John the Bastard," and is doubtless tired of it. But to kill his own brother?

"Are you all right?" William asks me. I must be pale.

I nod and glance at the floor, hating myself for lying to him. I never told him of the encounter I had with John Stewart and Thomas Paplay at the cathedral in Kirkwall, and I am yet wary of sharing my thoughts. Even among friends.

What if the blame for Earl Patrick's death is placed upon me?

"We all know that John Stewart wishes to seize the earldom," Ola says. "And if he succeeds, he'll be every bit as bad as his brother, if not worse."

"Surely the earl would kill Stewart," Dougal says, "if he suspects he was behind this murder plot?"

"It's a show of strength," William says. "Earl Patrick has many enemies. He will not simply kill his brother, regardless of whether he suspects his involvement."

"Aye," Isaac says, removing a pipe from his lips. "That is right. Thomas Paplay was tortured to death."

"Tortured?" I ask, an icy sensation creeping across my skin.

"The earl sends a message to anyone who dares to attack him," Ola says with a whisper.

"It has been one thing for Earl Patrick to set the skat so high that folk are starved to the bone," William says through gritted teeth. "And we know how much land he has stolen and how many of our people he has enslaved."

A murmur of agreement rises from our friends as Duncan recounts the earl's crimes upon our lands, for which he will never be held accountable: He destroyed the archives in the great library on the upper floors of St. Magnus Cathedral. Hundreds of years of Orcadian history, burned. He has taken land from the udallers, or the gentry who lay claim to their land through Viking heritage. And just last summer, he captured a merchant ship in Danzig. The rebels dispatched word of the earl's piracy to King James, and when Earl Patrick was called to stand before him at the court in Edinburgh, we thought we had at last succeeded. But somehow he managed to persuade the king to set him free.

He reminds me of an eel, too slippery to hold.

"I have learned that the udallers have the ear of Bishop Law,"

Will says, referring to the incoming bishop of Orkney. "Bishop Law has the ear of the king. Finally, if we play our cards right, he may listen. And act."

We look at one another for a long time, in silence. I dare not hope that this could happen. For a moment, I see the Orkney of my childhood—golden fields fat with wheat, the kilns in constant use for the grain. Cows that do not need to be carried from the barns for milking because they're too weak from starvation to walk.

Earl Patrick's reign has brought the islands to their knees, even more than the plagues that ravaged us in years gone by. Up here on the islands, so far north from the cities, we are powerless against such tyranny.

Twelve days later

I am making stew by the stove of my cottage when I hear horses hooves thundering up the hillside. I look out and see David Moncrief astride his horse. He is wearing an officer's uniform and a sword at his belt. My breath catches. Why is he here, approaching my home?

"Who is it, Mother?"

More horses appear on the bank—two more officers, and the broad shoulders of a man dressed in noble furs. It is John Stewart.

I give a gasp, and Edward is by my shoulder, peering at the scene before us. I meet his eyes, and his face is filled with panic.

"They are here for father," he says. "Aren't they?"

"Go to the loft," I tell him hastily. "Fetch your sister."

"No," he says, his eyes fixed on the men. "I won't let them take Father."

"Mama?" Beatrice calls, hearing the note of fear in my voice. "What is the matter?"

I hear a rattling sound, then see the square shape of a carriage. *They are here to make an arrest.*

I lean close to Edward's ear. "Wake your father," I whisper. "Tell him to hide. *Go.*"

His eyes are wide, but he turns sharply to do my bidding as I step toward the men.

"Good morrow," I call with a smile, using all my strength to remain calm in the face of whatever news befalls us. "What can I do for you, Master Stewart?"

John Stewart has halted his horse close to where I stand, his eyes meeting mine. *He remembers me,* I think, from our exchange in Kirkwall. I turn to David, who stays mounted. For a moment I wonder if this meeting has to do with Thomas Paplay and his request for a charm. *Surely not,* I think. *I have done no harm.*

But then one of the soldiers dismounts and with a grim look stalks toward me. A hand reaches for his sword, and his black eyes settle on my face.

"My husband is not here," I say, panicked. "He is in Kirkwall."

"We haven't come for your husband," John Stewart shouts with a sneer, and fear seizes me.

The officer seizes my arm and begins to pull me toward the cart. Beatrice darts out of the house after me, shrieking "Mama! Mama!" Edward is there now, and he grabs her. I try to pull away, but the officer is too strong. He drags me toward the carriage.

"We are instructed by the Earl of Orkney to arrest you and bring you to Kirkwall regarding an attempt on his life," the officer says.

"Sir, I have done nothing!" I want to say more to John Stewart, to remind him of how we walked and talked this past summer. He knows I gave him no charm.

But perhaps his asking me for it was a trap. He asked me in a public place, on a market day, with plenty of folk milling around.

William comes racing out of the house now, Beatrice in his arms, sobbing loudly.

"Have your bairns collect any personal items," the officer says, flinging open the doors of the carriage with his free hand. "You are to be delivered to Kirkwall on suspicion of witchcraft."

"Witchcraft?" I say, astonished. The air leaves my lungs. Though King James's witchcraft trials in North Berwick two years ago are well known, not a single soul has ever been arrested for witchcraft on the isles of Orkney.

"You will not take my mother," Edward says, stepping forward as though to snatch the warrant from the officer's hands, but the man lets me go and, pulling a heavy truncheon from his belt, he strikes Edward, hard, on the side of the head, sending him to the ground.

"Edward!" I scream, and I am on my knees beside him, pressing my hands to his head as the skin splits from the blow, spilling ribbons of blood to the grass, arterial and dark.

In a moment William is there, holding Beatrice close to him.

"My wife is innocent!" he shouts, but the soldier who bludgeoned Edward unsheathes a knife and holds it close to his neck.

"Calm," he tells the soldier, moving Beatrice behind him for protection. "Calm, sir."

David Moncrief strides toward me, holding open the doors of the carriage. I search his face. "No good will come of arresting me," I say, my voice trembling. I glance back at John Stewart, who stays mounted. "Please, there must be a mistake in this claim."

No one acknowledges I have spoken. I turn to William, holding him in a look. We are both filled with terror. Neighbors have gathered outside their homes, but no one rushes to help us—against John Stewart, we have no recourse.

"No!" Edward calls out, but William pulls him away, clapping a hand to his mouth.

My heart feels close to breaking.

David fastens iron cuffs around my wrists, ankles, and neck, like a dog. I stare at him in disbelief. He was there the day that John Stewart asked me for a charm to take a life. He saw me refuse.

He is Triskele. We are childhood friends. But his loyalty is not to me.

He opens the doors to the carriage, forcing me inside.

CHAPTER SEVEN

Glasgow
May 2024

CLEM

The police come to the hospital that afternoon: a woman in her forties in a gray trousers suit and brogues, her blonde hair tied back in a tight ponytail. A flash of a snake tattoo on her wrist. And a man in a navy suit, late fifties, dark-eyed and somber, who introduces himself as Detective Constable Sanger.

"How are you?" he asks Clem.

She takes a sharp breath and nods, the answer too overwhelming to speak aloud.

"This is Detective Constable Dorrit," he says, nodding at his colleague. "She's your family liaison officer."

"Call me Stephanie," the woman says, shaking Clem's hand.

"What's a family liaison officer?" Clem asks weakly.

"I'll be supporting you during the investigation," Stephanie says gently. "Any queries you have, anything you need, you come to me. I'm the point of contact between you and the other people involved in the inquiry."

"I know this is the worst possible time for you to have to answer questions from the police," DC Sanger says. "But it's also the most important time if we're to figure out what happened. Do you mind speaking with us for a few minutes?"

"Of course."

Clem follows them to a side room, the three of them still in their armory of yellow plastic. Stephanie closes the door on the small room, and Clem feels faint. She sits down and grips the sides of the chair to steady herself.

"We just wanted to get an understanding of what Erin and her friends were doing in Orkney," DC Sanger says, pulling off the plastic gown with a free hand while fetching a small notepad and pen from his pocket.

Clem nods. "Have you spoken to Arlo's parents already?"

"We have," DC Sanger says, and Clem's stomach flips.

"How are they?"

He gives a sad sigh. "About as well as you might expect."

She shakes her head, unable to speak at the thought of what Arlo's parents must be going through. "I'd like to speak to them," she says. "I don't have a number for them. Perhaps you can give it to me?"

"I'll pass on your number, how about that?" he says, and she nods.

"Can you tell us what Erin said about the trip?" Stephanie asks gently. "What plans she mentioned?"

"No plans, other than visiting Orkney," Clem says, her voice shaking. "She took a DNA test a few years ago and it said she had a huge link to Orkney. I think she wanted to trace some ancestors."

"And she wanted her friends to go with her?"

Clem nods. "She and Arlo were together for about a year, I think. She didn't tell me when they first got together."

"Why was that?" DC Sanger asks.

Clem isn't sure why they need to know this. "I don't know. She's always been secretive."

"How long were they gone for?"

Clem turns her mind back to the morning when she drove the three teenagers, happy, playful, to Glasgow Central. "They left the Saturday before last. April twenty-first? They took the train to Scrabster, then got the ferry to Stromness. They didn't book return tickets, just so Erin could come back earlier if she wanted to. She has a daughter, Freya. She's fifteen months old. Erin was anxious about going away, now that I think about it. She was excited at first but then more anxious as it got closer."

DC Sanger scribbles down notes. Clem sees the word *anxious* underlined. "Why do you think that was?" he asks.

Clem thinks back to the night before Erin left. She sees herself in the doorway of Erin's bedroom as she knelt by her rucksack, stuffing it with smalls, her face tight and flushed. She asked her what was wrong, thinking that maybe she couldn't find something she needed for the trip, or maybe that Senna had pulled out. Erin looked up.

I'm scared, Mum.

She glanced at Freya then, and Clem assumed she meant she was scared to leave Freya for a whole three weeks. It was a long time, after all, and she still remembered how nervous she had been to leave Erin when she was a baby, even for a night out.

But maybe it was something else.

"I encouraged her to go," she says tearfully.

"Why was that?"

Clem swallows back a sob, bitterly recalling her own words. *Go and have fun. Freya will be fine!*

"It's difficult to explain."

"Try." DC Sanger's voice is suddenly pressing.

How to put the last three years in a sentence?

"Erin got pregnant at seventeen," she says slowly. "It was just completely out of the blue. She'd been a grade A student, had a place at Oxford to read Politics and Philosophy. But then . . ."

"But what?" DC Sanger presses.

Clem bites her lip. "I don't know what happened. She bombed her Highers. Didn't even turn up for some. She's not seen much of her dad over the years but I was so desperate I drove her to his house in Wetherby for an emergency family meeting, you know, a crisis gathering." She thinks back, flinching as she remembers the three of them in Quinn's orangery on a hot August afternoon, surrounded by dead flies and lukewarm elderflower cordials, Heather and the boys hovering in the extension nearby.

"Quinn and I asked her what was going on," Clem says. "And she told us she was pregnant."

Stephanie nods sympathetically. "That must have been quite a shock."

"It was," she says. "And an extra shock because there was no inkling she was seeing anyone. Erin's bisexual. She's had a few girlfriends in the past but no boyfriend that we knew of. And when we asked who the father was, she just shrugged. We worried she was sleeping around, or being abused, or something."

"And was she?" DC Sanger asks.

Clem hesitates. "I don't think so. But we still don't know who Freya's father is."

DC Sanger writes that down. "What about phone calls and messages since they left? Was there anything that indicated another traveler? Someone they met up with?"

Clem feels her blood run cold. "No. I mean, I don't think so." The implication of this hits her like a rock. "Are you saying they met up with someone else?"

"We're still trying to work out what happened," DC Sanger says.

"Where is the site?" Clem asks. "Where were they when . . . it happened?"

"On the island of Gunn. Do you know Orkney?"

Clem shakes her head. "Not at all."

"Gunn's an unusual spot for a group of teenagers, I must say."

"I thought all of Orkney was beautiful," Clem says, looking across both their faces. "That's what Erin said."

"It is. But Gunn's a strange one. Hasn't been inhabited since the eighteen hundreds, since it was ravaged by plague. Not the prettiest island, either. There isn't a ferry service to it."

Clem draws a sharp breath, not sure what to make of this. "How did they get to it if there wasn't a ferry?"

"The island has a low tide," Stephanie says, "so you can wade across from Gairsay, which *does* have a regular ferry."

"God." She feels more confused with each answer to her questions, an endless spiral of mystery.

"The island does have quite a controversial history among the locals. Your daughter and the boy were found on a beach known as Fynhallow."

"I've never heard of it," Clem says, her stomach flipping at the word *found*. The thought of Erin helpless and vulnerable in some remote place for God knows what reason feels like her skin is being stripped off, very slowly.

"Would it be possible to take a look at the messages Erin sent you in the days leading up to the incident?" Stephanie asks.

Clem begins to say yes, then hesitates. "Why?"

The detectives share a glance. "We want to cross-reference the messages sent to the other parents," DC Sanger says. "To build a picture of their last activities. Senna's still missing, and Arlo's hands were bound when he died. This is now a murder investigation."

CHAPTER EIGHT

Orkney
November 1594

ALISON

The journey from Gunn to Kirkwall should take no more than an hour, but today the sea is furious, insistent on driving us back from the port, as though it knows as well as I do that the charges against me are spurious.

I watch John Stewart and the other men carefully as they sit at the far end of the boat, leaving me in the locked carriage, the iron bands on my wrists a sickening taunt. Over and over in my mind I think of Edward, how he fought for me, and the terrible sound of the baton against his head. It breaks my heart not to tend to him. Not to comfort him in my arms.

The boatman changes course, sailing east toward Stromness. White squalls slam down inside the boat, causing the skin of my wrists and ankles to chafe against my iron bonds, which are fastened to the bow.

By the time we arrive at the port, the sky is ink black, the wet streets quiet and desolate as the carriage moves over the cobbles, the horses' hooves echoing off the long walls of the palace. I start to shiver, fear setting in deep.

A shout from outside brings the carriage to a halt. Through the slats of the carriage I see thick walls that rise up, and with a sharp inhalation I realize where we are: this is Kirkwall Castle.

I hear the driver step down. He drags something wet from the back of his throat and spits it on the ground before unlocking the door. He tugs the chain, pulling me along the floor to the lip of the carriage, holding the chain around my neck to pull me close enough to smell his stinking breath.

"Rank witch," he hisses.

The orange glow of a second torchlight falls across the ground, showing the meeting of stone with grass, and the shadow of a figure headed toward us. It is John Stewart, his familiar swaying gait, the red scorch of his beard. I shrink back from him, but he ignores me, addressing the driver in a tired voice.

"Bring her hither, Mr. Addis."

We are at the back door of the castle, a looming door studded with sharp iron prongs. It creaks open at our approach. John speaks to the doorman, and at once we are led inside, the driver—Mr. Addis—tugging me behind him.

I have never been inside the castle, and the entrance hall feels consuming, muscular walls shrouding us closely, a dog's bark from somewhere deep in the structure echoing off the stone. Overhead is an iron chandelier as big as a cart, twelve candles guttering and dancing in the draft from the hallway. The air is scented with cloves and oranges.

Footsteps sound, a different pace to John Stewart's. Another light flares ahead, gilding the arch of a doorway wrought in dense stone, and the outline of a figure appears suddenly in the gloom.

"Your Grace," Mr. Addis says with a nod. "I brought your witch."

A man steps forward into the firelight. I see he is a parson, his robes made of sumptuous black velvet, the cassock of embroidered linen. A leather belt with a heavy brass buckle cinctures the cassock.

I flinch as he moves toward me, so close I can smell his scent— peat and earth, a faint tang of sweat.

"Well," he says to John, eyeing me with an arched eyebrow. "Bring her forward."

I feel myself tugged toward the parson, though I keep my gaze on the ground, allowing him to look upon me. If I meet his gaze, it may be taken as defiance. On this land, and within these walls, I am conscious of how I might appear as guilty. I am not, but that does not matter.

"My child," the parson says, reaching out to lift my chin toward him. His gaze is gentle, his blue eyes soft beneath thick white eyebrows. "I am Father Colville, the king's chamberlain. I believe you and I have much to discuss."

I nod, but this news terrifies me. The king's chamberlain! I am in grave trouble.

"Master John told me I'd be paid tonight," Mr. Addis says in a gravelly voice. He shuffles forward to my side, as though not wanting to be dismissed quite so soon.

"And you shall," Father Colville says. "God thanks you, Mr. Addis. Madam Alison Balfour," he says, with a gracious bow. "Follow me."

John gives me a long, silent look before turning to walk out of the castle.

The parson leads me up a staircase that spirals to the very top of the castle, stone steps ribboning into a confine so tight I must press my arms to my sides in order to climb.

The stairs deliver us to the upper chamber that sits out over the courtyard, a small window allowing the moonlight to pour across the wooden floor. Father Colville sets the candle on a table in a corner. Then he removes his cap and ruffles the thinning white hair on his crown, which is damp with sweat. The journey up the stairs has tired him. He has small blue eyes that seem to linger on me a moment longer than is common, as though he sees something that others do not. His manner is calming, though I am thrumming with fear. I watch how carefully he removes the scarf across his shoulder, folding it gently, with reverence, before setting it on a chair by the wall.

"Shall we begin in prayer?" he asks.

He lifts the hem of his robe and kneels by the small altar by the window, his palms pressed together and his face turned to the dark sky. I lower awkwardly and kneel beside him. I am shaking from head to toe, and I hope he does not notice.

"Father, we pray unto Thee for Thy Spirit to attend us this night." He speaks in somber tones, his eyes open and his head still held aloft, as though he converses with Christ in the flesh. "Bestow upon us Thy grace, and help us purge ourselves of the evil we hold within our hearts. Amen."

"Amen," I murmur. My mind is wheeling around ways to disclose to the parson what I believe—that John Stewart is trying to blame me for something I did not do in order to cover his own tracks.

"We shall read from Peter, in the New Testament," he says, opening the Bible. "First Peter, chapter four, verses twelve and thirteen. You know it?"

I open my mouth, willing some memory of this verse to come to mind. "I forget," I say at last.

"Saint Peter here is telling us that we are not to avoid fiery trials, but to embrace them, as Christ embraced His own suffering. It is by suffering that we are purified, and therefore find joy. Do you believe this, my child?"

"Yes," I say. "It brings us closer to God."

"You are right. The Devil can possess our bodies, but not when we suffer."

The air in my lungs seems frozen and spiked somehow, like sharp icicles. I nod, but my jaw is tight.

"Let us speak of the reason you are here," he says, folding his hands beneath his chin. "You are accused of a very serious crime, my child. An attempt on the life of the earl."

I begin to shake my head. "I would never . . ."

"Be careful that you mind who I serve," he says, cocking his head. "I serve God, and He cannot be deceived."

I force myself to look him in the eye, keeping my voice measured. "Father, I swear to God that I had no part in this."

"There are indeed many who would seek the earl's life," he continues. "And many who would pay handsomely for assistance. I see you are a woman of humble means."

"I have sufficient," I say, then thinking better of it: "But even if I were to starve, and my children to starve, I would not seek a man's life."

"Your children? How many?"

"I have two on the earth, Father. Three are with Christ in heaven."

"They were baptized?"

I swallow. "Two were."

"So one is in Purgatory, with the Devil," he says, nodding as though there cannot be any alternative.

His words feel like a knife to my flesh. "I . . . believe the child is with God. An innocent child taken to His grace."

He stares at me as though I am a fool, but I cannot take back my words. My mother has always said I was too honest, but then she has also said that I must always be honest. I have never found the distinction between these two rules.

"You know that Thomas Paplay was charged with conspiring to kill?" he says.

I give a cautious nod. "I heard he was arrested, Father. And that he was executed."

"He confessed. The caschielaws drove out the Devil from him, and he spoke the truth."

I lift my eyes to his, stricken. "Caschielaws?"

He nods, and smiles.

The caschielaws are metal bands cooked in fire until they gleam red as pokers, hot enough to strip the skin clean off with a single touch. They are set upon the skin of a criminal and left there for a time, then replaced with another freshly cooked set of metal bands, to ensure the pain meted by the heat against flesh is constant. I have only ever heard of the caschielaws used once, in Edinburgh, upon a man who had brutally killed a child. He died within hours.

"The earl survived the attack, though he was gravely ill," Father Colville says. "A physician attended him. He found an object, a hexed charm, beneath Earl Patrick's bed. Tell me, are you able to create a charm to hex a person?"

I draw a sharp breath, the implication of his question hitting me like a spike. "I would never . . ."

"I asked if you are *able*," he says. "Are you able to make such charms? Please, do not lie, my child."

The candlelight flickers, animate, as though a third figure is in the room. My cheeks burn. "My magic is for good," I say finally, the vise around my throat tightening. "Yes, I believe I may be able. But I did not."

"You are able," he repeats softly, trying the words out, like the sounds of a new language, fresh in his mouth. "What if I told you that Thomas Paplay said that you were the one who hexed the charm he used on the earl?"

My mouth falls open. "But that is a lie," I say.

"But you were seen, my child. In the cathedral, speaking with Mr. Paplay, merely days before the earl took ill."

"He did approach me in the cathedral garden," I say, wondering how to tell him what was said. I wish to appear helpful, eager to search out the truth with him. A collaborator in finding justice. "And he asked after a charm."

"Which charm?"

I stiffen. "He did not say, Father." It is a lie, but I feel panic at the thought of telling the king's chamberlain that a member of the royal family, the king's own cousin, approached me for a charm that would end a life. It will immediately implicate John in the earl's poisoning. What penalty will befall me if I make such a claim?

"Thomas Paplay told Earl Patrick that you provided him with a charm of wax," Father Colville says. "With something inscribed into it."

"I did not," I say, straightening.

"Others say you have provided them with a similar token in the past."

"I have, Father. But that was in the past."

"Why would he name you?" he asks. "He swore upon his children's lives and before God that *you* gave him the charm."

"I do not know, Father." This man does not trust me. That he sees I am lying.

"Thomas Paplay swore before God to tell the truth," Father Colville says tersely. "Let me remind you, madam, that this man was the servant of the Master of Orkney, John Stewart. A trusted, loyal servant."

But he tried to kill the earl, I think. His eyes move across my face, as though trying to read my mind. He does not have to say it—he does not have the charm to show to me, and it bothers him.

"Do you have the charm? Perhaps if I see it, I can understand who did make it."

"Perhaps you orchestrated this," he says, ignoring my request. "Perhaps it was not Thomas's will to kill the earl, but yours."

"Mine?" I say, shocked.

"My child," he says softly. "If you confess your crimes to me now, I will spare your life."

I open my mouth, confused. "But I . . . I am innocent of this charge, Father."

The look of softness slips from his face.

"Then I cannot help you."

I open my mouth to plead with him. He *must* help me. Surely he cannot insist upon a confession, if I am innocent?

But he rises from his chair, signaling that our conference is over. He nods at Mr. Addis, who steps into the doorway before turning to signal that I am to follow them down the stairs.

To the dungeon.

CHAPTER NINE

Glasgow
May 2024

CLEM

Strangers, so many of them, who are now on first-name terms, have become towering monoliths in Clem's life almost instantly. Surgeons, nurses, therapists, detectives, ophthalmic specialists, a cohort of experts springing from every corner of the country to assist Erin, who is not yet conscious. One doctor tells Clem gravely that her daughter may not make it through the night.

She feels as though she is falling down an endless hole in the center of the universe, reaching depths of horror she could never have imagined existed.

The experience of a child in emergency care is like someone ripping a skin off reality and inviting Clem to step inside another, a realm with new language and faces and a hierarchy arranged entirely around bacteria and luck. In this realm she is helpless and desperate; she forgets her life, her bills, the state of the planet. The pinching in her chest disappears completely, buried beneath the clamor of existential, unsurpassable dread.

Names and faces blur into one another, though she registers

three that stand out among the rest: Constable Byers, who stands guard at the foot of Erin's bed; Bee, Erin's designated nurse, a trained burns specialist and the one to whom all the doctors and surgeons consult about her care; and Stephanie, the detective assigned as their family liaison officer. Behind the scenes, and on the site where Erin received her injuries, are yet more people searching, analyzing, testing, deciphering, piecing together residual clues from the fire to help work out exactly what happened just after midnight on the night of Wednesday the first of May.

It is five o'clock in the evening, and the thought of going home is intolerable—Clem wants to be near Erin in case she wakes up, in case anything terrible happens.

She calls her workmate, Josie, breaks down in tears as she explains what has happened to Erin. Josie job-shares with Clem as a teaching assistant at the local primary school. Josie's little boy, Samuel, is a similar age, and Freya has had a few playdates. Josie offers to pick her up from nursery and keep her overnight. Poor Freya—she's too young to understand why she's suddenly being passed from pillar to post, but she does love playing with Sam, and Josie has nappies, baby food, milk, clean clothes.

Clem loves her for that.

She hears Quinn before she sees him, the sound of heavy, assertive footsteps on the other side of the door to the ICU family room announcing his arrival from West Yorkshire.

She steps aside, surprised by the state of her ex-husband: usually he is immaculately turned out, but today he looks like he's been dug up. Quinn is fifty-two, just shy of six foot tall, slender as the day she met him. He is ex-army, and although he has spent the last ten years working in IT, he still has the air of someone who is prepared to go on a weeklong trek across the desert at a moment's notice. His black hair has grayed at the sides, and he is unshaven, his face strained. She wonders if he still carries a tent in the boot of his car, just in case.

He hesitates before leaning forward to exchange air kisses and a half hug, which the occasion calls for. She is, after all, the mother of his firstborn child, his only daughter, though that hasn't stopped him from calling her a "callous bitch" in the past.

"How are you?" he asks, his eyes tracking across the hospital ward.

"Oh, fine," she says, because her anger toward him is multifaceted and too sharp to contain. She reins it in and softens. "Is Heather here, too?"

"No."

Clem almost says *good*, but stops herself. Heather is Quinn's second wife, mother of their three boys, Toby, Daniel, and Elijah. Heather is ten years younger than Clem, prettier, wifely perfection, as far as a man like Quinn is concerned.

"Where's Erin?" Quinn asks.

"Down here," she says, leading him along to the small room that holds the plastic gowns.

"We have to wear protective clothing," she tells him, ignoring the look of confusion on his face as she pulls the yellow sheet over her head. "It prevents us from infecting her."

"Okay," he says, copying her.

"Oh, hello," a voice says in the doorway. It's Bee.

"This is Erin's father, Quinn," Clem tells her. "Quinn, meet Bee, Erin's nurse."

Bee shakes his hand with the same warmth with which she greeted Clem.

"Lovely to meet you," Bee says, bewildering Quinn further. He's having to take everything in at a speed of knots, Clem thinks. "I'll be leaving soon, but I wanted to let you know that I'll be back in the morning. The night-shift nurse takes over at six o'clock so Erin won't be left alone."

"Can we stay overnight?" Clem asks.

"You can," she says. "But my advice is to go home. You won't sleep well here, and it's better for everyone if you come back in the morning as refreshed as you can be. It can be draining, all of this."

"I've got a hotel booked," Quinn murmurs. "Just around the corner."

"This way," Clem tells Quinn, and he follows her toward Erin's room. She opens the door, nodding at Constable Byers.

"I'll step outside," Constable Byers says. "Give you some time alone."

"Police guard," Clem tells Quinn, but he doesn't answer. His gaze is drawn to Erin in the bed, his mouth falling open. She realizes he hadn't expected it to be this bad. She hadn't mentioned the shaven hair, or the bandages, or the eyelids sewn shut. His face looks like a shattered mirror as he moves toward her.

"What happened?" he asks.

"She and a couple of friends went to Orkney," she says. "Erin, her boyfriend, Arlo, and Senna, one of her friends. They were exploring the islands. Beyond that, I'm not really sure."

"Did they light a campfire or something? And it got out of control?"

"Nobody knows yet. They were on some tiny island that no one lives on."

He scrunches up his face in puzzlement. "Why?"

"I don't *know*, Quinn."

She sounds angry now, all the relief at his arrival diminishing under the feelings of resentment she still harbors toward him. Erin hasn't seen her father since Freya was a few weeks old, when he came for an hour to see his granddaughter and barely looked at her. Erin has referred to him solely as *fuckwit* for the last year, and Clem has allowed it, partly because she agreed with the term for Quinn and because she felt soothed that, at last, Erin seemed toughened to her father's ineptitude. She dealt with being constantly let down by being sardonic and stoic, acting as though she didn't care.

"Sorry," he says then, and she starts, glancing up sharply. His expression is pained, apologetic, and he reaches out to place his hand on her upper arm. "We'll figure it out. Okay?"

She nods, reeling from this version of him.

He lowers silently into the chair next to Erin, his eyes tracking across her bandages, to her hands. Clem realizes he doesn't know about the amputations. He looks up at her in horror, and she holds his gaze. He is comprehending the extent of Erin's injuries in real time, taking it all in. After a few moments, his face crumples, and he begins to cry. She has never, ever witnessed Quinn cry before. Not even at his mother's funeral, though theirs was a complex relationship. But it is genuine, real tears rolling down his face and over his hand that stays clapped to his mouth, and she doesn't know what to say.

She moves to him, not speaking, then rests a hand tentatively on his shoulder.

"Sorry," he says in a crushed voice.

"It's okay."

"We're able to stay overnight, yes?" Quinn asks as they're taking off their plastic gowns.

"I thought you said you booked a hotel?"

He studies the floor. "I don't think I can leave her."

Clem draws another breath, surprised all over again by this new version of her ex-husband.

The nurses set up two camp beds in the family room. They take it in turns to sit with Erin in the still, small room, watching somberly as the night shift—Nurse Blair (*Please, call me Emma*)—scrutinizes the notes on Erin's chart, changes the catheter bag, attends to the IV. Clem finds her mind drifting to Arlo, exhaustion causing her to wonder why he hasn't come to see Erin, surely he must be worried about her, only to remember all over again that he's dead. And on the heel of that re-remembrance, a vision of the kind of flame that would kill someone, that would sheer flesh clean off the bone. She wonders how much Arlo suffered, how much Erin suffered. Does she already know he's dead?

She weeps softly, then thinks of Arlo's parents and mentally chides herself for crying when they have lost a child. Her mind turns to Elizabeth. She must be at her wits' end.

It is three in the morning when she climbs onto the camp bed next to Quinn's.

"How is Freya?" he asks. He's staring at the ceiling, and she wonders if he's slept at all.

"She's great. She's staying with a friend of mine. She has a little boy that Freya plays with."

"How old is she now?"

She bites back a retort. *She's your granddaughter. You should know how old she is.* "Fifteen months."

"How is Erin managing? Being a mum."

She almost gives in to the urge to ask him why he has been such a terrible, negligent father to Erin. Why has it taken a horrific accident for him to visit her? Why hasn't he been more present in her life?

"She's a brilliant mum," she says, deciding that now is not the time for the conversation about Quinn's parenting of Erin. "She makes me so proud." She chokes up then, emotion stealing away her voice.

"How long was she with the boy?"

"About a year," she says. "He is . . . was . . . a lovely kid." It happens again, the mental lurch from one state to another, as though she's hurtling through time. Re-remembering that Arlo is dead.

"And you thought it was a good idea letting three teenagers go off to Orkney, did you?" Quinn says.

"Excuse me?"

"I mean, yes, she has a baby," Quinn continues. "But given her history I would have thought you'd have known that a three-week hike with two other teenagers was a recipe for disaster."

His words land like a punch. Clem lies in the darkness, hearing the imagined echo of his words, searching them for anything that might alter their meaning. He is blaming her.

"I think you're forgetting that she's nineteen," she says. "I can't exactly prevent her from doing things."

"In hindsight, maybe you should have. Don't you think?"

At that, Clem gets up, her blood boiling. She folds up the camp bed and wheels it noisily toward the door. She'll drag it into Erin's room, sleep on the floor if she has to.

"What are you doing?" Quinn asks, but she bites her lip, forcing herself not to scream the words she longs to, a torrent of anger at the years of psychological manipulation he has meted upon Erin.

"I'm sleeping somewhere else," she says.

"Why?"

"You know why."

He sits up and stifles a yawn. "Oh, I see. I've touched a nerve, haven't I?"

Clem straightens and takes a deep, steadying breath. Her disappointment is crushing. The realization all over again that Quinn is and always will be the kind of person who blames everyone else, who is entirely self-interested. From this angle she can see Erin through the glass doors of her side room across the corridor, the night-shift nurse changing her dressings. She imagines what she would do if she knew her father was here. How that soft part inside that loves and will always adore Quinn no matter how cruel he is would fill up with hope that, just perhaps, he has finally decided to be a good father.

"Quinn?" Clem whispers, careful not to disturb the quiet.

"Mmm?"

"Go fuck yourself."

She moves her camp bed into the small kitchen next door, rage finally loosening enough for her to sink into a dark, dreamless slumber.

At dawn, she wakes. A few moments of wondering where she is before the disorienting, planet-colliding realization that she is in a hospital room, in an ICU, that her daughter is swaddled in bandages, intubated, unconscious. The knowledge of Arlo's death crashing down from the ceiling.

Clem gowns up and rushes to see Erin. She is relieved by the consistent bleep of the heart monitor, by the sunlight, but Erin's fresh bandages are already sticky, in need of being changed, and the bruising around her eyes has deepened, garish black fringed with red. For a moment Clem feels overwhelmed by the journey that lies ahead of Erin, a journey she can scarcely fathom: skin grafts, physiotherapy, counseling.

A knock on the glass of the door, the squeal of the hinge. "Morning," a voice says, and Clem sees Bee there, smiling and bright-eyed. "And how is our lovely girl?"

"She's in need of fresh dressings, I think," Clem says, gathering herself.

"Let's get those changed," Bee says, closing the door behind her and checking the night shift's notes. "Good morning, Erin darling. How are you today?"

Erin doesn't answer. Of course she doesn't, though Bee's chatter doesn't stop, musical and upbeat. She watches Erin closely for a moment for any sign of movement. The heart monitor bleeps steadily, the gasp of the ventilator.

"I think they'll try to bring her out of the coma tomorrow," Bee says, unwinding the gauze on Erin's right arm. The smell is immediate—meaty, sweet. Clem winces, and Bee sees.

"That's a good sign, the smell," Bee tells her.

"It is?"

"It signals that her body's responding to the silver creams. It's healing the way it should. It's when it smells like dead flowers that we get concerned."

Bee unwinds the gauze carefully, then the layer of cling film, revealing the full, brutal extent of Erin's burns. Clem winces at the sight of her daughter's arm, livid pink and wet from a layer of silver cream.

"Dead flowers?" Clem asks.

"Bacteria *loves* dying tissue," Bee says, unwinding a fresh roll of gauze and wrapping it gently. "It's a biggie for us, something we're always watching out for. Burn wounds leak and the bugs gobble it up. An infection smells like week-old cut flowers. Awful."

"And what happens if she gets infected?" Clem asks, immediately wishing she hadn't.

"We treat it with antibiotics. But she's doing okay just now, aren't you, my love?"

A figure appears at the door window: it's Quinn, and he looks ashen, dark circles under his eyes and a fresh patch of silver bristle covering his jaw. He is already gowned up. Bee opens the door for him, and Clem turns away. She's still annoyed about last night.

"Have you treated a lot of people like this?" he asks Bee. "Burns victims?"

"Burns *survivors*," Bee corrects. "Yes, I have. Hundreds of 'em." She says it as though she's talking about parties instead of patients, though Clem registers that it's precisely Bee's upbeat manner that sustains her in what is undoubtedly a tough job. "They stay in touch with me, too. I love seeing how they recover."

Clem and Quinn have breakfast in the canteen, sharing a table in mutually troubled silence. Clem texts Josie to check on Freya and is relieved to receive pictures of her happy, bathed granddaughter playing in a ball pit with Sam.

The family liaison officer, Stephanie, arrives, with some updates: Fynhallow, the bay on the Isle of Gunn where the fire happened, has been swept extensively for forensic evidence, and items have been recovered for analysis.

"What items?" Quinn interjects.

"We won't know for a few days," Stephanie says. "Most likely they'll have gathered the materials used for the fire and any fragments that can provide a sequence of events."

"What about Senna?" Clem asks.

Stephanie shakes her head. "Nothing yet. The family are frantic."

She doesn't look hopeful, and Clem knows what she's

thinking—that Senna has drowned. Two deaths. She catches her breath, shaken by the thought of it.

"What about the boy's family?" Quinn asks.

"Arlo's parents would like a meeting with the two of you as well. I'm happy to be an intermediary."

"I don't think that will be necessary," Clem says.

"Okay. Well, I have a few requests, if that's all right? It would be really helpful if we could get access to Erin's devices. Her laptop, tablet, if she has those?"

"Is she a suspect?" Quinn asks.

"It would just be useful for the investigation," Stephanie says. Then: "Of course she's not a suspect." Clem notices how her gaze lowers. "We're doing the same with Arlo's and Senna's devices. The smallest thing can have a huge consequence."

Quinn looks like he's about to repeat the question, then makes a conscious choice not to.

"Of course," Clem says. "Whatever we can do."

Clem goes home to collect Erin's devices for Stephanie.

The flat feels like a cave in the aftermath of Erin's hospitalization, a museum holding objects of her life Before, when Erin was fine, absolutely fine. Erin's clothes sit in the laundry basket, her keys hang on the hooks in the hallway, her cans of Diet Coke lie in the fridge. Clem finds she is more devastated at home than she is in the hospital, and perhaps it is on account of all the objects that call to her now, that remind her that Erin's life has been altered forever.

She trawls through Erin's belongings, not knowing what she's looking for. Something, she thinks. Anything that might throw up a clue, that might shine a light on the fire, on why Senna is missing, and where she might be.

There, just poking out from under her bedside table, is a black notebook with a silver owl cadaver on the front. She removes it slowly, flipping through the pages. It's Erin's notebook, mostly a scribble of thoughts, the occasional statement with a date beside it. A note of the day Freya took her first steps two months ago. A spider diagram with the word *SCHOLARSHIP* written in heavy lettering in the center of a page, scribbles about a *house of learning* and *continual progression.* A note about how much she loved Arlo, tarot readings accompanied by sketches of minor and major arcana, train times and ferry sailings for their Orkney trip.

And then a sentence that makes Clem's stomach turn.

Arlo's hands need to be bound.

She stares at it for a moment, confused. Why would Erin write this? Did someone else write it? No—the sentence is undoubtedly in Erin's handwriting, the looping *e*'s and leaning consonants.

Perhaps it is nothing, Clem tells herself, some kind of in-joke that needs context to be appreciated, or a lyric she thought of. But her throat is turning dry and her chest feels as though gravity has ceased to exist, and she thinks over and over of what Detective Sanger told her when they found Erin's boyfriend. *Arlo's hands were bound.*

Her mind races through the reasons why Erin would have written this. She wonders, feeling nauseous, if it was a description of a sex act. No, at least not in Orkney—Senna was present, and she highly doubts that Erin's closely guarded relationship with Arlo involved threesomes. An inner voice reminds her that she's biased.

She is Erin's mother, is therefore unlikely to suspect her daughter of illicit sex acts. She studies the word *need*. Why did Arlo's hands *need* to be bound? By whom, and for what purpose?

Before she can think further, she rips out the page and tears it in half. She picks up the fragments from the carpet and holds them in a cupped palm, heading quickly to the kitchen. There, she tips them carefully into the sink, takes a box of matches from the drawer, and sets the pieces on fire.

She watches the letters curl up and dissolve in the flame.

Then she runs to the bathroom and vomits in the sink, a flash in her mind connecting the sight of flame to the gut-wrenching sight of her daughter in the Burns Unit.

CHAPTER TEN

Kirkwall, Orkney
November 1594

ALISON

The dungeon beneath the earl's palace conveys none of the grandeur of its upper floors—it is nothing more than a cave, a lair for beasts and dark fears. At the end of the stairs is a stone chamber lit by a flaming wall sconce, a single fire for the jailer. At the end of the chamber is a cell gridded by bars, a series of squeaks signaling the presence of rats. I spy a window high up on the wall, glimpsing the road that runs along the castle toward the sea.

I am shaking so terribly that I cannot stop. I am not to be set free, not returned to my home. I will not see my children, or William. I am to be kept here, in the cell at the far end of the chamber. There is no comfort or warmth here. Stone, iron, rot.

"Search her," a voice says.

I jump with a shout. I had not seen the figures at the end of the hall, but now the light from Mr. Addis's torch reveals them: David Moncrief and John Stewart. I expect to see Earl Patrick, but only David, John, Mr. Addis, and Father Colville are here.

John Stewart was the one who ordered the earl to be slain, I am sure of it. His own brother! And as Thomas Paplay accused me, John Stewart is seeing to it that I stay silent.

But he and David both know the truth. They know I am innocent.

"Remove your clothing," Father Colville says.

I am panting, a prayer rolling off my lips. *Please, God, do not make me . . .*

"She is uttering a spell," Mr. Addis growls, reaching for the knife at his belt.

His accusation makes me start, and I turn to Father Colville. "My lord, I . . ."

But Father Colville tugs the chains, hard, metal against my joints forcing me painfully forward into the weak light. Meekly I pull off my cloak, then my apron and kirtle, my bodice, and my shift.

"And your coif, my child."

I hesitate.

He repeats the same order again and again, each time tugging the chain, until I have removed the shoes from my feet and the coif and forehead cloth from my head. It feels shameful to be without them, my long hair tumbling freely to my hips.

Father Colville offers a somber nod to Mr. Addis, who takes out his knife, the blade glinting in candlelight as it sweeps toward my face. Then, seizing my hair in his fist, he begins to cut.

Outside it has started to rain, and all the candles are quaking in their sconces. My long hair is shorn in minutes and lies folded about my feet like a wounded animal. It has never been cut; the same coal black hair I've had since I was a girl, shorn to the skin. My scalp prickles and bleeds from Mr. Addis's rough hand.

Never has any man seen me naked, except my husband. And

without my hair, I feel doubly naked. I stand now in front of John Stewart, Father Colville, Mr. Addis, and David, my skin shining like a ghost, the bones of my rib cage poking through like a comb. But then, John Stewart steps forward, raising his hand, and I flinch and give a cry. He means to strike me.

But instead he reaches down to gather up my shift. With a look of disgust, he throws it to me.

"Remember your children," he says, for my ears only, a warning look in his eyes. I hold my shift against my body as Father Colville steps forward into the light that pools from the moon on the stone floor.

"Alison," Father Colville says, "we offer you a chance to confess your sins before Christ the Almighty and his angels, here in this holy place." He nods. "You may speak."

"Thank you," I say meekly, my eyes on the ground. I am still shaking, and I can't feel my hands. I want to fall to my knees and beg him to let me go. Instead, I petition him softly.

"Father, if I may?"

He nods, and I strain to keep the sob in my throat from escaping. "As God is my witness, Father, I am not guilty of this charge."

My voice breaks, and there is a long, drawn-out silence as he considers my words. I am sincere, he must see this.

"We bestow this mercy upon you," he says, his voice brimming with pity and concern. "My child, I urge you to unshackle yourself from the wiles of Satan."

"But I am not in Satan's charge," I say. "I did not hex the earl. It is as I said."

Father Colville looks crestfallen, and I see him glance at John Stewart.

"We must search for marks upon the skin made by the Devil," John Stewart tells the parson, who nods.

Dare I say it aloud? That John Stewart asked me for a charm.

They would not believe me. I am only a woman, a spaewife, and he the Master of Orkney.

"Sit, please," Father Colville tells me, when Mr. Addis fetches a chair from the shadows. David lifts a candle from the wall sconce and brings it toward me as I lower into the chair, still covering myself with my shift as best I can. I feel like I am outside my body, drifting around the room. I try to fling my thoughts far, far away, as though I might cast my mind from this room, and with it, my soul, leaving only my body for this man to press and pry as he likes. *I am not here, I am not here.* I search for a place deep in my mind where I can hide.

Father Colville lays his hands on the crown of my shorn head, pressing his fingertips over the scalp. He runs his hands down to my ears, David's candle drawing closer to help him see.

"What is that?" he asks, finding something on my neck. He is addressing David, who lowers alongside him to see.

"I'm not sure."

"Let us check it."

Father Colville reaches into the pocket of his robe and produces a long, thin needle, which he raises to my neck. I jump with a shout of pain as he stabs the skin above my collarbone. The pain is like a beesting, a bead of blood running quickly down my chest.

I am in my parent's house, my father still alive. I am on the beach at Fynhallow gathering dulse for soup, watching the dolphins scythe the smooth water.

He finds another spot at my elbow, then several at my thighs, each time jabbing the skin with the needle, a hot sting followed by a thread of blood.

"Open your mouth," Father Colville says.

I am not here. I am not here.

"Wider."

David flinches as his candle drips hot wax on his hand. I tilt my head back, feeling the warmth of the candle close to my face, the hiss of the lilac flame. My heart is clanging in my chest.

Father Colville puts his thumb against the roof of my mouth, the fingers of his other hand pressing against my jaw. His thumb finds my tongue and lifts it, pushing it up. He lifts the needle and I squeeze my eyes tight, numbing myself out of the room, away from the presence of these men.

I am with William, laughing by the fire.

Edward is playing knucklebones with his friend Adam.

Beatrice is plaiting the hair of her woolen doll.

"There," Father Colville says with a gasp. He draws back, astonished, and turns to David. "And she gave no reaction."

"A mark," Mr. Addis hisses from the shadows. "The Devil's mark."

"You are certain?" John Stewart says.

"Under her tongue," Father Colville says, nodding. John Stewart steps forward and looks down into my mouth, then withdraws quickly.

Father Colville closes my mouth with his hands. I look down and see that my pale skin is streaked with blood.

My heart is thundering in my chest, and my teeth begin to chatter.

"My child, the evidence is plain to see," Father Colville says at last. "You cannot deny it."

A dull ache starts up in my mouth from where the needle was drawn. The rest of my body feels numb, as though I'm floating.

"When did He do this?" Father Colville says.

"Who?"

"You know very well who . . ." he says, but Mr. Addis interrupts.

"Beg pardon, Father. Perhaps the madam confers with the Devil by a different name."

Father Colville turns to me. "Is that true?"

"N . . . no," I stammer. "I do not . . ."

"It is said by some that he appears as a black dog," Father Colville says. "Or a cat."

"I have seen no dog," I say.

"So, a cat, then?" Father Colville says.

I fall silent, my mind spinning. The darkness shrouds the men's faces, their voices bouncing off the walls and punching the air from all directions. I am suddenly weary from the journey, and faint from the pricking. I struggle to gather my thoughts.

"Her silence is agreement," John Stewart says.

"I have not conversed with the Devil," I say, though my voice is weak, a ghost of a voice.

"When does He come?" Father Colville says, ignoring my protestation. "At night?"

"No," I say, shaking my head. David is looking at me close by with pity. He withdraws a handkerchief from his pocket and hands it to me, and for a moment I do not know why. I follow his gaze to my legs and see they are streaked with blood from Father Colville's needle.

"Thank you," I say.

He fetches my dress and boots from the corner of the room and sets them by my side. For a moment, I think he does this out of kindness. But then he holds me in a long, fearful look, his eyes narrowed, and I know his mind.

He fears I left the Triskele because I am the Devil's servant.

He believes I am a witch.

CHAPTER ELEVEN

Fynhallow
Isle of Gunn, Orkney
November 1594

EDWARD

He sits by the stove in his cottage, biting his nails.

It is beginning, he knows it.

Deep down, in that wordless place that speaks only truth, he knows that everything he saw is starting to happen.

"Edward?"

Edward's father, William, comes in through the door, carrying a bucket of fresh water from the well. He sets it down with a heavy thud, then lowers to check his son.

"Yes, Father?"

"How is your head?"

Strangely, the wound on the right side of his forehead has eased, but the muscles around his shoulders have started to scream, as though someone has tried to pull his head off his shoulders.

"It is well. Thank you, Father."

His grandmother stirs the pot on the stove before pouring it into a cup. She pauses to pluck out what Edward thinks are two sticks, before the shape of them makes sense—they are bones. She is making him a potion, not soup, as he'd hoped.

"Drink this," she says, passing him the cup, and he stares down at the murky liquid, his stomach turning. He has witnessed his grandmother grind animal bones to powder before pouring them into her brown bottles for various illnesses. On a wet night, she'll hasten outside to collect slugs to boil, or deer droppings, which she claims are wonderful for treating the sweating sickness. She'll scoop frogspawn or leeches out of the pond, though neither of these are as vile as the strange plants she grows in her garden. One of them is more beast than plant, for it has teeth and eats insects.

"Drink it," she insists, and Edward raises the cup to his lips.

"Do no such thing, Edward," his father says. William regards Mhairi with a cold eye. "I'll have no witch potions in my house."

"Now is not the time for this," Mhairi snaps. "The children have had enough fighting among the adults."

"Is Mother a witch?" Beatrice asks uncertainly from her bed.

"Of course not," his father says, and Edward sees his grandmother flinch.

"Orkney has never punished its magic folk," his grandmother says in a low voice. "Nor will it begin to."

Her voice is confident, and Beatrice is assured. But Edward sees the look that travels between his father and grandmother. He knows well that they do not like each other, that they have never seen eye to eye. But now there is a mutual knowledge that swirls about the cottage like a bat, so real Edward feels he could reach out and touch it—his mother's arrest has unleashed something on the island. Or perhaps it is spreading farther than Gunn. In his mind's eye he sees a shadow creeping over all of Orkney.

He lies in bed, barely breathing, listening to the sound of his sister's inhalation fall into a steady rhythm, the sticks crackling in the fire and the soft croon of the chickens in the rafters.

He thinks of that night in January, on the Wolf Moon, when he was initiated into the Triskele. His grandmother had told him and Beatrice what the ceremony would involve—that those members who lived in Orkney would come to welcome them, and that they would have to kneel before the bonfire while ancient melodies were sung, invoking the old gods and demons who once belonged to the clan. She warned him that *The Book of Witching* would require his "signature" in the form of a scream, and when Solveig held the book in front of him he had worried that he would not be able to produce a sound, given that his throat was tight with exhilaration.

But then Solveig had opened the book, revealing its strange, black pages without words, and an image had begun to stir.

And what he saw drew out the loudest, most harrowing scream of his life.

Later, he asked Beatrice if she had seen anything in the book, and she had shaken her head.

"It was just black pages," she said, disappointed. "I don't even think it's a real book."

She had pressed him then, curious as to why he would ask such a thing. But he didn't tell her what he saw.

He will never tell. But he knows he must, he *must* do something to stop it from happening.

CHAPTER TWELVE

Glasgow
May 2024

CLEM

It happens early the next morning, right after Bee wheels Erin into surgery to begin her withdrawal from sedation.

Clem hears voices outside the family room, notices that Quinn's bed is empty. The voices grow louder, the pitch telling her that the cacophony isn't nurses. It's an argument.

In the corridor, she finds Quinn in a confrontation with a man and a woman. They look familiar, and yet Clem is certain she has never seen them before. They are both in their late forties, dressed in joggers and T-shirts that look slept in, their hair disheveled, and their eyelids swollen from crying. The woman is gesticulating, her hands stretching out to Quinn, while the man stands behind her with his hands on his hips.

Quinn hears the door open and turns to Clem. "Allow me to introduce Arlo's mum and dad, Jim and Tracy," he says, and she sees Arlo's face in the woman's, his build in the man's.

"Oh," she says, stepping forward, a hand extended before she realizes how awkward, how awful this is. How their appearance and the emotion ringing in the air makes sense, given that they've just lost their son.

"I'm Clem," she says. "Erin's mother. I'm so sorry for your loss."

The man scowls at her, his eyes wet. His sorrow is so raw, so explosive, that she can feel it beating off him like a living entity. He doesn't speak, and she sees it is because he can't.

"Shall we take this to the family room?" Quinn says, and for a moment Clem is glad he is here, the air in the corridor crackling with frantic, chaotic grief.

"I'm not here for a chitchat, you understand?" Jim snarls. "My son has been murdered. I didn't even know he had a fucking girl-friend until two days ago, when two detectives showed up at my flat to tell me he'd died in a fire."

"I think we can all just calm down," Quinn says, but Jim is having none of it.

"We've seen the text messages on Arlo's phone," he snaps, hoarsely. "We *know* that girl talked him into it. She had something to do with all of this."

"That *girl* is my daughter," Quinn says, his own voice simmering with fury. "Now you've got a choice. You can either talk respect-fully with Erin's mother and me in the family room, or you can leave."

Suddenly, Tracy sprints past them, down the corridor, her trainers squealing on the linoleum. She has spotted Constable Byers going into Erin's room, has worked out where she is. As the door swings shut after Constable Byers she dashes inside, scream-ing at Erin.

"What did you do to him? Tell me!"

Constable Byers seizes her by the shoulders and begins to move her to the door, only to be confronted by Jim.

"Madam, you can't interfere with the patient," Constable Byers says, struggling to remove her.

"You have to gown up!" Clem shouts at him. "You'll infect her!"

But Jim pushes past, shouting at Erin.

"You know what happened to Arlo," he says. "Why won't you tell us?"

"Because she's in a coma, you moron!" Clem yells at him. She is in the room now, and none of them are wearing protective clothing.

Jim looks at her angrily, as though he's about to lash out. But suddenly the anger on his face melts and he sinks to the ground, sobbing and holding his head in his hands.

Clem looks on in shock, pity slowly replacing her outrage as another thought slips into her head: this man has had to identify his son's body, is having to talk about him in the past tense, is planning his funeral.

Bee bursts into the room.

"Right," she says. "Out, all of you. This is a burns unit, my loves, and Erin is at a very vulnerable stage in her healing journey. Not a soul steps inside this room until they're properly gowned up, got it?"

Constable Byers lets go of Tracy and moves toward Jim, helping him to his feet.

Slowly, they all move to the family room, Bee returning a few minutes later with some cups of tea and a box of fresh tissues.

"We're sorry for your loss," Quinn says after a few minutes. He is sitting next to Clem and opposite Jim and Tracy, tea growing cold on the table between them.

"We just want answers," Jim says quietly. "Arlo was at university. He wasn't living at home. We knew nothing about his relationship with Erin."

"What about the trip to Orkney?" Clem says, her mind turning to what she saw written in Erin's notebook. *Arlo's hands need to be bound.* "He must have told you he was going."

"He said he was going hiking with a couple of friends," Tracy says. "He didn't mention *which* friends. The police showed us the messages they managed to recover from his phone."

"What did they say?" Quinn says, sitting forward.

"One of them said he was nervous," Tracy says.

"Nervous about what?" Clem says.

"He was nervous about going to Fynhallow," Jim says. "Erin talked him into it."

"That doesn't make her guilty of anything," Quinn says archly. "Most likely they lit a campfire, and it got out of control."

"Why's Senna missing, then?" Tracy says, and just then the door opens, a nurse stepping inside, a woman following behind her.

"Here we are," the nurse says gently to the woman, and Clem sees she is sallow-faced and hollow-eyed.

"Elizabeth?" Clem says, recognizing Senna in her face. Same brown skin and wavy black hair, the same deep-set eyes. She stands and hugs her. "This is Senna's mother, Elizabeth," she tells the others in the room. "Elizabeth, this is Jim and Tracy, Arlo's parents. And this is Quinn, Erin's father."

Elizabeth looks as shattered as the rest of them, mascara stains on her face, black hair askew. Silently, she moves to each of them in turn, wrapping an arm around them, before bringing a chair from the corner and pulling it close.

"Any word on Senna?" Clem asks her.

Elizabeth shakes her head, her eyes wet.

"What about her phone?" Quinn says. "Have they tracked her calls? Her bank cards?"

"Her backpack was found at Fynhallow," Elizabeth says, dabbing her eyes with a well-used hankie. "Her wallet's still there, her bank card and money inside. Her phone is gone but it's turned off, or the battery's dead." She fixes Clem in a desperate stare. "I want to know where she is, and what happened. *Why* she's gone. Why she hasn't called me."

"I know as much as you," Clem says apologetically. She wishes she could help, that she had answers to give. But she doesn't.

"I want to speak with Erin," Elizabeth says.

"We all want to ask Erin questions," Jim says gravely. "Like how our son died."

"I think it's plain to see that Erin's going to be out of action for a while," Quinn says. "And I'm not liking the suggestion that Erin's at fault, here."

"Who said Erin's at fault?" Jim says.

"She's the only one who got out of there," Tracy mutters bitterly.

"Well, that's not true, is it?" Quinn says. "Erin's in a coma, with her eyelids sewn shut. Strikes me that if anyone's a suspect here, it's Senna."

"Quinn," Clem says, warningly.

"Are you joking?" Elizabeth says, her voice brittle. "Senna? A suspect?"

Quinn shrugs. "All I'm saying is, how odd that a boy has died and a girl is at death's door and Senna goes on the run."

Elizabeth gets to her feet, trembling with fury.

"I have a text message from Senna that she sent the same day as the fire, okay? And in that message, she said she and Erin had a fight, that Erin got violent with her."

"Oh my God," Tracy says.

Clem's mouth falls open. "Violent? You never said this before."

"Senna was fed up of being the third wheel," Elizabeth says. "She told Erin she was going home, and the next thing she knows Erin is grabbing her by the arm to stop her."

"Erin grabbed her?" Clem repeats.

"Not exactly an act of violence, is it?" Quinn says. "Grabbing her by the arm?"

"It depends on how she did it," Jim says. "Could have dislocated the girl's shoulder."

"Was that it?" Clem asks Elizabeth.

"I don't think it's anything to make light of," Elizabeth tells Quinn. "It's clear that whatever went on between the three of them that day resulted in Arlo's death and Senna's disappearance."

Jim and Tracy make noises of agreement. Clem can feel her heart pounding in her chest, and she eyes the door. She wants to escape this room before Elizabeth, Jim, and Tracy decide that Erin is to blame for what happened to their children. She wants to take her medicine.

But Quinn is standing now, yelling at Elizabeth. "So far, all you've said is that Erin grabbed Senna. That's hardly reason to fling accusations when Erin's in a coma, for God's sake."

Elizabeth pulls her lips tight, her nostrils flaring. "Well, I've shared the messages with the police. I should imagine they'll interview Erin as soon as she's awake." She narrows her eyes at Quinn. "Convenient, isn't it, that the only person found alive is still unconscious."

Clem excuses herself and makes for the toilet farther along the corridor. Outside the sky is darkening, storm clouds gathering—after a fortnight of unusually hot temperatures, heavy rain is forecast to sweep across the country.

Her stomach is churning, and she realizes she has left her medication in her handbag. She kneels down next to the toilet bowl.

The images that formed in her mind when Elizabeth told them of the girls fighting are vivid. She tries to imagine Erin grabbing Senna. Why would she do that? Was it a casual grab, or something more violent?

She thinks of that moment a month earlier, just before Easter. Waking at dawn to find Erin standing by her bed.

The memory is fragmented, dreamlike. She remembers thinking that Erin was there because Freya was crying and she needed help. But Freya was asleep beside Clem, and she remembered faintly waking at midnight to the sound of crying and fetching Freya from her crib in Erin's room to allow her a chance to catch up on sleep.

Erin stood, silent, her breathing labored. A pair of scissors held in her hand like a weapon.

The sight of the scissors in Erin's hand woke Clem up a little.

"What's wrong?" she asked. "Erin?"

Erin's face crumpled then, and she turned sharply and walked out of the room. Clem rose to check on her, but her bedroom door was locked. Later, she found Erin in the garden. She was sitting in one of the deck chairs, though it was raining. Clem pulled on a coat and headed out to sit next to her.

"What was all that about this morning?" Clem asked. "When you came into my room?"

"I was sleepwalking," Erin said. "I woke up and scared myself."

Clem nodded. That made sense. Erin had sleepwalked as a child, usually as a response to something stressful. Her father bailing on her, or conflict with her friends.

"I think I need to go away," Erin said. Her pink hair was soaking wet and stuck to her head. She was shaking from the cold.

"Go away? What do you mean?" Clem asked. "Where to?"

"Orkney," she said. "I've asked Senna and Arlo to come with me. I need to clear my head."

"I think that's a good idea," Clem said. She could see how worn out Erin was, juggling a baby and a part-time job. She had recently started a design course at night school, had mentioned that she wanted to reapply to university. A different degree pathway, this time. She wanted to go to Glasgow Art School to study interior design.

"I can look after Freya," Clem said.

Erin smiled at that.

"Thanks, Mum," she said. "Love you."

Clem reached out and squeezed her hand. "Love you, too."

In the toilet stall, Clem gets to her feet, simultaneously glad and disappointed that she can't be sick. Her stomach roils with hot liquid, sourness blooming in her mouth. The image of Erin standing by her bed with a furtive expression and a pair of scissors in her hand feels imprinted behind her eyes.

Until now it was such an out-of-character moment that she hadn't given it much thought. Erin was sleepwalking, and there was nothing more to be considered.

But Elizabeth's revelation has brought the moment back to her mind with a fresh layer of possibility. And Clem is forced to acknowledge the thing that has continued to nag at her since then, the thing that now blossoms into a warning: when Erin told her she had been sleepwalking, Clem read the microscopic flick of her eyes, the tilt of her jaw.

She had been lying.

She steps out of the cubicle, catching sight of herself in the small mirror opposite. But something else draws her eye, and she starts.

On the tiled floor of the bathroom by her feet is a strange object—some kind of book. It's large, about the size of an A4 sheet of paper, and the binding is old, like brown leather that is cracked and coming apart. She's alarmed at the sight of it. How did it get there?

Her eyes track to the cubicle next to the one she has just left, in case someone has entered the toilets silently and left their book on the ground. But no, she's alone. And she's certain that the book wasn't there before.

She bends to inspect it, noticing at once that the binding is not leather at all but a very good bark replica. Or perhaps it is indeed tree bark that has been pieced together, the ridges and gnarls of bark a disconcerting texture beneath her fingertips. A small green shoot pokes up strangely from the top corner, a seed that has found purchase. There is no evidence of stitching in the spine.

Gingerly, she reaches down and opens it, finding that the pages are completely black, the texture somewhere between fabric and paper. No writing. But then, as she stares down, something stirs on the page, like ripples on water. She suspects it's the bathroom lighting, a bulb flickering overhead. But then an image appears, and she steps back, alarmed.

She sees a woman, her mouth open and her head tilted back, the lines of her face shining in firelight. And then the scene expands, and Clem sees the woman is surrounded by kindling, her hands bound to a stake, a fire growing stealthily around her.

Her heart hammering, she reaches for her phone, glancing at the screen to open the camera. Then she points it at the object on the floor, her thumb hovering over the red button to take a picture.

But the floor is empty. The book is gone.

She takes a step back, startled. Did she have a blackout, a fainting episode? It was right there, the strange book with the cover made of tree bark with a tiny green shoot poking up, the delicate black pages.

The door bursts open, making her jump with a shout. It's Bee, and she's grinning.

"They managed to bring Erin round. She's awake!"

Clem bolts through the door and races along the corridor, her breaths ragged. Outside, the sky has darkened, rain lashing the windows and glossing the streets. A distant rumble of thunder rolls beneath the nurses' chatter.

Quinn is already gowning up in the small storeroom. He passes Clem a gown and ties it at the back of her neck. "The withdrawal went well," Bee tells them as they make for Erin's room. "She'll be a little woozy for a while and the conversation may not be in full swing, but it'll be good for her to see you both. Oh, and one thing you should know."

"What's that?" Quinn asks.

"They've left one eye sutured shut," Bee says. "The ophthalmic surgeon wasn't persuaded that it was ready to be opened. Just in case you're alarmed. It's not as bad as it looks."

"I think we're long past the point of alarm," Quinn says.

Constable Byers steps outside the room to allow them a chance to reunite. "Good luck," he says.

Inside, Clem sees that Erin is awake, though the wires and the machines are still in place. The stitches of her right eye have been removed, revealing a bloodshot but healthy eye. Clem is relieved at this, but despite Quinn's words earlier she can tell he's as alarmed as she is by the strangeness of Erin's appearance, one eye wide open, the other fastened shut.

A flash of lightning brightens the room, followed a moment later by what sounds like kettledrums.

"This *weather*," Bee exclaims, closing the rectangular window along the top of the room. "You'd never think it was May."

"Hello, love," Clem says, her voice trembling. She moves close, emotion overcoming her. "Oh, my sweetheart. How are you feeling?"

Erin turns to her and looks at her blankly. She doesn't answer.

"Can she see us?" Quinn asks, and Bee looks closely at Erin.

"Can you tell me what color my eyes are, darling?" Bee asks her.

"B . . . brown."

Her voice is hoarse and faint, but even so, it's Erin's voice. The sound of it breaks something in Clem, a metal plate she had carried inside her in the form of a thought—that she might never hear Erin's voice again. She presses her hands to her mouth to cover a sob of relief.

Bee turns to Clem and smiles. "I'd say she can see fine."

"Thank you," Clem says, overwhelmed by relief and helplessness. She is at once excited that Erin's awake and nervous about how she'll react when she realizes how injured she is. And when she hears about Arlo and Senna.

"Erin," Quinn says, a tremor of emotion in his voice. "It's Dad. I'm so glad you're awake now. Are you feeling all right? You're not in any pain?"

Clem registers that Erin isn't looking at Quinn, her eye swiveling around the room in a look of panic. The heart monitor begins to race. Erin makes a guttural sound in her throat, as if she's about to throw up. Clem steps closer, fighting the urge to hold her daughter, to touch her.

"Is she okay?" Clem asks Bee, who is busy with a tube of ointment. Her eyes rest on the heart monitor. Ninety-eight.

"I think she's just coming round," Bee says, nodding. "It's important that we keep her eye lubricated. Though the consistency of this stuff is always a menace. So hard to squeeze out . . . Ah, here we go."

She and Quinn watch patiently as the nurse applies a drop of gel to Erin's right eye. Erin gasps as it hits her pupil.

"Well done," Bee soothes. "It does sting a bit. But your right eye is doing well. I'm sure we'll have the other one open and working in no time."

Erin's face scrunches up, and she hisses something at Bee. Something in a different language.

"What was that, lovely?" Bee says, but Erin shrinks back, as if she's terrified. Bee smiles at Clem and Quinn. "It can take a few days for the reality of what's happened to register," she says. "Just be patient, yeah? This bit can be tricky. Let's start small. Ten minutes, okay?"

"Why ten minutes?" Clem says, sadly. She can't bear the thought of leaving Erin alone in here.

"Oh, love, I know it's disappointing," Bee says. "But her body needs lots and lots of rest to heal those wounds properly. You don't realize how much exertion a simple conversation takes for someone so badly injured."

"Come on," Quinn urges, patting Clem on the shoulder. "This is a good thing. Ten minutes will be fine."

The heart monitor begins to slow, but Clem can hear that Erin is whimpering, the same, strange nonsense-words that she heard before. She feels nervous, and as Bee shuts the door behind her Clem thinks about racing after her and asking her to come back in.

Quinn sits down next to Erin and smiles up at her.

"Hi, Erin," he says, his voice breaking with emotion. "It's Dad. I'm sure this must all feel very strange, and probably very frightening. I want you to know that I'm here, and your mother's here, and we're going to make sure you come out of this place as soon as you can and as well as you can."

Erin is breathing very quickly, as though she's having a panic attack. Clem moves to the other side of the bed.

"Sweetheart," she says, leaning close to her. "Can you see me?"

"Who are you?"

"It's Mum and Dad," Clem says, glancing at Quinn. Erin stares at her in a look that resembles horror. "Do you recognize us, love?" she says. What if Erin has amnesia? Or brain trauma?

"Where am I?" she whispers.

"You're in hospital," Quinn says evenly. "I know that might seem frightening. But you're in a very good hospital with excellent nurses and doctors."

Erin is still breathing in short, rapid pants, and Clem murmurs soothing words of comfort to her, wishing she could hold Erin, or wrap her arms around her.

"I saw her," Erin says faintly. "I saw the fire."

Clem throws a sharp look at Quinn, and he returns it. Erin remembers what happened.

"Okay," Clem says gently. "Let's just take it really slow. We're here for you, darling—"

She trails off, noticing that Erin is growing upset, her good eye tracing the heart monitor and the wires. It must be utterly disorienting for Erin, waking to find herself in such a state. She turns to Quinn. "Maybe we should call Bee back in."

"No," he says. "Just give her a chance to adjust." He turns to Erin. "Erin, we're right here, and it's all over. But if you can talk to us first before the police get here . . ."

"The fire was burning her," Erin whimpers. "And I couldn't stop it."

Clem is racked as she watches Erin's face crumple, all her relief shattered by witnessing her so frightened, so traumatized.

"I know you've gone through something utterly horrendous,"

Clem says. "But there's no pressure to go into it all, okay? We just want you to get better."

She pulls her chair closer and reaches out to place her hand on top of Erin's knee, the flesh there undamaged.

"Get away from me!" Erin hisses, flinching. She says something then, the same arrangement of sounds or words that Clem doesn't understand.

"Erin," Clem says soothingly. "It's all right. I promise."

"Who is Erin?" Erin says.

Quinn looks puzzled. "Erin's your name."

"My name isn't Erin," Erin says, in a tone so clear that Clem starts. She feels it then, a prickle at the back of her neck. Something about Erin isn't right. It's not the injuries, or her shock.

Erin tilts her jaw defiantly, her good eye fixed on Clem. "I am Nyx," she says.

CHAPTER THIRTEEN

Kirkwall, Orkney
November 1594

ALISON

Father Colville and the others leave the dungeon, Mr. Addis still petitioning for payment even as he bolts the heavy metal doors of the cell with a chain and lock.

And then I am alone, with only shadows and insects for company, my thoughts spinning rapidly.

I dress, pulling on my shift and stockings, my dress, and kirtle, wrapping myself tightly in my shawl. I pull my coif back over my bare head, the fabric sticking to the bloody cuts on my scalp.

The pain in my mouth is ferocious. I do not sleep, curled up in the dark pit of the cell. The air down here is foul, and there is no chamber pot or water. There are two hay bales teaming with insects. I push them together to form a bed off the wet stone floor.

I think of William and the children at home. They will be frantically wondering how to make sense of this. Our neighbors Angus and Maggie will have seen; Angus often gives us extra milk when our cow is too dwamly to produce more than a few drops. Agnes, too, may come to see me and find I am in Kirkwall.

For four days and nights, I am left without food or water,

though the soreness beneath my tongue from the parson's needle makes it too difficult to so much as open my mouth.

The dungeon walls are damp, and after the third day I am driven to gather moisture that runs along the stone. The taste is so bitter I can barely stomach it at first, but the thirstier I get the sweeter the taste. I can't help but think of Earl Patrick, who is said to have three trumpeters herald each meal.

My mother's stories whisper from the stones. The tale of the dragon who breathed water, not fire. The tale of the king's feast— bite by bite, plate by plate, the food revealed itself to be his own children, a spell put upon their bodies to make them appear as beautiful portions of fruit, freshly baked bread.

On the fifth day, I call out to Mr. Addis, who spends long hours at the other end of the hallway, sitting by the fire and using a knife to cut dead flesh from the soles of his feet.

He ignores me, so I call louder.

"What is it, witch?" he retorts in a gravelly voice.

"I have a petition," I say hoarsely. "If you please."

I cannot shout any longer, and so he rises from his chair reluctantly, grumbling and shuffling down the hall toward me, his lantern raised against the gloom. When he appears at the bars of my cell I see the deep lines of his face, the silver strands of hair smeared with grease across his scalp and the row of wooden teeth that click out when he speaks. He sneers at me, pushing his teeth in with a grubby finger.

"Go on, then."

"Please," I say. "I have not eaten."

He looks over the floor of the cell, his eyes landing on the long pink tail of the dead rat that has lain there since my arrival. I moved it beneath a bale of hay to keep it from my sight, but other rats have since disturbed the hay.

"Prisoners usually feed on the rats," he says. The thought of it turns my stomach.

"I need food, Mr. Addis. Surely it is the law to feed prisoners?"

He scratches his beard, puzzled. "Not witches."

"And it is the law that visitors are permitted?" I say. "Can you ask the earl to allow my husband and children to visit, and that they might bring food and water?"

His lips curl in a sneer of disgust, and I expect him to turn and walk away. But then his face softens, and he is lost in thought.

"What can you do for worms?"

"Worms?"

"Arse worms. I am sorely, sorely afflicted. Perhaps, if ye were to make a potion . . ."

I nod, eagerly, though my stomach is turning at the thought of it. "Yes, yes, I can help."

His face lifts into a beaming smile. "Oh, that would make me very happy. You see, I asked the physician and he gave me goose fat but it has not worked. Let me show thee . . ."

He makes to lower his breeches and present his arse to me, but I insist that he has no need.

"Can you fetch me wormwood, and orange water, some comfrey and garlic and—this is very important—eel grease."

"Don't you want to look at my pish?" he growls, lifting a hook-shaped eyebrow. "The physicians always look at my pish."

I shake my head. "That won't be necessary." Long ago, I began to recognize the instincts that rose up in me when I spoke with a person about their sickness. I would see that their particular sickness might require more of one herb than another, or a type of spell or charm that is for another ailment entirely. I suspect Mr. Addis's arse worms are to do with the pig's feet he eats in the evenings.

"I will fetch these things on the morrow," he says eagerly. And then he turns, his lantern casting a long orange seam along the corridor, and begins to return to his seat near the fire.

"Mr. Addis!" I shout after him, but he doesn't reply. I sink down to the floor, my head seeming to lift up and float across the room from hunger. A few minutes later, the orange seam returns, and I see Mr. Addis carrying a wooden trencher. He throws it down on the floor by the bars, and I pull it to me frantically, resorting at last to lowering my cheek to the floor and tipping the contents of the trencher into my mouth. It is gruel, but I eat it desperately, thank him weakly as I return to the corner of the cell.

Two nights pass. Mr. Addis brings slop once a day, and the ingredients for the potion. I pour it all into a glass jar, the smell of the orange water so beautiful that I have to bite my lips to prevent myself from drinking it.

"Here," I tell him, handing him the finished potion. He stares down at it with a doubtful look, then drinks it down.

"Please may I have visitors?" I ask him. But he turns and shuffles back to his fire without another word.

A week passes.

I am so hungry that I do not know if I am still alive.

I do not know if I will ever see my family again.

"Madam Balfour, wake up. Wake up!"

My grandmother's face looms close, a wavering shadow. I gasp, and her face bursts, revealing that of another. It's Mr. Addis. I can tell from the stench of his breath, his clicking wooden teeth.

My mind is swampy with dreams, my spine rubbed raw from sleeping on the hay bale. Nearby is a fierce light and an alarming heat, as though the sun has risen inside the castle. I squint at the source and find a row of candles against the wall to my left, dozens of little flames coalescing into a vibrant sunrise.

"On your feet."

Mr. Addis tugs at the chains around my wrists, pulling me sharply upright. I am still so immersed in my dreams that I stumble forward, and another pulls my arm to steady me. It's Father Colville, and behind him is David Moncrief.

"Walking and watching," Father Colville says. "We walk, and we watch. See?"

He strolls slowly alongside me until he's certain that I'm awake enough to continue. When I reach the far wall of the cell I rest my hands on it, then my weight, feeling my body sink down again into slumber. But Mr. Addis is there in an instant, hauling me up.

"No, you don't," he says, and shoves me away from the wall to walk. Why must I walk? Where am I going? I know not, only that he insists upon my walking back and forth across the wet stone floor.

Every time I have started to sway back into dreams Mr. Addis kicks me awake and makes me walk again. The candles hiss. The stone wall teases with its promise of support and rest.

Somewhere in the gloom, I know others watch. Is it William, or the children? I call out to them, though my voice sounds far away, an echo rather than a voice.

"She murmurs," a voice hisses from the far reaches of the dungeon. I recognize it as Father Colville's.

Mr. Addis pulls my arm. "What say you, witch?"

I open my mouth to speak but the words feel clotted in my mind.

"Look! In the corner of the window." David's voice. Four of them here with me in the middle of the night. My limbs ache and my mind swims with wild thoughts.

The room descends into silence. I lift my head to see what Father Colville has spotted in the cell window, high up in the far wall. The shadows thicken and move.

"It is a hare, I think," Father Colville says. A hare? I squint, hard. For a moment I think I see the shape of it, two long ears held aloft.

"By God, it is," Mr. Addis says fearfully.

"Take note of it," Father Colville hisses at David, who stands in the corner. "You see it, too?"

"I do," David says, his voice filled with fear. "I have heard that cunning folk often have familiars, animals that do their bidding."

"Mark you," Father Colville says. "That is no hare. It's the Devil."

Mr. Addis makes a low noise of fear in his throat, and I scuttle back into a corner, terrified. Father Colville turns to me, and I bury my head in my hands. I do not want the Devil near me. I pray silently to God that he will banish Satan from our midst.

Carefully, I raise my head and look at the window once more. Now I see that it is a hare-shaped shadow, but the men in the room are insisting it is a hare. Or rather, that it is Satan in the form of a hare.

"The Devil has come to save her," Father Colville hisses.

As I watch the shadows drift, a passing cloud unveiling the light of the moon, the shadow changes again. Just for a moment, it seems to take the form of a person. A tall man, striding through the small window into the night.

I flinch. Surely a trick of the light? The others react with gasps.

"Did you see that?" Mr. Addis says.

"It was Satan Himself," Father Colville says. There is fear in his voice. My heart is pounding so loud in my ears I would not be surprised if others could hear it.

"Perhaps He came not to save her," Mr. Addis growls. "But to ensure she is obedient."

"Aye," Father Colville says. "That is so."

I scan the corner of the window nervously, desperately trying to make sense of what I saw. Was it really the Devil? Or was it my own mind, so influenced by the pronouncements of the men that I *thought* I saw it?

No—I saw it, and the others did, too. My blood runs cold.

"Write that down," Father Colville instructs David. "We have all of us witnessed the most damning evidence yet. The arrival of Satan to spy on His servant, ensuring she remains at His bidding."

CHAPTER FOURTEEN

Glasgow
May 2024

CLEM

Clem and Quinn take off their yellow gowns and discard them in the small bin by the door of Erin's room before closing it.

"Everything okay?" Bee asks, approaching them from another room along the ward.

"Not really," Quinn says, nodding at Constable Byers by the water fountain. "Erin says she doesn't know who we are. And that her name is no longer 'Erin.' She wants to be called 'Nick.'"

"Nyx," Clem corrects under her breath.

"Oh, I'm so sorry," Bee says, her face falling. "I thought . . . I really thought she seemed okay."

"Definitely not okay," Quinn says.

"You know, disorientation after sedation is very common," Bee says.

"Really?" Quinn asks. "You've had other patients wake up with new names?"

"I've had *all* sorts," Bee says, which brings Clem a small amount of comfort.

"I suppose it is early days," Quinn says, running a hand across his face. "I just had my hopes up. She seemed to remember about the fire, but then she got more and more . . . confused."

His wording is careful, Clem can tell.

The reasons for her shock come clear now. She can handle Erin not recognizing her, though it's a blunt kind of pain. It's more than that: Erin's wounds lie deep beneath the surface, and whatever she experienced on that island was so horrifying, so beyond language, that she has disconnected from it.

The next day, Stephanie and DC Sanger arrive just after nine in the morning. Stephanie's wearing a gray COS trouser suit with black loafers, no makeup or jewelry, clean blonde hair streaked with gray and flat-ironed to her shoulders. DC Sanger is in a sharp navy suit. He looks friendly, but won't take any shit.

They ask Bee for a different room in the hospital where they can talk, somewhere other than the family room.

"We heard you had some visitors," DC Sanger tells Quinn and Clem.

"God, yes," Quinn says, rubbing his face. "What a nightmare."

"It's understandable, of course," Clem says. "I mean, they're frantic. I can't imagine what Jim and Tracy are going through. And Elizabeth."

"We've gone through the WhatsApp messages on your mobile phone," DC Sanger tells Clem. "And we've had a look at the messages sent from Arlo, Senna, and Erin. There seemed to be some friction in the group on the day that the fire happened."

Clem and Quinn share a look.

"What do you mean by 'friction'?" Quinn asks.

"Senna wasn't happy about going to Fynhallow," Stephanie says. "She messaged her mother and some other friends, claiming that Erin was forcing her." She takes a breath, letting the words hang in the air. "Look, I know that trips like this can be fraught at the best of times, and I know that teenagers fall out left, right, and center. I want to reassure you that I'm not meaning to insinuate anything..."

"It sounds very much like insinuation," Quinn says, and Clem finds she's glad that he's here. A strange turn of events, to say the very least.

Stephanie bites her lip, visibly contemplating her words. "I just want to know if you heard anything that might help us understand the dynamic between the group before the fire happened..."

"I didn't hear at all from Erin on Tuesday or Wednesday," Clem says, her throat tightening at the suspicion that Stephanie is pointing blame at Erin. "I had a message on Monday and it seemed things were going fine."

"And we're only getting one side of the story," Quinn points out. "We need to see what Erin says about it before we start painting her as..."

He doesn't finish his sentence. Clem lowers her eyes, her stomach turning as she thinks of what she found in Erin's notebook.

"What about when Erin called you?" DC Sanger asks. "Was there anything in her voice that suggested that the group were at odds with each other?"

Clem thinks back, though her mind feels too clouded by grief and confusion to pull details to the surface. Erin messaged on Monday, but the last time she actually spoke to Erin was on Saturday. They were in Papa Westray, and they'd just spotted dolphins off the coast. "When she called me, she said they were hiking," she explains. "It was sunny and she sent a few photographs."

"What about Fynhallow? Did she mention why they were heading there?"

Clem shakes her head. "They were exploring. I imagine there was no reason to it at all. Just another island to visit."

"One of Arlo's friends said that he FaceTimed Arlo on Wednesday at four o'clock in the afternoon. Arlo told this boy that he couldn't find something. He seemed quite upset about it. We think this is why they went to Fynhallow, to find whatever it was."

"The kid didn't say *what* Arlo couldn't find?"

"Sadly not. Did Erin mention something like this to you?"

"Couldn't find something?" Clem repeats, frowning. "No. Nothing like that."

"Arlo's friend said he made a big deal of it, particularly because the phone signal was bad and he was elated that he could make a call at all."

"That makes sense," Clem says. "Erin hadn't been able to call or message for most of the trip."

"Arlo's friend is under the impression that *this* was the reason they went to Orkney in the first place. That there was something that he and Erin had to find. And they specifically had to go to Fynhallow to do so."

Quinn looks to Clem for confirmation of this. "I think she would have told me if that was the case," she says.

Stephanie looks skeptical. "You're sure?"

"Am I sure of what?"

"Well, you indicated that it's been a rough few years with Erin. That she's been withdrawn, ditching school and university. Having a baby with someone who isn't still in Freya's life."

The words land like a punch to Clem's gut. They are true, but Clem had prided herself in getting Erin through her teenage years as a single mother. A single mother working two jobs and struggling with a heart condition and no family nearby. Her own parents are dead and, like Erin, she's an only child. She thought she had done her best, given the circumstances.

But now she feels like an abject failure.

"Erin has been better this past year," she says. "So this seems an odd time for her go off the rails."

"I'm not saying she went off the rails," Stephanie says gently. "I'm saying that, sometimes, people have secrets. Especially our children."

Especially our children. Clem's mind turns to the piece of paper she tore out of her notebook, to Stephanie's words about his phone call just before he died.

Arlo's hands need to be bound.

Arlo told this boy that he couldn't find something.

What was it Arlo couldn't find?

CHAPTER FIFTEEN

Kirkwall, Orkney
November 1594

EDWARD

Edward slips on the leather jerkin over his doublet, then the gaunt-lets, admiring the way they transform his hands—which he always found too scrawny, too feminine—into those of a giant.

"There you are, Edward," Mr. McNee says, patting him on the shoulder. "Ready?"

"Don't be afraid," his father says, and Edward's cheeks redden immediately. He has been nothing but afraid since the day he witnessed his mother dragged away to jail, though now his terror is distilled into the shape of a bird that Mr. McNee is tempting from a box with the entrails of a hare. The yellow beak appears first, piercing the darkness of the box like a flame, then the eyes like spheres of amber. Edward steps back, his body filled with a sudden call to flee.

"Be still," his father whispers in his ear, sensing his nervousness.

The eagle jerks at the bloody entrails dangling in front of it, shouldering into the open air and swallowing it back with a flick of its head.

"Good, Merlin," Mr. McNee says, offering his arm to the bird the way a suitor may to a lady. He nods at Edward. "You stay calm, and he will do your bidding, aye?"

"Aye," Edward says, swallowing hard. He mimics Mr. McNee's posture, straightening his knees and his back and lifting his head and his arm for the bird to approach. It is majestic, eyes like lanterns and smooth, shining feathers in all the shades of bronze and gold that he has ever seen. It is the feet, though, that surprise him most in their menace, hooked talons at the end of reptilian feet. It wears a leather harness and helmet, too, as though dressed for battle.

And in a moment, it is on his arm, close enough to peck his eyes out. It is much, much heavier than he was counting on, the bulk of it making his arm droop. The bird rankles, disturbed by the movement, spreading out its wings and giving a sharp shriek.

"Steady, now," Mr. McNee says, raising Edward's arm and taking the weight of it in his own hands as the bird settles. He glances at his father, drawing reassurance from William's expression of confidence, his nodding head and his soothing words.

"Good," his father says, smiling. "Good."

Edward takes in the knowledge that an eagle is sitting on his arm. A juvenile eagle named Merlin, with a wingspan longer than he is tall.

He counts in his head, subconsciously listing the words from the old tongue, the ones his mother taught when she was still part of the Triskele: *yan, tyan, tethera, methera, pimp, sethera, lethera, hovera, dovera, dick.*

"Let us walk," Mr. McNee says. "I have something I wish to talk to you about."

Edward puts one foot in front of the other, as though he is

walking a plank instead of the gardens of St. Magnus Cathedral, his eyes never leaving the bird on his arm. Mr. McNee keeps apace, still bearing the weight of Edward's arm and the eagle upon it.

"Your father is one of our most skilled stonemasons," Mr. Mc-Nee is telling him. "And he tells me you have been working alongside him since you were a child."

Edward starts at the last part of this comment. Is he no longer a child? He burns to be a man, to grow a beard, to have thick arms and a deep voice, but despite his best efforts he is still a boy.

"Yes, sir," he says, still walking in a way that insinuates he is sure the ground is able to crumble beneath him. "I find masonry very pleasing."

"That is good," Mr. McNee says, sharing a look with William. "I am also aware of some troubles at home. It is not good to dwell in misery."

The eagle turns, then, as though it is an extension of Mr. Mc-Nee, agreeing with him, and pins Edward with those ferocious amber eyes. Edward stops, careful not to move his arm or disturb the bird from its clutch on the gauntlet. Despite the thickness of the leather he can feel the sharpness of the talons pressing into his flesh, and his mind flings forward into grotesque images of the eagle tearing his guts out, a long, bloodied string of his inner parts drawn out with a single swipe. In an instant, the image shifts to his mother being burned alive at the stake, her mouth open to the sky in a dark, soundless maw, her hands tied behind her back.

He starts, realizing sharply that he is back in the garden of the cathedral, with Mr. McNee and his father, and he is covered in sweat, his knees trembling. He steadies himself, focusing on the ferocity of the bird. Oh, to be so fearless. To be so poised against one's terror, and one's enemies.

"I have invited your father to bring you to the cathedral," Mr.

McNee says, "to assist him in his work. You may live with him in his quarters."

"Yes," Edward says, and he understands at once that the conversation is more than the bird and the stones and the opportunity to be near his mother.

He is being initiated into another clan, another faction. One that seeks to overturn the earl.

And that, he decides, is how he unites the two halves of his being.

How he stops what he has seen from unfolding.

CHAPTER SIXTEEN

Glasgow
May 2024

CLEM

Text messages, phone calls, emails to everyone she can think of who might have information. Erin's employer and colleagues at the café, her former schoolmates, her midwife. All are sympathetic and saddened by the events, but there is little in the way of what seems like useful information.

"I've lowered her morphine dose," Bee says when they go back into Erin's room. "She seems to be comfortable but let me know if you need me to come and increase it, okay?"

Clem nods. "Of course."

"How about we try a twenty-minute visit today?" Bee says with a smile. "See how it goes?"

"If we see her start to look tired we'll call you back in," Quinn says.

"Great."

Erin looks better, brighter, her cheeks flushed and her good eye not as dilated and glassy as before. She is sitting upright, a remarkable improvement, the bed raised and pillows propping her up.

Clem sits next to her daughter, holding her breath. Quinn sits on the other side of the bed, similarly tense.

"Hello, love," she says gently. She is holding her breath.

"Good to see you sitting up, Erin," Quinn says. "How are you feeling?"

"I'm scared," Erin whispers.

Clem moves close to her, her heart breaking for her. "You have nothing to be scared of, okay? Dad and I are here for you."

"We can get you a lawyer," Quinn adds, holding Clem in a meaningful look. She nods—it's a wise move. "It would be great if you could tell us what happened on Fynhallow, though. Before we get you legal counsel."

Clem studies Erin's reaction. She seems lucid, her eye still scanning the room as if it holds some secret code. But her expression is unreadable, and Clem realizes that Erin hasn't mentioned Freya. It's so unlike her. It's all she asks about, anytime they're apart. But not a mention of her.

Stephanie's words ring in her ears. *People have secrets. Especially our children.*

"I think it's too early for that," Clem tells Quinn.

"Rubbish. That detective's going to interrogate her first chance she gets. That's why they've lowered the morphine, you know. It doesn't count as an interview if she's loaded on drugs."

"Is that even true?" Clem asks, but he's already moving his chair to sit closer to Erin, his manner firm and insistent.

"Erin?" he says. "What's the last thing you remember in Fynhallow?"

"I saw her burn," Erin says, her voice breaking. "In the book. I need to stop it."

"What book?" Quinn says, puzzled.

"Please don't burn her," she whispers. "I beg you."

Clem stands up, bending to Erin. She can see she's frightened, her face folded in discomfort. "Do you mean Senna?" she asks gently. "Or someone else?"

"I know I've been wicked," Erin says.

"What do you mean, 'wicked'?" Quinn says, glancing from Erin to Clem.

"I should never have given it to him," Erin whimpers. She turns to Clem, a look of pleading on her face. "Make it stop. Please."

"Oh, darling."

Erin reaches out to Clem then, and one of the bandages bursts open. The catheter tube scratches the raw flesh of her right arm, and Erin gives a shriek of pain. Clem grabs the tube and lifts it away, but the flesh is pink and wet, blood beginning to plume where the tube touched it.

"I'll get the nurse!" Quinn says, and he dashes for the door.

Erin's cries pierce the air, shrill gasps of pain bouncing off the surfaces. Clem watches on, helpless and frantic, still holding the tube. She dare not touch the bandage, and although she wants to wrap her arms around Erin and console her, she cannot touch her.

In a moment, Bee is there, administering morphine, and soon the room falls quiet, Erin's head dropping back as she falls to sleep.

It's seven thirty in the evening, but they manage to find Dr. Miller and ask him questions about Erin's behavior. In the family room, she and Quinn describe their encounter with Erin before.

"I don't understand," Quinn says. "I mean, I get that she's just come out of a coma but she's not the daughter we remember." He shakes his head, lost for words.

"Have you seen any other patients experience this?" Clem asks.

"We've had a variety of responses," Dr. Miller says carefully. "I'm not going to pretend I can offer a concrete reason for why Erin is saying these things. I think we can contact one of our consultants from the psychology unit and ask for some input."

"'Trauma' is such a small word for a massive range of events and responses," Bee says soothingly. "And remember, it's likely she witnessed Arlo burn to death. Horrific, right?"

"It's dreadful," Clem says, feeling shaken all over again at the thought of it. Her heart breaks for Erin, and for Arlo's parents.

"It would have been hugely traumatic for her," Bee continues. "The brain devises all sorts of coping mechanisms to protect us from mental collapse. It's just that sometimes those mechanisms look strange to the people around us."

Clem shivers at the thought of what Erin has gone through. She hadn't considered that she witnessed Arlo die, but it makes sense. And the burns on her arms . . . Did Arlo catch fire, and she tried to save him? Is that why she got injured?

Why did she mention a book?

Suddenly she feels a sweep of sorrow for Erin, the confusion stirred up by Erin's strange behavior resolving with this new knowledge. Of course she has blocked out what happened.

Another night spent on the narrow cabin bed in the family room, thin window blinds doing little to block out the light of the moon.

Clem's arms crave her granddaughter's soft warm body nestling close, the occasional squelch of Freya sucking her dummy. Despite how much Erin's pregnancy had confounded her, Clem has spent every second of Freya's life falling in love with her. It surprised her, that profound affection resurrecting itself for the small red creature that came out of her daughter.

Quinn snores loudly, something he never did when he was married to Clem. But that was almost twenty years ago. She suspects he'll go home later today, return to Yorkshire, to Heather and their boys. She is surprised he even turned up at the hospital at all, is positively staggered that he wept by Erin's bedside. Maybe he *has* changed, softened by his three boys and his perfect wife. Whatever quality Heather possesses that makes her so gifted at smoothing corners, at transforming the wilderness of her marriage into a garden, at raising three versions of Quinn with such balletic grace— Clem knows she hasn't got it. She has always felt wrong-footed by details, too focused on pragmatics to ever be elegant.

After several hours' tossing and turning she leaves Quinn to his deafening snores and tiptoes into Erin's room.

She stands at the foot of the bed, alternating between guilt at waking Erin from her much-needed rest and hope that she'll recognize her mother. Clem's shock at Erin's terrifying behavior earlier has lingered, all her maternal instincts and cravings brazen in their sudden want. What did Erin mean about stopping the fire? About seeing something in a book? She tells herself these are ravings induced by trauma, or morphine, but she feels there's something to it.

The uncertainty of the present situation feels like a stone dropped on a frozen surface, sending cracks in every direction of her life. And there is the matter of her heart, more of a ticking clock than an organ, stuttering and seizing in her chest. Reminding her with each flickering pulse that she is living on borrowed time.

She was thirteen when they first cut her open and discovered the defect in her valve. Dilated cardiomyopathy. She has had five surgeries since then, two myectomies and three septal ablations. Even so, the prognosis remains: her heart will give up before she's fifty. She'll need a full heart transplant. She's on a waiting list, has spoken to more cardiologists and consultants over the years than she can recall. She has a fifty-fifty chance of surviving the operation. If she does survive, the transplant may not take.

And now, with the new, unthinkable situation, Clem feels like everything around her is collapsing at long last into an endless vortex. And she is certain that seeing Erin's smile return, the spark in her eyes and the word *Mum* on her lips would give her the courage to face all of this.

CHAPTER SEVENTEEN

Kirkwall, Orkney
December 1594

ALISON

I have been in the dungeon for three weeks when Mr. Addis unlocks the cell, flinging the door open. At first, I think he has finally kept his promise and permitted me a visitor.

"How are the worms?" I ask him weakly.

He makes a noise that's difficult to discern, but I suspect he is healed.

"I'm to take you upstairs," he grumbles.

"Why?"

"The trial. It starts this afternoon."

I pull myself to my feet and follow him up the stone steps, a murmur of voices from deep in the castle making the muscles in my face tight with fear. On the second floor is the courtroom, a large room flooded with colorful light from seven stained-glass windows depicting saints.

At the far right is a gallery, twelve rows of seats wrought of oiled mahogany, filled with spectators. Facing the gallery is an ornate dais, gleaming woodwork carved with intricate depictions of cherubs praying, their clasped hands fixed, as though the prayer is eternal, never answered.

A chair sits on the platform at the top of four oak steps, upon which have been carved four large words in florid script: *fiat justitia ruat caelum*. I recognize it from my mother's schooling, when she drummed Latin clauses into David and me.

It means: let justice be done, though the heavens fall.

It means: seek justice, whatever the consequence.

As I am thinking of my schoolfellow, I see him: David Moncrief, standing at the side of the room, the familiar colors of his robe, one shoulder higher than the other. *Coward*, I think bitterly, though as I move closer to him I notice a look of shame pass across his face. It brings a sudden heat to my face—he pities me. But perhaps that is a good thing.

The spectators' whispered voices arrow through me as I shuffle past, chains squealing behind me across the wooden floor. A woman scowls at me before raising a hand to cover her nose. It strikes me that I must smell as foul as I look, the damp dungeon making the odors of urine, rodents, and rot cling to my skin.

The noise of the gallery rises as the spectators discuss the scene, and the charges against me. I keep my head bowed, my eyes on my bare feet.

"Where is he?" Mr. Addis grumbles, looking around. We pause by the wooden lectern, and as I glance over the gallery, I see John Stewart striding through the doors. My heart jumps into my mouth as he moves up the aisle to a seat at the front. As he sits down, he holds me in a meaningful look, his head tilted.

"Father Colville!" Mr. Addis shouts then, waving at the figures standing on a mezzanine that juts over the gallery. "I brought her up, just like you said!"

Father Colville stands by the railings of the mezzanine, in conference with two bishops. I realize they are here to oversee the proceedings, and William's words come back to me: *the udallers have the ear of Bishop Law.* Among the spectators I spy Jacob McVeigh and Peter Gauldry, both udallers whose inherited lands have been stolen by the earl. They watch me intently, and Peter gives me a nod.

I move my eyes nervously to John Stewart. He is still staring at me, and he draws a finger to his lips in a gesture filled with menace.

I am to be silent. That is why he is here.

It does not matter that the bishops are here, nor the udallers who have come to show their support. John Stewart is more powerful than them all, and his presence feels like a wolf in the room, waiting for his chance to devour me.

The murmuring among the spectators begins to die down in anticipation. My mouth running dry, I see more familiar faces— our neighbors, Angus and Maggie. They must have journeyed here by boat and by carriage. It is no small sacrifice to leave their farm; I've seen Angus and Maggie working the fields in all weathers, and through devastating sickness, precisely because rest comes at a high price under Earl Patrick's rule.

They must be here to show their support. It brings a little comfort, to see them here.

Maggie is wearing her blue cap, the one she's so proud of. I recall her showing it to me when she got it, soon after Beatrice was born. She has worn it only once that I recall, to her oldest boy's wedding, preferring to keep it wrapped in linen in a wooden chest. Angus's long copper hair has been combed and tied back, his farmer's shirt swapped for a smart gray mantle pinned with a silver brooch at the shoulder. I stare, hoping they'll catch my eye and see my undying gratitude for coming today. It means so much.

But then Maggie's eyes flick to mine. She does not smile, her face stiff and her gaze filled with metal.

My stomach twists. Has she seen me? I am sure she has. Angus glances at me, too, but he grimaces. All the friendliness is gone. My cheeks burn. Why have they come, if not to support me?

I scan the rows for my mother, and for Agnes, but I do not see them. At the back of the gallery, however, I see Solveig, his face almost hidden by his dark hood. So, the Triskele have come to spy on me. A burst of anger rushes through me at the cruelty of it. My mother insists that I cannot leave the Triskele, and that I am still part of the clan. Yet they will not save me.

Just as I am wondering where William is, he walks in, followed by Edward, both of them anxious to find a seat. Edward's face reddens when he catches my eye, his eyebrows rising and his mouth falling open. I lift my hands to my face, unable to stop the tears that wet my cheeks. Relief washes over me like a warm tide. How I wish I could tear off these iron cuffs and run to them. Edward grows upset, too, and I remember that he has not seen me since I was arrested. I must look frightful to him, bowed down by heavy chains, my head shorn and the bones at my chest rippling through the skin like weft work.

I touch my chin, and he does the same.

In contrast to my shameful state, Father Colville looks immaculate, a vision of godliness sweeping across the room toward me. He is clean-shaven, his silver hair brushed and set in fine waves atop his head. His sable cloak is lined with ermine, the white panels at his collar freshly pressed.

"Alison," he says gently, taking my arm and gesturing toward the dais. "Are you well?"

"I am . . . as well as can be expected, Father," I say, fear stopping up my throat. It is stunning to think that this is the same man who pushed a needle into my body over and over, the man who pushed a needle underneath my tongue. Now he is courteous and gentle, holding my elbow. The contrast between these two acts makes me dizzy, as though there are two of him.

From the cathedral across the street twelve loud tolls from the clock ring out, telling the city that it is noon.

"You may proceed," a voice calls out from the balcony when the last bell sounds. One of the bishops has given the order for the trial to begin, and my stomach clenches at the quiet that falls upon the gallery before me. A hundred pairs of eyes turning to me.

"State your name for Bishop Vance and Bishop Sinclair," Father Colville says, gesturing to each in turn.

I swallow hard. "Alison Margaret Balfour," I say, my voice hoarse after being silent for so long. The seats on the mezzanine creak loudly as the bishops lean forward to perceive me. Bishop Vance is a small, red-faced man with a hooked nose, preoccupied by the white headdress that keeps slipping down across his eyes. Bishop Sinclair has a thick jaw that he works as though chewing food, his black eyes shining like pebbles as he grimaces down. I offer up a silent prayer that they might be merciful. That they may discern my innocence and call a halt to these proceedings.

"Madam Alison Balfour," Father Colville says, turning his back on me on to address the crowd seated in the gallery. He moves to the side of the room and plucks a Bible from a table there, raising it high in the air. "Do you swear by God, upon this Holy Bible, to tell the truth during the proceedings of this trial?"

He moves the Bible toward me, standing close so I may lower my hand upon it.

"I do."

As my head touches the black cover of the Bible, I think of another book. A book with both a black cover and black pages.

I am a girl of twelve again, and there is a woman standing before me, wearing the antlers of a deer as a crown, her face hidden by a long veil of plaited hazel twigs.

Scream into the pages, the woman says.

She hands me what I think is a quill, but as I take it from her, I see it is a knife.

Write with a scream, not ink, she says. *Else you cannot be a Carrier.*

And then I am back in the courtroom, the Bible on the table, Father Colville's plush velvet robes catching blood reds and ochre yellows from the stained-glass windows as he strides between the dais and the gallery. On the wooden floor next to me I spy the face of one of the glass saints reflected, his eyes lifted up in solemn petition.

"Alison," Father Colville says in a loud voice. "You are indicted and accused of the sinful and damnable renouncing of God, your faith and baptism, enslaving yourself onto the Devil, following and practicing the fearful and abominable craft of witchcraft. Do you confess to these charges?"

The courtroom falls silent, and I flick my eyes at John Stewart. My heart is beating so fiercely against my chest that I fear it may burst out.

"I do not."

I see John Stewart shift in his seat, and I flinch. But I must stand my ground.

Father Colville turns to the gallery and calls out in a clear, loud voice: "You are further accused of consorting with Thomas Paplay, servant of John Stewart, to kill by poisoning Patrick Stewart, the Earl of Orkney. Do you confess to these charges?"

I glance again at John Stewart. His eyes bore into me, and I have to steel myself to tell the truth. "Before God, Father—I do not."

A sudden fervor swells throughout the gallery, as physical as the air that swells in the valley before a storm. I feel myself shake all over, but I know I am watched, my every movement read as though it might reveal some inner evil.

Father Colville looks wearily to the mezzanine. "Your graces, I ask that I may proceed with my efforts to draw out a confession from her, that her soul may perhaps be purged of these dark stains before God's holy judgment."

Bishop Sinclair makes a gesture with his hand for Father Colville to proceed, and he seems much relieved.

"Alison, you have long established yourself as a spaewife, a wise woman, having been sought out on diverse occasions by many for charms, spells, potions, and superstitions." He turns to me, his face saddened. "Is this true?"

I nod. "Yes."

"Have you, from time to time, provided charms, spells, and potions to the people of Orkney for the purposes of recovery from illness?"

"I have."

"Can you give examples of such occasions?"

My eyes search out Mr. Addis, who seems cured of his arse worms. I imagine it may be prudent not to mention that, for several reasons.

"I . . . I recall when I treated a child in our parish. A little boy named Malcolm. He had eaten a plant full of poison and was vomiting."

"And how did you treat him?"

"I made him a tonic of kettledock, vervain, and I placed the petals of a belladonna flower and the bones of a raven's wing by his head. I said an incantation and turned three times sunwise."

Father Colville nods, having heard me, but his eyes move to the faces of the spectators in the gallery, surveying their response. There is nothing outrageous about my treatment—this is an old remedy, and many here will recognize it. Some folk turn sunwise upon crossing the threshold of their own house in the morning, to bring fortune with them into the day. It is to harness the energy of the sun, turning the way light falls upon the sundial, from left to right. It is for this reason, too, that I was not permitted to write with my left hand as a child, but was instructed to use my right.

"Perhaps it might be said that the same power you possess to heal might also be used to harm," Father Colville says.

"I do not wish to harm," I say.

"But by your own words, you are a skillful practitioner in the magic arts. And all who are present will know that there are two forms of such arts: dark and light."

"Yes, but . . ."

"So it follows that anyone who is skillful at one must also be skillful in the other?"

"I do not practice the dark arts," I say quietly. From the corner of my eye, I see John Stewart murmuring to one of his aides.

"I am told that you spared the life of Thomas Paplay," Father Colville says. "Is this true?"

"It is, but . . ." I want to say that I did so out of innocence, not because I was consorting with him. The very idea makes me feel ashamed.

"When did you spare his life?"

"It was a year ago," I say. "He was gravely ill with smallpox."

"And what potion did you provide?"

"Sheep dung boiled in milk," I say. It is an old remedy. But it must be prepared under a spell. I open my mouth to confess this, but the words will not come.

"Why did you spare his life?"

"Because I..."

"Is it because you were lovers?"

I look from Father Colville to the bishops, appalled. "No!"

A murmur ripples across the courtroom, the spectators turning to one another, heated by this repugnant suggestion.

"And what of those charms you have prepared for those seeking to bring about harm?" Father Colville says, though it takes a long while for the words to sink through my shock at his former question. *Lovers?* I search out William in the crowd. He throws me a brave smile, but I know he must feel humiliated.

"You have provided harmful charms?" Father Colville continues.

"Never."

"But if I were to ask you for a charm to bring a foul wind upon a ship, or to cause an animal to fall foul of pest, you could provide these things?"

"I would not..."

He strides across the room, his footsteps pounding the wood of the floor, the sound making me jump. Then he hefts up the Bible, holding it aloft, and approaches me with such aggression that I think he means to bring it down upon my head. "Remember your oath, Alison," he hisses. "I asked you if you could provide such things, if it is within your capacity as a healer to do so."

I scan the faces in the room, my eyes settling upon other women I know to be capable of such a thing. I want to cry out, *But there are many healers in Orkney!* But then I wonder what might happen if I do. What might I unleash, if I say such a thing?

"It is," I murmur.

"It is said that you are a woman of low means, correct?"

"That is true," I say, though his question confuses me. Why is he asking this?

"Would you be willing to state to the court the annual income of your household?"

My eyes search out William in the crowd. I do not wish to bring shame upon him.

"Answer, Madam Balfour," Bishop Sinclair calls down from the mezzanine.

I see John Stewart smile.

"What say you to this, Madam Balfour?" Bishop Vance calls out. "Do you renounce Christ and His Holy baptism?"

"My husband's earnings are often in trade," I say. "And so we earn wheat and sometimes labor in our fields in exchange for his work in the cathedral, as well as money."

"And how much money is that?"

I falter. "I would say, five pounds each quarter."

The bishops consider this, weighing up among them whether it is enough to force me to seek other means of income.

"Do you renounce Christ and His Holy baptism?" Bishop Sinclair calls down after a few moments.

"I have not renounced God," I say loudly. And so there is no pain and no love on this earth that will make me renounce God.

"Madam Balfour has a mark upon her person that would surely prove her words sadly to be untrue," Father Colville says.

"What mark is this?" Bishop Vance asks.

"On the night of November twelfth, I inspected her and found the Devil's mark hidden beneath her tongue," Father Colville says, glancing at John Stewart. "This was witnessed by myself and three others, including the Master of Orkney."

John gives a deep nod to confirm this, and I shudder to think of that night, when I was standing naked in the dungeon before the men, blood drawn all over my body by Father Colville's long needle.

"I have sundry reports from various others on these isles

concerning Alison Balfour's misdeeds," Father Colville continues. "But perhaps the most damning evidence that she is a *malefica*, a harborer of mischief, was perceived when we witnessed her familiar enter the dungeon of this very castle."

"What familiar is this you speak of?" Bishop Vance asks.

"A hare, my lord, with a hide of darkest sable."

"All four men witnessed a hare in the dungeon of this castle?" Bishop Sinclair asks.

"We did, Your Grace," Father Colville replies. "A moment later, the same hare transformed into a man. I believe this dark figure to be Satan himself."

Somewhere in the gallery, a woman cries out: the spectators are unsettled at the thought of Satan walking the land of Orkney.

"I am not persuaded that the Devil would deign to visit His subject while she is incarcerated," Bishop Vance says. "This would seem to contradict scripture, whereupon we understand the Devil not to care a jot for those who do His bidding. Indeed, it is unheard of for Lucifer to trouble Himself at all, other than to have sexual relations with the witch. I am taking it that this did not happen?"

There is a long pause, as though the whole room is holding its breath. I watch Father Colville carefully as he considers his response. The smile never leaves his face.

"We did not witness such a thing, no," he says. I think of the shadow taking the shape of a long thin man as it passed through the window, and my skin crawls.

Was it really the Devil?

"Then I suggest we forget the last charge," Bishop Sinclair says.

"Have you any evidences that we may consider?" Bishop Vance says, pushing his headdress up his forehead. "Any of the witch's potions or tokens that may give us insight into her pact with the Devil?"

Father Colville hesitates, and for a moment I think that smile might yet slip from his face. "We have evidence in the form of Thomas Paplay's confession, Your Grace . . ."

"Has the witch's home been searched thoroughly?" Bishop Sinclair says.

"We will search again," Father Colville says. "Mr. Paplay mentioned that the charm made for him by the witch was wrought of wax. This may be difficult to obtain . . ."

"Try, Father Colville," Bishop Sinclair says, and Father Colville's eyes slide to John Stewart again. It strikes me then—he wishes me to be found guilty. It does not matter that his duty is to God, to save my soul.

He intends to see me to my death.

The cell door swinging shut will forever be the noise of doom, the toll of hell. Mr. Addis rattles the key in the lock and throws me a satisfied sneer, and I turn my face to the wall to hide the pain of being separated from Will and Edward. Seeing them in the courtroom before was the worst pain I have ever felt, but now, being returned to this cell, not knowing if I'll see them again, transcends even that.

"Open it again, if you please."

I turn to see Father Colville approaching, beckoning Mr. Addis to unlock the cell door. He smiles at me like a dear friend, as though he has not spent three hours relentlessly pursuing false ideas of my evilness, tearing me down in front of my neighbors, my family, the bishops.

He steps inside, allowing Mr. Addis to lock the door behind him before passing the keys through the bars. This is curious, though I do not feel assured by his presence. With a shiver, I find myself looking over his hands and the outline of his pockets for needles, or some such instrument of torture.

He is clutching to his chest the Bible I swore upon in the courtroom.

"I know you will wish to pray," he says, stepping forward, and I flinch. He sees, and his face falls.

"My child, I am not here to harm you. My intention is solely to bring you closer to God, to feel His love. I offer you a chance to pray and feel His holy peace."

I think of the way he looked at John Stewart in the courtroom, how I told myself he wished to see to it that I take the blame for Master Stewart's crimes. Perhaps I am mistaken. He is a parson. Surely he would not offend God by seeing an innocent woman burn?

He sits on the ground next to me and rests the Bible on his robes. It is too precious to place on the cell floor.

"Let us pray," he says, clasping his hands and bowing his head. "Oh Lord, Father in heaven, we humbly offer up a prayer to Thee upon this day . . ."

As he speaks, repenting to God on my behalf for my stubborn refusal to confess, pleading to God that my heart might be softened else my soul will be damned, I feel doubt rise up again. A parson may be swayed by the Devil to believe that lies are truth, that black is white. A thought drifts into my head, as real and as formed as a feather:

I see the crown of his head, his clean, soft hair.

I look down at the heavy chains and cuffs, the raw flesh around my wrists.

I glance through the bars at Mr. Addis, finding him already gone, and for a moment I think I have already lifted the chains and dropped them with all my might upon the soft part of Father Colville's skull before reaching for that knife I know is tucked in his boot, drawing it quickly across his throat. Then I filch through his pockets for the keys and let myself out, out into the night, my feet light upon the floor of the castle as the last drop of life pulses out of his veins.

"... and forgive her trespasses, Lord, if Thou wilt, for we know that within Christ all things are possible ..."

I give a jolt, landing back in my skin, realizing with equal parts relief and regret that the idea was just that—I have not acted upon it, I have not seized the moment and bludgeoned a man of God to death to purchase my freedom. But the temptation is still there, unfurling ever darkly in my heart—the way is open.

My husband's face springs to my mind. I imagine his anguish upon hearing that I committed such a terrible crime. His wife, the woman he has cherished and cared for all these years, capable of murder. He would wonder if he ever knew me at all.

"... in the holy name of our beloved Jesus Christ, amen."

Father Colville lifts his blue eyes to mine, the skin around them soft and fine as wrinkled silk.

"Let us read from the Bible. I think it will benefit you to learn of the Lord's plan for us. That oftentimes, it is the ones He loves most that He causes to suffer. For it is written, 'whoso I chasten, I cherish.'"

He reads with me until the curfew bell tolls at eight o'clock, and even when I am nodding off to sleep I hear his voice, the falling and rising pattern of his intonation lulling me, teasing me to slumber.

When I come to, he is already gone. I am lying on my side on the hay bale. I shuffle toward the cell door and find it is locked. With anguish I wish that I *had* seized my chance to escape.

And it is while I am marveling at this development in my character that I spot something on the ground, where the slate rises slightly. Something that was not there before.

A book. An old book, quite large and visibly heavy, many pages beneath its old wooden binding.

I recognize it instantly. My heart begins to clamor in my bones, a distant bell clanging in my ears.

Still, I approach it, eager to prove to myself that it is a figment of my imagination. I am dreaming. The book is not there. This is my conscience chiding me for my wild sins.

But the book is on the ground, rough to the touch. The cover is made from a tree, and inside the pages are black. The pages are pieces of night, for the book is from the dawn of time, before humankind, before love, and death.

With a trembling hand, I reach out and open it. The black pages appear blank, but I know otherwise. And right as I am telling myself this, the surface of the open pages quiver, as though a shadow has passed over them. I watch as an image appears there, a white light flickering with shadows that sharpen into figures.

I see a moving image of a white room, the items strange and shining. A silver bed with white sheets, a young woman with a shorn head, her limbs badly burned. Another woman is tending to her.

Her mother.

Why is the book showing me this?

But as I stretch my arms out to heft it, the book is no more. It is gone.

I stagger backward, falling to the ground. Then I lunge forward, sweeping my hands across the dark stone in case it has moved, been shunted by a rat, moved by my chains.

But the book is nowhere to be found.

And yet, I know I saw it. *The Book of Witching*.

It came for me, just like she promised.

PART TWO

UPON
A HARE MOON

CHAPTER EIGHTEEN

Two years ago

ERIN

Erin hasn't been nervous before now, but as she stares at the scene waiting for her through the trees, a thought crosses her mind.

If she runs, the darkness will cover her.

She will likely outrun the rest of them, and she knows where the road meets the woods. She can flag down a car, or find a phone signal and call someone. At the very least, she can hide out until morning and *then* make a run for it.

Maybe it's the fire that is making her wary, the heat of it beating through the trees. Or perhaps it's the voice in her head that says, *Your Mum would kill you if she knew where you were.*

The singing has started, a single drumbeat starting up. The melody is rousing, not sinister. It looks more like a party than a ritual.

She takes a breath, reminding herself why she is here.

How important it is.

What this *means*.

CHAPTER NINETEEN

CLEM

She wakes at dawn, checking her text messages from Josie.

> Morning! Hope you're OK. Freya is happy,
> went straight to sleep at 8pm last night. She's
> still in the travel cot, out for the count xx

A photo shows Freya from the night before, sitting on Josie's living room floor. She's wearing a pair of Sam's dinosaur pajamas and is grinning happily. Clem texts back.

> So glad to hear this. No change here. Thank
> you for taking care of her xx

Clem kisses her fingertips and presses them against the photo. Gorgeous girl. Freya looks exactly like Erin did when she was younger, a mass of soft blonde curls on her little head and wide blue eyes. She makes a mental note to share the photo with Erin, but then remembers Erin hasn't yet asked for Freya.

It's unthinkable, all of it. None of it makes sense.

She has breakfast in silence with Quinn, both of them standing in the small kitchen of the family room with toast that neither of them touches still in the toaster. The coffee is tasteless, all her senses dulled by the unfolding of another day in the hospital with their daughter.

Stephanie arrives at nine, just as they're gowning up to visit Erin. No sign of DC Sanger.

"Good morning," she says. "Might I join you?"

"I'm not sure that's a good idea," Quinn says.

"She's still out of sorts," Clem says, choosing her words carefully. "There was an incident last night . . . She managed to open one of her wounds."

Stephanie's face falls. "Oh God. What happened?"

"We tried to ask her some questions about the trip," Clem says. "It didn't go well."

"Hello," Bee says, coming out of the room and greeting them both. "She's awake just now."

"How is she?" Clem asks, noticing Bee's bright smile. Surely if Erin was acting strangely again, she'd be less pleased with her progress, more wary.

"She's a little groggy," Bee says, "but that's just the pain relief. I think she'd be glad to see you."

"Do you think she's well enough to answer some questions?" Stephanie asks, glancing at Bee.

"Absolutely not," Quinn says.

"I know it's difficult right now," Stephanie says, "but Senna is still missing . . ."

"I really think it's still too soon," Clem says, cutting Stephanie off. But she feels torn. Of course, she wants to find Senna, and perhaps Erin can help with some information that might lead them to her. But asking her poses a risk—Clem's worried that she'll only get distressed again.

"In my opinion, it's fine to give it a go," Bee says. "If she reacts poorly, then we'll leave it. Okay?"

Clem nods and glances at Quinn. Last night has shaken them both, and they don't know what to expect when they go inside.

Bee calls out Constable Byers and allows the other three to step inside. The room is quiet, the carbolic smell of creams and gels hanging thickly in the air.

Clem glances at Erin, noticing that she seems brighter, more alert, her eye turning to Clem as she steps inside. The swelling to her face has gone down a little, her features more recognizable, and the wound on her arm has been dressed. She lifts an arm as though to wave to them.

"Hello, darling," Clem says, sitting next to her. "How are you feeling?"

Erin turns to her but doesn't answer.

"Morning, Erin," Quinn says with a smile.

"Nyx," she replies.

The word hangs in the air between them, and Clem tries hard not to feel deflated. Stephanie looks at Clem for explanation.

"Nyx?" she asks.

"We think this is the effects of trauma," Clem says slowly, and Quinn nods.

"The doctor is aware of it," he says.

"What is it?" Stephanie asks.

"I am Nyx," Erin answers, louder this time, her tone brittle. She sounds hostile, not like Erin at all. Clem watches Stephanie for her reaction but she seems unfazed. Perhaps, like Bee, she has encountered such things often.

"We're here for you, love," Clem says gently. Erin looks straight ahead, contemplating Stephanie.

"Who are you?" Erin asks her after a moment.

"I'm Stephanie, and I'm a detective," Stephanie says. "I'm working with you and your family to make sure we bring Senna home safely."

"Senna?" Erin says. "What's that?"

"Your friend Senna," Stephanie says, and quickly she pulls out her mobile phone and shows Erin a picture of her friend. "Remember?"

"Are you able to tell us what happened in Orkney?" Clem asks. "How did the fire start?"

Erin turns drowsily to Clem, fixing her eye on her. "A bad man did it," she says, her words a little slurred.

"What bad man?" Quinn says, straightening. He looks at Clem, alarmed.

"She was tied to the log," Erin says wistfully. "Her wrists were bound."

Clem's throat tightens, and she sees Stephanie flinch.

"Okay," Stephanie says, tapping her phone to record Erin. "I'm going to caution you, Erin, that I'm filming you now."

"Filming me?" Erin says.

"Can you stop filming?" Quinn asks Stephanie. His voice is filled with alarm.

"Is it okay for me to film you?" Stephanie says, ignoring Quinn, and Erin nods.

"Her wrists were bound," Erin says again, "and then the fire grew. She died."

"Stop filming her!" Clem shouts, and Stephanie relents, lowering her phone. The tension in the room swells to a bursting point.

"Who bound Senna's wrists?" Stephanie presses Erin.

"Not Senna," Erin says, and Stephanie is puzzled.

"Not Senna?" she says. "Who, then? Arlo?"

"Who is Arlo?"

Clem rises to her feet, insistent that the questioning finish. "I'm really sorry," she tells Stephanie. "But it's clear that she's not well enough to answer questions ..."

"Arlo is your boyfriend," Stephanie says. "Can you tell us what happened to him? He died, you see, in the fire."

Clem looks with horror at Stephanie. "Stop. This is too much for her," she says, but Stephanie ignores her.

"We know this must be really tough for you," she tells Erin. "But it's so, so important that we bring your friend Senna home. And Arlo's parents ... well, they're devastated. Wouldn't you like to help them understand what happened?"

"I don't care about that," she says.

"About Arlo?" Stephanie asks. "You don't care about Arlo?"

"She didn't say that!" Clem says.

"I did," Erin says. "You said Arlo died. And I don't care."

CHAPTER TWENTY

Kirkwall, Orkney
December 1594

ALISON

It is snowing, white flakes piling up on the ground, just visible through the small window at the top of the dungeon wall. I shiver in my cell, huddled against the wall and holding my shawl around me for warmth. It is too cold for sleep, and I cannot stop the thoughts that beat inside my head.

Why did the book appear to me?

It was taunting me, reminding me that I cannot leave the Triskele, however much I wish to.

Or perhaps God allowed it to appear to me to remind me that I have a choice. But what was the image that I saw, of the woman in the bed, and the woman who I sensed was her mother?

Over and over, the questions circle my mind. My mother taught David and me that the book shows only what is needed, but I am inclined to believe it teases and mocks at will. The book could show me a way of escaping the dungeon, if it wished, or some foreknowledge that would give me advantage in the trial. But it does not.

It is a sin to complain, this I know, but I cannot help it. I know this is self-pity. But it gnaws at me, the absence of God that I feel here in the dungeon, and in the courtroom. When Father Colville speaks, I no longer believe he is serving God. And I recall what I saw, that night that Father Coville and the others claimed to see a hare in the shadows, a familiar.

I saw no hare, but I saw a tall man made of shadow, striding through the window and into the night. Was this the Devil? I believe it was. Why else would I find myself so caught up in this nightmarish situation? And yet, God has allowed it.

The next morning, I am woken by Mr. Addis banging on the bars.

"Wake up, witch," he growls. "You've a visitor."

"Oh!" I say, for behind him I see William.

"Not so fast," Mr. Addis says. "I'll need payment first."

I do not remind him of the potion I made for his arse worms. Instead, I pull off my stockings and pass them to him, imploring him to accept them. With a grunt, he turns and allows William to rush to me.

He kneels by the bars, setting down a basket and searching for my hands to take in his.

"My God," he says. "You are starving."

He passes the items of his basket to me: roasted plovers, raisins, a quail, and a cup of sack. I eat it all in one sitting, stuffing as much of it into my mouth as I can manage. It has been days since I last ate.

"Agnes sent you this," he says, passing something wrapped in linen through the bars. It is a hat, woven from brown wool. I pull it over my coif and immediately feel the benefit of its warmth.

"Blessed Agnes," I say, pressing my hands down on the thick wool. "Please thank her for me, won't you?"

"Beatrice sent a gift, too." Will slips a shell through the bars. I see she has drawn on it with charcoal. "She missed you," he says.

I hold the shell in my palm and look it over. This is no childish portrait—Beatrice has embellished the stone with a Triskele symbol of a hawk, its wings outstretched, a double arrow just beneath. The hawk means bravery, but the outstretched wings mean hope. The double arrow means unrestrained, constant love between two people. Her message strikes me hard: she wishes me to have courage, to know that there is hope, that she loves me and knows I love her. And she is calling on the gods, known so intimately by the Triskele, to set me free.

"What is it?" William asks, watching me study the shell. "She would not explain such an odd drawing."

I hesitate, because I do not wish to lie to him, and yet I have lied so much by omission: I have not confessed to William that my mother has taught our daughter the Triskele symbols. And now she is using it to pass me messages.

"I know not," I say quietly. "How are the children?"

He hesitates. "Beatrice is well."

"And Edward?"

"Edward is still not himself. He is staying away from the cottage for long stretches of time. Sometimes all night."

I think back to the initiation. Perhaps he is meeting with the Triskele. I dare not mention this to William.

"Perhaps I could bring him here," he says. "To see you."

I am torn at this. I am desperate to see my son, and William must be worried in the extreme to consider bringing Edward into this place.

I cannot eat another morsel.

"Will," I say, breathless. "I think you should leave the islands."

"What?" he says, his face falling. "I just got here."

He begins to recount his long journey from Gunn, how the ship home isn't until tomorrow morning and how he is staying with his employer in his cottage beside the cathedral.

"I mean, I think you should take the children and my mother and leave Orkney altogether," I tell him. "It's not safe."

"Where would we go?"

"Edinburgh," I tell him, and he laughs.

"Edinburgh? Where the tack is twice as much as Orkney? Where the king is intent on pitching stakes on every hill and burning witches?"

"Orkney is no better," I tell him quietly. "You know that."

"I'm told the pest is rampant there," he says. "The plague pits burn constantly, the cemeteries at capacity. All must stay inside for fifteen days to stop it spreading, on pain of death."

"The Highlands, then," I tell him. "Perhaps seek out your cousin in Inverness?"

"Inverness? You know we cannot, Alison . . ."

"I see what has happened," I whisper, my voice dropping. "Will, I know why I am here, why they have imprisoned me. John Stewart approached me this past summer, that day at the cathedral. He asked me for a charm to take a life. I believe he wished that charm for the earl."

His face falls. "Did you make such a charm?"

"Of course not. But likely the earl suspects his brother of this attempt on his life, and so John is eager to pass blame. He has killed Thomas Paplay. And now, because I am accused of aiding Thomas by witchcraft, he will also kill me."

My words hang like swords in the air. William blinks hard, taking this news into his thoughts.

"Oh, Alison," he says, taking my hand in his. "You must tell this to Father Colville."

"I *have*. I have told him, and he insists that I am guilty." I swallow back hot tears of frustration. "I believe he wishes me to be found guilty instead of John Stewart."

"I will procure a lawyer," he says.

I raise my eyebrows. "A lawyer?"

"Andrew Couper. You will remember his father is the clerk at St. Magnus Cathedral."

I nod, thinking quickly. Andrew Couper is a young, bright man. The last time I saw him he had barely grown a beard. "But how..."

My question trails off. I dare not ask. *How can we afford such a thing as a lawyer?*

"We have some friends yet, my love," he says. "I asked Isaac and Duncan to approach Mr. Couper. Next thing I know, someone has volunteered to cover his fee."

"Who was it?" I ask, thinking of the faces of our former friends in the gallery. I have felt so very friendless, so the knowledge that someone has paid for a lawyer brings tears of thanks to my eyes.

"It does not matter. What matters is that things are changing," William says. "I think the day is fast coming that we will pull the islands back from the lion's jaw. We will send our own message: Orkney will not be defeated."

I do not share his confidence, but there is a look in William's eyes and a power in his voice that heartens me.

The fight in him has returned.

CHAPTER TWENTY-ONE

Glasgow
May 2024

CLEM

In the family room, Clem sits with Quinn and Stephanie, shaking with anger and confusion.

"You shouldn't have filmed her," she tells Stephanie. "You don't know how paranoid she might be feeling, how traumatized."

"I did ask for her consent," Stephanie says, at which Quinn makes a loud *pfft*.

"I told you it was too early for her to answer questions," he says. "Erin is still on a heavy dose of morphine, so I think it's fair to say that whatever she said is not an accurate representation of how she feels about Arlo, or Senna. And we'd appreciate it if you could delete whatever you recorded of our daughter in there."

"I understand," Stephanie says, though she makes no effort to take out her phone and delete the video file. "We will take into account that Erin's a vulnerable patient and that she's heavily medicated. I'm sure you can both appreciate how urgent it is that we find Senna." She pulls her iPad from her briefcase.

"I think we need to be looking at ferry passenger lists," Quinn says. "Finding out who else was on the island that night."

"We have done that, actually," Stephanie says, and Clem senses she doesn't like Quinn. She flicks through her notebook. "We have another team currently reviewing any persons of interest on the two main ferry passenger lists. Another team are looking at all the boat traffic in and out of Orkney. What we do know already is that the Isle of Gunn isn't serviced by a ferry."

"You said they might have waded. How far is it from Gairsay?" Clem asks, pulling a map of Orkney up on her phone.

"It's half a mile," Stephanie says. "But I'm told that the tidal window is about an hour. So there's no messing about, otherwise you risk drowning. And Gairsay's ferry schedules mean that you need to camp overnight in order to cross."

Stephanie pulls out her own phone and brings up the timetable for Orkney Ferries.

"You see?" she says, pointing at the column for weekday sailings over the summer.

"The evening ferry from Gairsay arrives at six minutes past six, and the morning ferry is eight fifteen. There is also an afternoon ferry that runs at four o'clock. The low tide is at quarter to six in the morning. So if you want to get to Gunn, either you travel by boat or you get a ferry, camp out overnight, and then wade across before dawn."

"And why would anyone do that?" Clem asks. "What's so special about this place?"

"Well, that's what we're trying to work out," Stephanie says.

"Did they camp out?" Quinn says. "Did they have a tent?"

Stephanie shakes her head. "Senna had a three-man tent but it was found stowed away. But there are caves on both Gairsay and Gunn." She taps the map with her fingernails. "The fire happened inside a cave on Gunn, right here in the middle of the bay. So possibly they waded across at dawn then had a nap inside the cave."

"And maybe they disturbed a fellow explorer," Quinn says grimly.

"Possibly," Stephanie says. "Except we've checked the ferry passenger list for Gairsay. We know that's how Arlo, Erin, and Senna got to Gairsay. But they were the only people who stayed overnight. All the others got the return ferry."

Clem rubs her face and lets out a deep sigh. It is more exhausting than she can put into words, figuring it all out.

"What time was the fire?" she asks.

"Around midnight," Stephanie says. "Though the ranger found Erin and Arlo just before dawn. Arlo's phone conversation with his friend was the last contact they had with anyone."

"So they stayed overnight on Gairsay, waded across Wednesday morning, then spent the whole day there?"

"They would have had to," Stephanie says. "Unless they went over and came straight back, the next tidal window wouldn't be until Thursday morning."

Quinn studies the map. "And we still don't know who else was on the island?"

"No one else traveled by ferry to Gairsay," Stephanie says. "But we don't know if someone else traveled by boat to the Isle of Gunn. We're reviewing drone footage that should help create a visual map of the island."

"What about Gairsay?" Clem asks, making notes on her phone. "Is that island inhabited?"

"There's a population of about seventy."

"Well, surely we ought to be speaking to those seventy people?"

"We are."

"And?"

"No leads as yet."

"No suspects? No one saw three townie teenagers camping on their beaches?"

"They did," Stephanie says. "But beyond times and dates, we have nothing to follow up on. And no, no one is a suspect."

Clem looks down at her notes, feeling disappointed that nothing adds up. *Gairsay, tidal window, Gunn, cave.*

"What do *you* think Arlo couldn't find?" Quinn asks Stephanie.

"I really don't know," Stephanie says, but Clem's stomach drops. *This is no longer about a missing girl,* she thinks. *They're looking for a dead body.*

Clem's heart is tightening again in that sickening way that means her body is too stressed, and she rises to her feet, feeling the room spin.

"Sorry," she tells Stephanie and Quinn. "I need to take my medication."

"She has a heart condition," Quinn explains when Stephanie looks alarmed. He straightens then, reaching out to steady her.

"I'm fine," she says tersely.

"You sure?"

She doesn't answer. The hospital corridor lists and churns, but she makes her way into the small kitchen and presses two pills into her hand before swallowing them back. It all feels too much, the last nineteen years. She really thought things had come together when she married Quinn and had Erin, her perfect little girl. The sword that seemed to be hanging overhead with her heart condition was easy to ignore, what with her daughter and husband, and her parents living nearby. But then, her marriage ended abruptly, and both her parents died within three months of each other—her father in a mechanical accident, when he went to help an old friend, her mother of a heart attack. Their house swallowed up by debts that her father had concealed. Then Erin's pregnancy, and now this.

She gowns up and heads into Erin's room, where Constable Byers is standing in his usual spot.

"Can you give me a minute?" she asks him.

He nods. "Sure."

Erin is sleeping, silvery light from the window streaking across her forehead. The bruises are vivid, a fresh shade of yellow beginning to pool in the dip of her cheekbones, but the swelling is going down, the familiar lines of Erin's face beginning to reappear. She looks peaceful, and delicate. She looks like a child again.

Clem sits down in the chair beside the bed, feeling Stephanie's words roll like boulders in the wounded space of her mind.

She cries quietly, and there is the sudden urge to sleep, too, her body more pummeled than she can ever imagine feeling. As though the endless bad news is landing on her flesh like physical blows.

"Mum?"

The voice is so familiar that it makes Clem jerk upright, eyes wide. She turns to Erin and finds her awake, her head turned to her. Did Erin just call her "Mum," the way she used to? She sees that Erin's expression has changed, her face wide and searching.

"Erin?"

Clem moves closer to Erin, seeing that she is growing distressed. The heart monitor begins to race, her pulse hitting ninety, a hundred beats a minute. She lifts the wires around her, looking at them as though she's never seen them before.

"Mum?" she says again in a shrill voice, a series of questions folded in that one word, uttered with alarm. Clem stares, noticing how everything about Erin's demeanor has changed. Even the lines of her face have softened, her eye holding a familiar look. The girl dissolving into a panic attack on the bed in front of her is absolutely, 100 percent Erin, and Clem finds she is as relieved as she is confused.

"Let me get a doctor," she says, rising to her feet, but suddenly Erin lunges forward and grabs her arm.

"No!" she shouts. "Don't leave me!"

Clem sinks back down on the bed beside her, watching, frantic, as Erin's wide eye scans the room fearfully, her lips trembling.

"W . . . what's g . . . going on?" Erin says, stumbling over her words. "Where am I?"

Clem barely knows how to answer. She is desperately searching Erin's face to understand what she needs, why she has suddenly transformed into this sobbing, disoriented version of her daughter, the pendulum swung so far from the version that claims she is Nyx to this.

"You're in hospital, remember?" she says. "You were . . . you were hiking in Orkney, and there was an accident . . ."

"An accident?" Erin says, deeply puzzled. "Where's Arlo? Where's Senna?" She looks down at her bandaged hands, shock pummeling her as she seems to see the injuries there for the first time. "Oh God. Mum?!"

Clem is seized by the terrible awareness that Erin is beginning to hyperventilate, that she has at last asked for Arlo. A week ago, when Stephanie broke the news of Arlo's death, she couldn't care less.

"Mum, something terrible happened," Erin says, the words spilling out in a shrill tone, her whole body beginning to tremble.

"I know," Clem says soothingly. "I know it has."

Erin shakes her head. "No, no. No, you don't. We were on the beach . . . no, we went inside the cave and lit the fire. And it just . . . It went up, like an explosion. There was a black flash . . . I saw a *face*, Mum. And then it just . . ."

Her face crumples, her words dissolving into huge, gulping sobs of horror. Clem watches on, her mouth open and her thoughts racing. She doesn't know what to do, how to make sense of what she's saying.

"What happened at the beach, Erin?" she says, as gentle and as firm as she can. "Please, tell me. We need to know. We need to know what happened to Senna, and to Arlo. Can you tell me?"

Erin takes a gulp of air, tears streaming down her cheeks. "Oh God, Mum. Arlo was on fire . . ."

"I know he was, darling. I know . . ."

"Where is he? Where *is* he?"

"He's . . ." Clem can't bring herself to say it. She can see in Erin's eye that everything that Clem has already told her has somehow been rinsed from her memory, that she'll be shattered by this news. The strangeness of Erin's apathy when they first told her about Arlo seems welcome now. She can't face breaking her daughter's heart.

But in the time that she has hesitated telling Erin, it's as though another switch has flipped in Erin's mind. The racking sobs stop abruptly, and Erin falls silent. At first, Clem thinks she's in pain, or going to be sick, and she moves away. "Sorry, love," she says. "Are you okay?"

Erin looks up, and Clem flinches at the expression on her face. It is like flint, her eyes hard. "Don't touch me," she says.

Clem blinks, startled by the shift in her daughter's state. The room, too, seems to have chilled, as though a breeze has swept in from an open window. The windows are shut, as is the door. Clem steps back from the bed, watching, not sure what's happening to Erin. The heart monitor reports a drastically reduced pulse, too, dropping from the high nineties to low seventies.

"Are you okay?" she asks again, but Erin doesn't answer. She stares blankly ahead, her tears gone, her face like stone. The heart monitor slows. Sixty-four.

Clem sits down on the chair next to her, wondering if she can take Erin's hand. She decides not to touch her as she asked. "You were asking about Arlo, love," she says.

"Arlo's dead," Erin says.

"I know," Clem says. "And I'm so sorry."

"You're not my mother," Erin says. Clem jerks her head up with a gasp.

"You don't mean that."

"I do mean it."

"Erin?"

"I *told* you," Erin says, her expression fearful. "I am Nyx."

CHAPTER TWENTY-TWO

Kirkwall, Orkney
December 1594

ALISON

The trial is suspended until my lawyer arrives, and so I am in stasis, at once besieged with sorrows and yearning for sleep. The moment my body succumbs, Mr. Addis is charged with the task of rousing me by whatever means necessary. His current method is to throw a bucket of snow over me. Until yesterday he had taken to rattling a stick against the bars, but I was quite capable of sleeping through the noise. He brings candles upon candles to rid the dungeon of its darkness, forcing my body to react to the light, and sometimes he will wake me twenty times an evening, forcing me to pace. But he often is too lazy to do this, and so keeps a pail of snow by his chair to douse me if I doze off.

So little sleep has brought me into a world that is somewhere between dreaming and waking, a misty realm where the bars of my cell turn into drips of water, or black snakes that hiss, and the rats that dart about the floor develop human faces. I see my mother, and Solveig, and members of the Triskele I have not thought about for years.

A loud bang against the bars stirs me from my visions. It is

Mr. Addis. I see someone with him, and they both stand at the cell door, watching me. The man looks like a plague doctor, and it takes a minute or two for me to realize that he is wearing a cloak instead of a plague costume, a tissue held to his nose.

"Madam Balfour?"

I lift my head woozily and stare at him. "Yes?"

"My name is Andrew Couper," he says, and my senses sharpen.

"Andrew Couper?"

Mr. Couper kicks something with his feet. "Is this what the woman has been eating?" he asks Mr. Addis, nodding at the wooden trencher of slop that Mr. Addis has placed on the floor.

Mr. Addis is taken aback. "I made it myself."

"Dear God. Open this door at once."

With a choleric murmur, Mr. Addis unlocks the door and allows Mr. Couper to step inside. I watch as Mr. Couper pauses to study the wet floor, slimy with urine, mud, and rat droppings, before lifting the hem of his cloak to prevent it from being ruined. His clothing is expensive—the tartan cloak is made from finest tweed with brass toggles. We do not wear tartan in Orkney, but I always find the appearance of it on visitors from the mainland pricks a certain intrigue in me, and a reminder that Orkney sits somewhere between Scotland and Scandinavia—which is to say, we yet belong to neither.

Mr. Couper removes his cap—a little reluctantly, as though he is still cold—and clutches it in his hands. His nails are clean and trimmed. I look down at my own—brittle and torn, a thick line of dirt underneath and the skin around them raw and pink. I cannot remember the last time I washed.

He reaches into his satchel and pulls out a piece of bread wrapped in linen, then passes it to me.

"Take this," he says. "I will bring more, but you must eat now."

I am curled up in a corner, my knees drawn to my chest. I am too weak to move. The smell of bread rouses me. He squats close to me and reaches beneath my head, gently lifting me to a sitting position. I devour the bread, coughing and gagging as I do.

"You are my lawyer?" I ask with a hoarse croak, and he smiles.

"I am."

He appears younger than I remember. His eyes are round and thistle-blue, his skin unblemished by pox or wrinkles, his teeth white as milk. The picture of health and youth. I ask after his journey from Edinburgh.

"Oh, it was well," he says. "A long distance, but I traveled by carriage. It is good to be home in Orkney. I have missed it so."

"You have a family in Edinburgh?"

"A wife and three daughters," he says. "A fourth on the way. I am hoping for a son."

"They do not mind you being so far away?"

He shrugs. "It is my work. And Orkney is the home of my fathers." He lowers his voice, leaning close, to prevent Mr. Addis from overhearing. "I see that the situation here has become more precarious than ever."

"It is," I say. "There is talk of rebellion. I used to fear it, what it would do to us. How many lives it would cost our people. You must know of this, working with the rebels here."

He looks puzzled. "I'm afraid I don't follow."

"My husband said it was an anonymous benefactor among the rebels who paid you for my representation. One of the udallers, perhaps—Jacob McVeigh, perhaps, or Peter Gauldry?"

Mr. Couper remains puzzled and shakes his head. "I received payment from a man named Solveig," he says, and I fall quiet. He cannot mean Solveig from the Triskele?

"You must tell me," he says, "as honestly as you can, what role you feel you have played in this charge."

"None," I say.

"None?" he repeats, his eyes fixed on me. "You're quite sure?"

"I am innocent," I say. "I never gave any charm to Mr. Paplay."

"But you cured him of smallpox," Mr. Couper says. "Is that right?"

I look behind him, checking that Mr. Addis is out of earshot. "I believe John Stewart is the one who ordered the earl to be killed."

He blinks, as though he does not believe me. But then: "Go on."

I repeat all that has happened so far: the charm for Thomas's pox, the encounter in St. Magnus Cathedral, when John Stewart asked for a charm to take a life.

"Did he say the charm was for the earl?" Mr. Couper asks.

"Well, no," I say, but I tell him about the look between him and Thomas Paplay, how they pressed me, even when I told a lie and said such a charm could be performed only by one who has not seen death. I tell him about the arrest at my home, the interview with Father Colville, the pricking of my body. I show Mr. Couper the marks on my skin that have not yet healed, the sore on my tongue from where he plunged the needle. I tell him that Thomas Paplay is dead. He named me as his accomplice, for what reason, I know not. The first hearing.

"I think it is important that we present you to the court as a woman of healing," he says, tapping his pen against his satchel. "As someone who is concerned for the welfare of others and gifted enough to aid their recovery."

"Father Colville already knows I am a spaewife," I say.

"Yes, but perhaps the people in the gallery are not informed of your many efforts to heal people," he says. "They are mostly from Kirkwall, are they not?"

I nod. "Yes."

"So it's fair to say that the people of Gunn are the ones best qualified to bear testimony of your good character?"

"I believe so, yes."

"Then I think we begin there. We know that witches live in the world and that the Devil walks among us, so it is easy to fear that someone as skilled as you may potentially cause harm. I will call upon friends and neighbors who can testify of your goodness. They will persuade the bishops that you are not inclined to harmful practices, that the charge of attempted murder is far removed from your nature."

I think of the friends and neighbors I saw in the courtroom during the hearing, and my heart sinks.

"I am not sure they will be inclined to testify," I say.

"Oh, I am sure they will," he says, his voice filled with confidence. But I think back to the courtroom, to John Stewart watching me carefully.

"You must miss your family very much," he says then.

"Yes," I whisper. "I miss them every second of every day. And I fear most that I will never see them again as a free woman."

"You will," he says. "I will see to it."

He rises to his feet, our meeting finished.

"Oh, one more thing," he says. "Your husband tells me that the court has not appointed a notary to record the dittays. Is this true?"

"I do not believe so," I say. I know nothing at all about the processes of the legal system, but I have not yet seen anyone transcribe the trial. "If William says they have not, then I believe him."

"This must be rectified at once," Mr. Couper says. "The Privy Council at Edinburgh requires a transcript of the charges against you. I realize this may not be the traditional way in Orkney, but it is the law. I will remind the bishops of this procedure."

I fear his confidence comes too easily. Mr. Couper may have grown up in Orkney, but he has lived a long time away.

He does not know John Stewart, or what he is capable of.

CHAPTER TWENTY-THREE

Glasgow
May 2024

CLEM

Quinn's phone rings as they're heading back along the corridor. He cancels it, but immediately it rings again, and this time he answers, turning on his heel to take the call somewhere more private. But when he answers, Clem catches the note of frustration in his voice.

"For Christ's sake, Heather. You know why I've not answered. My daughter's in hospital."

As she heads to the vending machine for a bottle of water, Clem mulls over his words with a faint sense of satisfaction. All this time she has imagined his life with Heather to be idyllic. She realizes now that this was driven by bitterness at his abandonment of Erin. But still—to hear him speak to her with such anger, and to call Erin "my daughter" ...

She recalls a conversation, not six months ago, when Erin was standing in the kitchen, mashing up some vegetables for Freya. *I would have to do something drastic to get Dad's attention.* She said it lightly, and Clem agreed, because they both knew how much he preferred Heather and the boys over her.

A thought slips into her head: Did Erin do this to get her father's attention? A voice in her head shouts, *No! Of course not. She would never risk her life, not with Freya around.*

But the suspicion lingers.

Maybe she didn't mean for Arlo to die. Maybe she didn't mean for things to get so out of hand. But it is undeniable how much Erin wanted his attention, how much thought and effort she put into trying to work out the riddle that would make him love her, his only daughter.

But now Erin has his full, undivided attention.

No, she tells herself. The idea is ludicrous, and she feels guilty for thinking it.

"How're you doing?" a voice says. She looks up and finds Bee standing there, a hand on her arm.

"If I'm honest, I'm not doing great," Clem says with a weak smile. "It would be hard enough if we were just dealing with Erin's burns, but there's a criminal investigation going on, too. So many unanswered questions."

"I get it," Bee says. "This is not a quick process. It never is. You need to take one hour at a time. Not even a day at a time—an *hour*. That's the only way through this."

Clem considers this. It isn't the answer she wanted. "Thanks."

"Go home. Get some rest. Take a sleeping pill. You'll be amazed at what a difference it'll make, getting a good night's sleep."

Over Bee's shoulder she can see Quinn heading back up the corridor toward them, and the thought of a night with just her and Freya, in her own home, is suddenly tempting.

"I'm going home," she tells him, checking the time on her phone. "I want to see Freya and get some rest."

"Can I see Freya?"

She pauses, surprised at the request. "Well, yes. I'd have thought you wanted to head back to your hotel?"

"It's been a year since I saw her. Do you mind?"

"Well . . . No, not at all."

She reminds Quinn of her address and arranges to meet him after she collects Freya from Josie's. The house is noisy, full of toys and stray bits of laundry; a welcome respite from the hospital.

"Got your message," Josie says. "So good to hear that Erin's awake and talking."

Clem takes a steadying breath and smiles. "Yeah," she says. "It's great."

"God, you must be so relieved."

Clem swallows back a sob. She's not relieved at all. She feels battered, and broken, and wants someone to hold her while she cries her heart out.

"She's still a way off being better, but the doctors are hopeful."

Freya clocks Clem in the doorway and runs to her, arms outstretched.

"Gama," she says, her way of saying *Grandma*. "Gama!"

Clem scoops her up, breathing in her scent and pressing her lips against Freya's cheeks. "I've missed you, lady," she says.

Josie sends her away with a homemade lasagna in a large casserole dish and a bottle of elderflower cordial. "You just call me if you need me to have Freya again, okay?" she says earnestly.

Clem straps Freya into the car and drives home, where Quinn is already parked outside. He gets out and heads to the car, eager to see Freya. She looks up at him warily, then glances at Clem for explanation.

"Hello, little one," he says as Clem unclips her car seat. His face softens at the sight of her. "You're so much bigger than when I last saw you. Just like your mummy, too. All that blonde fluff."

Freya frowns, unsure who Quinn is.

"This is . . . Quinn," Clem says.

"Do you want to take my hand?" Quinn asks Freya, and she pauses before reaching out to curl her little fingers around his. They walk together like that to the front door.

It's strange, seeing Quinn in her flat, looking over hers and Erin's photographs on the living room walls. For years she has felt embarrassed that she lives in such a tiny flat in the wrong part of Glasgow. Compared to Quinn's Yorkshire farmhouse, with stables and a barn, three acres for his sons to play on quad bikes, she might as well live in a shed. Even now, when she is distracted enough by Erin's situation not to care about such things, she finds herself apologizing for it.

"Sorry it's a mess," she says, as Freya races inside.

"It smells like Erin," he says. "It looks like her, too."

"I gave her free rein with the decorating," she says, looking over the monstera-themed feature wall matched with pistachio green. All the house plants are Erin's, and the books in the bookcase are hers, too. A cabinet full of crystals is mounted on the wall, and the photographs on the mantelpiece are all of Freya. Clem realizes with a sting of embarrassment that there is hardly anything of her here at all, her life positioned behind Erin's. The main bedroom is Erin's, too, and that was before she had Freya and needed the space.

"Shall I put that in the oven?" Quinn says, glancing at Josie's lasagna.

"Oh. Okay," she says, though she's not sure either of them will eat it.

Freya toddles back into the room, holding a toy up for Quinn to take. He lowers to inspect it.

"Is this your owl?" he says, and she nods, shyly.

"Hello, Mr. Owl," he says, turning the owl to talk to him. "Are you Freya's pal?"

"Ollie," Clem corrects.

"Ollie," he repeats.

Freya beams, and then laughs, and the sound of it is the best sound Clem can remember.

They sit around the fold-out dining table overlooking the garden. Freya grins at Quinn shyly from her high chair while Clem pushes the lasagna around her plate.

"How the fuck is someone waking up and calling themselves 'Nyx' normal?" Quinn asks.

"Language," Clem says, glancing at Freya.

"Shit. Sorry."

They sit in silence, nothing but the sound of traffic on the road outside and Freya's occasional question. Clem realizes that, any other time, it would sadden her immensely that Freya is sitting with her grandfather but has no idea who he is. It's not like Quinn didn't know Erin was pregnant. Not only has he ruined his relationship with his daughter, but he seems set to do the same with his granddaughter. But Clem finds herself not caring, absolutely reconciled with the fact of it. What matters now is Erin. What matters is figuring out the puzzle of what happened on Orkney.

"Did Erin ever tell you who the father was?" Quinn asks.

"The father?" Clem repeats. She bristles at the way he frames it so bluntly. *The father* instead of *Freya's father*.

"You know what I mean."

"No," she says simply, and concentrates on cutting up Freya's food. "She didn't." Freya stares at him, unsmiling. Then she lifts a hand and waves at him. Quinn hesitates, before waving back.

"You haven't told her I'm her grandfather?" Quinn says.

"Would you like me to?"

He hesitates. Freya bursts into a laugh at him, and he can't help but smile back.

"I don't see why not."

"Freya," Clem says. "This is Granddad Quinn."

Freya stares, no sign of whether she has understood or not. "I think she's too young to grasp the concept of a grandfather," Clem tells him, though she wants to ask him, finds she is genuinely curious, why he is so keen to be a father or a grandfather now.

"The police are understaffed, undertrained. I don't rate that detective."

Clem bristles. Why can't he just call "that detective" by her name, like everyone else?

"She's the family liaison officer, and her name is Stephanie. She's not the one leading the investigation."

Quinn leans forward, his shoulders hunched, his eyes fixed on her. "You know as well as I do that this investigation is a shambles. And you know every bit as well as I do that we need to take this into our own hands now."

She studies his face, wondering what is driving this sudden impulse to go hunting for a killer. It's all very odd.

"I want to tell you something," she says then. "It's about Erin."

"Go on."

She takes a breath, wondering how to put it. "She had this moment where she just switched. Like she was back to being Erin again instead of . . . whatever is going on with her when she says she's Nyx."

"Right," Quinn says, but she can tell he doesn't get it.

"I don't know how to explain it. No one else was around. She mentioned Arlo. She said he was on fire, that she saw a face in the fire . . ."

He studies her. "A face?"

"Yeah. And then she changed again and went back to being weird."

He goes to say more, but just then Clem's phone rings, and she sees "Stephanie FLO" on the screen.

"Hi, Clem?"

"Yes? Have you found Senna?"

"No, sadly that's not why I'm ringing. I wanted to ask if you knew about Erin's TikTok account?"

"I know she sends me TikToks via WhatsApp," Clem says. "But I don't know anything about her account."

There's a long silence on the other end of the phone. "Are you at the hospital?"

"No, I'm at home."

"Would you mind if I come and speak to you just now?"

CHAPTER TWENTY-FOUR

Kirkwall, Orkney
December 1594

ALISON

Four days later, the castle bell tolls four times—today the trial is to recommence. Mr. Couper meets me at my cell an hour beforehand with a flagon of honey water, sweetmeats, and bread. I straighten my coif and dust down my kirtle, but he tells me not to.

"A state of dishevelment may gain the sympathy of the bishops," he says with a wink. "However . . ." He presents me with a bundle of lavender stalks, and after a moment I comprehend the meaning in this gesture—to remove the stink of the dungeon before we go to court. He turns away, allowing me to scrub the lavender into my skin before stuffing it into my bodice. A woeful appearance is one thing, smelling so is another.

I must still wear my chains, however, and with those heavy instruments I follow him up the narrow stone staircase. At the doorway of the courtroom, my breath quickens and my throat tightens as a sea of faces confronts me, a hush falling across the room as the spectators watch me enter.

Such is the look of disgust in their eyes that I cower, shrinking into myself as I am led to the dais and made to face the gallery.

There, sitting directly before me, is John Stewart. He seems angered by Mr. Couper's presence. I force myself to lift my eyes to his, and there is that same deep look, loud as words, warning me.

And for the first time, it strikes me that he is afraid. He tried to kill his brother to take the earldom, and he failed. And because of what I know, I can bring him to his death.

He must succeed in portraying me as a witch.

"Good morrow, Madam Balfour," Father Colville greets me as I sit down. "Are you well?"

"I am, Father," I say, though my stomach is in tight knots and my heart pounding. I do not like being so hated.

"I have been praying for you," he says.

I bow meekly. "I am grateful."

My eyes fall upon a hooded figure at the very back of the room. He is trying to keep himself concealed, but I recognize him—it is Solveig. My heart lifts a little, though I am curious—why did the Triskele pay for Mr. Couper? They were angered when I renounced my heritage, yet it seems they are trying to help me.

Mr. Couper strides to the center of the room, glancing up at the bishops.

"Bishop Sinclair, Bishop Vance," he calls up, drawing a hushed silence from the spectators in the gallery. "I would like to request a notary."

Bishop Vance grimaces from beneath his ill-fitting headdress. "A notary?"

Father Colville strides toward Mr. Couper in a bid to counter this request. "Your Grace, if I may . . ." he begins, but Bishop Vance silences him with a wave of his hand.

"Why do you request this, Mr. Couper?" Bishop Sinclair asks.

"My lord, you are no doubt aware that I practice the law in Edinburgh," Mr. Couper says. "And there we are instructed to assign a notary so that an accurate record of proceedings may be kept, should the king wish to peruse the order of events."

The bishops consider this gravely, sharing a look.

"Very well," Bishop Sinclair says after a moment. "Father Colville, Mr. Couper—who would you have assigned as this notary?"

Father Colville begins to speak, but Mr. Couper shouts over him.

"Your Grace, I would like to propose Mr. Moncrief," Mr. Couper says, glancing at David at the back of the room. The way David looks back at him tells me they have had a previous discussion, and I am wary. I know David can write, but it unsettles me that someone so involved in the case is possibly to serve as the notary. My words are already being twisted and used against me. If they are reported by him, it could be used against me, and my family.

"Father Colville?" Bishop Sinclair says. "What say you?"

"Very well," Father Colville replies, but I sense he is much displeased with Mr. Couper's request, a muscle tightening at his jaw.

"Good," Mr. Couper says, after a few moments, and David is given a table in the corner of the room, an ink pot and quill already awaiting him there. "Our notary is installed." Mr. Couper beams at me. "This is progress."

"I am informed that you wish to invite certain members of the public to testify of the woman's character?" Bishop Sinclair calls to Mr. Couper.

"That is right," Mr. Couper says. He turns with a flourish to the gallery. "I call as my first witness Agnes Glendinning."

The silence stretches out, and I search the room for sight of dear Agnes, my heart lifting at the prospect of her sympathetic face, her words of support and love. She is warm and articulate, and always seems to find the right words to speak her mind. I am so grateful to Mr. Couper for asking her to testify of my good character.

"Madam Agnes Glendinning?" Mr. Couper calls out again, louder this time. The spectators look from left to right, all of them scanning the room for Agnes. Where is she?

Mr. Couper calls her name again, but the silence stretches out, and I feel my courage falter.

"Perhaps she has been unable to make the journey from Gunn?" Bishop Sinclair says. I see Mr. Couper's certainty shrink. He stretches a smile on his face.

"I will call my second witness, in that case," he says. "Doubtless Madam Glendinning will be with us shortly. I call upon Alison's husband, William Balfour, to testify."

I start at this. William is to take the stand? Why did Mr. Couper not mention this?

William arises from his seat and walks confidently to the dais, the atmosphere in the room like the moments after a great bolt of lightning has streaked across the sky. Sweat gathers between my shoulder blades. I find I am fearful of his presence here. Agnes's failure to show up has unsettled me deeply. Perhaps something has happened, I tell myself, but I am on edge, a different concern creeping into my mind. *Was she too ashamed to be seen as my friend?*

Father Colville watches on, his hands pressed together and that same small smile on his face. I imagine he is determined to paint Will with the same venom as he has painted me, and the thought makes me nauseous.

William is wearing his best mantle, fastened at the shoulder with the swan brooch that he last wore on our wedding day. Beneath, he wears his linen shirt, which I dyed in saffron, his sable trews, and his shoes shined to glass. He has washed his hair, trimmed his beard, his eyes sharp and clear. He looks as though he has come here to negotiate, to go to war if necessary. Beneath the disappointment I feel at Agnes, there is a sting of pride.

"Good morning, Mr. Balfour," Mr. Couper says. "I wonder if you might tell us when you and Madam Balfour were married?"

"We were wed seventeen years ago next June," he says. "In the parish at Fynhallow on the Isle of Gunn."

"Where you continue to live, yes?" Mr. Couper says.

William nods. "We raise our family there."

"You are known in Kirkwall, too, I believe?" Mr. Couper says. "For your work as a stonemason?"

"I have worked at the masonry in Kirkwall for fifteen years," William says. "The stonework at the transept of the cathedral is my own work."

"St. Magnus Cathedral?" Mr. Couper says, impressed, though I'm certain he already knows this.

"The very same."

"So you are a man of considerable skill," Mr. Couper says. "And doubtless a man of excellent reputation."

William clears his throat. He does not like to boast, but he nods. I know he is doing it for me.

"Can you tell us about your wife?" Mr. Couper asks.

William pauses, thinking for a moment. "My wife has always been a kind, gentle woman. She has borne our five children, three of which are with God. She rises before dawn each day to take care of our animals and to fetch the milk from our cow. She makes the best broth I have ever tasted."

"Which broth is that?" Mr. Couper asks.

"It is one involving both trout and vegetables," William says, and I smile to think of the way his face lights up every time he comes home and smells the pot bubbling over our fire.

Mr. Couper turns to the gallery. "Surely no servant of Satan could make so fine a broth?" he says, drawing a laugh from the crowd. He turns his eyes back to William. "Tell us a little about Alison and her work as a healer, if you please."

William looks over at me, his eyes filled with tenderness. "I have known Alison to venture out in midwinter in the dead of night to help a neighbor on the other side of the island," he says loudly. "I have known her to sit up for days by the bedside of an elderly man who has lost his mind, whose life is slipping away. Although she knew there was not anything she could do to ease his illness, she wanted to be there to comfort him, to ensure he did not depart this life alone. She held his hand and whispered words of comfort, and even though she was large with child she did not complain, nor did she return home until the man had passed on and the body was interred in a coffin ready for burial."

The mood in the courtroom lightens, and I find myself recalling the night I sat with the old man, Brodie, in his home, his frail hand in mine. He had no family, no one at all to sit with him while he died. His home was dank, and the smell made me retch, but I felt honored to be the one to accompany his passing.

Mr. Couper asks William more questions about me, about our lives together, about our children and home. After a while, the discomfort of so much personal information being shared with a crowd of strangers eases, softened by the memories that are stirred up. William chronicles our relationship, offering up moments that I had forgotten. He tells them of the time our dog, Kelpie, was set upon by bees, his poor muzzle swelling to the size of the hive itself. I used a potion and a spell to take down the swelling and reduce the pain. Kelpie lived to the ripe age of sixteen, much loved by us all. We buried him behind our barn.

The afternoon light bathes the courtroom in a honeyed glow, and the air feels warmed by William's stories. His words about me have made the weeks spent alone in the dungeon fall away from me, just for a time; I am reminded of who I am. I am reminded that I am loved.

And then Mr. Couper's allotted time for questioning is over. Agnes does not appear, and while Mr. Couper delays, promising the bishops that she will yet arrive, they insist he give the time over to Father Colville.

William rises from the dais, but Father Colville lifts a hand to signal that he should remain.

"I have some questions also," he says, and William sits down again. I can see he is unprepared for this.

"It is very pleasing to hear you speak of your wife with such affection," Father Colville says. "But then, I suppose it would not be advantageous to speak ill of your wife, would it? Especially if you know she is a witch."

A noise of agreement sounds in the gallery, and I see the bishops nod at each other.

William flinches. "My wife is no such thing," he says, his voice measured but firm.

"I see," Father Colville says. "Though she is a spaewife?"

"She is."

"Pray, what is the difference between a witch and a spaewife?"

William falters. "One is led by the Devil, and the other is—"

"Both rely on magic, do they not?"

"Yes, but—"

"And how does one tell the difference between magic inspired by Satan and magic that is not?"

"Let the man speak, Father Colville," Bishop Sinclair calls down in a frustrated voice.

"Beg pardon, Bishop Sinclair. Perhaps the witch's husband

might clarify where the line is drawn between the practice of magic for good and that which is used for harm."

"I have never known Alison to harm so much as a flea," Williams says tersely.

Father Colville raises his eyebrows. "Is that so?"

I can feel William's ire from here. "It is so."

"Not so much as a flea?"

"No."

Father Colville lifts his eyes to the mezzanine. "Your Graces, perhaps I might call upon a woman that the witch treated in the past?"

"Aye," Bishop Vance replies.

Father Colville dismisses William from the dais. William strides across the room, his head held high and his hands in fists. I feel a prickle on the back of my neck as he takes his seat, and my eyes track the gallery again, looking for Agnes.

"I call upon Madam Elspeth MacGruer to bear testimony," Father Colville says. Elspeth's name causes my heart to lift a moment, fond memories of our childhood years flooding through my mind. Elspeth is a woman whose presence causes the air to shift; often I could sense her before I saw her, and she made me laugh like no one else. Her cheerful, vivacious nature always brought such color to my days.

But then I remember the terrible rumors her sister, Anna, spread, after I assisted in delivering Anna's first child. The babe died; a tragedy, but for years afterward, Anna blamed me for the child's death, though it would not have mattered who assisted. The bairn could not be saved. Very few people took heed of Anna's stories, but it was an uncomfortable period for a time.

Father Colville greets Elspeth warmly. "Thank you, Madam MacGruer, for coming today."

She nods, and my cheeks flush. My joy at seeing her fades quickly to wariness.

"You have said you are friends with Madam Balfour?"

"I *was* friends with her, yes," Elspeth corrects. "A very long time ago."

"Oh?" Father Colville says. "So you were friends as children but no longer?"

"That is correct."

"Forgive me, Madam MacGruer," Father Colville says. "But surely childhood friends have the strongest bond? What tore such a precious connection apart?"

Elspeth takes a deep breath, and I can see she is suddenly moved to tears. "It makes me sad to think on it," she says, reaching to her mouth. "Sad, and also angry."

"Why?" Father Colville says, in exaggerated, breathless shock. He steps closer to her, a hand pressed to his chest in a gesture of deep concern. "Pray, tell us, if you can bear it."

"It was Anna's first baby," she says. "My sister. She had fared well, but then seemed to struggle. I had promised to help her, seeing as I'd delivered my own six babies. I thought I knew well enough what to do in order to help a woman bring a child into the world. But Anna's birth was different, and I grew fearful. I sent word to Madam Balfour."

"And I believe it was Anna's husband, Simon, who fetched Madam Balfour?"

She nods. "Yes. But as soon as she stepped inside the cottage I knew something was wrong. She wasn't the same person I knew in my younger days. There was a darkness about her."

"But then, why let her into your home?" Father Colville says. "If you had such doubts?"

Elspeth hesitates, as though searching for the right words. "I was panicked," she says. "I needed help for my sister, and so I put aside my misgivings."

Her words are not her own, I think. I know Elspeth too well—she would never use this phrasing of her own accord. Even her accent seems different, her speech slowed so as to wrap her lips around the words that someone else has placed inside her mouth.

Father Colville turns to address the gallery. "You see how the Devil requires permission of entry into our homes, and our lives, so He can wreak havoc? And how deviously He finds a way to gain permission." He turns back to Elspeth. "Tell us, my child—did the witch assist in the birth?"

Elspeth's face crumples, and she gives a loud sob. Father Colville produces a handkerchief from his pocket and passes it to her. She dabs her eyes and takes a breath before continuing.

"I'm sorry," she says in a broken voice. "It was a dreadful, terrible time. That night has left a deep scar across all our lives."

She tells them that she saw a change over me, the very features of my face shifting. And at the moment she witnessed this physical alteration in my face, Anna's birthing went awry. Blood began to trickle from her, and her laboring stalled. The wind battered at the walls of the cottage, howling like a thousand demons.

"She shouted at me," Elspeth says, raising a hand to point at me.

It is the first true thing she has said of that night. I remember shouting at her to get some water, for I feared Anna was slipping away. "She shouted at me to leave her alone with Anna, but I begged her to let me stay."

"Why?" Father Colville asks, his voice barely a whisper.

"I was afraid," Elspeth says. "I felt a coldness enter the room. And when I looked at the window, I saw a personage."

She tells Father Colville that she saw what she thought were two horns rising from its head. She opened her mouth to scream, but then she saw me turn to the shadow with an outstretched hand.

"The shadow gave her a reversed cross," she says. "I saw it. I saw it as clear as I look upon her now.

"And then what happened?"

"The bairn came out," she says. "But he was already gone."

Elspeth's emotions overcome her, and she weeps into a handkerchief as Father Colville dismisses her sympathetically. Then he turns to Mr. Couper.

"Is it true, Mr. Couper, that you asked all of Madam Balfour's neighbors to testify in favor of her, and not a single one would agree to it?"

Mr. Couper's eyes dart away, and his face burns. He tries to recover himself, straightening and lifting his head in confidence. "It is true that I had but a short time to seek out some witnesses before the date of today's trial," he says.

Father Colville shakes his head, tutting. "To lie before God is shameful, and as a man of the law, you are doubly accountable . . ."

"Please, Mr. Couper," Bishop Vance calls. "Answer the question precisely, in the affirmative or the negative, if you please."

"I will ask again, to assist you," Father Colville tells Mr. Couper, clasping his hands. "Did you seek out a neighbor of Madam Balfour, or a friend, or *anyone* in the whole of Orkney other than her own kin and the witness who has clearly changed their mind, and found that not a single soul would attest to her innocence?"

"Yes," Mr. Couper says finally.

Father Colville turns to the spectators, his arms spread out wide, as though Mr. Couper's reply has made his point.

As though this proves that I am a wretch, too wicked for kith or kin to profess my virtue.

CHAPTER TWENTY-FIVE

Glasgow
May 2024

CLEM

Stephanie arrives at Clem's flat half an hour after her phone call.

"Thanks for seeing me so late in the day," Stephanie says when Clem opens the door to her.

"No DC Sanger?" Clem asks, and Stephanie shakes her head.

"He's up in Orkney, viewing the site."

Quinn doesn't look up when Stephanie comes into the kitchen, but she doesn't seem to notice.

"Can I get you some coffee?" Clem asks, but Stephanie shakes her head. She takes a seat at the dining table next to Quinn and flips open her iPad.

"We found this TikTok account of Erin's through Senna's," she says.

"What do you mean, *through* Senna's?" Quinn asks grumpily.

"Senna's account is active. She last posted about two weeks ago and we can see she was last active at eight o'clock on Wednesday the first of May."

"So—the night of the fire?"

"Correct," Stephanie says. "We went through the list of

accounts that she's following, and we came across this one by Erin. I wanted to know if you were aware of it at all?"

Quinn and Clem share empty looks. "No," Clem says, her heart sinking. "To be honest, I know very little about TikTok."

Stephanie opens an app on her iPad and brings up a screen of paused video clips, most of them showing Erin's face, her hair in various colors as time passes. Some of them show Freya, too.

Stephanie clicks on one of the thumbnails, and Erin's face fills the screen. She looks sullen, her eyes heavy and darkened with smeared mascara.

Erin lays out a deck of tarot cards in her bedroom. The room is dark, with a row of candles flickering on a chest of drawers in the background as Erin sits cross-legged on the floor. Her blonde hair is shoulder length, and she wears a vest top, revealing a new tattoo of a raven on her shoulder beneath the words *Second Skin*. From the hair and the tattoo, Clem pinpoints the video to be from five months ago. A song is overlaid on the clip of Erin selecting her tarot cards, and she looks happy, showing four cards laid out in a cross: the Ace of Swords, the Lovers, the Two of Cups, the Devil. Finally, she leans close into the lens and says, "The Green Man's hands must be bound."

Stephanie hits pause and looks at Clem, who tries not to show her reaction to the clip.

"What do you make of that?" Stephanie asks.

"What do we make of what?" Quinn interjects. "I'm not into tarot, personally."

"Arlo's hands were bound before he was burned," Stephanie says, and Clem tries not to show the sudden fear that leaps up inside her. "It seems coincidental that she would say this in the video here."

"Oh, come on," Quinn says. "I think that's quite a stretch."

Clem's breath catches. She thinks of Erin's notebook. It can't be coincidental at all, she knows that.

"We looked into the Green Man reference," Stephanie says. "It turns out he's a mythological figure from Beltane. Do you know what that is?"

"Is it a place?" Clem asks.

"No, it's a pagan festival," Stephanie says.

"A festival of what?" Quinn asks.

"It marks the beginning of summer. It celebrates fertility. The Green Man typically represents the new growth on earth. He's a figure associated with that festival. Usually there's both a Green Man and a May Queen. It occurs on the first of May, which, interestingly, is the day of the accident."

She lets that hang in the air. Clem keeps her eyes on the table.

Stephanie clicks on another thumbnail. "This is the last TikTok she posted," she tells them, and Clem sees that Erin has pink hair in this footage, the date stamp reading twenty-first of January this year.

Again, the footage shows Clem's face up close, the bars of Freya's cot just visible in the background. "I think I know what to do about my problem," she says. "But I have to wait until Beltane. It involves a fire ceremony." She crosses her fingers in front of the lens. "Here's hoping."

Stephanie presses pause and smiles. "Can I ask you what you make of that?" she asks.

"What is it you're accusing Erin of, exactly?" Quinn says in a hard voice. "I mean, I appreciate it's a coincidence that she mentions a fire ceremony, and then there was a fire, but . . ."

"It indicates that there was some sort of plan," Stephanie says gently. "Beltane is mentioned, and that's exactly the day of the fire, the first of May. We think they were performing a ritual, a fire ceremony, just like she mentions in the video. And it got out of hand."

"Even if they were performing a fire ceremony," Clem says. "It sounds like an accident to me."

"The fire, yes," Stephanie says. "But . . . it doesn't explain why Senna is missing."

"I think it's easy to take things out of context," Clem says. "Maybe they *were* performing a fire ceremony. But I think there are other things we need to consider before we connect this to Senna's disappearance."

"Yeah," Quinn says. "Like Senna's TikToks. What do they say?"

Stephanie clicks through to Senna's account, where Clem spies a split screen video, called a "duet." It features both Erin and Senna, laughing and chatting about something.

"This is *not* a recruitment video." Senna is laughing.

"Guys, the Triskele are the best, okay?" Erin adds. "I want to talk about them, seeing as I'm officially a member."

"You want to talk about the scholarship?" Senna interjects.

"Well, first I'll talk about who the Triskele are, and what it means to be a member, okay?"

"I think this might need to be a number of clips," Senna laughs.

"The Triskele is a special group of people," Erin continues. "The absolute best. They believe that we're all connected to nature, and that nature is basically magic. And we've all got so bloody consumerized that we've lost that connection, but once we get it back we realize there is *nothing* that we can't do."

"Okay," Stephanie says, hitting pause. "That's the first mention, there's another one." She flicks through to another clip from February. Just three months ago. Another close-up of Erin, chipped blue nail polish, no makeup, walking along the street. Clem can tell Senna is filming Erin as she's heading to her job at the café.

"I got amazing help from Paul," Erin says to the camera, animated. "Seriously, he has been the best in helping me out. It involves a fire ceremony. He told me the spell I need to do in Orkney to get rid of it."

Stephanie pauses the clip and looks over at them both. "Who is Paul?" she asks. "And why do you think Erin joined a pagan cult?"

CHAPTER TWENTY-SIX

Kirkwall, Orkney
December 1594

EDWARD

Edward is up in the rafters of St. Magnus Cathedral, in the small room where the ancient manuscripts are kept and where he assists Mr. McNee with carrying pieces of stone and ceramic from the cart on the ground floor. It is a backbreaking job, hefting pieces of red and yellow sandstone, some of the sections almost the same length as him, up and down the stairs. The hoist and pulley is still being set up by Mr. McNee, and Edward wonders what the delay is. It should never take this long to fit a hoist! The stone could easily be pulleyed from the cart directly up to the roof. He can't help but feel that the delay is personal—a punishment for being the son of a witch.

And so, he has taken to wearing his face scarf all day, not just when he's working the stone, or digging in the quarry, fearful of being recognized. With the scarf pulled all the way up to his eyeline and his fair hair stained by sandstone dust, he is able to blend in as another mason apprentice, hiding in plain sight.

The manuscript room will be seen by only the earl, for it is merely a storage room for the vast number of dusty manuscripts that are too important to be burned but too ugly to be placed on display. Nonetheless, Earl Patrick has commissioned a vaulted ceiling and four sculptures of heavenly figures holding scrolls at each corner, as though they watch over the old library, and so the task has expanded, requiring the finest craftsmen to teeter on planks of wood high above the ground, tethered by long lines of rope to the roof like puppets lest they fall.

A part of Edward is glad of the work, however tiresome it is. In fact, he enjoys the burning sensation in his arms and the screaming muscles of his legs, the repetitive manner of the task—up and down, up and down, like Sisyphus hefting his boulder—the sonorous groan of the oxen and the chatter spiraling from the cart driver and the men on the lower floor. His mother's accusation and trial, her internment in the bowels of Kirkwell Castle, has ripped through his life like a storm.

He is to blame. He knows he is.

Every single thought now is about making it right.

As Edward is climbing the staircase for the fifteenth time this morning, he sees a flash of deep red sweep along one of the cathedral's many narrow hallways. The flick of a rich burgundy cloak made of fine velvet, a glint of gold edging at the collar. His body reacts before his mind catches up. Gold clothing is reserved for royalty. It is Earl Patrick, right here in the cathedral.

He delivers the stone to the workers on the roof. The sculptor calls to him from farther along the line.

"Boy!"

He holds out a chisel, waving it as though he expects Edward to take it, which he moves to do, gingerly walking along one of the planks of wood striated across the open space of the new room. Below, the oxen are reduced to the size of chestnuts. The fall would kill him instantly.

"Swap this for a sharp knife," the sculptor says, passing him the tool, and Edward takes it with a nod before descending the stairs, slowing a little at the hallway where he spotted the earl.

There is no one around, no one watching, but from a room farther down the hallway Edward can hear voices. He glances over the balustrade at the workmen below, then up at the men in the roof space, before making his way down the same hallway where he saw the earl walk minutes before.

A door stands ajar about halfway along the corridor, an opening of about two inches. The acoustics of the chapel are at extremes—the vast open spaces of the quire and nave carry voices swirling in every direction in an echoing, bell-like fashion, often making it difficult to discern a message clearly. But the small, wood-paneled rooms in the upper floors compact even the slightest whisper, delivering voices in crisp tones.

"This new . . . installment is not to my liking."

It's the earl's voice. Edward freezes, every hair on his body standing on end—the way the earl said *installment* is chilling. The trouble he would be in now if he were found here, patently eavesdropping. He should turn back, right now, before he is caught, he knows the penalty is likely to be ten lashes, perhaps the stocks. But he can't move, can't persuade his body to turn away.

"What would you have me do, Your Grace?"

Another man's voice. Older than the earl.

"Get rid of him," the earl says, and something on the back of Edward's neck prickles. *Him?*

"It may be difficult to do so, my lord," the older man says. "The bishops are in favor of the woman's lawyer."

Edward starts. They mean Mr. Couper.

"Father," Earl Patrick says. "I expect such ministrations to fall within your remit."

The older man says something he doesn't quite hear, his pitch dropping. Edward leans forward, glancing around the corner. He must risk being seen if he is to hear more.

He wonders how terrible ten lashes would feel. He once saw a man buckle beneath a single lash, the skin of his back opened in bloody stripes.

He thinks of the way his mother looked in the courtroom. And what he saw.

Holding his breath, he tilts his head forward.

"I pray, you must not worry, my lord," the older man is saying. "I have already sent someone to ensure this stumbling block is removed."

"That is well," the earl says.

Edward hears the door open then, and ducks back.

"Oh, Father Colville?" the earl says, as though he has forgotten something, and the door closes behind him once more.

Father Colville, Edward repeats in his mind, his heart racing. and he suddenly feels like he might collapse, as though the sudden connections forged in his brain are more strenuous than a thousand flights of stairs.

Father Colville.

He forces his legs to move again, to take one step, then two, in the opposite direction, and quickly he is heading not up the stairs but down to the ground floor, where the oxen stand, two gleaming black creatures reeking to high heaven. He is still gripping the blunt tool that the sculptor wanted him to replace for a sharper one, but the thought of his task and even his whereabouts have flung out of his head, and all he can think about is Mr. Couper, Mr. Couper, the lawyer, the lawyer.

The lawyer's Kirkwall lodgings are two streets away, along the seafront, and Edward races there, praying in his heart that the lawyer is there, that he will receive him. He sees a figure through the window, and bangs on the door, and a moment later Mr. Couper is standing in front of him, puzzled.

Edward remembers his disguise and tears the cloth from his face.

"I am Madam Balfour's son, Edward," he says, though he has met Mr. Couper briefly some days before, accompanied by his father. "I . . . I . . ."

The run has left him out of breath, and he all but collapses into a chair by the lawyer's desk, his voice hoarse from dust and fear. Mr. Couper must see this, because he passes him a tankard with fresh, cool water, watching him with a concerned expression as Edward gulps it down.

"I have come from the cathedral," Edward says at last, his words slurred. Mr. Couper tells him to rest but he shakes his head, insistent.

"I overheard Earl Patrick speaking with Father Colville," he says, and Mr. Couper straightens, seeing the reason for the boy's urgency.

"What did he say?"

"I . . . heard him speak about 'the woman's lawyer,'" Edward says. "He wants rid of him. I think he meant you."

Mr. Couper's face changes. He grows paler, Edward thinks, and he repeats the exact words he heard.

Mr. Couper is silent for a long time. He turns away from Edward and approaches his desk, where papers have been set out, some in scrolls and some held flat by paperweights and filled with words. Edward wants to ask him what this all means for his mother, if it means she is doomed, but holds back, fearful of the answer.

"You know of Orkney's turmoil?" Couper says at last. "The rebels who wish to oust the earl?"

Edward nods. "I do."

"I had hoped they would have intervened before now. But they have already faced the earl's oppression, and they are frightened of what he will do next. I believe your mother's incarceration is an attempt on Earl Patrick's behalf to show what he will do to all who will withstand him. It is rumored he seeks to sell the Isle of Gunn, did you know that?"

Edward shakes his head.

"The whole island. And Gairsay, too. He will do it, if he isn't stopped. He will put every family on Gunn out of their home. He won't care where you go, or how long your family have owned the crofts and fields there." He looks over at Edward. "It is very, very important that we show Earl Patrick that this will not be tolerated. That Orkney will not stand for it. Do you understand?"

Edward nods, the full scale of events making his head spin. He imagines the whole island seized by the earl. The cottages in flames, the church . . . and the fairy glen, and the Triskele stones, old as time. All destroyed.

"Where are you staying just now?" Mr. Couper asks. "You are living in Kirkwall, yes?"

"I stay with Mr. McNee," Edward says. "Though sometimes I just sleep in the belfry."

Mr. Couper gives a short laugh, and Edward is confused. Has he said something wrong?

"It may be too dangerous for you to go back to Gunn," Mr. Couper says then. "Where is your father?"

Edward begins to answer, but his words are cut short by a thumping sound at the door. Footsteps, followed by voices. Mr. Couper nods at a crawl space in the wall opposite, only just big enough for Edward to squeeze inside. Mr. Couper moves the fire screen across the entrance right as the door swings open.

"Good morrow, gentlemen," Mr. Couper says. "How can I be of service?"

"Mr. Couper?" one of the men asks.

Edward holds his breath, silently begging his heart to stop its roaring.

"At your service."

"The witch's representative?"

Mr. Couper attempts a laugh. "I'm afraid I know no witches, sir."

His voice is closer now, as though he is moving backward across the room. Something rolls onto the floor, a sound of glass shattering and a splash—the inkwell, he thinks, being pushed off the desk. Then the rustle of papers.

"Stop that at once!" Mr. Couper says. "These are court documents. The king will hear of this!"

Edward does not hear an answer.

Instead, he hears the dull smack of fists pounding flesh, cries of pain, and Mr. Couper's unheeded pleas for them to stop.

Edward is trembling now, burying his fist in his mouth to keep from crying out. He hears the scraping of table legs across the wooden floor, followed by the heavy thud of a man's body hitting the ground.

CHAPTER TWENTY-SEVEN

Glasgow
May 2024

CLEM

Clem and Quinn sit in silence long after Stephanie leaves, both slightly shell-shocked. Clem downloads the TikTok app and tries to find Erin's account, then spends a long time silently watching her clips. Her mind feels like it's cartwheeling, the fragments of information colliding. Beltane. Paul. Who is he? What did he do to help Erin?

And why did she join this group? The Triskele?

"Erin's TikToks are mostly like diary entries," Quinn says, scrolling through the content on his own phone. He turns the screen to her. "Look. This one's from last October."

He shows it to her. It's Erin and Arlo in the living room of the flat, letting Freya put face paint on their faces. She keeps giggling, adding more and more colors to Arlo's face with her fingers.

Clem tears up, her voice catching. "It's lovely," she says.

"Ah, but the detective wasn't interested in wholesome family content, was she?" he says bitterly.

"She was part of a weird group," Clem says. "I think they're only interested in the stuff that might explain why she's in the hospital."

"All teenagers are into weird stuff," Quinn says. "And so what if she joined this group?"

"She mentioned a fire ritual, Quinn," Clem says. "It makes her look as though she's responsible for Arlo's death."

"Well, we contact this Paul person. Or the group she was part of. Find out what they know."

"I don't know how to do that," Clem says. "She never mentioned *any* of this to me."

Her voice breaks, and she realizes how hurt she feels about it. How wounded she is that Erin held something like this from her.

"Look," Quinn says. "This is from March this year."

He plays her a video of Erin with her hands cupped to her face, her cheeks wet with tears. She's in her bedroom, and it's dark. In the background, Freya is sleeping. Erin seems too stunned to speak.

"He's dead," she says flatly. "Oh my God, he's *dead*."

The clips ends, and Clem scans the comments from Erin's followers, all asking who she's referring to. One of them asks, Is Arlo dead? But there's no reply from Erin.

Clem gets to her feet, unable to stay seated any longer. "I want to show you something," she tells Quinn.

She settles Freya into her cot before heading into Erin's bedroom and fetching the notebook with the owl cadaver on the front.

"What is this?" Quinn says when she sets it on the dining table.

"It's Erin's notebook," she says. "There's a mention of the Triskele in there. Look."

She turns to the page where Erin has written *Triskele = scholarship*. Quinn stares at it.

"What does it mean?" he asks.

"I don't know," she says. "But I think it's all related."

"There's a page missing, here," Quinn says.

Clem chews her nail. Debates with herself and then decides to trust him.

"I tore it out."

Quinn's mouth gapes. "Why?"

She sighs. "Erin had written something in it that I didn't want the police to see."

"Which was?"

"She wrote the words 'Arlo's hands need to be bound.'"

"Was that it? Nothing else?"

She nods. "Obviously, the fact that Arlo's hands *were* bound when he died makes me feel sick to my core."

He draws a sharp breath, processing that. "Okay. So, you think this whole Orkney trip was about Erin and Senna killing Arlo?"

"No! God, no. Of course not."

His shoulders lower. "Then—what?"

"The police think that. That's the angle they're going to take."

Quinn clicks his tongue against his teeth. "I suppose her telling that detective that she didn't care that Arlo was dead didn't help."

"Well, no."

"But then why say it if she doesn't mean it?"

"I think she's messed up from the fire," Clem says. "And whatever happened to cause it."

"Maybe it was a fire ritual, and it went wrong. And that's why she's so traumatized."

"I think we have to go there," Clem says.

"Where?"

"Orkney."

Quinn doesn't answer, but picks up his phone. The light from his screen casts a glow on his face.

"I'm just googling 'Triskele,'" he says. "Some interesting stuff here."

"Show me?"

He passes her the phone and she sees the Wikipedia page, which is a stub, but nonetheless the words *ancient clan* and *Orkney* draw her attention. She googles on her own phone, the pair of them sitting for a few minutes clicking through the links. Clem googles "Fynhallow" and finds a page with drawings of a witch trial, right on the bay where Erin was found. She thinks of the book she saw in the hospital toilet, and the strange scene she saw of a woman being burned. She imagines the crackle of fire, and a scream, as though the image comes alive in her mind.

As though she knows that scene.

She turns to Quinn, the words almost tumbling out of her mouth. She knows she can't tell him that. She can't tell him what she saw, no way. He'll think she has lost her mind.

"Check this out," he says, turning his phone to her. "It says here the Triskele meet in Orkney. It's from last year. It says they meet on the mainland. So, not Fynhallow."

They stare at each other, the silence stretching out.

"We need to go to Orkney," she repeats. "You up for that?"

"What about Erin?"

"I mean, I don't want to leave her," Clem says. "But I think we need to get some answers before the police decide Erin murdered Arlo and Senna."

"It'll look, you know, heartless. Both Erin's parents up and leaving her while she's in hospital."

"We'll be quick."

"And Freya?"

"I'll see if Josie can watch her while we're gone. She likes playing with Sam. And it's better to keep things as normal as we can for her."

. . .

The flight from Glasgow to Kirkwall, Orkney's capital, takes a little over an hour. Clem downloads as many of Erin's TikToks as she can, making notes of what Erin talks about, and when. She mentions weekenders, and she remembers Erin going away with Senna every weekend for about six months. That was three years ago, not long after Erin and Senna first met, but long enough that the two girls were inseparable. These trips were always "camping with friends," but the weekenders Erin refers to in the videos seem more than that. Erin mentions Paul again, about his expert knowledge, and Clem feels sick. She can't quite shake the thought that Erin was seeing someone else. What if Paul made her do this, and Arlo got killed?

She can't bear it.

The plane lowers through the clouds toward Kirkwall airport, the North Sea meeting the Atlantic and the Orkney mainland coming into view. Night is falling, but she can make out a vivid patchwork of neat fields and rolling hills in shades of emerald and purple heather, dotted with freshwater lochs and fringed by colorful coastal towns. For a moment, she thinks of Erin, and how excited she was to come here. How beautiful she said it was.

In Kirkwall, they rent a car and head straight to the ferry terminal, determined to head straight to Fynhallow.

"I'm going to ask these men questions," Quinn tells her, nodding at a group of ferry workers by the dock. She watches as he pulls out his phone and shows a screenshot of the blog post he found earlier about the Triskele meeting, but they shake their

206   C. J. COOKE

heads. He shows them photographs of Erin, and they shake their heads. Then Senna.

"Oh yeah," one of them says. "Over there."

The man points behind Clem, and she turns sharply. Behind her are posters of Senna's face, the word MISSING in stark red letters, and a phone number asking for information.

None of the men know anything about either the Triskele or Senna, but Quinn isn't deterred from asking everyone in earshot.

They buy tickets for the Gairsay ferry, but the last sailing has already crossed. They'll have to wait until morning.

They check into a B and B for the night.

"You're here for some sightseeing?" the owner asks. She's an older woman with a friendly manner, short hair dyed vibrant pink with matching magenta glasses. Erin would love her, Clem thinks.

"We're here to visit Fynhallow," Clem says, and the woman's face falls.

"Oh my," she says. "I don't think that'll be possible. Terrible tragedy there recently. It's hard to get to at the best of times, but police are all over the place."

"We're one of the teenagers' parents," Quinn says. "Our daughter is in hospital. She was lucky. But we want to do our own investigating."

The woman nods. "I'm so sorry about your daughter. I heard a boy died, too."

"Arlo," Clem says, choking up again. "Sorry. He was my daughter's boyfriend. We really, really want to know what's happened. Particularly as a girl, my daughter's best friend, is still missing."

"It's been all over the news here," the woman says. "I'm afraid I don't know anything, but we get visitors here all the time, and you never know what folk hear. Do you want to leave a number?"

Clem writes hers down quickly. "Please. Anything at all, ask people to call me. And perhaps I can ring you, too, to chase up."

"Of course."

"Actually," Clem says. "Our daughter mentioned the Triskele. Do you know about that?"

The woman's smile fades. "Oh, I'm not sure I've much to tell. They're an odd lot, from what I hear."

"Do you know where they meet?" Quinn says.

She shakes her head. "I'm afraid not."

"We've heard there's a low tide between Gairsay and Gunn," Quinn says. "I don't suppose you know the times of the tide?"

The woman nods, writes down a name and number on the back of her business card.

"There's a local man with a boat who has been taking the police directly to the bay, so you don't need to wait for the tides. You tell him who you are, I'm sure he'll help."

Clem's dreams are fierce. She sees towering orange flames rising against black night, the sound of frantic screaming. Her daughter's voice. But she can't see her. She runs and runs, feeling the heat of the flames and hearing the screams, calling Erin's name. But she can't see her, can't help her.

She wakes, her heart pounding so fast she feels nauseous. With a trembling hand, she takes two pills, then a third, gulping them back with a glass of water from the bathroom tap in dawn's early light.

When she checks her phone, Josie has sent a WhatsApp video of Freya saying "Good morning" and waving at the camera. Clem's heart rate slows, and she sends a message back.

Good morning, Freya. Grandma loves you.

Mummy loves you too! Have fun at nursery,

my darling.

She thinks of Erin, how she hasn't once mentioned Freya.

People can have secrets, for sure. But she knows Erin loves her daughter. She adores her. Whatever happened on Orkney has affected her more than anyone can fathom.

"Morning," Quinn says when she meets him in the café. "How did you sleep?"

"Terrible. Nightmares all night."

"Me, too," he says. "Dreams of fire."

"I suppose that's par for the course when you've a child in a burns unit."

"Shall we contact this guy with the boat?"

"I'm doing it," she says, pressing send on the text message.

An hour later, they meet Ivan at the jetty. A retired ferry worker, he brings them aboard his sailboat and greets them warmly.

Quinn pulls out his phone, shows him the photos of Erin and Senna, then the posts about the Triskele.

"You're sure you didn't see three teenagers asking for a boat to take them to Fynhallow?" he says.

"No," Ivan says. "But I've got friends who do a lot of sailing in their free time. I can ask around."

"That would be amazing," Clem says. "Thanks."

The sea is calm today, vivid blue, Ivan's boat cutting through the waves. The rugged silver cliffs of Gairsay rise up beside them, then Gunn, the rise and fall of its green braes and thick forests.

And then, Fynhallow, its half-moon bay, milky sand leading to ultramarine ocean.

"This is it?" Clem asks as the boat pulls up to the jetty.

"It is," Ivan says. The jetty is muddied with footprints below her feet as she clambers out. Remnants of blue and white police tape flutter in the wind, a macabre reminder of the tragedy that happened here. Clem had expected to be met with police at the scene, perhaps the forensic team still sweeping for evidence, but the work is evidently completed, the beach deserted.

"I'll stay here for one hour," Ivan says as Quinn follows her off the boat.

"Two," Quinn says, handing him a wad of notes, but Ivan shakes his head.

"I've an errand to run. It'll have to be one."

"Do we know where the fire took place?" Quinn asks her as they head down to the beach.

"One of the caves," she says, and they turn to look over the cliffs. No caves are visible, at least not from this angle, and so they head closer, their backs to the tide. Clem finds she feels less closure than she had expected to feel, now that she's here. She discreetly checks her location on her mobile phone to make sure they really are on Fynhallow, for there is no sign, or indeed anything but Ivan's word that this is the right place. Only when the name appears on her phone next to a dot marking her location does she feel assured— but still, she feels unsettled. It is hard to reconcile such a beautiful place with the horrors that have unfolded in the last nine days.

They are almost within touching distance of the cliffs when she spots it—an opening. Drawing a sharp breath, she strides toward it and steps inside.

The smell of burning is overwhelming. It catches her so unawares that it feels like someone has grabbed her by the throat.

"You okay?" Quinn asks.

"You don't smell that?" she asks in a hoarse voice.

"Smell what?"

She swallows hard, directing her attention to the size of the chamber, to the wet floor and the slimy walls behind Quinn. Is she imagining the burning smell? Maybe it's not fire at all but something littoral, a confluence of kelp and calcium deposits.

Quinn scythes a torchlight along the walls and deep in the chamber, searching for anything that might remain. They both know the police will have searched this area, but it makes her feel purposeful, examining the place where their daughter almost died. She looks up and sees Quinn kneeling on all fours, lifting his hand to his nose.

"You found something?"

He pulls a face. "It smells like fire," he says. "I think this is where the fire was."

She stares down at the black sludge on the ground, a flash of something passing across her mind. An imagined scene of a terrible fire erupting. The walls of the cave turning bloodred. Arlo's clothes setting alight. His screams.

"Do you think it might be?" he says.

She nods. "It could be."

They share a long look. It holds paragraphs of meaning, all the terror and uncertainty of the past week held within it. They both know that it changes nothing, finding the remains of the fire. It doesn't bring Arlo back, and it shines no light on the mysteries surrounding Erin and Senna. And yet, by being here, it feels as though they are both a step closer to understanding what led to the tragedy.

Clem lowers the light of her phone to the spot at Quinn's hand, finding nothing solid, nothing but charred wood and ash. But then, as she swings the light to the ceiling, she seems something that looks out of place.

On the ceiling of the cave, about ten feet directly above Quinn and the charred wood, is a picture.

"Quinn," she says.

"What?"

"Look up."

He moves his own torchlight up, and she uses the camera on her phone to zoom in.

"Stay there," she says, moving close to him to show him what her zoom is picking up. Without torchlight, the image would be concealed. But with the white glare, she is able to pick up a large spiral, then another, another. Three of them, clustered together.

"What the hell is it?" he asks. "A trinity?"

Clem nods, a shiver passing across her. The cave suddenly feels cold. It didn't feel cold before.

"Who would go to the trouble of carving that into the ceiling?" she asks, trying to imagine the logistics of it. A ladder would be needed. Not an easy task. And you'd have to chip away at solid granite while angling backward, or perhaps lying down.

But why?

CHAPTER TWENTY-EIGHT

Kirkwall, Orkney
December 1594

EDWARD

Long after the thugs left Mr. Couper's office, Edward stays in the crawl space, rigid with fear. He thinks of the men who came twelve days after Samhain to his cottage and arrested his mother, the searing pain of the baton one of them cracked against his skull. He still gets blinding pains from it.

He waits, silently pleading for Mr. Couper to wake, to come and find him.

To tell him that all is well.

But he doesn't, and when Edward's leg muscles begin to shriek from the uncomfortable position of the small space, he finally pushes himself out into the room.

It is dark, but he can see the shape of Mr. Couper on the ground.

"Mr. Couper?" he says quietly. He lowers, touching him. Mr. Couper is cold, and he thinks about pulling the blanket that he lies upon to cover him. But then he realizes that the dark, glossy blanket is blood, sticky to the touch.

He gasps at the sight of it, spread far across the floor. When he finds the courage to look upon Mr. Couper's face, he knows he is already dead.

CHAPTER TWENTY-NINE

Mainland, Orkney
May 2024

CLEM

Clem and Quinn leave the cave to ask Ivan about the carving on the cave ceiling. On the jetty, she shows him the photographs on her phone.

"Probably just kids," he says, glancing down warily, but the tone of his voice isn't convincing, and he doesn't move from the boat to see the symbol for himself.

"It's carved into the rock," she says, zooming in to show him the detail. "You think kids would go to all that trouble?"

He shrugs. "Yeah. Why not?"

Quinn throws her a look. "Would you mind coming and having a look?" he asks Ivan. Very polite for Quinn, but the soft approach doesn't work. Ivan shakes his head.

Ivan shakes his head. "I'd better be getting back. Weather can change in a moment here in Orkney."

They climb back on to the boat. Clem watches the island pull away from them, and she feels strangely bereft. As though a part of Erin remains in the cave. And Senna, too. All the answers out of reach.

"You go boating a lot?" Ivan asks her as she approaches the cockpit.

She shakes her head. "Never."

"Have a try," he says, nodding at the helm. He smiles, and she senses he's apologetic for the trip to Gunn.

She takes the wheel in her hands, feeling the movement of the boat.

"Just keep it steady," Ivan says with a smile. "I'll make you some tea."

"Why's the island uninhabited?" Quinn asks Ivan when he passes them both their cups of tea. "Or not crawling with tourists?"

"There was a plague in the nineteenth century," Ivan says, his eyes on the horizon. "Folk left and just didn't come back. No cafés or hostels for tourists. Plenty of places to visit in Orkney that have infrastructure."

"You have any idea why a group of teenagers might visit it?" she asks him.

"Who knows why folk do the things they do," he says.

"Maybe that symbol has a history," she says.

"It does," he says, and she perks up.

"What history?" she asks.

"Well, it's three spirals," he says. "A trinity. It's an ancient symbol. The Catholic church use it, don't they?"

"I don't think Catholics carved that symbol in the cave," she says tersely, but just then Quinn holds up his phone, showing her something he has googled. It's an image of three spirals, with the word *Triskele*.

Ivan drops them off at Kirkwall, where the old castle has long been razed by Orcadian rebels, the thick stone perimeter buried beneath concrete.

"So the spiral is a triskele," she says, googling on her own phone now.

"That's the word for it, yes," Quinn says. "An ancient pagan symbol meaning life, death, and rebirth as interconnected states."

Her stomach flips. Was the fire a suicide pact?

"You okay?" Quinn asks, seeing her face grow pale as they move through the streets.

"Yes," she says. "Fine." She'd rather keep such thoughts to herself for now, at least until they've figured out where the Triskele—the group—might be found.

Clem had imagined Orkney to feel remote and underdeveloped, but instead it is surprisingly established, with thriving towns and a diverse population. St. Magnus Cathedral sits proud in the center of the city, light pouring through its reconstructed rose window, the aisles filled with American tourists from a cruise ship.

They speak to shopkeepers and tourist clerks, asking about the tragedy on the Isle of Gunn. About Senna, and the Triskele. They find sympathy and tales of the island, its history of witches, plague, famine, but no information about Senna, or the Triskele, though they manage to exchange telephone numbers with over a dozen locals who promise to contact them if anything arises.

At two o'clock, they get the ferry to Gairsay, and find a small town close by with a convenience store and an empty café. The convenience store owner tells them he was interviewed by the police in relation to the fire on Fynhallow.

"I told them I had CCTV footage of the teenagers," he says, pointing out the poster in his shop window featuring Senna's face, the word MISSING underneath in stark red letters. "The boy came in to buy a couple of Diet Cokes. Terribly sad. He was dead the next day. The ranger found him. I can give you her name."

"Thanks," Quinn says, but he sounds defeated. It's nothing they don't already know.

They stop for lunch at a café, the mood heavy. Visiting Fynhallow has taken its toll on both of them.

"I'm wondering if you might know anything about what happened on Fynhallow?" Quinn asks the woman running the café.

"No idea about that, I'm afraid," she says with a tight smile. She turns her eyes to Clem. "We'll be closing in fifteen minutes."

Clem notices a man sitting at a table in the corner, gesturing at them. He's young, midtwenties, wearing a rainbow-colored poncho with a guitar case in the seat next to him. She approaches him, and Quinn follows.

"I overheard you asking about the Triskele," he says.

Clem nods. "You know about them?"

"The Triskele own a lot of the land around here," he says in a low voice. "They control a lot of things. People won't like you asking so openly about them."

Quinn raises his eyebrows. "Okay. Well, do you know where we could find them?"

The man glances at the café owner, makes sure she's not listening. "Can I ask why you're looking for them?"

Clem takes the seat opposite him, and Quinn copies her, taking the seat beside her. "There was a fire on Fynhallow, and a boy got killed. Another girl is still missing. We have reason to think there's a link between these events and the Triskele. We want to ask them a few questions, see if we can find out where the girl is."

The man looks puzzled.

"Our daughter, Erin, was seriously injured in the fire on Fynhallow," Clem tells the man. "We know she was researching the Triskele. I'm starting to wonder if she joined them."

"No one just *joins* the Triskele," he says. "It doesn't work like that."

"Well, that's what seems to have happened here," Quinn says.

"Maybe different branches do different things?" suggests Clem.

He gives a small laugh, as though this notion is insane. Clem shares a look with Quinn. She's not sure whether to trust this man. They don't even know his name.

"Are you a member?" Clem asks, the penny dropping.

He eyes them with a small smile. "I am, yes."

"Oh, wow," she says. "Okay. So—"

"You'd be best talking to Edina," the man interrupts. "She's the leader, if you like. Tonight's a hare moon."

"A what moon?" Quinn asks.

"A hare moon. The elders will be meeting tonight in the old byre in Scarwell Woods."

Clem scrambles to write that down on her phone.

"Scarwell Woods?" she checks, and the man nods.

"It's about forty minutes from here. I can give you directions."

"Yes," Clem says, her heart lifting. "That would be amazing."

His face darkens, and he looks them both over. "Fine," he says then. "But I caution you both to take this extremely seriously. The Triskele doesn't take kindly to strangers. You need to be prepared."

They have dinner in Gairsay, in a diner opposite a set of church ruins, watching tourists pose for photographs on the steps outside. Strange, she thinks, how Erin never mentioned St. Magnus Cathedral, or Skara Brae, or the ancient standing stones at the Ring of Brodgar. Back in Kirkwall she could see they were exactly the kind of places Erin would like to visit, given their Viking connections, their importance to Orcadian history—but Erin didn't say anything about these places.

They ask for the check, and Quinn glances at his watch. "Did Poncho Guy give us a time for the meeting?"

"He mentioned a hare moon."

"Oh, hare moon, not hair?"

He spells out the one he means. Clem googles it. "It's to do with fertility and new beginnings. Sounds like a pagan thing. Poncho Guy said they would be here tonight. I don't recall a specific time."

"Well, it's six o'clock. Sunset is eighteen minutes after nine."

"We'll go and scope the place out first. See what Poncho Guy means by being prepared."

They find Scarwell Woods about ten miles from the town, a small sign pointing toward it. No sign of any houses nearby. A field, and a metal gate. No signage to indicate if it's private.

"Should we park here?" Quinn asks, pulling into the field.

She steps out and opens the gate. They park up, and when she steps out of the car it feels colder than in the town.

They head toward the woodland, finding an old stone building among the trees.

"The byre?" Quinn asks.

"I guess so," she says, though the doors are closed. No sign of anyone around. Thick roots snaking through the understory, mossy boulders gathered between the tree trunks making it difficult to walk anywhere but a single path that leads from the byre to the mountains at the north of the island. And the trees are gnarled and ancient, the branches twisted over many years by strong winds.

About ten minutes later, she notices an etching on a tree trunk.

"Quinn!" she hisses, waving at him.

"What?"

He strides up to her and inspects the tree trunk in front of her.

Three spirals in the shape of a trinity.

"Well, that's certainly a coincidence," he says.

"It's exactly like the one in the cave," she says, bringing out her phone to compare the carving on the tree with the image on her phone.

"Looks like we're in the right place."

As she reaches up to touch the carving with her fingers, she sees something moving through the field just below the border of trees.

A hare.

She gasps at the distinctively long ears, the gleam of a gold eye.

"Look," she whispers to Quinn.

"What?" he says, looking up.

But when she looks again, the hare has gone, out of sight.

CHAPTER THIRTY

Kirkwall, Orkney
December 1594

ALISON

No one has been to see me for three days. Has something happened to William, or the children? Why has Mr. Couper not been to see me?

Never before has the uncertainty of my situation felt so grave.

It is dawn when David Moncrief appears in the dungeon. I feel my stomach churn. I suspect his presence is to inform me of something terrible, but instead he unlocks the door and passes through a basket. He says nothing, but touches his chin. The Triskele gesture for *I wish you well*.

So he is still Triskele.

But he has stood by as I have been abused, vilified, watched as Father Colville made me stand naked before him, David Moncrief, and John Stewart, as he pricked me, as he made Mr. Addis cut off my hair.

I inch toward the basket, smelling salted pork. I suspect it may be poisoned, but I devour it anyway and drink the milk in one go, followed by the water. There are apples inside the basket, and oranges, and as I peel the fifth orange, something falls out of the middle.

I stare, confused. It is a piece of paper that has been folded meticulously and slipped inside the core of the orange, part of the rind removed and then replaced to conceal it.

Gingerly, I open it.

It is written in Triskele, but the meaning makes me gasp.

> *Mr. Couper has been murdered.*
> *You must hold fast. Do not confess or Orkney will fall.*
> *The Triskele are still with you.*

I rip the paper into tiny bits and secrete them individually into the gaps of the stone wall, fearful in case Mr. Addis sees.

Then I hold my head in my hands and weep for Mr. Couper, and his family. He is dead because of me.

And I do not know whom I can trust.

CHAPTER THIRTY-ONE

Scarwell Woods, Orkney
May 2024

CLEM

It is almost nine o'clock, the trees filling with birds coming to roost. Clem and Quinn find a dry spot on a bank overlooking the byre and decide to wait there.

"So is the operation scheduled yet?" Quinn asks after a long silence.

She waits a long minute before answering. "What operation?"

"You know what operation."

She wants to ask, *Why do you care? You've not asked about this for over a decade, and now it's important to you?*

"I'm on the waiting list. I'm scheduled to have a LVAD fitted if a donor heart doesn't become available."

"Remind me what an LVAD is?"

"A left ventricular assist device."

"Okay. I'm taking it that's a major operation in itself?"

"It's heart surgery, yes, Quinn."

"I see. When?"

"A week after my birthday."

"Which birthday? This one?"

"Yep."

"And how do you feel about it?" he asks.

She laughs. "Fuck off," she says. Then, when he looks at her with a thoughtful expression, "Since when do you ask anyone how they *feel* about something?"

"I suppose since a minute ago."

"You care how I feel about having a heart transplant?"

"Yes. I do."

She takes a long, deep breath, far more unsettled than she cares to reveal. She wants to shut the conversation down, tell him she'd rather not go there, not now. The operation is six months away—less than six—and in her mind the date is like the barrel of a gun pointed at her face.

"I have feelings about it," Clem says finally. Then, before Quinn has another chance to ask another inane question: "I worry about leaving Erin to raise Freya alone. I worry how she'll manage financially, logistically, emotionally, without her mother to guide her. Her life at this point looks completely different. She's lost fingers and toes. I've no idea how that's going to affect her, both emotionally and logistically. And she doesn't have a father, does she?"

She lets that settle.

"What are you talking about?" he says in a tone of genuine confusion. "She *does* have a father. Are we talking about Erin, here?"

"Yes, we're talking about Erin," she says. "God, Quinn. Are you really that stubborn that you can't acknowledge how shit you've been as a father?"

He keeps his eyes straight ahead, though she reads his body language. He wants to put his fist through something.

Instead, he sits in a long silence, the noise of birds and leaves all around them. After a few minutes, his voice is measured, as though he's compressed the anger that almost burst out of him before. "Do you realize you do that?" he asks.

"Do what?"

"Lash out when you're scared?"

"I didn't lash out. I spoke the truth."

"So you don't realize it, then."

"Don't twist my words, Quinn. You haven't bothered with Erin for most of her life. She has felt like a second-class citizen in your eyes, like a kind of distant cousin-by-marriage instead of your firstborn child. She has *suffered*." Her voice breaks, and she's horrified to find she's crying. Quinn watches her, not taking his eyes off her. "It has been soul destroying, watching her ache for you, only for you to let her down time and time again. And I blame you for everything, Quinn, I do. I blame your complete and utter neglect of her because she fell pregnant. I blame you for her self-harming. I blame you for *this*, whatever happened here in Orkney. It's all connected. And most of all, I wish I could turn back time and fall pregnant to someone who gave a shit about our daughter. Because it's highly likely that I'll die on that operating table in six months' time, and I have to do so knowing that my beloved girl has no one else to care for her when I'm gone."

Her words hang in the air; he is stunned, utterly speechless. Never has she spoken such truth to him, with such raw, untarnished emotion.

"I know you must be terrified," he says after a moment, and the look on his face is of such concern that it can only be sarcasm, or hatred, or spite, because Quinn doesn't do empathy, and she wants to punch him in his goddamn smug face.

But instead, she turns away, tears coursing down her cheeks as she stares out the window at Orkney's enormous sky, beyond which is nothing, absolutely nothing. "Of course I'm fucking terrified," she whispers. "Who isn't afraid of death?"

"It was the first thing I thought of when you called me," he says. "I thought of how you'd be thinking about the operation, and who would look after Erin."

She closes her eyes at this, hoping it's true, then reminds herself that it's probably bullshit, like everything else he says.

"Heather asked for a divorce," he says then, and she starts. Heather, perfect, patient Heather actually asked him for a divorce?

"Sorry to hear that," she says, trying her best to sound genuine, and she finds she is sorry. It explains a lot. And she knows how crushed he must feel about it. Heather made him feel proud. She holds his and their children's lives together, a tirelessly dedicated Quinn-champion. And she knows that Quinn's mother left his father when he was about the same age as Quinn. Come to think of it, Heather is very similar to Quinn's mother, and Quinn is a carbon copy of his father, Eric. Eric never got over the divorce. He retired early, drank heavily, died early.

"Have you separated yet?" she asks gently.

"She wants me to move out," he says. "I've asked for six months." He makes a noise at the sound of it, the echo of Clem's own timeline.

"Six months for what?"

He shifts his feet. "To change. To . . . be better."

She lets the silence drift. She suspects he has no idea what *be better* means, an abstract goal.

"I've signed up to an anger management coach," he says. "And I'm seeing a therapist. We're working through my issues with my father."

She almost bursts out laughing, but holds back. A huge part of her feels deeply for him. She always knew a lot of Quinn's problems were to do with the damage inflicted on him by his father. A cold, emotionally distant, heavily fisted alcoholic, whom Quinn desperately wanted to please.

"Do you think it's helping?" she asks. "The therapy?"

He sighs. "I don't know. Maybe."

"When is your six months up?"

"September."

"You've still got a few months, then. To turn it all around?"

"Sometimes I think the damage is done," he says with another sigh, leaning his head on his hand. "Maybe I should just call it quits, move out. Let her get on with her life."

She bites her lip. The advice she wants to give comes from a place of experience, of how well she knows him—or knew him. And yet it contradicts her feelings of bitterness. She is still furious at him for how he has treated Erin. A voice in her head tells him he deserves this, all of it. Heather has been a stoic. His path, running parallel to his father's, is laid out.

But the words come anyway. "If you want my opinion . . ." she begins.

"Please," he says, turning his blue eyes to hers. She can see how physically similar he is to his father, too, the likeness striking. "I'd like to hear your opinion."

She takes a breath, startled at her own compassion for him, and how much of it has lain buried beneath her feelings of resentment and frustration. How a person can still care for another despite how much they betray them, over and over and over again.

"I know you'll hate me saying this," she starts.

"Go on."

"You need to work on your marriage," she says. "And on your relationships with your children—all four of them."

He nods, taking it in.

"You're doing all the same things that your father did. Repeating his mistakes."

She sees him wince, though the observation doesn't come as a surprise—he has seen it in himself, but to hear her say the words aloud is the confirmation he needs.

He thinks for a long moment, inspecting his fingernails. "I'm sorry for neglecting Erin," he says quietly. There is a sudden roar in Clem's ears. She wants to say, *Sorry, did you just apologize? Could you say that again and let me record you saying it?*

But instead, she says, "That's a good first step."

"I know I could have been a better father. You're right. I've been a shit dad."

She holds her breath, wondering if she's dreaming or if he's actually becoming self-aware.

"Heather says I could do better for the boys."

"Funny, Erin thinks you've been an amazing dad to the boys."

"Not according to Heather." He rubs his chin. "I know I stand to lose everything," he says. "My wife, my daughter, my sons, my house. Actually, fuck the house. I don't care about the house." He turns to her again, lifting his eyes to hers. "And I'm sorry for how I treated you," he says.

She isn't sure how to take that, and for a moment she considers that he's being sarcastic. But she nods. It seems the right thing to do, the appropriate response.

Just then, a light moves across the hillside in front them. The sky is dark navy, the trees silhouetted, but a gold light is moving through the trees like a jewel.

The light is a flaming torch, held aloft.

CHAPTER THIRTY-TWO

Kirkwall, Orkney
December 1594

ALISON

I am still weeping about Mr. Couper's murder when Mr. Addis leads me inside the courtroom.

The windows at the back of the room are blotted out by a line of spectators on their feet, three rows deep. On the mezzanine, more have been allowed to congregate behind the bishops. In the very front row, John Stewart sits in his usual spot. And beside him sits Patrick Stewart, Earl of Orkney.

I tremble ferociously at the sight of them both. My stomach clenches, and I feel I might be sick.

Mr. Addis marches me toward the dais, directly past John Stewart and his brother. I keep my head bowed, but as I pass by Earl Patrick I see him from the corner of my eye, tilting his head at me, his black cap removed, revealing the same feathery blond hair as his cousin, the king. Patrick is younger than his brother, John, but as John is illegitimate, Patrick received the earldom when their father Robert died. Earl Patrick is broad-shouldered, his skin remarkably clear, a flaxen beard groomed to a point at his chin. I remember he is newly wedded, and a sudden hope stirs that perhaps this fresh union of the heart might make him tender toward me.

Does he suspect his brother, I wonder. Or does he regard me as the instigator of his attempted murder?

As I sit upon the dais I notice that the open fireplace to my left is stacked with wood, red flames licking the mantelpiece. The heat is welcome, though I see some spectators in the front row remove their shawls and mantles at the warmth of it. That is why the earl has removed his cap.

"Your Graces," Father Colville calls up to the mezzanine. "I trust you are well."

"Where is Mr. Couper?" Bishop Sinclair calls down.

"Your guess is as good as mine, Your Grace." Father Colville beams, and it is as though a bucket of ice water falls upon my skin. *He knows*, I think. *He knows Mr. Couper is dead. And he is lying.*

The realization that he lies brings with it another thought. That Father Colville was involved in Mr. Couper's death.

I slide my eyes from him to John Stewart, then to his brother. I sense I am caught in a trap, and I know not the reason for it.

"Does the witch have an alternative representative?" Bishop Vance asks. I shake my head, feeling exposed, and vulnerable, as though they are all bears and I am waiting to be consumed.

"She does not," Father Colville answers.

"Very well," Bishop Vance says, waving his hand.

"Your Grace, I have here an object which you may wish to consider as we proceed today," Father Colville says.

He nods at Mr. Addis, who passes a hemp sack to Father Colville. As he holds it in the air for all to see, I start at the sight of it—it is my sack, the familiar twine of red wool around the fraying handle.

He turns to me, a look of satisfaction on his face.

"Madam, it appears you recognize this sack?"

I decide it would be best not to lie.

"I do."

"Whose sack is it?"

I swallow, but hold his eye. "It is mine."

He reaches inside, though his eyes do not leave my face. The object is so small that I can't make it out, so he brings it to me. It is a piece of wax, about the size of a robin's egg. I realize it is the charm he described to the court. The charm sent to harm the earl. The evidence he could not find.

"You recognize this, Madam Balfour?" he asks.

I shake my head. "I do not."

He turns the wax over, revealing lines carved into it. At first, I think it is a rune, the slant lines forming a symbol. But then I realize it is a word.

"Can you read this?" he asks, bringing it to my eyes.

"It says 'Nyx.'"

He cocks his head, watching me in a way that is creating heat around my neck.

"What is the object, Father Colville?" Bishop Sinclair calls down.

"Your Grace, it is a piece of wax."

"And what is the significance of a piece of wax?" Bishop Vance asks impatiently.

"I am told it is a method commonly used by cunning folk to cast a hex," Father Colville answers. "Wax is melted over a flame, Your Grace, with sundry objects inserted into the mixture while it is yet soft. Then it is fashioned into the shape of whosoever is to be hexed."

"Madam Balfour," Father Colville says in a loud voice. "Do you understand this word, 'Nyx'?"

I glance warily at him. "I believe so."

Bishop Vance glowers down. "It would be most helpful if you might share your knowledge with the court, madam."

"It is a Triskele word, Your Grace. It means 'vengeance.'"

A murmur rises up among the people in the gallery.

"Vengeance," Father Colville repeats loudly, turning toward the gallery so that his voice might project all around the room.

"How does the woman know the meaning of this word?" Bishop Sinclair calls down, and I feel my cheeks burn.

"The woman is Triskele, my lord," Father Colville says. "And as you know, the Triskele are among the fiercest and most powerful sorcerers in the isles of Orkney. Not only that, but this sack and the wax were found in Thomas Paplay's possession." He turns to me, eyes gleaming. "Pray you, madam, why would your sack be in the possession of a man who attempted to kill Earl Patrick?"

"I know not," I say quietly.

"Madam?" Father Coville says. "Are you suggesting Thomas Paplay stole it from your cottage?"

"No, but . . ."

"When you renounced God," he shouts in my face, "what was the price? Judas fell for thirty pieces of silver. What was your price?"

"I had no price," I say, my throat tightening with panic. I see the earl sit forward, and his brother reaches out to place his hand on his arm in a motion of brotherly affection.

"I did not give it to Mr. Paplay," I say.

Father Colville nods at Mr. Addis then, and he collects something from the side of the room and returns, tying it around my waist.

"What is this?" I say, but he says nothing, fastening me to the chair. He tugs at the bonds, ensuring they hold fast before turning and walking out of the room.

A bronze light bathes the courtroom this morning, the stained-glass windows drenched in winter sun. My heart is beating fast, a film of sweat forming at my shoulder blades. The earl stares impassively, turning his head to one of his guards and having a quiet word in the man's ear.

I search out David and find him sitting at the desk in the corner, his inkpot and quill laid on the wood and the parchment set out. To his left, I find William, and my breath catches. It is a relief to see him here, though I recognize at once the pain on William's face. He knows as well as I that Mr. Couper is dead.

He holds my gaze, unblinking, and for a long minute there is no one else in the room with us, no words or sound but the communication that travels between us. He tells me: *I am sorry.* I tell him: *It is well. Please do not fear. I love you.*

Father Colville's gaze turns to Mr. Addis, who has returned and stands next to the fireplace. He pulls on a leather face covering, then long protective gloves, before reaching into the flames and withdrawing what I think are two red swords, the room filling with hot steam from the glowing metal. As he steps closer, I realize—they are not swords at all, but thin strips of metal that bend as he walks.

They are caschielaws.

I start to whimper, thinking of the man in Edinburgh who died when they used caschielaws upon him. Father Colville leans toward me, making a soothing noise, as though I am a child receiving a scolding. "Hush, now. Remember what I said. If you confess, I will spare your life. Please, Alison. You *must.*"

"Stop this!" a voice shouts from the back, and all heads turn to a boy who is attempting to stride across the room toward me.

With a gasp, I realize that the boy is my son. It is Edward. Immediately two guards are upon him, seizing him as he shouts and dragging him to the entrance of the room.

Mr. Addis approaches me and, with a glance at Father Colville that seems to confirm something, crouches by my legs. Then he lifts my skirts and wraps one of the strips of metal around my ankles.

My focus was on Edward, on his shouts of protest, but then bright, radiant pain sends sparks shooting behind my eyes into the black void of my skull. I give a loud, high-pitched shriek, but someone is quickly behind me, fastening a leather belt across my mouth, dulling the sound of my screams to a muffled growl. Mr. Addis binds the second strip of metal around my knees, up around the flesh of my thighs.

"I remind you that the Devil cannot inhabit a body in pain," Father Colville shouts over my screaming. "This may seem cruel, but it is the *only* way we purge this woman of Satan and bring us closer to the truth!"

I feel like I am outside my body, someone else screaming. The steam rising from my blistering skin is so thick and tinged with blood that it is as though a great billowing cloud has gathered all around me, that I'm being taken up to heaven by angels. But I see a person coming close—he is no angel. He is Mr. Addis, his face covered with the leather helmet, and he unpeels the metal strips, which have already cooled.

"Alison, do you confess?" Father Colville calls through the veil of smoke, and I open my mouth to howl *Yes! Yes, I confess, I confess!*

But then a scene flashes before my eyes. I see myself at the edge of a high cliff, a chasm between me and the other side. The ground is so far below my feet that clouds gather in the abyss. William and the children stand on the other side of the cliff, and I know that if

I confess, we will forever be separated. I will never see them again. Not even in the next life.

Mr. Addis returns with two different strips of metal, glowing red.

The courtroom collapses to the size of a pearl, and I am swimming in darkness, plunging under to that place where neither prayer nor thought is found.

CHAPTER THIRTY-THREE

Scarwell Woods, Orkney
May 2024

CLEM

"Bloody hell," Quinn whispers. "It's a torch procession."

"I don't like the look of this," Clem says. She regrets sitting on the bank now. The car is on the other side of the trees, so even if they dash back now, they will easily be spotted by the oncoming procession.

"Let's just hold tight," Quinn says.

They watch a long stream of people dressed in flowing robes move through the forest, several more flaming torches held aloft, bright as comets through the silhouetted trees. Long shadows pour down the field toward them, and in the sky above a full moon silvers the branches.

"I think we should go," Clem says.

"They're probably Druids, do you think?"

"Well, they're Triskele."

"Druids are peaceful, aren't they?"

"Oh yes," Clem says dryly. "They look very peaceful."

Clem and Quinn move behind a tree trunk, watching on as the group stops at a clearing opposite the byre and slowly forms a circle, the heat of the flaming torches carrying across to the bank where they hide. Clem counts thirty, maybe forty people, some children among the group.

Suddenly they start to sing, no words and no melody, just a long, sustained note that splits into a harmony of two notes, then three, and so on, a dark chord that send chills up Clem's spine. It's a chilling, ethereal sight, the woods thrumming with the voices held in harmonic unison.

She sees a small figure moving into the center of the group. A young woman, she thinks, judging by the slender form and long hair silhouetted against the trees.

"Is that Senna?" she whispers to Quinn.

"I'm not sure," he murmurs.

There's something familiar about the way she moves, the outline of her face. Clem squints into the gloom as a tall man strides toward her from the opposite side of the circle, his long cloak sweeping behind him and something grasped in his left hand.

The humming changes tone, a minor chord, and suddenly the man holds the knife high above him and sweeps it across the girl's throat. Clem shouts out as the girl's knees buckle, and as she folds to the ground, several of the group turn toward the bank.

"Shit," Quinn says. "I think they've seen us."

They bolt down the bank, though the earth is loose, making it difficult to gain purchase. They manage to cross the clearing toward the car, but close behind her she can hear voices, fragments of exchanges between the group. *Over there! That way!* She sees the glint of the car roof in the field below and races for it, but suddenly she slips on long grass and goes down, hard, her elbow cracking something cold and wet. A rock, she thinks as she rolls to her feet and continues to run, a burning sensation announcing a bloody wound.

Quinn manages to find his car keys—for some reason he has locked the goddamn car—and quickly they're inside, the engine turning over, the wheels spinning and the headlights revealing figures advancing on them.

"Move!" she shouts, and Quinn shifts the car into reverse, flinging them backward down the hill toward the road, the engine roaring. She keeps her head turned to the rear windscreen, searching out the gate they drove through.

Quinn manages to put enough space between the car and the advancing figures to turn around, the headlights picking out the gate. They're so close, only seconds away, and she feels the first stirrings of wild relief as the car picks up speed.

But just as they reach the gate at the entrance to the field, it swings shut.

Quinn slams the brake and jerks the car to the left, a reflex movement calculated to stop them from crashing. But too late—the car smacks the concrete pillar holding the gate, bringing them to a stop.

A moment later, the car doors are opened, many hands reaching inside, pulling them out of their seats.

The byre, a long, single-floor building like a scout's hut, is old and dirty inside, iron rafters exposed and lined with pigeons and cobwebs, leaves scattered around the room. An oil lantern is placed in the center, and around them stand at least thirty men and women, all of them dressed in long black robes, their faces covered in black and white paint. Some have their faces concealed entirely by masks made of animal skulls, four with long horns that spiral upward, others with chain mail masks. The room smells of earth and fur, of flame and wood.

Clem is terrified.

She thinks of Erin, and Freya, her stomach tightening at the thought of them being left without either her or Quinn.

They have both been thrown on the floor, the group of strangers towering over them. Clem feels herself begin to shake. They are trapped in here. No chance of escape.

"What is this?" Quinn says hoarsely. "Let us go or I'll burn this fucking place to the ground."

Someone kicks Quinn, hard, in the chest, the slam of a boot knocking him against Clem, his head thrown back into hers. She lets out a cry of pain. Quinn groans, and she hisses at him to shut his mouth.

In front of Clem is a woman of about eighty years, a wild mane of white hair to her shoulders, the top half of her face covered in black paint. Her sharp blue eyes stare out garishly amidst the black makeup.

"We saw you watching," the woman says, bending down with surprising ease. "A pair of spies." She glances at something in her hand, and Clem is horrified to see that the woman has her wallet, the driving license removed. They've found her backpack in the car boot.

"Clementine Woodbury," the woman reads. "From 32A South-end Street in Glasgow. And this is Quinn Ferney, from Harrogate. You're married but living apart?"

"Divorced," Clem corrects.

"I see," the woman says. "Well. You're both a fair distance from your homes. We don't usually get visitors unannounced."

A flash of the scene amidst the trees springs to Clem's mind. The man slashing the girl's throat. She wants to be sick.

"We're just looking for information," Quinn says. She can hear the fear in his voice.

"Information?" the woman says. "I hear Google is good for that."

"There was an incident on Fynhallow last Wednesday. A fire. Our daughter almost died, and her boyfriend, Arlo, was killed."

The silence stretches out, the smell of blood reaching Clem's nostrils. She swallows hard, realizing that neither the woman nor the people around her are reacting to this information, certainly not with any sympathy. It strikes her that they are responsible for the fire. They killed Arlo. And she and Quinn are next.

This is all a trap.

CHAPTER THIRTY-FOUR

Three years ago

ERIN

Erin meets Senna online when Senna comments on her tarot Tik-Toks, asking for a reading. Sure, she messages back. It's fifteen for a three-card read. We can do it by WhatsApp?

It turns out that Senna lives in Glasgow, too, that she's into paganism just as much as Erin. They decided to meet up for a bubble tea in Partick. Erin admires Senna's black space buns and the badges pinned to her velvet blazer, which are a mix of goth Barbie-core and pithy statements about Trump and late capitalism. They have some of the same pins, too, one for the TV show *Good Omens* and one that says "Socially Awkward."

"I'm part of a pagan group, actually," Senna tells Erin when they sit at the window table looking out on to Dumbarton Road.

"Really? Like, Druids?"

"Better than Druids," Senna says. "I was a Druid but this group is way better."

"Oh my God," Clem says. "Tell me it's not some Dungeons and Dragons thing?"

"Course not," Senna laughs. "We meet up every week, usually in the park. We have picnics when the weather's nice, sometimes bar-becues. Chat about nature and shit. Everyone's super chill."

"You chat about nature?"

"Yeah. And life. And magic."

"Do you do spells?"

Senna smiles broadly. "You'd love it. The Triskele. That's the name of the group."

Several things happen after that first meeting in the bubble tea café that change the course of Erin's future:

First, her best school friend, Bella, tells her that her father has booked a daddy-daughter trip for the two of them to Egypt af-ter her exams. A week in Luxor. Nothing to do with grades. Just a chance to hang out together. When Erin tells her how lucky she is, Bella pulls a face and says she wished he'd booked Ibiza in-stead.

Second, she stops sitting with Bella at lunch, then stops speak-ing to her entirely, because every time she looks at her she's re-minded of how unbearably shit her own dad is, and how much his absence burns her.

And last, Senna messages her constantly, telling her all about the Triskele. They have a leader known as "the Brother," and he has specifically said that Erin can come to their next meeting, even though she's not a member.

Erin feels alive with excitement as she takes a bus with Senna to the Triskele weekender. She had expected the meeting to be some-where central, like Kelvingrove or Queen's Park, but they end up in the Trossachs National Park, on the grounds of a derelict castle. There are tents and gazebos set up, more than a hundred people gathered together, like a mini-festival. There are dogs of all breeds—Rottweilers, Alsatians, cute little dachshunds wearing hand-knit jumpers.

"It's not a cult," Senna had said, very early on, when they met over Zoom. "You'll hear people say it is, but it's not."

"Why do they say it's a cult?" Erin had asked.

"People are so fucking narrow-minded," Senna said. "It's because we have a so-called leader, right? And he's a guy with long hair and robes."

Erin smiled. She'd seen photos of the leader. She liked the idea of someone heading up an organization but calling themselves "brother." And there was nothing in the Triskele's code of ethics that she disagreed with. Triskele was like coming home. She liked the emphasis on tarot and spells, the strong connection to nature. She liked the feminist edge and the environmental advocacy. Most of Triskele's work was based on rewilding and pressurizing big corporations to stop killing the planet. She was absolutely in favor of that. She'd heard rumors that Greta Thunberg was connected to Triskele, which made her heart stir with hope.

The more she found out, the more it seemed that Triskele was where she was meant to be. Everything was falling into place since she found it. She knew it wasn't a cult. No one was asking for money, for a start. They invited donations, but that was to pay for the workers and the venues. It was just like Patreon or Ko-fi. Triskele wasn't a MLM or a Ponzi scheme. They weren't asking her to sell stuff for them, and they weren't controlling her. They were a community. They weren't a cult.

They were a family.

. . .

The Triskele meetings are intoxicating. Sometimes the Brother will talk for five hours without stopping. He'll sit by the campfire, getting up only to pace and light a spliff, and talks without a single note about what life really is, about who all of them really are, about their real identities. He shares all his wisdom about the world, which means everyone who isn't Triskele, and how they are all blind, and stupid, a herd of dumb sheep.

She comes to love the weekenders nestled in the woods. Everyone like one big happy family, enduring the Scottish weather, eating soggy sandwiches and smoking spliffs, talking about the important stuff. She learns about the Crossing. The Brother tells her there is so much more to learn, an ocean of knowledge into which she can dive. He tells her that sometimes he offers scholarships to students who are sincere in their efforts to learn. It doesn't involve money, but it involves time, and attention, and education.

"How do I get a scholarship?" she asks.

The Brother grins. "You have to commit," he says. "Are you ready?"

Three weeks later, he tells her she has been accepted. She is taking the most important first step of her entire life.

"The first lesson of the scholarship is very simple," the Brother says. "No Google searches. No reading anti-Triskele stuff. All that shite will poison your mind. It's *intended* to poison your mind, so don't fall for it. We're hated, remember?"

She nods, feeling the sting of those words. *We're hated.*

"No school," he continues. "No university. Stay away from that shite. Mind rot. Your friends who aren't Triskele? They aren't friends. Don't tell your family about the Triskele because they won't get it. We're your true family."

The scholarship is intense, with many hours of personal study required. The Brother's seminal text is six hundred pages long, and she is required to read it three times, cover to cover, a kind of Bible for Triskele members. Stories. There are multiple exams, none of them written—everything is done in person, interview style. She is examined by the Brother and once by Senna. A few times she comes close to failing, and has to take the exam again, faced by a panel of six members.

When they tell her she has passed, she cries with relief.

Her graduation is called "the Crossing," before she becomes proper Triskele, part of the clan.

But as Senna helps her into her robes, and the Brother tells her what the Crossing involves, the word "cult" crosses Erin's mind for the first time since her first meeting.

"People have made sex so taboo," he says, "but think about the way plants and trees do it. Sex is natural. It's a celebration."

"Yes, but in front of, like, everyone?" Erin says. "With a stranger?"

Why had no one mentioned that the Crossing would mean she had to shag someone? And not just shag them but as a kind of performance, with an audience. Was it too late to back out? They'd think she was a coward, or a traitor. Her palms turn clammy.

But then Senna wraps her arms around her, pulling her close for a hug. "Oh, babe. I know exactly how you feel. I was nervous, too."

"You were?" Erin says, followed quickly by: "You did this, too?"

Senna pulls back. "Yeah. I did. And I remember feeling like I wanted to back out and run away." She giggles at the memory of it, at how silly she'd been. "God. If I'd only known what lay on the other side. I think that's part of the reason for it, you know."

"For what?" Erin asks. "The Crossing?"

Senna nods. "Yeah. Like, if it was easy, everyone would do it, and they wouldn't be ready. Not really."

"But if you have the balls to do something that society deems so illicit, so *pagan*," the Brother adds, "then you're halfway there already."

Erin takes a breath. That makes sense. It is about courage, and thinking with your higher brain, the one that hadn't been conditioned by society. She'd always known that school was just a conformity vehicle, churning out lots of obedient little workers who would never challenge the system. And adulthood was like that, too. Her mum struggles with council tax and water bills and bin day and bloody income tax, for what? The whole world is set up as a distraction from the Truth. No one is who they think they are. Triskele is a groundbreaking project aimed at getting people to wake the fuck up and realize who they really are.

"So who do I have to shag?" she says, sniggering a little as her own words reach her ears.

"You know Arlo already, yeah?" Senna says, and Erin follows her gaze to the boy standing in a huddle, about thirty feet away, closer to the fire.

"Oh." Erin is a little relieved. She likes Arlo. She is slightly disappointed that she doesn't get to have sex with a girl, as that is her preference, and they already know she is bisexual. For a moment she wonders why the setup is so heteronormative.

"What about, you know, contraceptives?" she asks, but then Senna is asking her to get to her feet and the drums are louder and she realizes it's time, oh God, she is really doing this. She feels excited and sick: her body wants to go into the circle where the people are waiting and to run away, all at the same time. And then she's drinking something from a wooden goblet that instantly makes her head feel light as a feather, and she thinks of a line from *Romeo and Juliet*, "Thy drugs are quick" ...

It all feels like a dream, the Crossing. Erin is conscious of people standing in a circle, at least forty of them, all dressed in robes like hers, but masked, too, black cloths covering their faces. Some of them wear helmets made of deer antlers, while others wear elaborate vests and aprons made of braided twigs. Four guards stand in a square holding flaming torches around a large wooden platform, about the size of a double bed, made of logs and padded with black blankets, and beyond that is a small bonfire, the heat of it beating through the forest like a living heart. It strikes her that the whole thing is a health and safety nightmare, but then the drumbeat ratchets up, pulsing through her, shaking the very ground beneath her feet and rustling the trees overhead.

She senses Arlo's nervousness beneath his ardor, but she focuses on him, pretending he's a lover instead of someone she'd chatted with once or twice. She's just glad it's over quickly, a wild shout rising up from the crowd. And instantly they are covered again, her and Arlo, and Senna is there, saying, "Well done, well done."

But she does not feel accepted, or swept up in a beautiful sense of belonging. She feels used, and nauseous, and tearful, even when they stumble forward into the midst of the well-wishers and the Brother shouts, "Tonight, we drink to love!"

CHAPTER THIRTY-FIVE

Kirkwall, Orkney
December 1594

ALISON

William comes to me that night, when I am lying on the floor of the dungeon, swaying between two worlds. One is a realm of dark mists and screaming, the other of light clouds and ecstatic pain-lessness.

When I see him, I cannot move. My legs are sticky, raw wounds, the slightest movement sending arcs of pain through every muscle.

William sets down a basket and removes the contents quickly, passing me a bundle.

Inside is a clutch of living snails, trapped inside the stitched cloth. I know the reason for their inclusion—I am to use their slime to treat the burns on my legs. There is also a poultice of honey and bran, which I use once the slime has dried.

I lift my skirts hastily and place the snails on my bare flesh, gasping with pain as they find their way across the livid welts left by the caschielaws.

William unstoppers a bottle and passes it to me. The taste of cold rose water sweetened with honey is so relieving on the tongue that for a moment the pain lifts.

"I'm sorry," he says after a long silence.

"Why are you sorry?" I ask.

"You should not be in here."

"It is not your fault that I am here."

"It is," he says. He keeps his eyes on the ground. "I resolved to have you sprung from these bars within days. It has been weeks. And now you are wounded."

"Do you know what happened to Mr. Couper?" I ask.

"He was beaten to death," he says. "Edward was there. He witnessed it."

My mouth falls open. "Edward?" I whisper. "Are you sure?"

He nods. "They did not find him. He is lucky."

"But what if they find out?" I cry. "William . . ."

"I am meeting with the rebels tonight," he says. "Edward is safe, and we will find you another lawyer. This is not over."

I tell him about the visit from David, telling me I yet have friends. How Mr. Couper said that David offered to be the notary.

He begins to object. "I don't trust David Moncrief. He is working for John Stewart. *None* of them are to be trusted. They work only for their own gain. They will see you thrown to the dogs before they act to help you."

"Perhaps we ought to speak with him," I say. "An army made of two factions is better than one."

He considers this.

"I have learned that the earl owes the king money," he whispers, "and it is for this reason that he fears a rebellion. He has wriggled out of both the king's grasp and that of the Orcadian elite for many years, but he cannot contend with both at the same time."

He tells me that Earl Patrick paid six thousand pounds for the title of earl, and continues to pay exactly two thousand and seventy-three pounds and six shillings annually—a revenue which the king has found useful enough to overlook the earl's indiscretions, including piracy, the murder of tenants, and theft of udal lands. Patrick has borrowed money from the king several times before, but has defaulted on his most recent sum of ten thousand pounds, the punishment for which is beheading. Earl Patrick is therefore under considerable pressure either to find the money to pay the loan—which he cannot—or to provoke the king's sympathy to extend the term and avoid beheading.

"We know that the king is fresh from the Berwick witch trials," William says. "He is still paranoid, however. He fears witches above all else. The rebels believe that Earl Patrick is intent on launching his own witch campaign here in Orkney specifically to persuade the king that he is too busy fighting witches to pay off the loan."

"I do not understand," I say. "You believe that the earl has imprisoned me because he owes the king money?"

"I believe that the king has many advisers," he says carefully. "And they all seek power, and money. Why do you think Father Colville is so intent on painting you as a witch?"

"He is the king's chamberlain," I say. "So will do his bidding."

"I do not believe Father Colville serves anyone but himself," William says, raising his eyebrows. "I believe he is working for all three men: the king, John Stewart, and Earl Patrick."

"But why?" I ask. "Why would he do that?"

"For money," he says. "He holds a position of trust, and therefore commands a high price. John Stewart has attempted to kill his brother in order to take the earldom, and now he must regain his brother's trust. I would imagine he is paying a very high price indeed to Father Colville for this task."

I feel my heart drop. I have no hope at all if what he says is true.

He must see the look of despair on my face, for he reaches through the bars and takes my hand. "My love, you must hold fast. You must not confess, no matter how much they try you. Promise me, Alison."

I nod. "I promise."

CHAPTER THIRTY-SIX

Scarwell Woods, Orkney
May 2024

CLEM

Clem's eyes are on the machete held by the man directly in front of her, next to the white-haired woman, who follows Clem's eyes to the knife.

"For goodness sakes, Russell, put that away." The woman shoves him away and as he turns, Clem's gaze is drawn to his Rangers top peeking out from beneath his black cloak.

"My name's Edina," the woman says, ruffling her hair and looking faintly abashed. "Though perhaps you already know that, given you've been snooping around."

"We're not snooping," Quinn says. He sounds in pain, and from the corner of her eye Clem can see he's clasping his bad knee. "We were told the Triskele run things around here."

"You make us sound like the Mafia," the man with the machete says from farther back in the crowd.

"You killed Senna," Clem says. "In the woods. I saw you cut her throat."

Edina stares blankly for a moment, before turning to the man next to her questioningly. "Did you cut someone's throat, Russell?" she asks him.

He shakes his head.

"I saw it," Clem blurts out, though a voice in her head shouts that she should probably keep quiet. She feels close to tears, unable to control her emotions. Everything from the last week is bubbling up inside her, about to spill over.

"What you saw was a reenactment," Edina says through gritted teeth. "A ceremony that we only perform on a Hare Moon, signifying the death of winter."

"You staged a murder?" Quinn says hoarsely.

"This is Winter," Edina says, holding a hand out to a young woman in a long black dress. She is short of stature, her face painted black, like Edina's—and messy black hair, just like Senna's. It's the girl, and her throat is intact. "And she is very much alive."

Clem drops her head with a sob of relief. It doesn't answer the mystery of Senna, but the horror at this cold-blooded murder that has been coursing through her veins begins to ebb away.

"Please tell us where Senna is," Clem whispers at last. "She's still missing. We want answers. Our daughter is badly injured, and her boyfriend was killed."

"Slow down a moment," Edina says. "This is a different thing we're talking about here, correct?"

"Nothing to do with the Hare Moon," Quinn says.

"Senna is the name of one of the teenagers?" Edina asks. "From the incident on Beltane?"

"Beltane?" Clem asks. Then, remembering what Stephanie said: "It's a festival, isn't that right? On the first of May?"

Edina nods. "The night of the fire." She says it in a tone of voice that suggests the two things are connected.

"What do you know about it?" Quinn asks, a little too direct,

Clem thinks, given the circumstances. She is terrified of these pagan strangers, with their bizarre costumes and horned masks.

Edina doesn't answer, and Clem can sense the air changing. Something is being communicated among the members in glances, without words.

"My d-daughter, Erin," she says, stammering. "We think she joined the Triskele."

"Do you, now?" Edina says, cocking her head.

"Yes," Clem says. "I'd never heard of you before that. She joined in Glasgow."

"I can assure you that she did not join the Triskele," Edina says.

"She came to Orkney," Clem insists. "And we heard that the Triskele meets here. So we wanted to speak to you—she came to see you." This last feels more like a stab in the dark, but it feels impossible to break through to these people how serious this situation is.

"The Triskele is as old as time," Edina says. "But there are many fraudulent groups. Your daughter joined one of them—not us. And we'd like to know more about them—we're always interested in speaking with these individuals to persuade them that the misuse of our name and our values is taken seriously."

"What about Senna?" Clem asks. "She went missing from the Isle of Gunn. And someone killed my daughter's boyfriend, Arlo."

"I'll tell you the situation, as far as we see it," Edina says. "Several years ago, something of great importance was stolen from us."

"By Erin?" Clem asks, puzzled.

Edina cocks her head. "We know a group of people visited the Isle of Gunn and took the object in question. A book. A very old book."

"Erin mentioned a book," Clem says. "But I don't believe she stole anything."

"We want the book to be returned," Edina says in a low voice.

"I think that's going to be a bit difficult," Quinn says.

"Why is that?"

"One of them is dead, one of them is missing, and the other's in a hospital bed."

"You must believe me when I tell you that your interpretation of what is 'difficult' would change radically if you know what I know," Edina says.

"Which is?" Quinn asks.

Edina smiles, her eyes glistening. Clem feels a shiver crawl up her spine.

"I see the book is still in Scotland," Edina says, her voice far away. "It is angry with the person for possessing it, and yet it knows she did so unwittingly. She was tricked by another and attempted to destroy it. And now, if she does not return the book in a matter of days, she will die."

"A matter of days?" Quinn says. "Where is this book?"

"You mentioned you were told about us," Edina says. "That someone told you the Triskele run things around here. I'm taking it you're expecting us to help you find your young woman. Senna. Perhaps we can help each other, in that case."

Clem nods. "Yes. Yes, we can."

She thinks of the book she saw in the hospital bathroom.

The strange scene of the woman that sprang up from its pages.

"Let us go," she says. "And I swear I'll do everything I can to return it to you."

CHAPTER THIRTY-SEVEN

Kirkwall, Orkney
December 1594

ALISON

The year tilts toward the winter solstice. I feel the drag of the days, darkness and ice creeping ever closer and the earth preparing for her long sleep.

The trial is suspended, no one has told me why, and I lie and wait in my cell for something, anything, to happen.

My sleep is thick with dreams. I dream of the time my mother taught me about the gifts of a Carrier. When I said I would not follow her path and become one, that I would have nothing to do with *The Book of Witching*, she grew impatient and told me a story.

"The book is many things," she said. "It is a storehouse, a map, and it is also a door."

In the dream, I see the book transform into its many variations, springing from a square binding made of bark to a vast storehouse in which shadows bustle and pour through the stones like smoke. Then it spreads outward, revealing the cartography of evil. It morphs again, taking the form of a black door, at which I stand, my hand on the door handle, fashioned to resemble a claw made of iron.

"The book allows a Carrier to soul-slip," my mother whispers in the dark. "If you need, you may pass through it and reside in the body of another Carrier for a time."

"Why would I do that?" I ask.

"There are many reasons why a Carrier would need to escape," she says. "You might be in danger. Ravens are Carriers. A human Carrier has been known to soul-slip into the body of a raven in times of danger."

"Into its body?"

"Yes."

"And then what happens? Where does the raven's soul go?"

"They coexist. A body is just a portal, a container for all that a soul is. The raven and the Carrier become one."

In the dream, I see a burst of black feathers as I open the door, and suddenly I am lifted high, high above the earth, the trees and fields shrinking beneath and the clouds arranging themselves around me like a vast white dress.

The trial recommences when I am yet suffering from the scorching of my legs. I can walk very slowly with the aid of a stick. Mr. Addis leads me up the stairs, and it takes me a long time to follow.

In the courtroom, Earl Patrick is not present, which is a relief, though John Stewart maintains his usual seat before me, eyeing me sourly. When Father Colville approaches, I notice he is wearing the smile that doesn't reach his eyes, the one that tells me he is about to do something terrible. He turns to the gallery and holds his hands out wide.

"We wish to apprehend William Balfour," Father Colville bellows. He looks up, and I see Bishop Vance give a nod of approval.

For a moment the name doesn't mean anything, because why

would he be calling to apprehend my husband? But then a stramash starts up at the back of the court, and in the middle row the spectators make way for two guards who wrestle William off his seat, pulling his coat and his hair. My heart thuds in my throat as I watch William thrashing against the guards, the scuffle terrible to witness. The guards haul William up the aisle, his feet dragging, and for a desperate, jagged moment, we make eye contact. I cry out as two more guards walk toward Will, their heavy boots squealing on the wooden floor. The four of them wrestle him down, tying his hands and ankles together. I can scarcely breathe for fear of what they plan to do to him. I glance nervously at the fire. It is lit only a small amount, and no metal strips are visible.

But then Father Colville orders the guards to take William outside, and a commotion sweeps across the courtroom. William's shouts ring off the stone staircase as the guards heft him into the hallway. The spectators follow, pushing and shoving to see what is happening.

Mr. Addis leads me behind the crowd. I am too stricken to speak, to breathe, the pain from the burns in my flesh gone entirely. I am too afraid of what is to become of William to feel anything other than terror. Has he been taken to the dungeon? Surely a charge would have had to have been made for that to be the case?

We follow the crowd not to the dungeon, but to the front of the castle, out into the street. The spectators have gathered all the way to the archway joining the castle estate to the marketplace. From out here the castle is a looming, black specter, slick with rain and old snow, but the crowd remains, despite the weather, growing thicker as onlookers from the marketplace and the fishing boats are drawn near by the commotion.

At Father Colville's bidding Mr. Addis tugs me roughly through the throng to the front, where I find my husband. He is pinned down on the ground by the guards close to a cart laded with stones and, bizarrely, a door. William is fighting them, and I cry out.

"Stop!" I plead. "Please, leave him alone!"

"Don't confess, Alison!" he shouts with a strained voice. "For Orkney!

His cries break my heart. I have to cover my mouth with both hands, so desperate am I to make them stop, to set him free. Father Colville signals hastily to the guards to gag him. They fetch a hangman's hood from the cart and slip it over his head, then fasten it secure with a belt across his mouth. I fall to my knees, sobbing.

"Madam Balfour," Father Colville calls out to me. "Do you still deny your crimes before God?"

I open my mouth, willing myself to say the words. *I confess.* I look at William, straining to get up, telling them to get off, and I call upon God to save him.

Father Colville steps closer. "Say the word, Alison, and it can all end."

But William's shouts have lodged in my mind, stopping up my words. *For Orkney!* I remember what he said when he visited me last—that my confession may be a tool that Earl Patrick can use to deepen his plundering of Orkney.

How can I allow it?

"Say it," Father Colville hisses.

I shake my head, but it breaks my heart.

Two more guards fetch the door from the cart and place it lengthwise across William's body. Two others gather heavy stones. They heft them and stagger back toward him before dropping them with a loud clatter on the door.

With a horrible grunt, William stops bucking against the door. The sound he makes is unlike anything I've ever heard.

THE BOOK OF WITCHING

Some spectators look away.

"Alison?"

Father Colville is before me. His face is wet. It has started to rain in earnest, the light spit from the sea escalating to a heavy lash, pooling darkly in the nooks of the road. William's clothing is soaked through, his hands in fists, the tremor and clenching the only things I can still see moving below the weight of the door, the boulders. My stomach roils as I eye the stones on the cart. There must be the weight of a house on that cart. Enough to crush him.

Spectators cluster together, watching my husband on the ground beneath the door and the stones. Birds cry overhead. On a wall opposite sits a large black raven, its darkness hooking the scene as it watches on.

In my mind's eye I see my mother, pleading with me to sign the black book. Had I signed it, perhaps I would have had powers to escape. Perhaps I would have foreseen the dangers to come.

A stream of dark liquid runs from under the door, down through the cobbles like a snake. The rain falls hard, the sky a silver shield.

And I look up and meet Edward's eyes through the crowd. My son. It breaks my heart to witness him here, watching on as his beloved father is killed before him, and in such an unspeakable manner. Edward's mouth hangs open in a wordless howl, his eyes sightless and streaming with tears. I should confess. But even as I open my mouth to scream out the lies, I cannot—to do so is to damn my soul forever. I will not see my family in heaven.

Father Colville turns his head and nods at the guards. A moment passes before I realize what is meant by this exchange, and then I gulp back air to scream it out again in a long, single word.

"No!"

Father Colville pays me no heed. The wind unfurls as it does, no pause in the rain, the insistent movement of light. The birds call above, stars winking in the firmament, that old, death-defying pulse of light. And wherever He rests, God's ear does not turn to my cry.

The guards make for the row of boulders and heft one each. They don't stop until Will's groans cease. Until the crowd grows quiet and disperses, Edward disappearing with them. Until Mr. Addis drags me away, Will's body lifeless and still beneath the weight of the stones bearing my silence.

CHAPTER THIRTY-EIGHT

Fynhallow
Isle of Gunn, Orkney
December 1594

EDWARD

Edward walks across the beach of Fynhallow, stopping every now and then to pick up dulse on which to chew. He is hungry and afraid, but he can't risk being discovered, not even by the boys he has grown up with or the people who live by their cottage.

And now he weeps for his father, and for Mr. Couper. He is terrified, and wrung out with guilt. He wants to see his mother, and his grandmother, and his sister.

When he sees his cottage on the hill, he starts to run, his body propelled toward it. He is crying noisily now, and so exhausted that he stumbles and falls to his knees several times before he reaches it. He can smell the peat burning, sees the shaggy kyloe gifted by Agnes. The sight of her burns in him, the familiarity of home an overwhelming comfort.

Just as he reaches her, a girl comes out of the cottage. It's Beatrice, his sister, and he is astonished. Her fair hair is braided in a long plait that hangs down one shoulder, catching the light of the sun. She lifts her eyes to him, then shouts out his name.

"Edward!"

They run toward each other, colliding in an embrace, and he is laughing and weeping and she is asking question after question. Where is Father? How is their mother?

She leads him inside the cottage, where a fire is blazing. Porridge is bubbling in a pot over the stove and the smell of it pulls him close.

"Where is Grandmother?" he asks as Beatrice serves him. She is so little, he reminds himself, not yet seven, and yet she is so capable. "How long have you been alone?"

"Not long," she says. "Grandmother is looking after me."

"Where is she?"

"I think she's with Solveig. The Triskele are helping get Mother out of prison."

Edward's heart lifts. "Is that true?"

She smiles and nods. "It is. But we must not tell anyone. Do you want to see something?"

He nods.

"You have to promise not to tell anyone," she says, suddenly cautious.

"Just show me."

She moves to the space under the fire, the space he knows neither he nor his sister is to touch, for his mother uses it to keep her potions and strange powdered bones and any extra coin that comes her way. He watches as Beatrice lifts out a large object wrapped in black linen, peeling back the fabric to reveal what looks like tree bark.

"Look what I found."

His breath catches. "*The Book of Witching.*"

She is disappointed, having hoped to astonish him. "You recognize it from the initiation?

"No," he says. "I am the Carrier. That is why it's here. I have been keeping it safe in our cottage."

"Not safe enough," Beatrice says. "The soldiers came and pulled everything apart, looking for it."

"I do not think they were searching for this," Edward says. "And besides, it can hide of its own will. It can vanish and travel without us knowing."

Beatrice looks puzzled, and he realizes—she has not seen what he has seen.

She does not know what will befall their mother.

Edward is asleep when he hears it, the drumming sound. He is entangled by dreams about wild dogs rushing inside Mr. Couper's office and biting his ankles, and in the dream, one of the dogs—a large black one—noses the crawl space and begins to bark, alerting the others.

The snort of a horse outside draws him sharply out of sleep. He shakes his sister awake.

"Go up into the roof," he says, and she does so, quickly and quietly, right as the door opens.

And though he climbs after his sister, the soldiers stride across the floor of the cottage, grabbing Edward before he has time to make a sound.

CHAPTER THIRTY-NINE

Orkney
May 2024

CLEM

They are in the car, driving away from the Triskele in a hurry, the car swerving dangerously across the muddy pathway. Quinn narrowly misses a metal cattle gate that swings toward them, the headlights glinting off the aluminum posts. He gives a shout and manages to right the car at the last minute.

"Why did you promise them that?" Quinn says finally. "You said you'd find the book and yet you've no bloody clue what they were on about."

She turns to him. "I do, actually."

"You do." He doesn't believe her.

She draws a sharp breath, recalling the book she saw in the hospital bathroom. She knows better than to attempt to explain that. *I saw a ghostly book in the hospital that showed me a woman in flames and then it vanished.*

"I need to talk to Erin," she says finally.

. . .

It's the next morning, just after eight o'clock. They've not spoken since leaving Orkney. She can sense that Quinn is angry at her. That he blames her for the confrontation with Edina and her crew.

"What was Edina's last name?" Quinn presses.

"I've no idea. Why?"

"We need to tell the police about what happened."

"I thought you said the police were shit."

Quinn says nothing. She checks her phone and sees a number of missed calls from Stephanie. First, she rings the hospital to check on Erin. She's just been in surgery. They've removed the stitches from her other eye, and her vision is clear. Clem breathes a sigh of relief.

"Morning," Stephanie says when she calls her back. "Just checking in. Everything okay?"

"Yes," Clem says, and she suspects Stephanie is wondering where the hell she and Quinn have been for the past two days. She holds back from mentioning their trip to Orkney. "I was hoping there had been some news of Senna."

"No, sadly not," she says. "I have some updates from the SIO," she says, the sound of rustling papers in the background.

"SIO?" Clem asks.

"Senior investigating officer," Stephanie says. "And some things I wanted to follow up on. In particular, we managed to track down Paul, the guy Erin mentions on her TikTok. Do you want to come to the station?"

"Oh," Clem says, taken aback. They've not met at the police station before. "Yes, of course," she says, and they arrange a time to meet, but she can't help but feel uneasy.

Stephanie greets them at reception and takes them through to her office.

"This man," she says, bringing an image up on the screen of her desktop, "is Paul Renney."

Clem looks him over. He's a heavyset white male, midfifties, black hair with silver temples. Deep eye bags and a bovine expression. An old leather jacket, the lapels curled from use, a blue shirt.

"He's an antiques dealer based in Stratford," Stephanie says. "We brought him in for questioning."

"And what did he say?" Quinn asks.

"We can show you some of the recording," Stephanie says, opening a video file. Clem watches intently as an image of a man seated at a desk appears, the back of DC Sanger's head as he faces him. The camera is mounted high on the wall, looking down. Stephanie scrolls a little into the footage, then presses the play button.

"Erin contacted me about a book she had been given," Paul says.

"When was this?" DC Sanger asks, writing something down.

"Last summer. July, I think. Maybe August."

"She contacted you how?"

"I have several social media accounts in relation to my antiques business."

"And she contacted you about a book?"

"A very unique book."

"What was unique about it?"

"It was cursed."

"Cursed?"

Paul leans back in his chair with a sigh. "I know you probably don't believe in such things."

"Do you believe it?"

"As an antiquarian, I have come across many strange things.

And more than one cursed object. I have seen the consequences of possessing something that is cursed."

"And what did you do to help Erin?"

Paul is silent for a long time. "I had to do some research. This was a very unusual object, and I had to be sure I gave the correct advice. Also, I was a little bit frightened."

"Of?"

"Well, of what might happen if I intervened. Curses are often put on an object for a reason. And if I intervened, I feared I, too, may be cursed."

"In what way was Erin cursed?"

"She told me she had suffered nightmares," Paul says. "And then, one day she began imagining herself harming her mother, and her baby daughter. She felt the book was the cause of it. And so she tried to get rid of the book, as anyone would. But each time she threw it out, it would return. She tried everything."

"Where did she get this book, then? Couldn't she just give it back?"

"Apparently she attempted to, but the fellow who gave it to her— a man she knew only as the Brother—had committed suicide."

Clem thinks of the TikTok she watched from March, where Erin announced simply "He's dead." Maybe she was referring to the Brother.

"What did you advise her?" DC Sanger asks Paul.

"I researched a little and found that the book was connected to a witch," he says. "A woman who was a magnificent healer, and a Carrier of the book by birth. She was killed at the stake at Fynhallow, a beach in Orkney. I found a spell that Erin would have to perform on Beltane on the exact spot where the burning took place."

Stephanie presses pause and looks to Clem and Quinn.

"A witch," Quinn says, folding his arms. "Great. I suppose you're going to charge Erin for witchcraft next?"

"Regardless of the fantastical statements made here," Stephanie says, "it seems we have a motivation here for the trip to Orkney. Erin was in possession of a book she thought was cursed, and she was in touch with someone who told her that she had to perform a spell on the first of May on the beach at Fynhallow, which is exactly what appears to have happened."

"Okay, I get that Erin thought the book was cursed," Clem says. "But Senna and Arlo went with her to perform the spell willingly."

Stephanie doesn't look convinced.

"Why do you think Erin has said multiple times that she is glad Arlo is dead?"

"Oh, for God's sake," Quinn snaps. "She almost died not so long ago. She watched her boyfriend burn to death. She's dissociating, or whatever that psychologist said." He glances at Clem, a flash of anger. She knows he still blames her for Erin's state.

"That may be," Stephanie says. "But as it stands, Erin is now a person of interest in this case."

CHAPTER FORTY

Kirkwall, Orkney
December 1594

ALISON

Mr. Addis leads me up the stairs to the courtroom. The room is dimly lit and the gallery full, the air thick with tension and fear. At the doorway, I lean against the frame for a moment's rest. My vision is full of stars.

"Move," Mr. Addis says, tugging my chains, but I shake my head, turning my head to the cold wood, wishing I could disappear. The thought of facing the townsfolk after what has happened to William makes me want to howl and beat the door with my fists. How could they have stood there and watched an innocent man be crushed to death?

And yet, the voice in my head reminds me that the only person to blame for William's death is Father Colville. It was not Earl Patrick who called to apprehend William, nor the bishops. Father Colville did, and he was the only one with the power to stop it— and now I think upon it, he was likely the one who organized the carts and the boulders. The people are scared. They fear I am a helpmeet of the Devil, that I will cause more pain and suffering than they have already experienced in the last ten years, with rising teinds and skat, poor crops, murder. Father Colville presides over this grim assembly.

The fire is lit again, and I begin to sob. The caschielaws are to be used on me again today. My legs are still agonizing from the last time, the wounds still raw and weeping. I cannot go through it again.

My heart is galloping so fast I can scarcely breathe. I look across the blurred faces in the courtroom, though one hardens into a recognizable shape. It is Solveig.

He nods at me, and touches his chin. I feel my heart slow. *Courage.*

"Over there," Mr. Addis says, shoving me to the left of the room, away from the dais. There is a chair in the far corner. He pushes me toward it, and I sink down in relief, my eyes searching out the fire nervously. Perhaps I am not to be tortured today. It is biting cold outside, with the winter heavily upon us. We are but a week away from Yule, and many of the spectators are wrapped up in hats and mittens despite the blazing fire.

"Good morning, Father Colville," Bishop Vance calls down. "I see the woman is here. You may proceed with your questions."

"Thank you, Your Grace," Father Colville says with a bow. He moves toward me. "Madam Balfour," he calls out in a loud voice. "I remind you of your charges. That you are accused of assisting in the attempted murder of His Grace, the Earl of Orkney. We have heard testimony after testimony attesting to your wickedness, your talents for dark magic. We have proof that you aided Thomas Paplay in attempting to kill His Grace, the Earl of Orkney. Furthermore, you allowed your husband, William, to die a most terrible and unnecessary death, rather than own up to what you have done."

He is shouting, and I am trembling, utterly pierced through by his words. To hear him say that I allowed my husband to die is worse, far worse than any accusation he could ever make against me.

He kneels before me, whispering now, his eyes soft. "Remember, Alison. I can make this all end. I can let you return home to your children. All you have to do is confess before the court."

It takes everything in my power to shake my head. He looks pained, deeply wounded by my response.

Suddenly, the heavy doors creak open. The spectators turn to survey the scene. A voice rings out, and my heart lurches, recognizing the sound instantly.

It is Edward, I rise to my feet to catch sight of him as two guards drag him thrashing and shouting along the back of the gallery. Many of the spectators are on their feet to catch sight of the commotion.

"Let me go!" he cries, his feet clattering against the stone floor. He reaches out and pulls over a chair. One of the guards trips over him, and the remaining guard seizes Edward by the hair, another arm locked around his neck, hooking him up upright.

He faces me, and at once, our eyes lock.

"Mother!" he shouts, a look of gladness on his face.

"Edward!"

"Do not confess!" Edward calls to me as the guards haul him to the dais. He manages to break free of their grasp, slipping his arms out of his shirt and jacket, leaving them clutching his garments as he stands, bare-chested, arms raised, on the raised platform.

Suddenly Mr. Addis lunges at Edward, his fist drawn, slugging him hard across the face, and I give a shout of pain as Edward's knees buckle and he collapses to the ground like a fallen sapling, the punch knocking him out cold.

Father Colville stands over him and nods to Mr. Addis, who makes for the fire with the guards. A moment later, they approach

Edward, still out cold, and I realize they intend on applying the caschielaws to his bare flesh.

My heart races, terror gripping me. "No!" I shriek, scrambling toward them. Father Colville wraps his arms around me, holding me back.

"He's just a child!" I scream at the guards.

"Madam Balfour, are you ready to forsake your sins and confess?" Father Colville hisses in my ear.

I keep my eyes fixed on Edward. He lies on the ground, unmoving, as Mr. Addis lowers the caschielaws to Edward's breast. There is a terrible moment where the room is silent save for the hiss of the iron against his tender skin, and then he wakes with a scream so loud it seems to fly around the room, and the sound of it makes me tear free of Father Colville. I throw myself upon Edward's legs with a shriek.

"Stop!"

One of the guards hooks both hands under my arms and throws me roughly aside, a loud crack ringing out as I fall face-first, breaking my nose.

I try to move but I can't.

"He's just a boy," someone from the crowd shouts. The sentiment spreads like wildfire, the room erupting in protests.

"Stop this!"

"He's innocent!"

"This is barbaric!"

I manage to sit up, witnessing the whole courtroom now on their feet, their voices rising. Even the bishops get to their feet, their expressions grave as they peer down from the mezzanine at my son, who writhes in agony.

"He's a child!" a woman shouts loudly, her voice ringing above Edward's shouts. "He's done nothing!"

"Enough, Father Colville," Bishop Vance commands. "And give the witch a rag, will you?"

Father Colville passes me a handkerchief. It is only when I see the white linen turn red that I realize my broken nose is fountaining blood.

"We are satisfied that the woman will not confess," Bishop Sinclair says. "Let the boy go."

Father Colville signals the guards to stop, and they drag Edward from the room, the only sound his sobs. I watch, frantic to know he will be well, but the doors swing closed.

"The trial is suspended until tomorrow," Bishop Vance calls. "We will return in the morning with clear minds and strong hearts."

"As you ask, Your Grace," Father Colville says.

CHAPTER FORTY-ONE

Glasgow
May 2024

CLEM

Clem takes the lift to the Burns Unit, alongside two visitors who chat about the news—politics, riots, war. She had forgotten about the outside world, about everything beyond the small hospital room in which her daughter lies.

She thinks of Edina, and the byre, and the book. How she has promised to return it to the Triskele. Except, of course, she has no idea where the book is now. She tries to piece together what she learned from the interview—Erin had the book, had tried to get rid of it, but it kept returning. And then she went to Orkney to destroy the book in a fire which killed her boyfriend and put her in hospital. Maybe the book burned in the fire? But would Edina and the Triskele be so convinced it still existed somewhere? How would they know?

Perhaps the book doesn't exist at all.

Paul Renney seems an odd character, and his claims about witches and dark magic seem more of a distraction than anything else, an attempt to come across as eccentric rather than predatory. With a shiver, she wonders if he and Erin *were* involved. And her mind turns to what she found in Erin's notebook. *Arlo's hands need to be bound . . .* Did Paul ask her to kill Arlo? Was that part of the ritual to destroy the book?

She feels a migraine beginning its sharp pulse behind her right eye as she makes her way to Erin's room. Bee is just leaving, and Constable Byers greets her with a smile.

"She's slept all morning," Bee tells her at the doorway. "That eye has healed well since you've been gone."

"Thanks," Clem says, feeling uneasy about the reference to her being away. It will have looked heartless, both of Erin's parents not visiting for two whole days. But she doesn't want to tell anyone they were in Orkney. Not while the police are ramping up their interest in Erin.

She sits quietly beside Erin, feeling equal parts relieved and doomed. She wishes she could shake Erin, shake the truth out of her. She knows Erin is vulnerable and lost and so desperate for her father's love that she'll go to any lengths to achieve it, and perhaps this really has led her down a dangerous path, one that has resulted in murder. Or manslaughter. A boy is dead, and Erin is hellbent on telling anyone who will listen how much she doesn't care that Arlo is dead. She hasn't once asked about Senna, or Freya. It is heartbreaking. And yet, Clem knows her daughter through and through. She isn't evil. She isn't capable of murder.

But she didn't know that Erin had joined a cult. Maybe she doesn't know her daughter as well as she thought she did.

"Mum?"

Clem looks up, seeing that Erin is awake.

"Where am I?" she says, sitting forward. She looks over the room with panic, at the wires in her arms, at the machines around her. "Mum?!"

Clem can't believe it; Erin is back again. Her voice has the same cadences of the voice Clem knows so well, her eyes are animated, and she surveys the hospital room as though she's never seen it before. She is confused, and in a state.

"Freya!" she cries. "Where's Freya?"

"She's with your father," Clem tells her. She shares a glance with Constable Byers, who looks as startled by the shift in Erin's demeanor as she is.

"Is she okay?" he says. "Should I call the nurse?"

"Would you mind giving us a moment?" Clem asks Constable Byers. He looks wary, and it strikes Clem that he has only ever seen Erin snarling at everyone around him.

"You're seeing this, aren't you?" she asks him, checking she isn't imaging it, and he nods.

"Your camera is on, isn't it?"

"Yeah."

She turns back to Erin, glad that Constable Byers is here to witness the change in her. Perhaps it'll counter the claims against her, about Arlo. She watches Erin begin to cry, noticing her bandaged, ruined hands, her face crumpled. Clem knows she has only so much time before this shift fades.

"Erin," she says quickly. "I need to know where Senna is. Can you tell me."

Erin is crying loudly. "I don't know! She ran away while I was trying to save him!"

Erin is somehow *back*, she is lucid, and Clem must take this chance in case it doesn't last again. "Where's the book, Erin?" she says. "The Triskele book?"

"The book!" Erin gasps, pulling at the wires in her body. "I felt I was going out of my mind. I need to get rid of it. The Brother's dead so I can't give it back. I've tried and tried . . ."

She tells Clem in a wild stream of words of all the ways she tried to dispose of the book. She put it in the wood-burning stove and set it alight, watching it burn for twenty minutes. But when she opened the stove door, the book was intact. She waited for the bin lorries to come and chucked it in the back. But when she came back to her bedroom, the book was in her room again. She and Arlo went to the Clyde River and threw it in, watched it—filmed it, even—being carried off downstream, the pages swelling with water. But when they came home, the book was in the hallway. As though it was proudly announcing that it would not, could not, be destroyed.

"Is this why you went to Orkney?" Clem asks. "You found a way to get rid of it?"

"I contacted someone," Erin says. "I found a man called Paul who knew about the Triskele. He told me what I had to do. It could only be done on Beltane, the Scottish first day of summer, in a place called Fynhallow in Orkney. He said we had to do a fire ritual to burn it."

"That's what caused the fire, then," Clem says, and Erin nods again.

"We did it in a cave because it was really windy and we worried the wind would put the fire out." She gives a choked sob.

"Tell me," Clem says quickly. She can't waste a second in case Erin becomes Nyx again. This version of her, and the story she's telling—the truth, at long last—could all vanish in a moment.

"But it went wrong," Erin says, her voice rising to a high pitch, as though her throat is squeezed tight by fresh terror. "I tied his hands together."

A noise makes Clem turn. It's Constable Byers, aghast at what Erin is saying. But she can't stop now.

"Go on," Clem tells Erin.

"We tried to save him," Erin says. "We did everything that Paul told us to do. Arlo was nervous about performing the role of the Green Man because of the hand binding. But I told him it was okay. I promised him, Mum. I said, 'You can trust me.'" Her face falls. "Those were the last words I ever said to him."

She tells Clem that they lit the fire in the cave. Senna was there on lookout. She was by the cave mouth, watching out across the beach as Erin and Arlo stood by the fire with the book. Arlo knelt down by the fire, which was small, flickering meekly amidst the bundle of logs. Erin said the words of the spell. And all of a sudden, the fire erupted, shooting out toward Arlo.

"I saw it climb up his clothes," she says. "It just climbed straight up to his neck. He started shouting to get his T-shirt off. I pulled it over his head but it literally melted onto his skin. I was screaming . . . I didn't even notice that I was on fire at this point. I couldn't get his T-shirt off. He fell down and I was throwing sand over him but nothing worked. Nothing! Senna ran down to the shore to get water but by then he was completely on fire, I mean, every single part of him. He was clawing at me, begging me . . ."

Erin folds forward, gasping for air, her face crumpled. "I couldn't save him, Mum! I tried, I tried so hard!"

"And where did Senna go?" Clem asks her, glancing at Constable Byers. "Do you remember?"

"The fire . . ." she repeats. "I've never seen anything like that. It just leaped out at us and . . . Poor Arlo. It burned and burned. We tried everything."

Erin breaks into uncontrollable sobs at the memory of it, feeling frantic. Clem glances back again and Constable Byers now wears a deep look of suspicion. But the feeling that Erin could slip away again persists: This might be Clem's only chance to hear what happened. To get information about Senna.

"Erin, Senna's parents are sick with worry," she says quickly. "Do you know where she is? Did someone take her?"

Erin shakes her head vehemently. "I tried to help him!" she sobs. "We beat the flames until I had blisters up and down my arms!"

Clem tries to console her, but Erin is lost to the memory of it. Suddenly, she freezes, something on her face shifting.

"I saw someone," she says in a small voice. "Mum, I saw someone in the flames."

"Who?"

"A boy," she says. "A . . ."

But then, Erin seems to shrink back. Clem watches, astonished, as her daughter's crumpled face slides into a look of fear.

"Please help me," Erin says in a low voice.

"Erin," Clem says, trying to reason with her.

"I need them to stop the fire," Erin whimpers. "Please."

"Stop *who*, Erin?"

"Stop calling me Erin, I'm not Erin!"

A loud knock on the door startles them both, and Clem sees Stephanie through the window, gesturing for her to come out.

She steps outside, reeling from Erin's shift in demeanor, but the look on Stephanie's face conveys a distinct urgency.

"What's happened?" Clem asks, her gaze stuck to Erin, cowering in the bed inside.

"It's Senna," Stephanie says, and Clem's eyes dart to her. "They've found her."

PART THREE

CROSSING
THE BOUNDARY

CHAPTER FORTY-TWO

Two years ago

ERIN

The pregnancy test shows up positive.

She does another one, then another. She stares at the lines on the tests for a long time, her whole body numb. She has no reaction at all. It is as though her brain won't compute the result, won't calculate the next steps.

She tells Senna.

"Oh my God," she says when they meet up in a café. "Are you okay?"

"Not really, no," Erin says with a nervous laugh. "You're the only person I've told."

"How far along are you?"

"Well, I've only had sex once with a guy this year. So I'd say I'm a month along?"

"Still time to get an abortion, then."

"Yeah."

"Is that what you think you'll do? Get rid of it?"

"Probably. I don't know."

Senna's head tips to the side and she fidgets with the sugar packets.

"Do you . . . mind if I speak to the Brother about this?"

Erin bites her lip. A voice in her head asks her why she is telling Senna instead of a GP, booking in for a termination. Or perhaps her mother. The answer is there, though difficult to accept—she needs the Triskele's approval before she acts. She needs their guidance. This baby was conceived while she was crossing the Boundary, after all. And she asked them for guidance about everything now, because they had the Truth. Life was one long maze, and the Triskele was like the watchtower, with a view over the maze.

They know the way out.

A week later, Erin meets with the Brother at a derelict castle in the Trossachs.

"The baby is a very, very special being," he tells her while they are walking through the old drawing room. "A child has never been conceived during the Beltane ritual, and a child born to someone living beyond the Boundary is incredibly gifted." He turns to her with his big soft eyes and his bushy Santa Claus beard and takes her hands in his.

"I'm so happy for you, Erin," he says. "So, so happy." She melts. It's not a sexual thing. Rather, she wishes he'd adopt her.

"So I'm to keep it?"

"Yes. Definitely."

"What about Arlo? Should I tell him?"

"That's entirely up to you."

They walk toward one of the windows, where a tree has grown through the frames, all the glass long gone. The enormous stone mantelpiece was still intact. It makes her think of her grandparents' cottage on the Isle of Mull, where she'd often curl up in the inglenook fireplace and her grandmother called her a little bean. Her grandparents died within three months of each other, both of them, when she was nine. Her mother's parents. Her paternal grandmother lives in Australia and her grandfather is an even big-ger asshole than her dad.

A voice in her head tells her, *You're too young to have a baby.* The other says, *But it means you'll have a bigger family.*

"I want to remind you of two things," the Brother says, turning back toward the front entrance of the castle.

"What's that?"

"The Triskele is your family."

She looks up sharply, her heart burning inside her. Did he just read her mind?

Another gentle look, and that fatherly smile. "We are here for you, and this baby."

Erin sighs deeply, a sob rising to her throat. "Thank you," she says, her voice breaking.

"Secondly, I want to extend an invitation. Remember I told you about the dark book?"

Erin tries to recall. Her training had covered a lot of things, a lot of mystical stuff. She nods anyway.

"This is no accident, Erin," he says, taking her hand and press-ing it between both of his own. "You conceived on Beltane! This is your destiny. Your child is a fire god or goddess of the natural world. You're amazing, Erin. This is your journey to the Truth!"

She opens her mouth to say something enthusiastic in re-sponse, but just then he says, "I have something I want to give you."

"What is it?" she says.

"Remember the book with black pages?"

She nods. "Yeah?"

"I'm giving it to you for safekeeping."

He walks her to his car and opens the boot. There, wrapped in a blanket, is the book. She glances at the Brother and notices he seems nervous.

"Take it," he says. "Please."

She finds herself lifting it out of the boot, and the look of relief on his face is striking. She shivers.

"What do I do with it?" she says.

"You just hold on to it," he says. "It's a valuable item, as you know. And you've been initiated, and now you're carrying a child conceived on Beltane! It's only right you should have it."

She wants to say that there are plenty of Triskele members who have been initiated.

"Can't someone else take it?" she says. "I'm pregnant and this looks fragile, and . . ."

He shakes his head. "You got your scholarship for free, Erin. The least you can do is take this thing out of my fucking hands."

She reels at the sharpness in his voice. He'd been so kind, so jolly a moment ago, like a big friendly bear. A father figure. And now he is all sharp edges and brittleness. She tightens her hold on the book and nods.

"Okay," she says.

"It's yours," he says firmly. "Okay?"

She nods. "Okay."

He smiles, but it's an odd, broken smile.

"Good luck, Erin."

CHAPTER FORTY-THREE

Kirkwall, Orkney
December 1594

ALISON

"I summon Mhairi Ness to the stand," Father Colville bellows.

The courtroom buzzes with chatter, and I search across the room for any sight of my mother. I find myself looking for William, too, before the horror hits all over again. How can he be dead?

I expect the silence to stretch out, for Father Colville to be confounded by the failure of his first witness to appear. But then, she is there. My mother. My blood runs could, and I want to shout to her, *Stop! Don't you see? He wishes to tarnish you with the same brush as I!*

But she makes her way to the front of the room, eyes fixed ahead as she walks up to the dais.

Mother stands before the crowd, wearing her best white dress beneath her mantle, a brooch bearing our family's crest at the shoulder. She clasps her hands, sunlight from the window falling upon her face. My heart begins its fearful flutter. Her presence here is wrong. She is walking into a trap.

"Good day, madam," Father Colville greets her.

"Good day, Father."

"Mhairi, please tell the court who you are in relation to the accused?"

My mother takes a breath, her eyes flicking toward me. "I am Alison Balfour's mother."

She says it in a small voice, and so Father Colville prompts her. "May you repeat your last?"

"I am Alison's mother."

This time, her voice rings out across the courtroom, an announcement that stirs a rumble among the spectators and the bishops seated on the mezzanine. I watch Mother carefully, wondering why she will not look at me. Perhaps it is to spare herself from being overcome. But why is she here? Why has Father Colville called upon her?

"So, it is true to say that you know the accused very well indeed?"

"Yes, very well."

My cheeks begin to burn, a bell ringing in my ears. I fear Mother is putting herself in danger.

Please be careful, I scream in my mind, hoping that somehow the message reaches her.

"I would invite you to tell the court about the night you saw Alison consort with a man outside her cottage."

I snap my head up. Consort? Outside my cottage? My eyes travel to my mother, willing her to glance at me, to tell me why she has been called as a witness without uttering a word of it to me beforehand. She presses her chin to her chest, drawing a deep breath.

The crowd stares on at her, their attention fixed.

"I was in the byre behind my cottage on the evening of October nineteenth," she says. "I had heard a noise and believed it to be my cow, who has a habit of getting her leg stuck between the wooden slats of the gate. If I don't attend to her, she'll break the slats, or injure herself. And so I went to check on her."

"And what did you see?"

"I saw a man riding up the hill toward Alison's cottage."

"Which man was he?"

"Thomas Paplay."

"The servant of John Stewart?"

"The very same, Father."

My mouth falls open. Why would my mother never mention this to me? Why is she saying this?

Another murmur spreads throughout the court. Father Colville takes a step closer to her, his arms folded thoughtfully. "Please, share what you witnessed," he says.

She hesitates. "Well, I wondered what business this man had with my daughter, or indeed her husband, and so late at night. It was close to midnight, the sky dark, and I could not imagine any business that would draw anyone across the parish so late. And when I saw who he was, I knew he would have had to come all the way from Kirkwall. It was a mystery."

"Did you ask Alison about the meeting she had with Master Paplay?"

"I did not. I wished to see if she might mention it. And she did not."

"Did you see him leave with anything?"

"He had a sack with him, tied with a red ribbon."

The bishops huddle together in fervent discussion.

I want to slide off my chair and sink deep into the earth. I cannot believe that my own mother is saying these words.

Unless she is trying to protect someone.

There is a long silence as Father Colville processes her words. "Madam, there is one thing I cannot quite understand about your testimony. You say you believe your daughter to be such a powerful witch, capable of hexing the Earl of Orkney?"

She nods. "Yes, I do. She is a most powerful witch."

Fervent whispers spiral up from the gallery, and I am dismayed all over again. My own mother, speaking so wickedly against me! How cruel she is, how hateful to stand before the bishops and gallery, declaring me a servant of the Devil Himself. But another thought stirs me—is she speaking out against me to protect Beatrice? They've already harmed Edward, but perhaps she fears for Beatrice, too? And it's as though a candle is lit in the darkness of my mind. *Is she sending me a message:* Beatrice is at risk?

I've come so far now. Surely my mother can hide my daughter away until I am safe?

"But yet, she lost three children," Father Colville says, recalling me to the room. "She tried to use magic to restore them to health, yes?"

"Certain magic only works if the witch is of a certain condition."

"Such as?"

My mother glances at me for the first time. "Well, there are hexes that only work if performed by a witch who is dying." She tilts her head up and clicks her tongue against her teeth. "The hand of fate will not be turned on a whim, my lord. Magic requires sacrifice."

I squeeze my eyes shut, tears streaming down my face. I think of my little ones. The boy I named William, and my two daughters, Eliza and Viola. My own William, who will never hold me in his arms again. My poor Edward, burned to force a confession, and Beatrice, who may yet grow old without either parent there to comfort her.

My mother is wrong. Sometimes, no magic in the world can save a life.

She leaves the room without looking at me. I feel the earth close in, the wind rattling the windows as though it brandishes knives. Inside I am filled with darkness. Regardless of her intentions, my own mother has rejected me, to see to it that I burn.

The whine of metal pulls me from my sleep, and I wake to see a dark shadow by the bars of the cell, the door opening.

It's Mr. Addis. "On your feet," he says gruffly.

"What's happening?" I ask. I did not hear the cathedral bell toll at dawn, nor the four tolls that tell me the trial is to recommence. The window high up on the dungeon wall is blocked by snow, and my breath clings to the icy air like a cloud.

Mr. Addis does not answer, but tugs my chains roughly to hasten my pace. My head feels as though it's filled with wool, but the thought slips into my mind—perhaps I have been freed. Perhaps I am being let go. The townsfolk have raised their voices to the earl, having witnessed the terrible and wrongful torture of my son and the murder of my husband, and I am finally being freed.

William's death has not been in vain.

But then he takes me quickly across the castle courtyard, and I see a light in the tollbooth opposite. No carriage awaits me. Mr. Addis knocks at the door of the tollbooth, and Father Colville opens the door.

My heart lurches. Why are we here? Father Colville's eyes travel to me, and he smiles. As the door widens, the lantern he is holding illuminates several others behind him, two guards I recognize from the courtroom. The last time I saw these men they were hauling my husband from his seat in the gallery, and my stomach turns to see them again.

"What is this?" I ask Father Colville. "Why am I here?"

I hear a noise in a corner. "Mama!"

I give a gasp as Father Colville's lantern reveals Beatrice sitting in a chair by one of the guards, clutching the doll I knitted for her.

"Beatrice!" I say, making to run to her, but Mr. Addis holds the chains at my wrist, preventing me from going to her. My blood running cold, and my mind thrumming with my mother's warning in court today, I turn to Father Colville. "Please, I beg you. Do not burn her little flesh."

He nods. "As you wish."

He answers by nodding at the guard, who takes her small hand in his and slips it in a metal contraption.

She grows panicked. "Mama, please!" she calls. "Make him stop!"

Father Colville stands by, his eyes fixed on mine, as the guard winds the machine with her fingers inside, and I see what they mean to do—they will crush her soft hand, destroying it forever.

"Stop," I gasp.

The guard continues winding the machine. Beatrice gives a shriek like I have never heard, a high-pitched scream of pain.

I cannot bear it. First William, then Edward, and now our precious girl. My resolve is shattered.

"I will speak!" I scream.

I am sorry, William. I failed you.

The guard pauses, glancing at Father Colville. Beatrice's scream vanishes in a deep exhalation of breath, her mouth open wide in terrible pain. Her eyes flutter, and the guard catches her as her knees buckle.

"I will confess," I whisper. Then, a yell, from the bottom of my soul. "I will confess! But you will stop this now."

I had to. Please understand.

I cannot abide her suffering. I cannot abide the crushing of her little hand, the fear on her face, the cruelty, oh, the cruelty against so innocent a being. Should the very gates of hell throw open wide before me I should withstand the flaming pits more than I can the harming of my daughter. I know now what my mother was trying to prevent—and yet despite the hurt she has caused, I am still in this room, still trying to save my daughter from harm.

Father Colville nods at the guards, who release my daughter. She slumps to the floor, shaking in breathless terror. In a moment I am with her, cradling her head in my arms. So long, so long have I craved her in my arms. Her body, all but broken.

And then I see *The Book of Witching*. It is in Father Colville's clasped hands, though he does not see it. The book is there, capturing this moment in text scripted upon its pages, and I wonder how long it will stay.

"I confess," I say.

Beatrice sobs. "Mama, no," she whimpers.

"To which charge?" Father Colville asks me, and I almost want to laugh, to howl in his face. Does it matter? Every single charge against me leads to one destination: the stake.

"All of them," I say in a low growl, a sudden ferocity springing from deep inside as I crouch over Beatrice. "Every single last one of them, if it means you'll not hurt my bairn."

The book vanishes from sight.

CHAPTER FORTY-FOUR

Glasgow
May 2024

CLEM

Two days after Stephanie tells her about Senna, Clem takes Freya to stay with Josie before heading to Elizabeth's flat in the west of the city.

Erin has not resurfaced again in the last two days—whenever she is conscious, she seems more frightened than anything but won't talk about the fire or Senna or Arlo. Most of the time, she seems entranced by the machines that monitor her condition, tracking the lights and the beeps with unblinking eyes.

Elizabeth and Senna live on the fifth floor of a tenement flat in Greenock, and when Clem knocks, Elizabeth opens the door and pulls her into a long hug.

"I'm so glad she's home," Clem says, holding her tight. "This has been a terrible time for you."

"God, it has," Elizabeth says, pulling away and dabbing her eyes. "She's been seen by the doctor this morning. They said she's fine to recover at home. No injuries, just dehydration and shock."

They stand for a moment in the kitchen as Elizabeth pours Clem a cup of tea from a freshly boiled kettle.

"She wasn't hurt by the fire?" Clem asks, and Elizabeth shakes her head.

"No, thank God."

"Did she say what happened?"

"She says they were doing some kind of silly ritual. It was Beltane, which is apparently a pagan festival, and they'd had a few beers and thought it would be hilarious to act out the ritual and light a fire. And Arlo must have got too close, because the next thing she knew he was on fire. She tried to throw water over him but it wouldn't go out. And she panicked and plunged into the sea. She said she swam the whole way to the isle of Gairsay, then hid in an unlocked caravan. The police found her."

Clem takes a sharp breath, imagining it all. Part of her is glad that, so far, Erin doesn't seem to be to blame. It was an accident.

"So no one else was there with them?" Clem asks. "It was just the three of them?"

Elizabeth nods and sighs with relief, covering her face with her hands. "I thought she was dead. That someone had murdered her and buried her corpse. I've aged about thirty years."

"I'm so sorry."

Elizabeth smiles weakly. "Senna's such a shy girl, too. So straitlaced. Not one of these rebellious teens you hear about. Never had any trouble with her. Wouldn't say boo to a goose."

Clem nods, but she gets the impression that Elizabeth doesn't know her daughter very well.

"She's been asking about Erin. She didn't know that Arlo had passed away. She feared it, obviously, given how bad the fire was. But I think it's really tough on her, now she's back here, giving police statements and that sort of thing."

"I think it would do Erin a lot of good to see her," Clem says. "Do you think she'd be up for that?"

Elizabeth looks wary. "How is Erin?"

"She's doing a lot better," Clem lies.

Elizabeth searches her face, as though checking that she's being honest.

"Well, as long as Senna's feeling well enough, it's okay by me."

She takes Clem through the flat to Senna's bedroom, and knocks on the door.

"You're got a visitor, love," she says. "Clem is here."

"Okay," Senna answers weakly, and Elizabeth opens the door.

Clem steps through the threshold into Senna's bedroom, which overlooks the West End. It's tidier than Erin's room, a pile of laundry neatly folded on the chair by the wardrobe and a bookcase arranged by color, the spines of novels and textbooks graduating through the shades of the rainbow. It all looks very unlike Senna, all so *girly*—peach wallpaper, a pile of soft toys on a white armchair. One thing stands out—a textured poster on the wall that mimics the one in Erin's bedroom. Unlike Erin's, which reads PROTECT ME FROM WHAT I WANT, Senna's reads ALL IS FALSE.

Senna is sitting in bed, her gaze distant. Her black hair is messy and her face is drawn, but she looks well. No burns or bruises. Clem finds herself wishing it was Erin sitting in her bedroom like this, no bandages or creams, her body untouched by flame. A flash crosses her mind, a scene of Arlo up in flames, the terrible screams. What Erin would have done to help him.

"Senna," Clem says, taking the chair next to her. "It's *such* a relief to see you safe and at home."

Senna's eyes flick to Clem's. She seems nervous, which is to be expected after what she's gone through, but Clem notices she seems especially wary of Clem, her body language telling her she doesn't want to speak to her. Elizabeth sets a cup of tea on the bedside table.

"Can I ask what happened?" Clem asks gently, turning from Elizabeth to Senna.

"The police have already questioned me," Senna says guardedly.

"Of course," Clem says. "I'm not here to interrogate you. I was worried about you. And I'm so relieved you're okay."

"She got scared when the fire grew out of control," Elizabeth explains, eyeing Senna. "She swam to the next island. Poor thing was exhausted. She found a caravan park and one of them was open. So she was staying there. The mental health nurse thinks she dissociated for quite some time."

"That's horrific," Clem says.

Senna nods. "I can't really remember much," she says in a hoarse voice.

"Erin will be over the moon to know you're all right," Clem says with a smile. "I think she will be so, so glad to see you."

It's a lie—Erin has still not asked about Senna—but her words manage to sound genuine. Elizabeth nods, but at the same time Clem sees Senna tense up.

"I'm still very weak," Senna says haltingly. "Maybe you should come back another time."

"Perhaps when you're feeling better, then," Clem says, unable to hide her disappointment. She glances at Elizabeth. "I know Erin would love to see you."

Senna nods, but she doesn't make eye contact. Something's amiss, Clem thinks. She's clearly been through a lot, but there's another element in the room with them, something she can't quite place. A secret. Senna is holding something back.

Clem makes a motion as though to get up to leave, and she sees Senna's shoulders lower—she's relieved that Clem is going.

The flat's buzzer sounds, and Elizabeth rises to get it. "That must be your father," she tells Senna, glancing at her watch. "He flew in from Jamaica," she tells Clem. "He'd have been here sooner but the flights were canceled due to the strikes." She continues talking as she moves from the bedroom into the hallway, and Clem sees her chance.

She turns to Senna, who is resolutely ignoring her, studying the bed quilt.

"Erin mentioned a book," Clem says.

Senna lifts her eyes to Clem, visibly panicked.

Clem presses her. "She said the book was yours," she lies.

"It wasn't mine," Senna blurts out, but then she visibly closes up.

Outside the room, Clem hears Elizabeth open the door to the flat, greeting the caller. She leans forward.

"Does your mother know about the Triskele?"

Senna shakes her head. Of course Elizabeth knows nothing.

"We need to find that book, Senna," she hisses, holding her gaze. "I know the group you're in is a cult. If you want me not to mention it to your mother, I suggest you tell me where the book is."

Senna swallows, hard, and shakes her head. Then she flicks her eyes up at her mother. Clem turns to see Elizabeth coming back into the room, followed by Senna's father. Her face falls—she can see something has changed while she has been gone. The atmosphere has become charged.

"Everything okay?" she asks Senna, who nods briskly.

"Fine," she says.

"Perhaps I can come again tomorrow," Clem asks Elizabeth. "I can have Quinn set up a video call with Erin so you two can chat."

"Oh, that would be lovely," Elizabeth says, but Senna visibly squirms.

"Sure," she says. "Though maybe . . ."

"Great," Clem says, cutting her off before she has a chance to renege.

"Can I come and see her?" Senna calls after her. "At the hospital?"

Clem looks to Elizabeth, who looks cautious. "Maybe tomorrow," she says. "You need to rest today, love."

"I can pick you up in the morning, if you like?" Clem offers. "I'll bring Freya."

Senna seems reluctant. "Okay," she says finally.

Clem smiles at Elizabeth. "Great. I'll see you then."

CHAPTER FORTY-FIVE

Kirkwall, Orkney
December 1594

ALISON

The sun has barely risen today, as though it cannot bring itself to bear witness to what I am about to do. If I confess, Orkney will fall. The king will be persuaded by Earl Patrick that the same witchery that almost claimed his life in the North Sea also exists here and must be eradicated. And Earl Patrick will use this as license to increase his tyranny on our land.

But what choice do I have?

"Your Graces," Father Colville calls from the court. "The witch informed me last night that she wishes to confess at last." He turns to me, throwing me a look that lies somewhere between scorn and pity.

"Oh?" Bishop Sinclair says, raising himself slightly on the mezzanine. "Her conscience has been pricked?"

"It has, Your Grace. I am only saddened that she allowed the passing of her husband and the injury of her son before we reached this arrangement."

The bishops murmur in agreement, and I squeeze my eyes shut. *Do not answer it, Alison. Do not tell the truth.*

"As the witch is dull of intellect and has the voice of a mouse," Father Colville says, "I will repeat her confession for the benefit of the scribe and the court."

He throws a meaningful look at David, who prepares his parchment and quill to transcribe my words.

I swallow hard, trying to recall the words that I prepared in my mind last night. The words that will bring this all to an end and spare my children's lives.

"Your Graces," I begin. It is difficult to speak. My nose is badly swollen, and my teeth are still loose from when I tried to protect Edward, and the guard knocked me to the floor. I use my tongue to hold them in place as I speak, and close my eyes.

"I wish to share my confession . . ."

Father Colville repeats this in a loud, clear voice, his eyes on David as he writes it down. He emphasizes the word *confession*.

". . . that I am indeed a witch," I say. A small murmur rises from the gallery. I keep my eyes on the floor as Father Colville repeats it, unable to conceal the tone of satisfaction in his voice.

"I am as w . . . wicked as Father Colville has suggested," I say, tripping over my words. "I . . . I plotted with Thomas Paplay to k . . . kill the earl. I would have killed many more if Father Colville had not caught me. My desires . . ." I falter, my mouth so dry that I find my voice diminishing with each word. "My desires are black as coal. I am a vengeful spirit, a servant of darkness. I know that God has shielded His face from mine forever."

The truth of this severs my heart. I feel it deeply, the fear that I am forever separated from everyone I love. That I will not see heaven.

"Madam Alison Balfour," Father Colville says gravely. "You are hereby charged with the practice of witchcraft and an attempt on the life of the earl."

I stare ahead, lest I give in to the urge to tell him that everything I said was a lie. I expect the courtroom to erupt into a frenzy, for the name-calling and whispers to begin. But it is silent as a grave. Father Colville sweeps his eyes over the crowd, and I sense he is disappointed. At last, he turns to me, fixing his eyes on me a minute longer.

"May God have mercy on your soul," he says.

CHAPTER FORTY-SIX

Glasgow
May 2024

CLEM

Clem is driving to the hospital with Elizabeth and Senna. They are going to see Erin, and Clem is clinging to the hope that a visit from Senna will coax Erin back to the surface.

Senna looks more rested than she did in her home yesterday, and her eye contact with Clem is better, too. She and Elizabeth gown up and follow Clem into the room.

Erin is awake, her eyes turned to the window.

"Erin?"

Clem watches as Senna takes in the sight of her friend with horror, her face falling. Elizabeth nudges her, and she reins in her shock.

"Hi, Erin," Elizabeth says softly. "Are you feeling any better today?"

Erin stares blankly. But then her eyes turn to Senna.

"You see Senna?" Clem asks her.

"Who?"

"Oh God," Senna says, breaking into tears. "I'm so, so sorry I left you. I freaked out. Honestly, I didn't even know what I was doing. I just ran."

"It's you," Erin says, her face changing, "You know about the fire. You and Erin."

"Erin?" Senna says, confused. She looks to Elizabeth, then Clem, who steps forward.

"Erin, the fire is over, love," she says gently. "This is Senna. She's safe, and she's here to see you . . ."

"You have to stop it," Erin says angrily.

"I'm sorry," Senna whimpers. "I didn't mean to leave you like that. I never would have. And Arlo . . ."

"I'm going to give you one last chance," Erin says. "If you don't stop the burning, I'm going to hurt Erin."

"Stop what?" Senna asks. She turns to her mother. "What is she talking about? Why is she like this?"

Erin opens her mouth wide and gives an earsplitting scream, before lifting her left arm and bringing it down, hard, on the metal side bar of the bed. With another hellish scream, she brings it down again and again, until Senna and Clem lunge at her, grabbing her arms and holding her down while calling for help.

"Erin, *stop!*" Clem shouts. Her eyes fall on the arm Erin pounded against the metal bar, writhing under Senna's desperate grip. Blood begins to bloom through the bandages.

"I'll get the nurse," Elizabeth says.

As the nurse tends to Erin, Senna bursts out of the room and races down the hospital corridor, past Quinn, who has returned from the café downstairs. Clem follows, pulling off her protective clothing.

"Senna!" she calls. "Hold on a minute."

She catches up with her as Senna reaches the end of the corridor.

"Stay *away* from me," Senna snarls.

"Stop lying, and I'll stay as far as you like," Clem says.

Senna hesitates, catching her breath. "What the fuck was that?" she gasps. "What's wrong with her?"

"You tell me," Clem says in a low voice. "What happened in Orkney to make her say these things?"

Senna's aggression shifts a gear. "I don't know," she says, bewildered.

"You're lying," Clem says, leaning into Senna's face. She knows what she risks by acting so forcefully with her, that she's a grown woman intimidating a teenager, but she hasn't got time for this bullshit. "Where's the book, Senna? I know you know."

It's a bluff, but it works—Senna's eyes move nervously to hers, and Clem realizes she knows after all.

"I promised her on my life I wouldn't tell anyone," she says, glancing at her mother and Quinn over Clem's shoulder.

"Whatever promises you made, forget them, okay? Erin is seriously ill and she needs you to be honest."

Clem looks behind her and sees Elizabeth, Quinn, and Bee heading toward them. "We need to speak in private," she tells Senna, and to her relief Senna nods.

"I need a minute," Senna tells her mother.

Clem looks at Quinn. "You'll look after Erin for us?" She nods to Senna and hopes that Quinn understands what she's doing. Quinn frowns but then gives her a swift nod. He takes Elizabeth by the elbow and they follow Bee back toward Erin's room, where nurses are working on Erin's arms.

Clem and Senna take the lift downstairs. They don't speak until they're outside, in Clem's car.

As soon as the passenger door closes, Senna breaks down into huge gulping sobs. Clem senses this is the first time she has cried since the night of the fire. She has held it in all this time.

"Senna," she says gently, "I know this has all been very hard on you. But please . . . you must see how urgent this is. Erin is really, really ill, and the police think she killed Arlo."

Senna gulps as she seems to take that in.

"Can we take a drive?" Senna says, looking nervously at hospital visitors crossing the car park.

"Sure," Clem says. "Where do you want to go?"

"I don't care," Senna says. "Actually, McDonald's."

Clem starts the engine and types "McDonald's" into Google Maps on her phone.

"I know about the Triskele," Clem says. "Or the fake Triskele, rather."

"Fake?"

"The cult you belong to isn't the real Triskele."

There's a long silence as Senna takes it in. "I don't believe that."

"You need to tell me if that guy—the Brother—ever laid a finger on Erin."

Senna shakes her head. "No. He never did."

"You sure?"

"Yes, but . . ."

Clem's heart begins to pound. "But what?"

Senna covers her face with her hands for a moment. "I can't believe I'm telling you this," she says.

"Go on. I can take it."

"Do you know how Erin and Arlo first met?"

"Erin said they met online."

"They met at a Triskele weekender. Erin got a scholarship . . ."

"What scholarship?"

"It basically means she was trained by the elders of the group about life and magic and things."

Clem rolls her eyes. Such bullshit. "Okay. And then what?"

"The graduation ceremony is called Crossing the Boundary. Basically, when Erin and Arlo met, they had to have sex. As part of the ritual."

Clem has to grip the steering wheel, as though she might veer off road at this information. Senna all but whispers it, and the car feels as though the doors and roof and windscreen have pulled closer together, squeezing the inhabitants.

"Were you there?" she asks Senna, who doesn't answer. "I'll take that as a yes."

They pull into the McDonald's drive-through, which feels disorienting in its banality. But the shift in the journey—the drive-through intercom reminding them of why they're here—gives Clem time to think. She has questions of her own, questions that hurtle through her mind like bullets. Was Erin forced? Why did she go through with it? Was it filmed? The timing of it hits her. Was this how Freya was conceived?

"She wasn't forced," Senna says once Clem has paid the cashier and passed her the food. "She joined the Triskele because it made her happy."

Clem reads the tone of Senna's voice. "You were the one who got her to join," she says, thinking of the timing. "Aren't you?"

"I never forced her. And anyway, she left." Her tone shifts again, and she sounds disappointed.

Clem processes that. "And you're still involved?"

"Yes, I'm involved."

"Then why did Erin have the book?"

"Not long after Erin got pregnant, the Brother gave her this old book and asked her to look after it. But as time went on, she said it was driving her mad. She said it made her think about killing people."

Clem thinks of the night she woke up to find Erin standing next to her bed, clutching the pair of scissors. How she'd lied when she said she was sleepwalking.

"She tried to give the book back," Senna says, haltingly. "But the Brother had killed himself. Really awful. Erin thought the book made him do it. No one would take it, so she threw it in Loch Lomond. And it came back."

"Came back?"

"I watched her do it. She literally threw it into the water and we watched it go under. And then, when we got back to your flat it was sitting on her bed." Senna shudders. "Every time she threw it away or chucked it in a manhole or tried to shed it, it would reappear." She looks at Clem. "I know what you're thinking, I do. But honestly, I saw it happen. I hadn't believed her. How can a *book* just reappear? And it didn't even look like anything special. Just this old, strange book. But nothing, and I mean *nothing*, would get rid of it."

They pull up in the hospital car park. Clem presses her face into her hands.

"So what was the ritual in Orkney about?" she asks. "On Fynhallow. What really happened?"

"Erin contacted someone," Senna says. "She tried to speak to people in the Triskele but nobody knew anything about the book. She finally found this bookseller who knew about the Triskele. He knew about the book."

"Paul Renney," Clem says, and Senna nods.

"Yeah, the antiquarian. He said the book was probably *The Book of Witching*. He told Erin that the book was cursed, and the only way to break the curse was a spell. It involved a fire ritual."

"Arlo's hands have to be bound," Clem mutters.

"Right," Senna says. "He was to perform a role. The Green Man. And it had to be on Beltane. Erin and Arlo were counting down the days." She falls silent, recalling that terrible night. "It all went wrong. I don't know what happened but it did."

"And where's the book now?" Clem asks.

Senna bites her lip. "I put it in the fire on Fynhallow," she says, growing upset. "I saw Arlo and Erin were burning and there was nothing I could do but put the book in the flames. They'd said the words of the spell. I watched it burn, and then I ran for my life. But it came back. It followed me."

"Where, Senna?"

Senna's voice drops to a whisper. "It's in my bedroom."

CHAPTER FORTY-SEVEN

Kirkwall, Orkney
December 1594

ALISON

"We have some concern about the burning of the witch's body here in Kirkwall," Bishop Sinclair proclaims after Father Colville has passed my sentence. "This has been raised by the earl, who notes that oftentimes the wind draws leaves into his courtyard. He does not wish the ashes of the woman's body to end up drifting upon his dwelling place. Therefore, we propose the witch to be taken to her own island of Gunn for the execution."

"Very well, Your Graces," Father Colville says with a deep bow. "We will see to it that her execution is implemented on the morrow at the Isle of Gunn."

The darkness of this small, dank room feels deeper than ever tonight. I am numb, through and through. I have been sentenced to death but it does not feel real.

I think of *The Book of Witching*. How one becomes a Carrier not by signing their name upon its pages, but by screaming into its void. The howl of pain. I wish to scream, but I cannot. I think of

Edward, and Beatrice. It astonishes me how so much relief is brought to me by the fact that they did not meet the same end as William. They are doubtless alone. I fear that my mother has abandoned them, as she has abandoned me. They must be terrified. They are both so young, and have only each other.

"Mother?"

I look up, recognizing the voice before I see the face.

"Edward?"

I squint into the gloom, making out a figure beyond the bars. He steps closer.

"Just a second," Mr. Addis says, putting a hand on Edward's shoulder. He wants payment. I offer him my coif, but he shakes his head. "I don't need no women's clothing."

His wooden teeth click as he talks. Two teeth at the front of my mouth are loose from when the guard tore me away from Edward in the courtroom, and so I remove them from my mouth, holding the cloth of my kirtle to my gums to stop the bleeding. He takes them, beaming brightly.

"Take all the time you need," he says, shoving Edward forward.

I rush to him, taking his hand when he slips it through the bars.

"My son! Are you well?"

He nods, though still I look him over, checking his injuries. He wears a clean tunic and waistcoat, his cap pulled low over his eyes. I notice that he grimaces when my hand brushes across his chest from where he was burned.

"Mother, I need to tell you something," he says. My heart drops.

"What has happened? Is it Beatrice?"

He shakes his head, and I feel weak with relief.

"Beatrice is well," he says. "Grandmother is caring for her at the cottage."

"Grandmother?" I feel panicked—my mother betrayed my children when she betrayed me. "She is not to be trusted, Edward."

"Not to be trusted?" he says. "She was protecting me, Mother."

"What?"

He begins to cry. I reach out and take his hand in mine, clasping it tight.

"Edward, what is wrong?"

"I am Nyx."

"What?"

"The charm for John Stewart. I made it. And I gave it to Thomas Paplay."

He is weeping, his voice shaken with pain. I glance quickly at Mr. Addis along the corridor, in case Edward's words reach him. He is busy cleaning his new teeth, trying to fit them into his wooden mouth brace.

"Why do you say such things?" I ask Edward.

"I saw something," he says. "In *The Book of Witching*. It happened the night that Grandmother initiated Beatrice and me into the Triskele."

"What did you see?" I ask, studying his face. A memory flashes in my mind of the day the same book appeared here in the dungeon, almost where I sit now. The woman tending her daughter in bed.

"In its pages, I saw a . . ." He falters. "I don't know what to call it. It was like looking through a window. As real as though it was happening in front of my very eyes."

"Tell me."

"I saw you speak with Thomas Paplay and John Stewart in the gardens of the cathedral," he says. "And when you left, I approached them to see if I could help. Thomas Paplay recognized me, and he asked me if I knew how to make a charm. He told me it was to cause death." He stops, his eyes wide, as though seeing something deeply profound. "I knew then that *this* was the reason I had seen you being burned at the stake. The earl needed to die in order to save you."

Edward tells me he made the charm and placed it outside our cottage as promised, watching as Thomas collected it. He had hexed it for Earl Patrick. He had intended to kill him, so that I would be spared the fate he had witnessed in the pages of the book.

"That is why I made the charm. I knew the rebels wanted the earl gone, because he has robbed our lands and killed the people of Orkney. And I thought that, if he died, the burning I witnessed in the book would not happen. You would be saved." His voice is stolen by gulping sobs. "But... But... I think I only made it worse."

I try my best to soothe him, and after a moment he calms.

"You are not responsible for my imprisonment," I tell him firmly. "That is entirely in the hands of wicked men. Not you."

He shakes his head in disagreement. "I have learned what the book can do, Mother. I have learned soul-slipping."

His words rattle me, and I think back to what I learned when I was a child of his age, how my mother said that Carriers could slip for a time inside the bodies of animals, such as ravens and hares.

"You have soul-slipped?" I ask him softly.

"I became drawn to this idea," he says, lowering his voice. "And when you were arrested, I thought that soul-slipping inside a raven would allow me to come and save you." He grows upset again, and I reach for his hand. "But the spell went wrong. I found myself not inside the body of an animal, but inside a girl."

"A girl?" I say, disbelieving. "How?"

"I was in an evil realm," he says with a whisper. "The people there were evil spirits, and so I told them I was Nyx, so they'd know that if they continued with the burning I would take revenge..."

He begins to weep again. "I was so confused. I didn't know what had happened. I did the spell again and again, each time finding myself in the body of the girl. And she was in pain, but I endured it . . . They gave me potions and I thought I might die." He lifts his eyes to me. "And I could not find you there. I was so lost, Mother. And now they are to take you to be burned at the stake, just like the book showed me. I have failed you."

I speak gentle words to him, my thoughts flinging in many directions because of the things he has told me. I think of my mother and Solveig, counseling with him. And the woman tending to the girl in the strange white bed. I did not recognize either of them. But there is always a reason for the book doing what it does. It is not by accident that Edward and I both saw what we saw.

Perhaps the woman is a Carrier, or the girl. Perhaps the book wishes her to be so.

But why show *me* this, when I have left the Triskele?

As I am wrestling with the vision of the mysterious mother and daughter, I think of my own mother, and her betrayal of me in the courtroom. She did so to protect Edward. She knew that was what I would want. If he was found to be the one who made the wax effigy, with the name "Nyx" scored through, they would exile him, or burn him at the stake. And she knew I would want to protect him from that fate.

Or perhaps, she knows that Edward must continue to be a Carrier. Or Beatrice.

"I have seen things," he says. "Through the eyes of the girl."

A shiver crawls up my spine. "What things?"

"I know she is badly injured, her body spoiled by fire. She is in a white room in a metal bed, the floor and walls wrought of whitest stone, and she is surrounded by strange lights and machines."

"Machines?"

"I cannot explain them, Mother. It is a wicked place. But I know the fire was caused by a spell she cast to be rid of the book. It backfired and killed a boy."

An image is unfurling in my mind. The picture the book showed me when it appeared on the floor of my cell. Of the woman attending to a girl in the bed. Is what Edward has seen?

"There may yet be a way that you can help," I tell him. "You and I know that David Moncrief is on my side. I believe that, if we can get David to testify that John asked me for the charm, that *he* is the one behind this plot, I may yet be set free."

He nods. "You want me to approach him?"

"Yes. Once it is done, you and Beatrice must leave Orkney. As soon as you can. If they find you, they will kill you."

"You will follow?"

"Of course." I smile, trying to hide the lie in my words. I sense he knows I lie, that it is the last time I will ever hold my son.

"I love you," I tell him, pressing my lips to his hand. "Now go."

CHAPTER FORTY-EIGHT

Orkney
May 2024

CLEM

Clem drives to Senna's house in the west side of Glasgow. Elizabeth is still at the hospital, but Senna lets herself in with her key. Clem follows her into her bedroom, holding her breath as Senna opens the door to her wardrobe and lifts out a shoebox.

"I didn't know what else to do with it," she says. "I mean, I thought it had been burned, but when I was hiding in the caravan park, I woke up one morning and it was there, on the end of my bed. I was terrified."

"So you brought it home?"

Senna nods, opening the box. "I didn't know what else to do with it, and it freaked me out too much to think I'd got rid of it and then have it appear again out of the blue."

She lifts out the black cloth inside the box, then stares down. "Oh no."

"What's wrong?"

Senna looks up, frantic. "It's gone. I swear I had it. I brought it home and I put it in here."

She reaches inside the wardrobe, removing clothes and shoes, searching for it. She claps her hands to her face, growing tearful. "Where is it?"

"You're sure you put it in here?"

"Swear to God, I did." Senna pulls out her phone and dials. "Hi, Mum," she says. "Have you been in my wardrobe at all?"

Clem can hear Elizabeth on the other end of the line, asking where Senna has got to. Exasperated, she hangs up and begins searching the rest of her room, under the bed, in her chest of drawers. She begins to cry. "Where is it?" she says with a sob. "Where the fuck is it?"

Clem pulls her into a tight embrace, calming her. "We'll find it," she says. "I promise."

When Clem returns to the hospital, she's shocked to discover Erin is in surgery. The injuries she'd inflicted on herself have opened some of the burn sites, and surgeons are battling to prevent the delicate wounds in her hands from becoming infected.

Bee takes Quinn and Clem into the family room and holds the door open for Dr. Miller, who has spoken to the surgeons involved in Erin's operation.

"How is she?" Erin asks.

"We've managed to perform an emergency skin graft on her right hand," Dr. Miller says. "But she's broken a bone at the knuckle and fractured three of the metacarpals there."

"What does that mean?" Quinn asks.

"It means there's good news and bad news. Which do you want first?"

"Good," Quinn says, at the same time as Clem says, "Bad."

"I'll start with the bad, which explains the good," Dr. Miller says. "She's essentially pulped her hand. We're trying to save her thumbs at the minute, but the other four digits of her right hand are lost."

Clem covers her face in her hands and tries not to cry. "And the good news?" she whispers.

"As long as we hold on to the thumbs, she can retain use of her hand with a prosthesis. It really is good news, I promise you. Without the thumbs a lot of movement is completely gone and it involves quite complex prosthetics, which, to be frank, a lot of young people can't get along with. But with her thumb, I have confidence that we can make this something she can manage."

Clem allows herself to feel glad, and relieved, but she is far from it.

"There is one more thing," Dr. Miller says. "Erin's emotional welfare. It's clear that there are some complex issues here. We simply can't afford anything like this to happen again." He eyes them carefully.

"Go on," Quinn says.

"We propose to restrain her, very carefully. It's not an ideal scenario but the alternative isn't ideal, either."

Clem feels faint, the room suddenly closing in. "What's the alternative?"

Dr. Miller pushes his glasses up his nose and clears his throat, hesitating. "We place her back under sedation. Not a coma, but close to it."

The room is silent. Quinn must feel as torn as she is, as though each step forward sends them ten steps back.

"How long?" Quinn asks.

"A week, in the first instance," Dr. Miller says.

Quinn contemplates that. "What if she's as … out of sorts when she wakes as she is now?"

Dr. Miller sighs. "I think psychiatric intervention will be needed," he says. "I don't really feel I can give a full picture of that outcome. But let's hope we don't need it."

CHAPTER FORTY-NINE

Fynhallow, Orkney
December 1594

ALISON

Mr. Addis comes to fetch me from the dungeon, and I wrap my hands around the bars and pull myself to my feet before he can tug the chains or force me. If I am to die, I will face the flames without duress. For so long this has been my greatest fear, leaving my children alone. And now they have neither their father nor their mother to look after them, and yet I will not let them believe I fear it.

"Come on then," Mr. Addis says. I look him over, wondering if he has no remorse, or conscience. I sense he is eager for the stake, that perhaps he has helped to build it, relishing the death that is to come there.

Father Colville is waiting in the atrium, his hands clasped and his head turned to the light.

"Madam," he says mildly. "The carriage awaits us."

It is a relief to step outside the castle into the December sunlight, strong and portentous. A crowd has gathered to watch me, the usual call of the chapel bell and the voices in the marketplace stilled as they stare, rows of them. Father Colville climbs up beside the driver while Mr. Addis locks me inside the carriage.

"Drive through the streets," I hear Father Colville say, and I know he wishes to make a show of me to the people of Kirkwall, letting them see that the evil that has lived among them is now to be wiped out, burned this day at the stake.

A loud cry of jeers rises up and the carriage is pummeled with stones. None of the stones reach me, though several find their way through the bars of the carriage door, landing at my feet. After a while, I do not hear the clanging of the stones against the bars or the cry of *witch!*, for my mind has swept me off again to other places, other times in my memory, rendering them with bright sounds and sharp colors, as though I have traveled there—my marriage ceremony in the small chapel to the east of Gunn. A bright June morning, as crisp and golden as today. How handsome William looked, his face unmarked by care, in the cloak he wore at the trial. I had thought at the time that he wore the cloak because it was his finest garment, because he wished to look smart, but now I think he wore it for one reason only: to remind me of our wedding day.

A crowd meets us at the shore of Fynhallow. Bishop Sinclair, Bishop Vance, Father Colville, David, Mr. Addis, John Stewart, and Earl Patrick. Agnes is there, though she won't meet my eye. Elspeth, Angus—families who have lived with us on Gunn since I was a girl. They are somber. No name-calling or throwing of stones, but they watch silently as I am led along the cliff.

My mother is not here, nor is Beatrice or Edward. Perhaps he has done as I asked and left the islands, heading to Edinburgh.

And there is the stake, and the hooded executioner, holding a belt. The sight of it makes my heart lurch, all the calm I had before wearing thin at this stark reminder of what is to happen.

I must not fear. I must *not*.

The crowd follows us, a gathering of fifty. I see David among them, and my heart lifts.

In my pocket, I carry the piece of slate with the Triskele symbol. It is a message without words, a symbol, just like Beatrice drew on the shell to me. I have a plan: to pass on the slate to David Moncrief. He is the only one who could interpret the message. And he is perhaps the only one who can do what the message asks.

I wait until I am near enough until I drop it close to his feet. My heart is in my mouth. What if someone sees that I have deliberately passed him a message? What if David does not see it?

When I reach the executioner, I glance back at David, who is bending now, lifting the slate. I have drawn a sun with an arrow facing west, and above is a crown. It means, deliver the truth to the king, but as I see the look of puzzlement on his face my stomach drops. Perhaps I have mistaken his loyalties.

In which case, all is lost. Orkney will fall, and our deaths will be for nothing.

CHAPTER FIFTY

Glasgow
May 2024

CLEM

The phone on Clem's lap starts to buzz. She ignores it until she spots the word "Josie" on the screen. Freya, she thinks, her skin turning cold. Something has happened to Freya.

"Hiya," Josie says when she answers. "Just a quick one—what's with this old book? Is it a toy?"

"What book?"

"This old book she's playing with. She pulled it out of her changing bag. Did you put it in there by accident?"

Clem's mouth falls open. "Describe it to me."

"Well, it's blank, for a start. Just these old black pages. Looks like it belongs in a museum. Weirdest toy I've ever seen!"

She drives to Josie's, where Freya is playing happily with Sam, her mouth smeared with tomato sauce and her hands sticky.

"This little madam has only eaten half her dinner so she might be hungry later," Josie says, stuffing the changing bag with Freya's bottles and bibs. "And we had a bit of a nappy explosion so she's wearing Sam's clothes."

Clem looks Freya over and sees she's wearing a T-shirt with a dinosaur print and denim dungarees.

"You mentioned a book?" she asks Josie, trying to sound casual.

"Yeah, I thought it was odd that you put it in her changing bag. Definitely not mine. And she was playing with it."

Clem's heart lurches. She watches, holding her composure, as Josie fetches an old book covered in bark from a sideboard lined with framed family photographs.

"Look," Josie says, surveying the cover made of bark with revulsion. "It's even got things *growing* out of it."

She reaches down with finger and thumb to a small green shoot poking out of one of the folds, plucking it out. "Moss and everything. Is it yours?"

Clem nods, mouth dry. "Yes. Yes, it is."

"Well, let me know if you need me to look after her tomorrow. I'm taking Sam to soft-play."

"Thanks."

She hugs Josie, puts Freya in her car seat.

Then she pulls out her phone and finds the driving route for Orkney. Seven hours. If she leaves now, she can be there by midnight.

CHAPTER FIFTY-ONE

Glasgow
May 2024

CLEM

Clem takes the A9 from Glasgow toward Inverness, the book in the changing bag on the passenger seat beside her. Freya was extra clingy, and Clem has been missing her. After an hour of babbling, she falls asleep in her car seat. Quinn rings six times, eventually leaving her a voicemail that Clem resolves not to play until she parks up at the byre.

She has voices in her head, shouting at her the whole way to Thurso.

The police will arrest you at the ferry terminal.

What if Erin's infection gets worse?

You've brought Freya to deliver an evil book to violent pagans. What are you thinking?

She has no idea if she can even trust the Triskele.

She is utterly convinced that the book will disappear of its own volition by the time she gets to Orkney, vanishing once more into thin air as it did in the hospital bathroom. But it's there when she stops for petrol in Dingwall, when she boards the ferry at Thurso, and when she stops to buy food for Freya in Stromness. And then, as the moon appears in the sky, she pulls into the same field that she and Quinn fled just four nights ago. She can still see the tire marks running through the grass from where Quinn veered wildly toward the exit.

As she parks up, she feels nervous. She doesn't have Edina's phone number, just this knowledge of the byre—the Triskele's meeting place.

She takes Freya out of the car seat and tucks the book under her arm, trying to swallow back the tight knot of fear in her throat. The voices of panic in her head are louder now, but when she hesitates, Erin's shouts return to her mind, the terrible scene of her bashing her hand again and again on the metal bar, until it bled. Erin is under sedation, recovering from surgery, she reminds herself, and if she doesn't stop this bizarre behavior, God only knows where she'll end up.

If she hasn't already managed to infect her wounds.

But as she approaches the byre, she sees two figures moving through the woods behind her. Freya begins to cry, and she holds her tighter. The figures are silhouetted, but the way they move toward her—stealthily, one of them holding something—sends shivers down her spine. She glances nervously at the car parked down the bank.

She's come too far to make a run for it.

CHAPTER FIFTY-TWO

Fynhallow, Orkney
December 1594

ALISON

David lifts his eyes to mine. He touches his chin. With relief, I see that he understands my meaning, even as Mr. Addis pushes me backward against the stake and tethers me there.

The executioner is hooded, his face covered and two brown eyes peering through the holes. He carries a belt of leather. Mr. Addis sets twigs around the base of the pyre. I am to be strangled, my body burned. There will be no burial, no grave. I feel my knees quake, but force them to be still. I keep my eyes on the sea before me. I think of William.

Wait for me.

The executioner is so close that I can smell him: earth, leather, wood. "Father Colville," David calls out, and all heads turn to him.

"It is customary for the accused to speak before execution. The Privy Council requires a record of her confession."

John Stewart steps forward. "We have no need for such a thing here in Orkney."

"Beg pardon, my lord, but the Privy Council may request it,"

David says. "Never before has a witch been executed on these isles. Doubtless the king will wish to commend us all for our efforts in ridding the land of witchcraft."

"Let her speak her final words," Earl Patrick says, overruling his brother.

"Speak ye, Madam Balfour," Father Colville shouts then. "And let God be praised that your wickedness ends this day."

I look over the group of witnesses here on the hill. Bishop Sinclair, Bishop Vance, Father Colville, David, Mr. Addis, John Stewart, and Earl Patrick.

On the banks overlooking the beach are groups of villagers, straining to see.

David stands upwind, his parchment and quill ready.

"I renounce my confession," I say loudly. "I am no witch. I am no murderer. My confession was a lie, offered only because my daughter, all of six years of age, was to be tortured in front of me. And before her, my son was tortured, and my husband, who died from his injuries. All of these things have been done to force me to confess to a crime of which I am not guilty. I know I will be killed today, but before God and all who stand before me I declare that I am innocent!"

I scream out the words, my voice louder than it has ever been, the wind carrying it to the people far on the bay. John Stewart strides toward me, his eyes blazing. I see his hand is in a fist, ready to strike me.

"I curse you," I hiss at him. "I curse you that you will *never* claim the earldom. Your brother is the last earl to breathe on the land of Orkney."

John falters, his eyes boring into me.

"Mr. Addis," he says in a loud voice. "Burn this witch."

Mr. Addis begins to light the kindling, impatient, and there is a moment of tension between him and the executioner, who does not wish his shirt to catch fire when he strangles me.

I turn my head, fixing my eyes on Father Colville. I want to tell him that this is not the end. Does he not realize this? That his own end will yet come? That he will have to explain this before God?

This short life is wasted only when one does not use it for good. Even the moon waxes and wanes. Even the earth, immeasurable in her wisdom and brimming with secrets, is yet turning.

In my hand, I hold Beatrice's shell, which I kept in my mouth as I was removed from the dungeon. I recalled my mother's words during the trial—*Surely she has charmed shells and pebbles on her person*, and when Edward came to see me, I realized that she was telling me that she had charmed Beatrice's shell. I was to use it for a hex. The other thing she told me is there in my ears, too: *There are hexes that only work if performed by a witch who is dying.*

I may not be a Carrier, but I am still Triskele. And I know how to hex. And this hex is especially powerful.

Digging a ragged nail deep into the flesh of my palm, I blot blood across the shell before dropping it into the flames by my feet. Then I whisper the spell.

By the will of blood and sea
A second Yule you shall not see.

The smile slides from Father Colville's face as he sees the flame darken for a moment, accepting the gift. I do this for Orkney. If he is not stopped, these hills will be alive with stakes, innocent men and women in the flames. The damage may yet be done.

He strides forward to see what I have thrown in the fire. But the hex is done, and he cannot undo it. He will not live more than two years hence.

The cool leather belt is slipped around my neck.

A flash of black feathers amidst the swirling smoke.

William. William.

CHAPTER FIFTY-THREE

Six months ago

ERIN

"I'm thinking of leaving the Triskele," Erin says.

"What?"

Arlo turns over in bed and looks at her. Their daughter, Freya, is between them, just nine months old. He has one of her little feet in his hands and is staring down at it.

"I don't know," she says. "I just don't feel the same about it. I liked it at first but . . ." She tails off, trying to gauge his own feelings.

"It feels less fun," he says. "Doesn't it?"

"Yeah. More and more like being told off."

The previous weekend, they'd asked Clem to babysit while they went to the meeting in the Trossachs. The Brother asked Erin to hold an art workshop. She tried to explain that Freya was still feeding all night, that she still felt ragged, but he got arsey with her. Started bringing up the scholarship and how she was indebted to him, how the money she paid in each month didn't even cover the basics. She wanted to scream at him. She was handing her maternity pay over to this man, who didn't work, but somehow drove a Land Rover. She sensed the only reason he asked her to give the art workshop was to ensure she felt part of something. She had missed the last nine meetings because of the baby and he was pissed off about it.

That weekend, when she saw a thin, balding man walking across the grass, she didn't recognize him until he spoke. It was the Brother. She'd not seen him for months, and in that time he'd shaved off his long hair and beard and lost a ton of weight. His eyes were no longer soft and kind, and he looked haunted, dark circles beneath his eyes. She wondered if he had a terrible illness.

He spent two hours shouting at the whole clan, telling them they were blind, they were stupid, they were going to be punished for how lazy they were. And then she stood at a table under a shoddy gazebo teaching new recruits how to make a poster while her breasts filled with milk and her body ached. Her own poster said PROTECT ME FROM WHAT I WANT, and she stared at it, realizing that she was telling herself something.

"I'll leave, too," Arlo says.

"You don't have to do that because of me."

"Actually, I've wanted to leave since you got back in touch," he says. "Since you told me that Freya's definitely mine."

"Rubbish," she says, though her heart swells at his words.

"It's not rubbish," he says with a smile. "I only stayed because I thought you wanted to."

"It is a cult," she says then, and finds she's relieved to say this out loud. "Senna made this big deal about how it *wasn't* a cult when I first went along. But it is. They control everything we do."

She holds his eye, feeling flooded with relief. How glad she is that he feels the same. "I wanted to be part of something," she says quietly. "I think I wanted a family. But the Triskele wasn't it."

Arlo and Freya were.

"I want to give back the book," she says, kissing Freya's head. "It's creeping me out."

She thinks back to when she met the Brother at the derelict castle in the Trossachs and he convinced her to keep the baby.

The least you can do is take this thing out of my fucking hands.

She took it, albeit reluctantly, and tucked it under her bed. But since then she has felt haunted. Terrible whisperings in her head, in her bones, in her heart. And a few months ago, she woke up to find herself standing over her mother, scissors in her hand, imagining the thrust of them into the soft flesh between her jaw.

She has to get rid of the book.

Later that morning, while Arlo takes Freya in the stroller to the corner shop, she messages the Brother via WhatsApp. He doesn't reply. Impatient, she messages the Triskele group chat, which was now at over two hundred members.

Erin: Hey @TheBrother, I need to see you asap.

Rodge: Not possible. Can I help you?

Erin: Why isn't it possible?

Lois: 😭 😭 😭

SJ_Clarke: 😿

Roadman_2005: OMG soooo sad

Her phone starts to vibrate with messages and emojis that she doesn't understand from various members of the Triskele. A few moments of confusion before Rodge videocalls her. She can see su-permarket shelves behind him, a flash of a yellow vest. He's at work.

"The Brother is dead," he says.

"What?" She can't believe it, both literally and emotionally.

"Suicide. Monday night."

"Oh my God."

"I'll message you about the next weekender. There's going to be a shift in how the group works."

A colleague interrupts him, and he tells Erin he has to go.

"Wait, Rodge!"

"What? I'm at work."

"I want to give the book back!"

He hangs up. She drops the phone and holds her head in her hands. The Brother killed himself. What the actual fuck? She stands for a moment, staring at a spot on her bedroom wall, feeling the ground beneath her move a little, the air ionizing with the im-possibility of this news. Is it real? She doesn't know what to do.

She pulls the shoebox from underneath her bed and opens it, then takes the book out. She is shaking now, bile rising up her throat. Sometimes she can feel the book's presence in her room, like another person, and she can feel an energy coming off it, as though it has thoughts. But today, it's just a book. It's such a gnarly old thing, too. So ... ugly. The bark is old but not worn, bits of lichen falling off it and a fresh shoot poking out from the spine as though it's still growing. Carefully, she opens it and looks over the black pages. Hard to say what they're made of—like fine charcoal paper that she expects to leave marks on her fingers. They don't.

With a sigh, she puts the book back in the shoebox. Fuck the Triskele. The rumble of a bin lorry sounds, and she springs to her feet, the shoebox under her arm. The idea is bright in her mind, the chance to be free of the weird dreams and the strange pull she feels to the book, its horrible whispers.

Maybe she's just going mad.

She runs downstairs and outside before she realizes that she's made a decision, and throws the shoebox into the back of the lorry, delighted by the sight of it tumbling amidst the trash. She waits until the lorry has emptied all the bins on the street, watching it pull away into the distance.

"You look pleased with yourself," a voice says.

It's Arlo, returning from his walk. He kisses her, and she looks inside the pram. Little Freya is still asleep. For a moment she forgets the news about the Brother, the shock of it momentarily removed by the book finally being carried off down the street. Gone, forever.

"I am pleased," she says, and he kisses her.

Hand in hand, they head back to the house, where she will find the book waiting for her on the bed, fully intact, as though she never threw it in the lorry at all. All its shadows and whispers as tantalizing and inescapable as ever.

CHAPTER FIFTY-FOUR

Scarwell Woods, Orkney
May 2024

CLEM

"You looking for Edina?" a voice calls through the trees.

Clem squints at the figure emerging from the silver mist that has gathered, veillike, between the trees. The tall thin man who was among the people who pulled her from the car last time she was here is walking toward her. Before she can answer, the burr of an engine comes into earshot, and she turns to see a van idling across the field, parking up behind her car. Freya begins to cry. The knot in Clem's throat tightens.

"I brought the book," she says, holding it out to him.

He stops a few feet away from her, looking down at the book, as though he can't believe what he sees. Stepping forward, cautious, and he takes it from her, running his hands over the bark. Then, seeing people get out of the van, he puts two fingers in his mouth and whistles, before lifting his hand high in the air and waving.

"Come inside," he tells Clem.

She follows him into the byre, where a wood burner is lit. On a table an electric stove with a large silver pot steams something aromatic. He gestures at an old sofa in a corner.

"We saw you coming," he says. "We knew you'd be here. So I made some soup. Would you like some?"

"You saw me coming?" she says.

"We have cameras on the ferry," he says. "So we see who comes and goes to Orkney. Soup for the baby, too?"

She is cautious, but tries not to show it. The man seems friendly toward her, going to the trouble of plumping the cushions for her to sit down.

"Oh, she's just eaten," she says, glancing at Freya. "Thanks."

"Ah, visitors," a voice says, and she looks up to see Edina entering the byre. She's not wearing the cloak from last time, and there is no black paint on her face. Her white hair is still long, and she still wears the purple fleece and jogging bottoms but without the disguise, she's a rather ordinary-looking woman of about eighty years old. She moves toward Clem with the aid of a walking stick.

"Clementine," she says with a smile. "Nice to see you so soon."

"I brought the book," Clem says haltingly.

The tall man passes Edina the book, and she stares at it in her hands, before pressing it to her chest. "Thank you," she says. "We will perform the ceremony tonight."

"Ceremony?" Clem asks.

"I see you've met my grandson, Thorfinn," Edina says, nodding at the tall man who is passing a spoon to Clem. "And who is this little sprite?"

"This is Freya," Clem says. "She's my granddaughter."

"Ah, *Freya*," Edina says. "A Norse name."

"Is it?" Clem says.

"It means 'noble woman,'" Edina says, taking the baby's hand. She smiles at her, then turns to the others who filed into the room behind her. There are six of them, three men in their twenties, and three women of the same age. None of them are wearing the costumes that Clem saw the first night she was here.

She dips a spoon into the soup and tastes it. Hot French onion.

"Can I ask you something?" Clem says.

"Of course," Thorfinn says.

"Why is this book so important to you?"

"This book holds all the darkness on earth from the beginning," Edina says. "It has been looked after by the Triskele for centuries. Fear, hate, every form of magic that is designed to do harm—it's all in here."

"I found out who stole the book," Clem says. "It wasn't my daughter. A man I only know as 'the Brother' was leading a cult in Glasgow, they were calling themselves the Triskele. The one I told you about last time. He was the one who stole it, and then he gave it to Erin."

Edina holds her in a long look, as though deciding whether to believe her or not. "And where is this man now?"

"He's dead. He committed suicide. Erin tried to bring the book to Orkney. I'm just wondering if you can help me . . ."

"Help you?" Edina says. "In what way?"

Clem lowers her eyes. She turns to Freya, who is mesmerized by something on Thorfinn's hand.

"I think she likes my ring," he says, smiling.

It's only when he takes it off to let Freya handle it that she realizes the yellow stone set into silver is a tooth.

"Maybe not," she says, plucking the ring from Freya's hands as she attempts to put it into her mouth. She smiles at Thorfinn as she hands it back.

"Strange, how she is drawn to the witch's tooth," Edina says thoughtfully.

Clem looks up sharply. "The what?"

Thorfinn passes the ring back to Clem, who looks over it cautiously. "This is the tooth from one of our clan who was burned as a witch. I'll pass it on to my son, and he'll pass it on to his."

"We don't forget our dead," Edina says. "They live on through us."

"Arlo is dead," Clem says impatiently. "A boy of just twenty. He was Erin's boyfriend, and he was helping her attempt to get rid of the book on Fynhallow. That's how he lost his life." She stares at Edina, silently pleading for her help. "Please. Erin is very, very ill. I don't think she'll get well unless you find a way to stop whatever this book is doing."

Edina runs her fingers over the book, her eyes fluttering. "The book is capricious. It is thousands of years old, and it knows its mind. We can attempt a spell to remove the attachment it has to your daughter."

"What attachment?" Clem says.

"Well, you say Erin is ill," Edina says. "My guess is that she wasn't a Carrier, and neither was the man who stole it. Therefore, the book haunted them both. Giving them nightmares, perhaps driving them to do terrible, terrible things . . . And it would never stop until it was possessed by one who is authorized to carry it."

Clem considers that. "I think it's worth trying anything," she says.

Edina glances at Thorfinn, and Clem notices something pass between them.

"My mother is the clan chief," Thorfinn tells her. "She is the one who must do the spell. But it may backfire."

"Meaning what?" Clem asks, glancing from Thorfinn to Edina.

"Just as the book claimed the life of the young man," Edina says lightly. "So, too, may it claim mine."

Clem feels her stomach drop. The last thing she wishes is to risk more lives. And she has Freya with her, too—will she be injured? What if Edina is right, and the book kills her?

And hundreds of miles away, Erin lies in the hospital, still under the book's spell.

"I can see you're worried," Edina says. She glances at Freya. "Come and watch. We'll make sure the bairn is safe."

They move outside to the clearing just outside the byre.

"Sit here," Thorfinn tells her, pointing at a large tree stump. She sits down, clutching Freya to her, who has begun to fall asleep. Thorfinn puts a woolen blanket around her shoulders, then removes the ring and places it on Freya's thumb.

"Just while she's sleeping. For protection." He smiles. "It's why my mother makes me wear it."

Clem watches as the clan put on large, heavy cloaks of bearskin, helmets made of stag horns and tree branches, chain mail face coverings. The fire is lit, glowing red against the dark trees. Edina sets the book in the middle of the pyre, and the group forms a circle around it. They begin to chant, a rhythmic incantation of words that Clem doesn't understand.

Edina approaches the flame, her arms held out wide and her face lit orange, determination writ upon it. An instinct tells Clem to move farther away, and so she rises, Freya still bundled up in her arms, and moves back, behind the corner of the building, peering out as Edina chants loudly over the fire. The rest of the group hold hands, the humming changing key again, growing louder, tall red flames spiraling up into the canopy.

Then a terrible scream pierces the air. Freya jolts awake, startled. She begins to cry, but another scream rings out, and another in a different voice. Clem steps back, soothing a hysterical Freya. Her heart races.

As she glances back out from behind the byre, it seems the screams are not coming from the group, who are still chanting in low voices. Edina drops her arms, her face aglow from the fire. She looks astonished, or terrified, her eyes fixed on the flame. And yet the screams spiral into the air, one after the other, until the night falls silent.

She stares at the group, who have ceased chanting.

"Come," Edina calls her. "It is safe."

Clem finds a dummy in her pocket and gives it to Freya to console her, and she falls back to sleep on Clem's shoulder.

"Is everything okay?" she asks Edina, who nods, her face shining with sweat. But Clem can tell she is shaken.

Edina points at the fire, which has tamed to a low flicker. Clem squints into the fire, expecting to see the old book charred, the bark cover blackened by flame. But it has vanished, the fire diminishing until all that rises from the logs is a thin wire of smoke.

A rustle draws her attention to the understory. A hare looks up at her, its head tilted toward her and a paw lifted, before darting into the field.

CHAPTER FIFTY-FIVE

Fynhallow, Orkney
December 1594

DAVID

He watches the stake burning long after the families and neighbors have left, forcing himself to look on her. Alison's body will be burned until it drifts high across the sea, landing on the hills and the fens and the forests. They will stoke the flames until her body cannot be inhabited by the Devil, until it is ash.

He keeps his eyes on the birds that circle nearby, wondering, hoping.

When the stake collapses, the body gone, he watches the guards poke at the bones within the rubble, as though they might become animate. Even now, he thinks, after they have tested, tortured, and wrung every last hope from her, when they have killed her and burned her body, they still fear her.

Under his cloak is the record book, the ink still fresh.

He takes the boat back to Kirkwall to fetch his belongings. The risk of traveling alone is great. He is John Stewart's servant—the king will not look kindly upon him.

He returns to his quarters, packs his satchel, fetches his knife.

He will need to report to Father Colville before he leaves, and so he makes for the castle, his stomach roiling with nerves.

He finds Father Colville not in his study, but in the courtroom, standing by the steps leading to the dais.

"My lord," he says, sweeping forward in a deep bow to avoid making eye contact. "I will hasten to Edinburgh."

"You recorded the woman's retraction," Father Colville says, an arched eyebrow. "Why?"

David straightens. "I believed it was what you wished, my lord."

Father Colville holds him in a searching look. "Why would you have thought that I would wish the retraction of something we worked so hard to achieve to be *written down*?"

"You are right," David says, after a pause. "I only did so because I believed the woman was about to confirm her wickedness, or perhaps speak treason."

This seems to satisfy Father Colville. "Show it to me," he says, holding out a hand.

Without hesitation, David removes the book from his satchel and hands it to Father Colville, who flicks through the pages. Finding the record dated 16th December, he scans the text briefly—then rips out the page.

He takes it to the fireplace and throws it in, watching the flame curl around the edges. He doesn't move until the page is ash.

He turns to David. "You will send the rest of the record to the king."

"Yes, my lord," David says with a deep bow. "I will deliver it myself."

As David leaves the room, he closes his eyes, his heart beating hard. He is glad, so very glad, that for once he listened to his instinct. He suspected that Father Colville would find a way to destroy the record of Alison's words, and so on the boat back to Kirkwall, he created a copy on a page folded within his shirt. To-night, he will sail for Edinburgh, and deliver the book to the king.

He slips the copied page carefully back inside the book, closing the record.

CHAPTER FIFTY-SIX

CLEM

She wakes early in Edina's cottage in St. Margaret's Hope, the silver waters of the sound lapping at the cobblestones of the front garden. It's peaceful, and she feels strangely calm.

"Would you like coffee?" Edina calls from the kitchen.

"Yes, please."

"What about oats for the little one?"

"She's still asleep. The drive really took it out of her yesterday."

Clem sits at the kitchen island as the coffee boils in a moka pot on the stove. Edina looks different in this setting, less clan chief than happily retired artist, her colorful paintings depicting animals and ancient stones hanging on every wall.

"Gama!" Freya calls, and she heads into the bedroom to find her sitting up and bleary-eyed, her little arms reaching up.

"Can I ask what Freya's surname is?" Edina says.

"Woodbury," she says.

"I see. Is that your father's surname?"

"Yes."

"And what was your mother's?"

"Balfour. Why?"

"Interesting. Have you Orcadian ancestry, perhaps?"

"Actually, yes. My daughter, Erin, did a DNA test that said her family line is from these parts."

"Look a little deeper into that," Edina says. "A lot of Triskele folk come from Orkney." She moves closer to Clem, taking her hands. "You might find this journey has brought you full circle, in a way."

Edina's voice is tender, the suggestion one of kindness. Clem nods.

"I'll do that."

She pulls out her phone with a sigh. Four messages from Quinn. He's probably angry that she's gone without telling him where. And he probably needs to head back to Yorkshire to save his marriage, so she needs to let him know she'll be back tonight.

But when she rings him, he doesn't shout, doesn't demand to know where she is.

"It's going to be okay," he says.

"What's okay?"

"Senna made a statement. She went down to the police station last night with a lawyer and told them exactly what happened on the night of the fire. She said that Arlo's death wasn't Erin's fault. They all participated in the ceremony willingly and Arlo allowed his wrists to be bound."

Clem claps her hands to her mouth. "Oh God," she says. "What did the police say?"

"Well, they said they'll get back to us. But I think it's a good move in the right direction, wouldn't you say?"

She nods at the phone. "Yes. Yes, it is."

"And I'm here in Erin's room," he says brightly. "She's doing better. Sleepy, but they lowered the sedation last night and she's doing well. You want to speak to her?"

She doesn't know if she's answered or not, she's that surprised by the tone of the call, by the news of Senna, and of Erin.

"Mum?" a voice says. It's Erin, *Erin*, not Nyx.

"Erin?"

"Mama?" Freya asks.

"Oh God, is that Freya?" Erin shouts.

"Yes. She's here with me." A sob forms in her throat. "How are you feeling, love?"

"Groggy," Erin says. "And wet."

Clem laughs. "Wet?"

"It's all the creams they have to put on."

"She's on a lot of morphine," Quinn says in the background. "And she's still under some sedation. But we're hopefully coming off that tomorrow."

"Mama!" Freya says, trying to get the phone from her. Clem hears Quinn speak to someone and realizes he's having an exchange with Bee.

"Clem, stay on the line," he says. "I'm just letting the nurse change Erin's dressings." She waits, not daring to hope that Erin has improved, that whatever Edina and the Triskele did last night has had an effect.

"Are you there?" Quinn says.

"Yes, yes I'm here."

"Good. I'm just outside the hospital. I didn't want anyone to hear what I want to tell you. Are you sitting down?"

"No."

"Sit down for this, trust me."

"Okay. I'm sitting. What is it you want to tell me?"

"Erin told me who Freya's father is."

Clem stiffens, barely able to believe this news.

"Who is it?"

"Arlo," he says.

CHAPTER FIFTY-SEVEN

Fynhallow, Orkney
December 1594

MHAIRI

The soldiers barge through the door of the cottage before she has a chance to pack the few valuables that Alison and William owned. The first soldier sweeps the old wooden wall unit to the floor, sending the chicken shrieking to the rafters and a torrent of glass bottles across the carpet of ferns, their contents bursting out in a shower of poultices and powdered insects. Another soldier raises his sword and strides toward Mhairi; she cowers with a yell, a hand raised to defend herself, the other hand pressed against the wooden chest against which she leans.

There are six soldiers in the small cottage now, so much movement and aggression in such a small space, scattering the lanterns and the spinning wheel, splinters of wood spiking the floor. The lieutenant steps forward and places a hand on the shoulder of the man with his sword raised above Mhairi, urging him to be calm.

"Where's the girl?" the lieutenant demands of her.

"Please," Mhairi begs, crouching over the chest, her arms stretching across it. "Please don't take her. We'll leave the islands, I promise."

The men share a glance before pulling her off the chest with a cry.

"No!" she wails. "Take me! Take me!"

"Out of the way, hag!" the first soldier says, shoving her out of the way. But Mhairi won't be deterred. She scrambles to her feet and lunges at him with a cry, sinking her teeth into his hand. The back of his fist connects with her cheek in an explosion of pain, sending her to the ground like a sack of twigs.

Mhairi gasps, breathless from the shock of it. "She's only a child!" she pleads.

A shriek sounds from inside the chest as the soldiers try to lift the lid of the chest. It is fastened shut, and Mhairi throws them a wild look as they handle the iron bolt, finding a heavy lock at the end of it.

The lieutenant approaches her, his gloved hand finding the handle of his sword. "Where's the key?" he asks her.

Blood blooms at the split skin on her cheek, and she shakes her head. The lieutenant sighs, disappointed, before unsheathing his sword. His blade is sharp and quick, piercing Mhairi through her breastbone.

She feels only the heat of her life force leaving her in a steady pulse, soaking her back, her neck, her eyes fixed on the soldiers as they heft the wooden chest on their shoulders and stride outside. She hears a shout, then a strong waft of smoke brought to her by the wind. They have set the cottage on fire.

It matters not. Inside the chest is a calfling, not Beatrice. As the flames lick the baskets and hay mattresses inside the cottage, Mhairi utters a spell that will distract the soldiers, keeping their minds on good ale and jesting and women all the way back to Kirkwall, preventing them from unlocking the chest until they reach the palace.

That should be long enough to allow Beatrice to escape and make her way to Edward, who is waiting for her by the shrew ash in the hills. He has *The Book of Witching* in his keeping. From there, he'll take her to the Triskele deep into the mountains, then on to the far north, where many of the Triskele live and thrive.

Where they will be safe.

CHAPTER FIFTY-EIGHT

Glasgow
Six months later—November 2024

CLEM

Clem sits alone in the changing room, taking a moment before she replaces her jeans and shirt with the hospital gown and slippers provided by the nurse. She has envisioned this moment for years, anticipating the terror she'd feel, the crushing sense of dread . . . But now that she's here, about to have her heart operation, confronting the moment of her possible death . . . she feels calm. And although she'd never say it out loud, she feels grateful.

After all, Erin survived. She retained her sight, and her mobility. Her recovery is slow and frustrating, and she was heartbroken when they told her that her fingers could not be recovered. But her thumbs were okay, and she has adapted to the prosthetics very well. Youth is on her side. It will help her bounce back before she knows it.

She has Freya to raise. And Senna is still her friend. Loyal to the very end.

And now that Clem sits in this changing room, looking back over her almost fifty years of life, she feels angry at herself for allowing fear to take up so much of her energy. So much of her time, nursing terror. What is there to fear, really, when death is the only certainty?

A knock on the door.

"Are you ready?" a nurse asks.

Clem looks up and smiles. "Yes," she says. "I'm ready."

CHAPTER FIFTY-NINE

Glasgow
November 2024

ERIN

Erin is walking—very slowly, and with the aid of a walking stick—with Quinn through Kelvingrove Park. It's a glorious autumnal day, bright sunshine peeling through the gold spaces of the park that are populated with people meeting up with friends and walking their dogs. Nearby a young boy in a green overcoat kicks a pile of yellow and red leaves. She is already out of breath, and so Quinn tells her to sit down. The bench overlooks the city. It's a nice spot to stop, close to a coffee van, too.

"You want anything to eat?" her father asks.

"Just a cappuccino," she says.

He returns a few minutes later with two cappuccinos and two flapjacks. She raises her hand and takes it carefully from him, amazed all over again by the prosthetic hand that opens and closes around the cup. She cried when they first showed the fake hands to her, and even when they put them on she felt it was impossible, that she would never get used to it. That she could never feel okay with it. But here she is, doing normal stuff, like a normal girl. She is different. She grieves her old self, and she still cries herself to sleep over Arlo.

But today feels normal, and nice, and maybe that is enough.

Across the park there's a little girl about three years old walking between an older couple. She holds their hands: they must be the child's grandparents. She watches, intently, thinking of the day she introduced Freya to Arlo's parents, explaining she is their granddaughter. The look on their faces is something she will never, ever forget. In a moment, all the anger and hurt between them all seemed to melt away. They are good and kind to Freya, and she is getting to know them, too—surprisingly, her family seems to have tripled in size. She used to be jealous of people who said they were part of a large family. And yet now she falls into that category, and it's a beautiful feeling.

"I was thinking," Quinn says, sipping his drink. "Once your mum has recovered, maybe you could come and stay with me for a while. And Freya, of course." He clears his throat, visibly awkward. "I just think it's time to get to know her. And you. I mean, only if you want to. Heather would love it . . ."

"I think that's a great idea," she says, cutting him off as he starts to meander into reasons that are secondary to the real one. She smiles at him, eager to encourage this new show of vulnerability, at his willingness to try. "Once Mum is better."

Yesterday, Clem had her heart transplant. It took eight hours—the longest eight hours of Erin's life. Even Freya was worried, despite them all taking extra care not to tell her too much about what was going on. But she could read them all, could work out that they were gearing up for something. Erin told her that Grandma was going into hospital for a few weeks, that they could go visit her once she was well enough. She found herself keeping her fingers crossed behind her back when she told Freya this, because she had literally no idea how she would explain death to a child so young. She couldn't think about how it would feel to lose her mother, let alone to have to deal with a grieving toddler.

When the surgeon called to say the transplant was successful, she cried for an hour, the full force of what she had faced hitting her like a tsunami. To lose both her mum and Arlo in less than a year—she might not have recovered from that. She's going to save up and take herself, her mum, and Freya on a holiday somewhere gorgeous, once they're both recovered enough to travel. Maybe Greece, or the Seychelles.

But for now, she's focused on her physiotherapy sessions and rebuilding her relationship with her dad. This new version of him seems cool. Chastened, patient.

"I'd like to get to know the boys," she says.

"Your brothers," Quinn corrects.

Erin stares at him, realizing that he has never acknowledged this until now. Toby, Daniel, and Elijah are three little boys who share her green, feline eyes, and 50 percent of her DNA.

"Freya's uncles," she adds, and Quinn visibly takes that in.

"Oh yeah," he says. "I did know that. But I'd also forgotten it."

"A visit sounds lovely," she says. "What should Freya call you? 'Granddad' or 'Grandpa'?"

He winces. "I'll think about that one."

A raven has been watching them from the other side of the park. Quinn tears off a few pieces from his flapjack and throws them toward the bird, but it simply stares at them, uninterested in the food. Erin admires the iridescent gleam of his coat, shades of teal, lilac, and navy striated within the black feathers. She thinks of Arlo, a lump in her throat. But the raven stays put, and even when an enthusiastic Labrador bounds up toward it, the magnificent bird only waddles a few cautious steps away, only to turn back to face her. She finds herself thinking of what the Brother said about the book. About it enabling Carriers to soul-slip into the bodies of birds, particularly ravens.

Could Arlo have done that, right before he died? Was that the strange black flash she saw before he fell to the ground?

Either way, the images in her head feel a little easier, less disruptive, with this new possibility lacing through them. She likes the thought of it—Arlo as a bird, free to fly wherever he wants.

She watches the bird unfold its wings and fly off, soaring high above the city toward the gothic prongs of the university tower.

EPILOGUE

Freya is in her bedroom, playing with the LEGO sets her mum bought her for her fifth birthday. She's got a massive box of pieces, and now that she has her own bedroom she can tip the whole thing on the floor and build a castle, if she likes, or a spaceship.

So she does just that—she turns the box over and lets the pieces rush out.

But she's surprised to find something amidst the pile. It's an old book, with a tree-bark cover, and strange, black pages.

She looks it over, at once repulsed by the rough binding and drawn to it. The room is silent, but as she sits quietly, trying to work out how such an object ended up in her new box of LEGOs, she hears what sounds at first like the rustle of leaves. It graduates to whispering, and she looks around, expecting to find her mother or grandmother there.

But she is alone, and the whispers are soft and vaguely familiar. It says, *Hello Freya.*

She giggles. How does it know her name? Is it like her Alexa device?

Open me, it says, and she hesitates before reaching out to peel open the cover.

Now scream.

In summer 2023 I traveled to Orkney to carry out research for this book. I spent a few days in the archives at Kirkwall, trawling through weathered papers from the 1500s, struggling to decipher the records of the witch hunts. As well as trial records, I found documents that captured old Orcadian folklore. Among these were several mentions of the *Book of the Black Art*, a book with black pages full of sinister secrets. The book couldn't be destroyed, though many had tried. Once the keeper of the book died, Satan took their soul into his keep, and the book passed on to someone else.

This was the inspiration for *The Book of Witching*.

I was also inspired by the trial of a woman named Alyson, or Alison, or Allyson Balfour, who was born in Orkney, Scotland, around 1560. She was the first of at least seventy-two people to have been executed on charges of witchcraft on the Orkney isles.

In 1594—notably just two years after the North Berwick witch trials—Alison was implicated in a plot involving witchcraft to kill the king's cousin, Patrick Stewart, the Earl of Orkney. Patrick was nicknamed "Black Patie" for the tyranny and destruction he meted on Orcadian communities. We know that Alison insisted on her innocence, even under torture. Not satisfied with her claim, the king's chamberlain and parson of Orphir, Henry Colville, tortured her husband, then her son, and finally her little girl in front of her. It was the torture of her daughter that finally broke Alison, and she "confessed."

What happened to Alison's family, if they died, or if they survived the torture, is unknown. History tells us nothing about Alison's life, beyond her work as a healer. We know nothing about her childhood, or where or when she was born. She was living in Stenness at the time of the trial, but I have changed this to the fictional island of Gunn. We don't know where she was held during the trial—secondary sources will tell you that she was imprisoned in St. Magnus Cathedral and that the trial took place in an upper chamber of the cathedral that is now filled with silver. My own research led me to understand that she was either held in the castle dungeon, or in a tollbooth, perhaps the one close to Castle Street, opposite where Kirkwall Castle once stood (a bank sits on the site, and the street is named Castle Street for its absent structure). Accused witches could be imprisoned for months or even years. Given the inhumane conditions in which they were imprisoned, it is not surprising that some died of disease or suicide. The imprisonment, in short, was torture in itself.

On 16 December 1594, Alison Balfour was executed in Kirkwall, Orkney—both Fynhallow and the Isle of Gunn are fictional. A memorial now stands on Gallow Ha' to commemorate her and the others killed on charges of witchcraft. Her husband's name was Taillifeir, and he was in his eighties. There is no record of her children's names.

Eighteen months after Alison's execution, John Stewart and his men tracked down Henry Colville in Shetland and murdered him. Earl Patrick was imprisoned in 1609 and finally beheaded for treason in Edinburgh in February 1615. John Stewart died sometime after 1640, though the cause is unknown. Orkney's earldom was founded in genocide, from the Viking raiders who pillaged the lands of indigenous Orcadians and established themselves as earls (known as jarls), followed by a dynasty of Scottish earls commencing in 1232. Patrick Stewart's death marked the end of the earldom in Orkney.

Sometimes the detective work we undertake for a historical narrative can lead to breathtaking revelations. For example, it is extremely unusual that Alison's retraction was recorded. No record of the trial proceedings exists; indeed, the only record we have of Alison's trial at all is her retraction. But why was Balfour's retraction written down by the notary? She was a woman, after all, and typically only the indictments against the accused "witches" are recorded, with few utterances made by women. It is hard to imagine what value a recording of her retraction held for a prosecution so intent on condemning her.

During my exchange with Professor Julian Goodare, an expert on the Scottish witch trials, he mentioned that the recording of Balfour's declaration indicates that the prosecution had lost control of the trial. I find the prospect of this fascinating, and full of meaning.

When we think of the witch trials, we must remember that early modern societies were fervently Christian, that the pervasive belief in and practice of magic coexisted with religious faith. Even a healer like Alison would have practiced Christianity, and therefore believed that a soul ascended to heaven to live in the eternities with God and their loved ones. For a condemned witch, however, the possibility of an afterlife was obliterated. The families of convicted witches had no body to bury, no tombstone to mourn at, the hope of a heavenly reunion gone entirely.

While Alison had to endure unspeakable horror and injustice, I like to imagine that a notary—one who had witnessed the torture of Alison's husband and children, and who stood by as she was tied to the stake—took the opportunity to transcribe her last words, hoping they would one day set her free.

C. J. Cooke

ACKNOWLEDGMENTS

I am indebted to so many people for this book.

Thank you, Katie Lumsden, Jessica Wade, and Martha Ashby, for helping me pluck a finished book from the mulch of a first draft. Thank you to Lynne Drew, Morgan Springett, Maud Davies, Meg Le Huquet, Rhian—copy editor extraordinaire—and the rest of my book family at HarperCollins UK. Thanks also to Claire Zion, Loren Jaggers, Kaila Mundell-Hill, Gabbie Pachon, Hannah Engler, Craig Burke, and all at Berkley/Penguin Random House US.

Thank you to my champions, Alice Lutyens and Deborah Schneider.

Thank you, Olivia Bignold, Emma Jamison, Samuel Joseph Loader, Anna Weguelin, and Theo Roberts.

Professor Julian Goodare, thank you for enlightening email exchanges that really sunk deep into my brain and made pieces come together.

Professor Marion Gibson, thank you for chatting by Twitter and email and for your marvelous research.

Graham Bartlett, thank you for assisting with my queries into police work and answering last-minute calls for help.

Professor Niamh NicDaeid, thank you for assisting with my queries into forensics.

Krissie Stiles, thank you for assisting with my queries into burn injuries.

James Paterson, thank you for suggesting "Triskele."

Dr. Ragnhild Ljosland, thank you for speaking with me in Orkney and for a wonderful impromptu history tour.

Thank you, Ali Macleod, for insights into sumptuary laws and other early modern matters.

Thanks to the archivists and librarians at Orkney Central Library and Archive, and huge thanks to Fran at St. Magnus Cathedral, Orkney.

I can't thank the booksellers, book bloggers/champions, and readers of my work enough. I had a particularly hard year with my anxiety, but I was often reminded that I have a community of book lovers behind me, who supported me and cheered me on. It made a huge difference, so thank you. A special shout-out to @HollyReadIt, @PhillyBookFairy, Dan Bassett, @TheJerseyReader, @DiveIntoAGoodBook, @The_Constant_Reader, @KayliesBookshelf, @xRubyReadsx, @CherylPois, @JessHeartsBooks, @FictiousKayla, and @Betwixt.The.Pages.

My Instagram community, beloved online collective who cheered me on—thank you.

Agnus MacRae, whose beautiful music inspired me while I wrote—thank you.

Thanks to the authors and editors of the following publications: John Warrack, *Domestic Life in Scotland, 1488–1688* (London: Methuen, 1920); Peter D. Anderson, *Black Patie: The Life and Times of Patrick Stewart Earl of Orkney, Lord of Shetland* (Edinburgh: John Donald, 1992); John Gunn, *Orkney: The Magnetic North* (London: Thomas Nelson, 1946); Robin Noble, *Sagas of Salt and Stone: Orkney Unwrapped* (Glasgow: Saraband, 2018); Sir Walter Scott, *Letters on Demonology and Witchcraft, Addressed to J. G. Lockhart, Esq.* (London: John Murray, 1830); Dr. Ragnhild Ljosland, ed., "Special Edition: The Victims of the Orkney Witch Trials," *New Orkney*

Antiquarian Journal 9, 2020; Brian P. Levack, *Witch-Hunting in Scotland: Law, Politics and Religion* (New York: Routledge, 2008); *Orkney Presbytery Book, 1639–1646* (Orkney Archive OCR/4/1); Sigurd Towrie's website, Orkneyjar (OrkneyJar.com); Maria Hayward, "'Outlandish Superfluities': Luxury and Clothing in Scottish and English Sumptuary Law from the Fourteenth to the Seventeenth Century," in *The Right to Dress: Sumptuary Laws in a Global Perspective, c.1200–1800*, edited by Riello and Rublack (Cambridge University Press, 2019), 96–120. All errors are mine.

Heartfelt and big love to my husband, Jared, and our children, Melody, Phoenix Summer, and Willow. As always, you have all been so supportive and encouraging, and I could not (and would not) do any of this without you.

Finally, to you, reading this. Thank you.

C. J. Cooke is an award-winning poet and novelist published in twenty-three languages. She teaches creative writing at the University of Glasgow, where she also researches the impact of motherhood on women's writing and creative writing interventions for mental health.

VISIT C. J. COOKE ONLINE

CarolynJessCooke.com
X CJessCooke
CJCooke_Author

Ready to find
your next great read?

Let us help.

Visit prh.com/nextread

Penguin
Random
House